Novels by Thomas Savage

THE PASS

LONA HANSON

A BARGAIN WITH GOD

TRUST IN CHARIOTS

THE POWER OF THE DOG

THE LIAR

DADDY'S GIRL

A STRANGE GOD

MIDNIGHT LINE

I HEARD MY SISTER SPEAK MY NAME

HER SIDE OF IT

Her Side of It

THOMAS SAVAGE

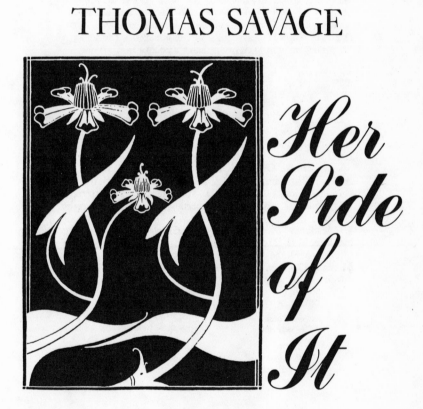

Her Side of It

LITTLE, BROWN AND COMPANY — BOSTON — TORONTO

Acknowledgments

Lines from "The Harpy" by Robert Service, from *The
Collected Poems of Robert Service,* reprinted by permission
of Dodd, Mead & Company, Inc., and McGraw-Hill Ryerson
Limited.

Lines from "Out Where the West Begins," words by
Arthur Chapman, music by Estelle Philleo, reprinted by
permission of Forster Music Publishers, Inc. Copyright
1917, renewed 1945. Used by permission of the copyright
owner.

Lines from "Montana," words by Charles C. Cohan, music
by Joseph E. Howard, copyright 1910 by the Montana
Children's Home Society, copyright assigned 1941 to the
Montana Children's Home and Hospital, Inc. Used by permission of the copyright owner.

LIBRARY OF CONGRESS CATALOGING IN PUBLICATION DATA

Savage, Thomas.
  Her side of it.

  I. Title.
PS3569.A83H47   813'.54   80-25755
ISBN 0-316-77157-0

BP

Designed by Susan Windheim

*Published simultaneously in Canada
by Little, Brown & Company (Canada) Limited*

PRINTED IN THE UNITED STATES OF AMERICA

For
Camilla McCormick
who knows why

Her Side of It

 ALL THE WORLD KNOWS that Mr. T. S. Eliot has written, "April is the cruelest month," but in New England March can knock the spots off April. In March, whatever was good of winter is forgotten — the purity of the first sheltering snow calling up scenes from Currier and Ives, the New Year's resolution to be a better person — and tedious months remain before the end of classes and the merciful departure of the students.

In March, students are the most querulous; pregnancies are discovered among them, stemming from an excess of good will during the Christmas recess. There is backbiting behind closed doors. It is in March that contracts are renewed, or not, and promotions made, or not. One's entire future may be assured or ruined in March, as Caesar knew.

What remains of the snow is filthy.

In March I am most susceptible to head colds.

I felt this cold coming on when I stopped at the student store for coffee and went over my notes for my three o'clock on Emerson — not Emerson the essayist and philosopher but Emerson the poet. Those familiar with *Brahma* can't but agree that Emerson was influenced by both Donne and Waller. The coffee was worse than usual; they are careless about cleaning the Silex machine.

I felt a pressure behind my eyes and a tension in my back and shoulders that must give way to the aches and pains I have suffered since I was a child, and yet each new onset seems a new experience to which new defenses or fresh understanding must be summoned. It takes my colds three days to incubate; I have three days to set my house in order before I isolate myself, three days to set up appointments with students, to correct blue books and to get in foods and drugs and reading material. I will not be caught without books.

I could pinpoint my contracting this most recent cold. Three days earlier, Etta Murphy had stopped by at my office.

"What is this row between Truman and MacArthur?" she asked.

"MacArthur is an ass," I said.

"Had you also heard he is an Episcopalian?" But she was there to talk about her sabbatical, to begin the next fall, not about politics. Like many setting off on high adventure, Etta began to live it even before she experienced it by discussing all aspects with whoever would sit still. It excited her that, thanks to wash-and-wear, traveling was simpler. She pressed her palms together. "I won't even need an iron."

Sloan, the head of our department, was in favor of Etta's doing her work on Southey at the British Museum, and much as I dislike Sloan for a narrow-minded pedant and clever trouble-maker, I can follow his argument that the BM has the largest and most important collection of Southeyana, including the so-called "lost" diaries. It was all very well for Etta to fly in the face of Sloan and opt for a year in New York; Etta had tenure and I did not. But I suspected, as I'm sure Sloan did, that she would spend most of her time at the Museum of Modern Art because of her passion for the Impressionists and for old silent movies, and at Lincoln Center because of the opera. She would have little time left to pick old Southey's bones.

"Sloan came dancing in this morning," she said. "It's remarkable that with all those children he has kept his figure. I told him how I hate the English winter." And then she sneezed so suddenly I hadn't time to turn away from the blast. "I hate sweaters, the feel of wool against the skin and the pressure about the wrists." She raised her hand to push her glasses back up on the bridge of her broad nose. For one who thought of herself as responsible because she had not missed a class in two years' time, she was quite irresponsible in bringing her head colds into the classroom and into the offices of colleagues. She knows of my extreme susceptibility to viruses and their physical and emotional effect on me. That is not to say I do not sometimes welcome the altered consciousness that head colds give me.

"New York winters are no picnic," I reminded her. "And that black grit finds its way into the room. The soles of one's feet are filthy from November to March." I had taken my Master's at Columbia. "You ought to be in bed with that cold. There's pneumonia around. There have been deaths."

"I don't know," Etta said. The wan north light touched her glasses, and I could not see her eyes. For a second I felt the embarrassment one feels before the blind. "It may be an allergy," she said. She stands close when she talks, trusting neither the carrying power of her voice nor the worth of her listener's ears. To be certain that you attend her, she will touch your arm and feel the cloth of your sleeve. "One of my students traipsed into class this morning in an old fur she'd picked up somewhere. Do you realize what a business these thrift shops do? If you want a waffle iron or a set of electric feet to dry out your shoes, that's where to go. Where do you think the kids pick up all those clothes. I wonder why so few furs are worn by other people now. My mother had a lovely Alaskan seal but it rubbed off at the elbows before she passed on. She simply could not sit down without resting her elbows. Eventually she had it made into a cape, and a little hat of what was left of the sleeves."

"The new ecology," I said. "Women now hesitate to dress in what suffered death in a trap or by suffocation."

"Is that what they do? Suffocate them?"

"With gas, so the fur won't be damaged. No death throes."

"This student had on an old silver fox, I believe, but it had lost its character. Its élan. She'd been having trouble with the Dean. I'm sensitive to certain pelts. Anyway, you couldn't kill me with an ax."

It puzzled me, how she could be so sensitive to furs and not to my colds. She is a large woman — the kind word was once "statuesque" — and I had heard that while she was doing her graduate work at Oberlin she had toppled downstairs and had had both kneecaps removed and replaced with plastic disks, and that accounted for an unsteadiness on her feet; you could not help but wonder if her knees might suddenly bend backward and, if so, would it be safe to try to pick her up.

But I well believed that one could not kill her with an ax. Women like Etta live into their nineties in the same apartments they lived in in their forties and fifties and gather the same people about them and the same potted plants. She boasted that she drank ten cups of coffee a day and often forgot lunch — people do boast of how they abuse their bodies — but I know her dinners are more than liberal. She cooks. Her kitchen is an arboretum of healthy green herbs growing in pots, a museum of copper utensils hanging on hooks. Late one evening when we had been laughing and drinking and talking about Proust, she handed me a pan in which madeleines could be made — it was a madeleine that Proust dipped into his tisane and that caused him to recapture the past. At Christmastime she mails off little cookbooks, the pages held together by red silk ribbon, of favorite cookie recipes she has had Xeroxed on the office machine, at no expense to herself.

"Perhaps not," I said.

"Perhaps not what?" Etta asked.

"Perhaps nobody could kill you with an ax."

"Oh, that," Etta said. "My entire family was healthy, you see. My father had a farm for a while as the result of a foreclosure — some improvident person, I guess. I can't recall any processed foods until I was eighteen and then Mother didn't allow us to eat them. She had sound, even primitive values. You see, Sloan has this English thing like so many of our colleagues who have not set foot in London. I think he feels it looks better to the Trustees if I do my work at the BM but it's no secret that our two richest Trustees never got through high school. To see them there at graduation in cap and gown and wearing borrowed hoods — falsehoods, you might say — is enough to make my blood boil. You know very well how Sloan likes to have his hand in things, and by the way, I'm truly sorry about that ruckus you had with him over Shakespeare in freshman English. They were talking about it in the faculty lounge." Etta glanced toward the closed door.

I'll bet they were talking it over, Etta included. I could hear and see them talking of it, wandering to and from the coffee machine.

"Of course," Etta said, "it may blow over, or some of it. I imagine you heard last week that Sloan did his Chicken Story. Just a few of us over there at dinner. It was truly hilarious. You've never heard him do it, have you?"

She knew quite well I'd never heard him do it. She knew who was close to him and who was not, who had heard him do it and who had not. As I get it, the Chicken Story concerned a daft farmer who is in love with one of his hens and confides in her his troubles. The narration is accompanied with much clucking and stumbling and posing and cocking of the head as an attentive chicken might do. A part of the fun, I believe, is the privilege of a favored few to observe Sloan let down his hair, for ordinarily he is much concerned with his amour propre. Further, his telling of the story makes it clear that he is perfectly comfortable with his small-town Indiana background and need make no effort to hide it as many of us might, and those who have been allowed to see him perform are a kind of aristocracy among us. Apparently he is much gifted as an actor.

"I do hope you don't get this cold," Etta said.

"You said it was an allergy."

"I said it could be one. I don't know the precise nature of the fur the girl was wearing."

So she was not quite certain it was fox. My hope of not getting the cold was vain. In the student store, my notes on Emerson before me, I felt it approach headlong. Fortunately, it was a Friday; I had until the following Monday to attend to it. I begin by drinking fruit juice — the frozen — I don't dilute it as thoroughly as the directions insist. I take Alka-Seltzer regularly and stay in bed. I sterilize the thermometer before taking my temperature, against self-infection. One is, alas, not even immune to oneself. I dip it in rubbing alcohol, but it is not good to keep a thermometer in rubbing alcohol too long; the paint comes off and you can't see the numbers or the arrow. Rectal thermometers are more accurate but I have not yet come to them.

My circulation is not good; I wear white athletic socks to bed until late in May — the wool, not the nylon. I am allergic to all synthetics. The thick socks serve as slippers when I walk the cold floors. Death begins with the feet.

My colds not only raise the temperature of my flesh and alter my sense of smell and taste; they also disarrange my sense of time and place, throw me back in time to a town in western Montana, and once again I know the cracked sidewalks of Rife and South Pacific streets, chalked up with lines for games of hopscotch. I see the Ford garage and the Grayling Implement Company where a life-sized wooden horse sometimes trussed up in harness, sometimes bearing a stock saddle, stares with bulging eyes across at the City Drug Company. I feel myself a child again and hear the striking of the courthouse clock, the sound moving out in everwidening circles, past the Hale Memorial Hospital and at last dying away over the sagebrush at the far edges of town. Again I wait for the dusk and the shriek of the Union Pacific traveling west or east, bearing lucky passengers. At last I was one of the lucky ones.

Now I am thirty-five. I teach in an excellent small New England college and, except for circumstances, would now have my doctorate. Without a doctorate one is vulnerable to slings and arrows, and except for my ability to hold the attention of a class and to listen to problems, I would be lost. Yes, I am a good listener, and what I hear I remember. What I remember makes me understand something of other people's lives, if not my own.

Etta called Sunday evening to ask if I had got her cold, and I said yes, I had, and that I was reading Milton Hindus's *The Proustian Vision*. Proust, shut up in that cork-lined room of his, would have perfectly understood my preoccupation with that horse in the big window of the Grayling Implement Company and my hope, since it was part of my childhood, that it had not been hauled off to the dump as passé.

Etta laughed over the telephone and I heard "Voi che sapete" in the background.

Each fall Etta gathers about her the more attractive of the new instructors. They are glad to be gathered about, for they cannot afford the liquor she offers, and under her aegis they are not so vulnerable as those who have no old hand to support them in faculty meetings. They empty Etta's ashtrays, exclaim over her record collection, which includes jazz later on in the evening when scholarly inhibitions are set aside. They remember Etta's birthdays, the date if not the number, and they bring a potted plant, a jar of jelly or a box of incense. There was no great thing they could buy her, and anyway she bought the great things. It has always struck me as unfair that professors should be allowed private incomes. Professors with money have the advantage of not much caring whether a contract is renewed or not; they can put their furniture and books and music into storage until they decide what next; they can travel from one end of the earth to another by jet, or by freighter if time is no object. With Etta, it was something about the lumber business. Her grandfather had owned trees, a great number of trees, but Etta with her emerald rings and oriental rugs and heavy silver had clearly risen above sawdust and the howl of circular saws.

I had once been one of Etta's young favorites. I had scarcely unpacked my suitcase before she was at my door. She had rushed in, smiling. "I know your name! I already know your name!"

I had taken the place furnished; the two chairs, the couch and the table were of oak — "Mission" I think is the word — a style that might have been chosen for a private library at a time when there was such excitement about motorcars and electricity. I had brought with me two Toulouse-Lautrec prints, and a Maxfield Parrish print because it had hung in my house when I was a child. It was a landscape no grown-up had ever seen. I had brought my clothes with me, and an ironing board, an iron and my letters.

I started to take Etta's coat as she began to slip out of it, but she pulled gently away from me. "No, don't bother, really. I know where the closet is. I've known several who've used this apartment. I'm familiar with many places here." And with her coat she moved toward the little closet. She opened the door and groped in the cramped darkness, and my ironing board slid out; flushed out of hiding, it lay there on its back, its complicated legs exposed. Etta stared at it, and then she began to laugh. "You don't!" she cried, hugging herself. "You honestly don't!"

"Don't?"

"You don't really have an ironing board."

"But you do see I have?"

She put her finger to her lips and looked into the corner of the room. "I want to see your iron."

"It's just an old iron."

"I want to see it."

"It's on the shelf just above you."

She took it down. "Heavy," she said. "I think you're the only man I know who has such equipment."

"Is it so unusual? I like to touch things up."

She laughed. "Oh, lordy! Touch things up!"

"May I make you coffee?"

"If you have a little sherry, no. It's that time."

Etta was plump and dusted over with powder. Content, she sat with her bracelets and her rings and her sherry. Then her eyes

[*8*]

squeezed shut and her shoulders shook. "Touching up!" she breathed. Suddenly she rose and picked up from the windowsill what I think is my only treasure — a heavy, hollow glass globe the size of an orange; it rests on a round, delicately carved ebony base.

"I adore paperweights," Etta said. "Valuable? Looks it."

True, these glass globes were used as paperweights, but children a hundred years ago got them as toys at Christmas, and as mementos of Christmas they were appropriate; shaking them caused flat, white particles to swirl in a clear liquid: you held a tiny blizzard in your hand. At last the particles settled back to the little earth around a house or a snowman or a bundled-up figure in a sleigh.

"I don't think this one is a paperweight," I said. "Paperweights had the base attached. I've heard them called snow scenes."

"Or snow globes," Etta said. "I wonder what the true name is. I should have sworn it was on the tip of my tongue. Curious we shouldn't know the true name of so common an object."

The particles in the globe Etta held appeared to be chips of opal and they changed not only in space as they swirled but in hue and color, and the liquid that supported them was not thin like water but viscous like glycerine; the small storm prevailed a longer time and the fairylike flakes lay still at last around a carved carnelian pagoda, whose eaves tilted up to cause those evil spirits bent on sliding down the roof to be hurled harmless back up into the air. In the background was a fanciful jade mountain. Just outside the entrance of the pagoda stood a human figure so small it was impossible to guess its age or sex. My whatever-it-was was by no means common.

"Have you ever seen one without a figure of some kind?" Etta asked.

"I've seen them without a human figure, but never one that didn't suggest human habitation. The craftsmen appear to make a point of humanity."

"I wonder why that is?" Etta said.

"I have a friend who would know."

Now, seven years later I was no longer young. No longer a favorite of Etta's but still a friend, I heard her voice and "Voi che sapete" struggle for control of her telephone. "Can you hear me at all?" she cried. "I'm having people over for drinks. I hope it won't be the way it was the last time." I remembered. I was there. One young, pretty, pregnant faculty wife had slumped over in the bathroom. It was thought that the husband should have been watching her, but the husband, following a grotesque argument about the value of physical education in a liberal arts college, was attempting to do a handstand in limited space. Etta herself, suddenly recalling that her now favorite young instructor had recently married and had moved into new and connubial rooms, had rushed into her darkened bedroom and had thrown herself supine on her broad bed; I covered her over with an afghan her mother had made, the ultimate creation of the old lady's faltering hands, and once again I emerged to do the honors. But the honors were already being done for me; the party had moved into the kitchen, where they were getting into the reserves of gin under the sink, and they had begun to touch each other.

Etta is revived by very little sleep.

Now she stood framed in her bedroom doorway. Thunder might have marked her appearance and lightning have played about her. Her appearance was like that of the Queen of the Night. Afghan draped about her shoulders, she cried out, "Get out of my house! Trash! Varlets — jades!" And everybody but me did get out of the house, fairly falling down the steep, narrow stairs into the waiting snow, but everybody forgives Etta because of the size of her heart and the extent of her booze. Her broad, forgiving smile still hung over the campus like a cloud; the briefly vindictive clutched to themselves the thought that perhaps she would have preferred to have a man rather than a Ph.D.

"I've never known anyone so sensitive to colds," she said over the telephone.

Since I was up, having had to answer her call, I went downstairs in my old Pendleton robe to see about Saturday's mail. I found it unpleasant, as I padded down to the first landing, to contemplate my mail lying there unattended and examined by the other tenants as they came and went to their jobs in the Mammoth Mart and the Mobil station, perhaps wondering why I had not yet picked it up. I do not like to be thought of.

I didn't get much mail. I heard regularly only from my brother, who wrote twice a month, and I appreciated the mental and physical effort he made. I had considered writing him that a single letter a month would do, but a single letter would not have allowed him the opportunity to show me that, although duty was becoming increasingly difficult for him, he was the kind of man who persevered, in pain.

I had not made friends who might write, except for one. I was not good-looking. Few saw in me anything to cultivate or understand. No one was attracted to my ambition; when once I realized I would never write, I put ambition aside and hoped only to live from day to day, to anticipate breakfast, lunch and what dinner I might arrange or what the kind might arrange for me, to teach what facts I had learned, and to plan vacations. My closest friend was a woman, and Etta was not she.

The mail was deposited at 9 Silver Street in a cramped entryway closed off from both street and dwelling against the bitter cold. The entryway was ripe with the nostalgic odor of rubbers, overshoes and such woolen outer garments as one would not mind having carried off by the needy. The postman tossed letters and packages onto an oval mahogany table whose top was supported by four alert griffons, wings poised for instant, directed flight. It was a piece meant to grace the center of a baronial reception hall. It so crowded the entryway that the broad of hip or the unsteady must consider it, and the sensitive must ponder who had chosen and bought it, who in that northern New

England town had owned a house to match such elegance. The clue, I think, lay in the hotel in the town, the Maple, the renovated mansion of a tycoon who had manufactured shoes before industry fled south to cheaper labor.

Now the griffon table had fallen into the hands of a fiercely clean French-Canadian woman who tacked up signs ordering tenants to turn off the lights and to see that the toilet did not go on running after it had been flushed; she was ever busy with pine-scented disinfectant, bottled under pressure; she lived below in rooms bright with plastic flowers, a parakeet and the Infant of Prague, its gilt-trimmed red robes protected by a layer of cellophane. She listened, contemptuous of the college community, of the students who lived off their parents, of the faculty with their books and shabby cars. Her son, a big hairy fellow, and his pretty wife with the curls and children never missed a Sunday dinner. Her son had left high school to found his own construction company. He belched.

On the griffon table this cold, sunstruck morning was my fresh copy of *PMLA*, which threw fresh light on the *Lusiads*. Having only Spanish and French but virtually no Portuguese, I have read it only in translation. The classics lose a good deal in translation — I have heard it said that poetry is what is lost in translation.

And a letter from my friend Liz. A long one as usual — three single-spaced pages, carefully contemplated, read over after she had written them, to judge from the neat corrections in ink. Her letters were an excuse for not getting to her own work. I think she had come to value my instant response more than the eventual response — I hoped — of the critical reading public.

She seldom dated a letter so that anyone would know at once what day it was written, what week or even what month. She seldom used the Gregorian calendar or even the Julian. I have letters from her dated 1 Brumaire — the twenty-second of October — and 1 Messidor — the nineteenth of June. For Liz, January 1 was Horses' Birthdays. August 1 was Lammas. Feast of Esther. Ramadan.

For twelve years I had been Liz's sounding board, confessor, scapegoat. I had more than four hundred single-spaced pages of her letters, all of them sensitive, some grotesque, some shocking. Little she had thought or done that I couldn't put my hand on simply by crossing the room and unlocking a metal file cabinet. Because she was so great an artist, although so little known, I felt pride in being the only one who knew what her life had been — her terrors, her loves — and how, unless she changed her ways, her life would end. She had a chilling knowledge of why anybody did anything. I once told her I'd noticed that when somebody is about to take a bite of a sandwich he will first lift the top slice and look inside even when he already knows what's there. I said I wondered why that was.

"*I* know," she said. "Anticipation. The eyes prepare the taste buds. The senses perform better in concert."

The letter I now read was headed Lady Day, which comes late in March, and it concerned Liz's close friend Helen.

"She has ordered her husband out of the house again. She is qualified to do so, since she owns the house."

Helen and Claude-Michel had been married twelve years. They were held together by a fierce, mutual antagonism that they could not bring themselves to resolve, for its resolution would have left them lost in an intolerable vacuum like the death of an only child. Helen was fastidious. I had seen her eyes bright with concern at the sight of an ink stain on her hand; she was a compulsive handwasher and a liner-up of pencils on a desk. Certainly she used shoe trees. She would rise from a chair and straighten a picture on a wall not her own. She was fragile and beautiful but she did not believe in her beauty. Once, quite drunk, I tried to convince her that she was beautiful and began the gestures meant as proof, but she was staring out the window, listening to an engine screaming to a fire on a Village street. This was not the time to babble of beauty when someone, somewhere, was about to be burned alive, another left an orphan. She thought in capitals; she felt in italics. She was more or less my friend, but one who, I felt, was standing beyond a scrim of unspeakable experience.

I had never heard her tell an off-color story, never heard her speak the words toilet or john or even Little Girls' Room. Needing that facility, she would simply vanish and return from her brief errand with the same smile or frown with which she had left. She must not, as a child, have missed Sunday School in Michigan, where she lived in a big white house with a smooth rolling lawn she often spoke of.

"I see her," Liz wrote, "playing croquet or sitting in the shade of the lilac tree twisting the ring on her finger, the opal birthstone Daddy gave her, the son of a bitch. Her crayons would not have strayed beyond the lines."

Helen had once announced that we were all lost in New York. She was sitting at Liz's "dining" table in the one-bedroom apartment high up over Twelfth Street. (An overnight guest or anyone too drunk to get down the five flights of crazy narrow stairs slept on a daybed.) Liz called it her dining table, but it was seldom laid with more important food than Habitant pea soup — easier than other soups because you didn't even add water. It was served — dished up — in liver-colored Mexican pottery, each piece of a different shape as if the potter didn't give a damn. The clay used in making this kind of pottery contains sufficient lead to poison anyone using it regularly, but Liz did not. Often she ate directly from the can.

"We're lost here in New York," Helen had said.

Helen often wore white linen that had the charming impracticality of cut flowers; she sat carefully to avoid crushing or soiling it. As she spoke she was moving her fingers slowly over the surface of the table as if reading Braille. The table was constructed of pine planks held up at either end by two pine X's. It had been stolen from a public picnic ground. One imagined an outraged public official in the background. The table had not come to them a tabula rasa. The names and initials and symbols carved deep into the top went far beyond Liz's acquaintances,

[*14*]

including him who cut in a swastika to remind the Jews that hate still walked abroad, and him who cut in an ace of spades. Kilroy was there on the tabletop, and "Tex" K-T, a phantom who chalked his name on the flanks of boxcars at least as far west as Grayling, Montana. Over these names and symbols Helen's fingers passed, over those lost ones who, in identifying themselves with pocketknife or shard of glass, said, "Here, at least, I am. Here, not lost."

Helen had spoken of our plight in New York in words distant and hushed, like a medium's.

"Lost, shit," Liz said.

Helen was a sitting duck for Liz who, from the internal evidence of her first novel, had been a cruel child and remained a cruel child, and she had retained a child's love of holidays. All of them — Valentine's, Fourth of July, Halloween, Christmas, New Year's. I remember a valentine she fashioned from a painting of a Sacred Heart, dripping with expiating gore, which she had cut out from a conservative Roman Catholic magazine and decorated with lace sheared from a cast-off piece of female underclothing. She invented holidays that, like the Saturnalia, excused unspeakable behavior. She celebrated Grace Coolidge's Arrival in Washington, President Harding's Coupling with Nan Britton — condoms were distributed as favors — and the Puberty of Al Capone. She fancied Easter and displayed a clutch of sawdust-stuffed yellow chicks. I had seen similar birds, and the true beaks had been replaced with sharp wooden pegs; black glass beads replaced the perishable eyes. But the skin, the yellow down and the feet — if a bit withered — were authentic.

"As a child," Liz said, "I couldn't see what the cuddly birds had to do with Easter except as a logical outcome of the egg as a tiny tomb from which Life illogically bursts forth. Only years later I saw the awful symbolism of the stuffed chicks. They, no less than Christ himself, had died for me." She sent out invitations on a colored print of the Stone Rolled Away from the Empty Tomb — one of the early Italians — and over it she had printed with a felt-tipped pen, GRAND OPENING. People came for drinks and were invited to search, one by one, for eggs that she and her husband Hal had spent weeks decorating. They guided each guest by the you're-getting-hotter method to his own egg. Because I admire Melville, I was guided to an egg decorated with a whale, a clever imitation of scrimshaw.

A set designer, often in and out with his unsolvable problems and insolvent lovers, once retrieved an egg with an exquisitely executed drawing of the Globe Theatre. Poor Helen, one year, searching and searching, her face pale under the dusty skylight, breathing a little hard, her Best's lilac tweed new for the occasion, her pearls murmuring purity, came at last on that egg done only for her. She had assumed the breathlessness of a child, the anticipatory smile, the mask expected of her, and she put her hand on the egg. It was one of those pure white ones said to be laid by the dark among the hen tribe — Anconas, I believe — white it was, pristine. Except for Old English script that spelled out 𝔉𝔲𝔠𝔨 𝔜𝔬𝔲.

Helen was an almost constant theme in Liz's letters to me, a point of reference, a visible thread, and I wondered why; and why, as the years passed, Liz was more and more critical of Helen, more and more mocked what I can only call Helen's essential purity and reserve. I questioned the exact nature of their relationship, but of course none of us, from time to time, is above being witty or amusing at the expense of even his closest friend.

As I slipped this latest of Liz's letters back into the envelope, I considered my own relationship with Helen: it was somewhat distant; possibly she disliked me. Many do. Possibly she considered me a cipher. But it was at Helen's elegant little house in the Village that I first met Liz, and so I owe her much.

Helen was then living with her first husband, who was French. He wore little pointed shoes, fussy dark suits with whimsical lapels and cuffs peeking out just so. I supposed he was literary or social and was surprised to find he was in business, importing or exporting something. I did not then know he was a first husband since I had met him and Helen only once, and Helen had introduced him as "my husband" and not "my first husband," a phrase she might have used if she were not or did not expect to be satisfied with him. Helen believed in permanence in those days, but in another way she remained starry-eyed right up to her end.

I had seldom come down from Columbia to the Village; I had seen the inside of a few apartments down there, but never the inside of a house. Helen's house was small and old and charming. It was of brick and squeezed in between two new, tall apartment buildings. It had a tiny lawn surrounded by a brick wall, and a birdbath, should birds arrive from God knew where. The small living room was elegant with the gleanings from antique shops up and down Third Avenue; mirrors, set with sconces in which tapers burned, reflected a Chinese chest of carved teak; a shoji screen was inlaid with pressed flowers; a captain's desk was bound in brass; prayer rugs hung on the wall; hurricane lamps dripped with crystals. There was an imperial Russian samovar, an ancient Japanese scroll on which a foreshortened tiger crept out from a bamboo grove. A tall clock told the time and the phases of the then-virgin moon. Helen had friends in the antiques business; she listened to them and harbored them overnight when they had tiffs and they responded with vases and inkwells blown by Gallé and Lalique, penholders of gold and mother-of-pearl, peacock feathers and jade eggs. Charming, useless, sterile elegance.

She had met her little Frenchman during her junior year abroad when she was studying the Imagists at the Sorbonne. A French family, afflicted by the hands-across-the-sea syndrome, had invited Helen into their apartment on the rue Madame for a certain fee, and there beside a tall, narrow window had introduced her to Claude-Michel. At that moment the heavens above Gaul parted and delicious music quite like Gounod's descended, for Helen confided to Liz with a look of ecstasy that she had never before been so completely treated as a woman.

[17]

"Exactly what she meant by that," Liz wrote me, "I do not know. Do you suppose he goosed her? Or is that the Italians? Maybe it's as well she didn't explain because, after all, there must have been other people there. Or maybe he simply took and kissed her hand, not the palm of it but the back of it. And you know how Helen felt about Courtly Love. She knew — of course she knew — that once they married, if they did, he would suggest they sleep together, but that was not the part she liked. It was the kissed hand, the flowers, the bonbons, the *petit bleu* dispatched and received at some crazy, pretty hour."

It was all a far cry from the state of Michigan and Wellesley College.

Two years later, Claude-Michel followed Helen to New York, a lapse of time that hardly suggests pursuit, and in truth he had been sent by his family to look after the American wartime interests of the family business. And so they were married.

"The fact was," Liz wrote me, "that he had married her because she was the only girl he knew in America and he could not be expected to remain unmarried here, and she had married him because she could not have allowed him to say the things he had said to her unless marriage was the end of it." That they both spoke French was to the point: although he spoke English, French was easier, and because she was married to him, her French was not likely to get so rusty that she might be pointed out as one whose French had gone downhill.

Early on in their marriage, he restricted his criticisms to America as an abstraction and of Americans to Americans other than her. He attacked plastic, supermarkets, chrome trim, vaginal douches, showers, orange juice, Sunday driving, billboards, baseball, hamburgers, our baffling preference for cream in coffee instead of milk, our coffee perversely unmixed with chicory, Wonder Bread, the filth in our subways, and Mrs. Roosevelt, whose teeth offended his sense of symmetry.

"He approved only of our Red Indians and our buffaloes," Liz wrote. "He had read of them as a child."

But then Helen herself became a target. He did not like her pastel tweeds, her Peter Pan collar or her linens. Frenchwomen wore quite different shoes, and they did not remove them and sit cross-legged. Must she hum when she prepared his dinner? Humming indicated she was distracted, that her mind was far from food. Why was she so improvident with leftovers? In France she could have rescued entire meals from them. Must she surround herself with queers?

"And you will quit your job," he announced, using the forceful American vernacular.

She had paused and looked at him. "Quit my job?"

"No married woman of our class," he said, "works." In business, he knew, women were routinely approached by men, and women were naturally tempted. Further, business so exhausted them that they had not the sexual stamina their husbands expected, and could not prepare a proper nest for a husband and little children. "Un nid juste," he said, "pour un mari et des enfants."

"Enfants, my eye," Helen said, suddenly gone crude. "I've got news for you. For some time my authors will remain my children, and I will not quit my job, as you call it. Why on earth do you think I left Michigan and came to New York?"

In the argument that followed, neither of them mentioned the word love; to do so would have put them both on pretty thin ice. It was obvious that in marriage he was seeking convenience and that she liked to say she was married, for she had been taught in Michigan that after a certain age it is shameful to be single. After a certain age an unmarried woman is unmarried simply because she has never been asked to marry, because something perhaps unspoken is wrong with her; she can no longer be included at parties unless her parents are asked and she comes as a shy appendage fit only to pass the hors d'oeuvres.

Claude-Michel had sulked like a child who had never before been crossed; he had been reared to believe that a wife refused a husband nothing — owing everything to him as she does, includ-

[*19*]

ing her money. What was the good, otherwise, of having been born a man? He believed the answer to such mulish recalcitrance was to turn unpleasant, and he initiated periods of silence, some of them lasting a week and underscored by carefully slammed doors. He refused foods.

Helen suspected he consoled himself by the French method of taking a mistress; that would account for his absences. She kept busy filling the little rented house with her grandmother's midwestern antiques and the other antiques and with editors and authors and friends. He would disappear upstairs at the arrival of guests and flush the toilet and call down to ask, in the middle of a string quartet, if she had the toenail clippers. He had disappeared to mistress or detective story the evening I got there with a fellow who had known Helen when she was at Wellesley.

"Want to take in a literary bash?" he had asked me. "Helen doesn't drink but she has booze on hand for those as do. It's for the guy who wrote *To the Windward*."

I'd read it. The author, I knew from the Sunday *Times*, was scarcely older than I. Worse, there were rumors that the movies were interested.

I had wanted to write a novel about the West I believed I understood — the small-town West, the social strata, winter afternoons in the Public Library and the midnight striking of the courthouse clock. Thousands, maybe millions, have wanted to write that novel, one that would lend wings to fly from the Philistines and to join ranks with other artists, for artists are judged only by themselves and are the envy of all those left back home. But, in fact, we have no more credentials than once having been praised by Miss Merchant or Miss Eastman. We had a poor relationship with our peer group, who considered us grinds or sissies and scorned our professed preference for Tchaikovsky over "Flat Foot Floogie" and "Stardust." But oh, we meant to show Montana or Colorado or Texas a clean pair of heels and head for New York where our talents would thrive.

Mine had not. I lowered my sights, and hoped one day to find a teaching job. Others like me you find selling books or running failing boutiques with names like Ampersand.

But the author of *To the Windward* had made it. He had not had to show the East a clean pair of heels. His novel was his key to immortality.

Halloween wind in the Village; in the entryway of Helen's little house the tapers guttered and caught on bits of crystal and brass. Mirrors caught reflections. How I longed to mingle regularly with these people — painters, sculptors, writers and editors, the clever and amusing who pad gatherings and are comfortable with red caviar and the social kiss.

I disliked the author of *To the Windward*, a blond young man casually dressed; he stood, he touched the mantelpiece, he smiled, he pondered. I suspected that the rumor about the movies was true. He would walk easy in the shadow of Faneuil Hall (he came from Boston) as I had not walked easy in the long, blue shadows of the Rocky Mountains.

Since it was his party, I had no business feeling hurt that no one noticed me — why should anyone? Until that moment I had thought I had given over being envious. But I did not add my applause to that of his claque. He said, "Oh," and looked into his drink when I remarked that I had come from Montana, a state whose mention sometimes commands brief attention in eastern circles because it is the Big Sky Country:

Out where the handclasp's a little stronger,
Out where the smile dwells a little longer . . .
*   That's where the West begins.*

There's more of giving and less of buying,
And a man makes friends without half trying . . .
*   Out where the West begins!*

These sentiments I had often seen burned into wooden plaques and stamped on rayon pillows stuffed with pine needles.

When I lived in Montana, I hated it. Now, having left it, I was as defensive of it as I was of myself. Nor could I, in New York or New England, see a Montana plate on a car without a pang of homesickness, of loss, an urge to speak to the driver, as if he and I had more in common than the crowd of strangers around us simply because he and I knew that Route 2 runs along the top of Montana and Route 10 through the middle of it, and that the area of Montana is a hundred and forty-seven thousand square miles, quite big enough to swallow up the whole of New England and most of New York State.

The truth is that it is a mistake to abandon one's roots unless one is so self-confident he has no need of roots, or so talented or so capable that he can put down new and different roots.

Someone spoke. I turned to a young woman who sat on a daybed that was disguised as a sofa with silk and velvet cushions.

"Did I hear you speak the word Montana?" she asked.

She was tall, dressed in a black sheath, an enormous black hat, and a pumpkin-colored scarf I knew later was a nod to the ghostly season; what she wore was not an outfit but a costume, and she was an elegant witch who might blight a jolly gathering by merging suddenly from the shadows, or laughing in the wings at some transpiring horror. Her hair was heavy and glossy. She was posing a little, her arm extended; she held her cigarette close to the tips of her index and middle fingers which arched back toward the blue veins of her unusually white hand. She was a stranger to the sun.

"Yes," I said. "I said Montana." And was alert to defend it.

"Montana, Montana," she said, "glory of the West."

"Of all the states from coast to coast," I said, "you're easily the best."

"Montana, Montana, where skies are always blue."

"M–O–N–T–A–N–A . . ."

"Montana, I love you," she finished.

"You love Montana?" I asked.

"Of course not," she said, "or I wouldn't be here. But for a second I thought I did, and I smelled the sagebrush and heard coyotes yelping at the moon. What I loved was myself, as a child."

"Have you read *To the Windward?*"

"I read everything. Lists of ingredients. Directions. The *Elks Magazine*. Letters not meant for my eyes. I'm a storehouse of obscene information."

"How did you like *To the Windward?*"

"The book is — how shall I say — ?" and she made a tent of her long, slender fingers and touched the peak to her full lips. "The book is pure shit. Had Edna Ferber been born in Newton Center, Massachusetts, instead of Appleton, Wisconsin, that is the novel she would have written. And written and written."

I felt a leap of premature affection that so definitive a judgment was based either on a refined critical sense, or on envy.

"You've stated my opinion," I said.

"Oh," she said. "Oh, the lovely old Paisley shawls passed down from Grandmother to Daughter to Granddaughter. And Granddaughter with all that proud lineage lusting after a no-good handsome hunk! The vile letter in the trunk that exposed Grandmother's own past! The brother, turned away from the Porcellian Club, turning to that willing little waitress in Hayes-Bickford. My God — the disillusionment!"

"Do you write?" I asked.

"I'm Liz Phillips."

"Elizabeth Phillips?"

"Indeed."

"I'm Bill Reese, but no matter. May I sit at your feet?"

Where I came from in Montana, almost everybody was white, Anglo-Saxon and Protestant. Apart from the red Indians, WASP eyes had first looked on the mountains and WASPs owned the water that greened the fields. As a WASP myself, I felt no envy of anyone who was not one. If a Catholic or a Jew or a Latin succeeded—and success in Grayling, Montana, meant money or land, there was no other standard — I assumed that such success was compensation for not being like the rest of us and had been achieved through the bestowal by Nature of some special ability as she rewards the blind with an extraordinary sense of touch and pigs with the gift of sniffing out truffles.

Because Liz was a woman I could not envy her success. As a woman, she possessed some special gift it was pointless for a man to envy, but Grayling, Montana, would not have named her a success. I doubt that her novel, *Masquerade*, sold a thousand copies. It concerned a group of actors in a summer playhouse who lived the parts they played and addressed the problem of identity.

Patients sinking into oblivion under anesthesia speak of a moment of revelation when they feel possessed of an Answer to a Cosmic Question. They speak of euphoria, of freedom, and the answer is on the tip of their tongue. But on returning to consciousness they find that it has vanished like smoke and nothing remains but loss and frustration.

But I have read of a man who could pass between the conscious and the unconscious as over a bridge, and at that moment of revelation he cried out, "Think in other categories."

I had been charmed by his call to break out of the mold, to cast aside the shell, to break the habit. The dusty pall of habit forever threatens to smother us; habit dulls the senses and blinds us to mystery and beauty. Thinking always in the same categories, we tire even of Beethoven's late quartets.

Liz's work was a very expression of thought in other categories; in reading it, my eyes looked through magic spectacles. Over her stunning prose, wit and perception and humor played like fire. (Later on I found almost equal delight in *The Marble Orchard*, a novel by Margaret Currier Boylen.)

"May I sit at your feet?" I asked her.

"Dear heart, please do for a little while. But then why don't you sit here beside me on this false divan, where it's more comfortable and we will tear people apart as they pass to and fro."

Before midnight I went with her to the five-flight walk-up, once a small town house and now somewhat in ruins; it had been a long, long time since a horse-drawn cab had stopped there. On each stair landing was a niche set deep into the thick plastered wall to accommodate urn, epergne or plaster bust. Liz said Hart Crane had lived on the fourth floor, having escaped Cleveland and his mother Grace, and there he had written parts of *The Bridge* shortly before he threw himself off the end of a boat.

I was out of breath when we reached the fifth-floor landing. On it was a wrought-iron bridge lamp with a dusty parchment shade; the weak light behind it seeped through a colored print of nosegays; such light had once fallen on folding tables, scorepads, ashtrays shaped like diamonds and clubs, tiny pencils and bonbons, and I thought of the sibilance of female voices and of marcelled hair.

Liz opened her purse, took out a key and worked with the lock in the door. The doorjamb bore old scars healed over by layers of cream-colored paint, evidence that lock after lock had been replaced when key after key had fallen into the wrong hands. The door itself was sheathed in a painted metal that had withstood the coin-shaped blows of a hammer and the wedge-shaped wounds left by an ax.

"Hal is still overseas," she said.

I felt it proper to take some note of Hal's patriotism. "Army or Navy?"

"Army. He's in a jungle with MacArthur."

So we went to bed together.

I think that even in New York City a common knowledge of the state of Montana is no excuse for adultery. When the pale light of morning pressed against the windows, I was glad I didn't know Phillips. I dressed as quickly as so androgynous a confusion of cloth allowed and went to look for the bathroom. It is thought-provoking when you have slept with a faceless man's wife to see your face in a mirror over the washbowl, where countless times his faceless face had observed himself growing older.

I relieved myself carefully against the porcelain of the toilet bowl, wishing no unnecessary splashing to remind me of my humanity; for the moment I preferred to be a cipher. I had no toothbrush. I had never before spent a night out without a tooth-brush. Worse, from a cosmetic point of view, was my lack of a razor. I had begun shaving at thirteen, not regularly because I had no beard, but it was said that shaving hastened the need to shave. How I had longed to have a beard like my father's. He had seemed to me at once proud and exasperated that his beard was so active he had to shave twice a day if he was going out in the evening for pinochle; nothing is so sharp a reminder of how much in common we all have with the skid-row bum or the child abuser — led off shackled by the police — as a stubble of beard. A stubble of beard after eight in the morning advertises that one has abandoned self-respect, can expect public scorn, and is lucky not to be exhibited in a cage.

I hesitated to further invade Hal Phillips's privacy by opening the mirrored cabinet over the basin, but a second look at my sprouting face made me cast compunction aside. And there among the liquids to sweeten the soured stomach, pills to quiet the reeling brain, salves to facilitate penetration, was a razor, shaving brush and squat wooden bowl of lavender-scented shav-ing soap. Would he return to use them — strengthened by brushes with danger, proud of his camaraderie with those who had fought with him shoulder to shoulder? Or would they gather dust, objects of bathos like the Little Toy Dog?

But it was some time before I shaved, for Liz was beside me to make her own use of the bathroom, and I stepped out in order to keep my image of her as a woman intact; it is intolerable to concede that the women we admire defecate. Some women, perhaps — bad women, women who have had no advantages, who are not, perhaps, loved; possibly foreign women, or those so close to the soil they have the example of livestock ever near them. Some women, yes, but not the beauty caught arranging spring flowers or whose profile is seen at the opera window of her town car. Not a sweetheart or a mother, good God, no.

I stood looking out the window, insofar as it could be looked out of. Village grime clung to it like filthy frost. Through it, the high, narrow window across the street had the delicate opacity of a photographic negative, and like a negative it revealed a ghostly figure: someone was standing over there watching me watching, the narrow abyss of a Village street a no-man's-land between us. Neither he nor I could ever possess it; it didn't really exist. It had no more substance than a thought, no more permanence than a word just spoken, inconsequential as a rose petal falling in an empty room. For I guessed that he, like me, like me and Liz and Helen, had fled some hometown where life had been intolerable. For the Village had had a style of life that had vanished and was but legend even when we were all little children. Sometimes in a bar called the Stirrup or the Bagatelle, where soft lights touched the face like cosmetics and rendered it perfect like the face in a dream now impossible to call and never forgotten, there might suddenly pass among us a woman much like Edna Millay, who burned her candle at both ends, and doing so became immortal.

But Liz was twenty-three then, and I was twenty-five, and we didn't know that home was home because of us, and that we took it with us.

Here.

RAZORS, LIKE FOUNTAIN PENS, have personalities and are strange in a strange hand; my hand was strange and shaking after the previous tawdry hours and I nicked the upper edge of a depression in my face to the right of my mouth and I began to bleed. Luckily I had removed my shirt and undershirt; blood is a cranky stain and must be washed out at once with cold water; hot water sets the stain. Bleeding is a problem with me; I haven't sufficient coagulant material in my blood.

I controlled the flow by pressing against the wound a bit of toilet paper, which acted as a temporary scab; it darkened and was conspicuous. Now, a race walks the earth whose singularity is its quickness to point out things that the kind and the sensitive among us overlook. Those of that race want to know how we came to cut ourselves and expect a reasonable and detailed answer. They draw attention to a loose thread, the missing button, a bit of food clinging so high on a necktie that it would have gone unnoticed but for them. No eruption on the skin escapes their interest; the words "pimple" and "blackhead" and "pus" fall rich from their lips. Do not be surprised when they greet you with the observation that your hair has thinned, that a paunch strains over your belt.

Except for feeling egregious, I should have known that Liz was not one of that tribe — she was one who took it for granted that everybody cut himself and sometimes woke to find new bruises or a sprained thumb. Now she was sitting on the edge of a chaise longue discarded by a theatrical warehouse when even from the back rows it could no longer suggest opulence; one of the fussy legs lacked a caster and had been replaced by a textbook on the Victorian poets, those whom one has once read and never reads again. I wondered why she and Hal had not simply removed the three remaining casters to allow the piece to find peace on its original legs and do away with the distracting book. That ravished settee was hardly more movable on three casters and a book than on no casters at all. All the sparse furniture was odds and ends and I took it to imply not poverty but a gypsy frame of mind that refuses death, refuses the ownership of anything so valuable or durable that it hinted at their own mortality — how different an attitude than that of the Chinese, who are said to begin very early to save funds for a coffin.

Liz was filing her nails, and from time to time she extended her hand to get an idea of how they would appear to one who viewed them from a distance. "It's a relief not to have Hal here in the morning," she said. "He expects breakfast, or used to."

I should have thought that her relief at not having Hal there would have been other than his expecting breakfast. As for me, I had rather expected breakfast. I had been counting on the homely aroma of perking coffee, frying bacon and burning bread to fumigate the dark, unhealthful corners of my mind and to allow a return of innocence. Nothing really awful can have happened to people who sit down to a good hearty breakfast.

"Hal is one of your men," she said, "who would starve before he'd carry a brown paper bag down the street from the grocer's or drop a slice of bread into the toaster, or he once was. He was reared gently. He's the only man I ever knew who as a child really had a rocking horse. Oh, you see them on Christmas cards and in Schwarz's and you assume every child but you had one, that every child has the right to a piggy bank and sparklers on the

Fourth; I guess many parents are tempted, not having had the advantage of a rocking-horse ambience, to make one available for their child. But in the end they hold back. Maybe the arguments run that the child will outgrow the horse and it will have to be stored somewhere — who has the heart to toss out a child's toy on the dump? And should something tragic happen to the child, the horse would be a hideous reminder of happier days." She said Hal's mother had somehow been a Bradstreet of the colonial Bradstreets who gave us Anne Bradstreet, lately known as the Tenth Muse, but to be truly Bradstreet you had to have a sailboat. Hal had learned to sail off the Cape as a child, but they had lost everything in one of those panics that sometimes surprised people with money, and he'd never had a boat of his own, but a couple of fellows he knew at Harvard had, and they all exchanged cards at Christmas. "And now," Liz said, "it's time for a milk punch."

It was clear there were defined times for a milk punch, and that there would be no breakfast. I had never had a milk punch. I had never thought of one, and had I, I should have thought of winter holidays when one had been lately frisking about in the snow all bright-eyed. But no snow had fallen on West Eleventh Street and my eyes were not bright.

Liz had come a long way from the West we had known, where from the age of fourteen until you were eighteen you drank beer and after that, one day, whiskey and water — no ice — a drink we called a "ditch." The bars I knew in Grayling, Montana, and those outside of town called roadhouses, were stocked with gin, but I don't recall a bottle uncapped. Bottles of crème de menthe and Cherry Heering added color to a basic brown scheme, as fancy jars of colored water perked up the otherwise dismal atmosphere of the City Drug Company. The levels of the Cherry Heering and crème de menthe dropped but slowly as some troubled woman, late in the evening or watching out the window as the sun rose again over the Rocky Mountains, turned to a cordial to recapture a time when she had drunk for taste rather than for effect, or simply to express a pretty feminine caprice. A man would no sooner have ordered a cordial than he'd have fitted himself with a garter belt. Probably a milk punch was equally suspect, but I accepted the first of a garland of milk punches. You mix equal quantities of ice-cold milk with ice-cold gin, and over the first one or two you scatter a few grains of nutmeg to show you still care about the looks of things.

Throughout the morning and the early hours of the afternoon — there was no lunch — I faced a dimension of my life I had almost forgotten — the years when I was fourteen down to the age of five, those years when you must eat what they tell you to eat. As she talked of childhood, Liz might have been directing a pageant. And of course the years of childhood do recall pageantry in their strangeness, our willingness back then to accept toads and trolls and monsters as our peers.

"Remember the Thanksgiving Pageant?" Liz asked. "What was your Plymouth Rock made of?" She sat back on the ruined chaise longue, hugging her knees like an excited child.

The curtains that hid the Grayling Public School's Plymouth Rock from the audience until the proper time were not quite long enough to hide the ankles of those who hurried across the stage — ankles well enough known in ordinary circumstances. The sight of disassociated ankles prompted titters, as if something already had gone wrong. The theater was so little practiced except at Thanksgiving and Christmas, so little understood even by Miss Snodgrass, who was in charge, that no production was without flaw — the crash, say, of a stepladder backstage, the failure of lights, the snapping of a string on the piano in the midst of a sacred anthem. The curtains did not part on cue.

"That's the way it was, yes," Liz said. "The machinery never worked. But a sentimental tradition insists 'the play must go on.' The play must go on in spite of failing powers, an aching heart and collapsing scenery. If it is not believed that the play must go on, it follows that plays aren't worth the playing, and an actor's life is meaningless. In the airy reasoning of actors, the play is life.

No wonder society is slow to accept actors. Who can take seriously a bunch of people who make a living pretending to be somebody else?

"But you were saying about your curtains."

The curtains opened on a Plymouth Rock constructed of folding chairs brought up from the basement. Down there the janitor had a small, warm room beside the furnace. He smoked his pipe and read *Western Story* magazine.

The chairs had been unfolded and placed, some upright and some on their sides, to make a nice rocky effect, and the whole covered over with gray crepe paper of the same shade as the clothes of the male Pilgrims. It was a rock as Montanans knew rocks — rough and craggy, not worn smooth like the old Appalachians. The Pilgrims approached the rock from the wings to the right, the males in their gray and the females in mercerized cotton outfits of mocha brown. They trudged as if weakened by the long voyage, slogged ahead as if wading through hip-deep water. The true Pilgrims must have come ashore by dinghy, but to introduce a dinghy, perhaps a rowboat mounted on roller skates, would suggest that the entire voyage had been made in it, and to leave the false impression with the younger children that maybe the Atlantic wasn't so wild after all.

Halted, the Pilgrims flung themselves cautiously against the rock, and they knelt in prayer. A chord from the Ivers & Pond brought them to their feet and they sang "We Gather Together to Ask the Lord's Blessing" and then "The Star-Spangled Banner," which brought the audience to *its* feet. As Americans we could claim the Pilgrims, their perseverance and triumph; by extension we might claim Pocahontas, Harvard University, and a thousand statues of generals on prancing horses in public parks. We need not settle for the dust and dung of the County Fair, nor for winter evenings at the varnished oak tables in the Grayling Public Library viewing cathedrals and bazaars through the stereoscope.

"Yes, yes," Liz said. "And some saw more in the Pilgrims than a possibility of escape. As evidence of our beginnings, the Pilgrims assured us we did indeed exist. They made reasonable a search for a pedigree. They and their counterparts in other countries gave point to the rites of ancestor worship. That they themselves had emerged from darkness explains archaeology.

"I was a tall, awkward child, never certain of my balance. I was never called to play a Pilgrim. I was a bad bet. I might stumble and fall and bring down the house as the house was not meant to be brought down. An audience of children is critical and punishes imperfection with such laughter as only another child understands. But each year through grammar school I stared at that stage, a stage empty except for Plymouth Rock, and each year I felt the same apprehension as the Pilgrims in the wings prepared to enter.

"Who has not caught his breath at feeling he has just now exactly relived a moment of the past? But some — and I was one of them — have been shocked at having glimpsed the quickly averted face of the future. We need not wonder, or be surprised." She rose, moved to the window, stood in profile, and looked down into the street. "The future is no less an integer in the sum of a human life than the past or the present. Signals of the future are everywhere. Oh, yes. Portents stand just out of reach. Harbingers hover and dive like terns. Adumbrations appear. Cigarette ash is pressed between the pages of a book thought never to have been opened. Earnests wait under every other stone.

"Each year as the curtains parted and the Pilgrims landed on Plymouth Rock, I had the irrational conviction that they had directly affected my life. Well, it turned out they had." She smiled. "It had been better for me if Plymouth Rock had landed on the Pilgrims."

We talked of pencil boxes that held more than pencils — a pencil sharpener that spewed out tiny spirals of fragrant cedar when a new pencil was introduced into its aperature and turned around and around; a compound eraser — one end for pencil and one for ink; a little can with a slot big enough to receive pennies, nickels and dimes but not quarters, for quarters were seldom available to children. From this primitive bank I learned that if I was foolish enough to drop in a coin, I could slide it out on the flat surface of a table knife. In each box was a ruler, good for lightly penciling in left and right margins. Teachers were crazy about margins, and if margins were not good they might write MARGIN! in a margin: boundaries were clear and respected in those days. Against the edge of a ruler paper might be torn evenly from right to left or top to bottom. Sophisticated pencil boxes had a compass — of no practical use in grammar school, for the perils of geometry lay ahead. But with a compass you could draw stylized flowers satisfying in their symmetry. A compass had a special meaning for Liz and me, who had gone on to college: a compass was a part of the future when we would read "The Compass" by John Donne and be flung back into grammar school at three of a winter's afternoon, snapping shut a pencil box whose cover was embossed with a picture of a rushing locomotive, the profile of a horse, or Jackie Coogan in that cap of his.

"And if you were good, you got to do things," Liz said.

"Many were called, but few were chosen."

If you were good? You didn't whisper or pass notes. You got stars for spelling — who can count the pupils who have fallen with the word "fragrant"? And if you were good you were chosen to pass out paper, carry a message to the principal, open the windows with a window stick. You were glad to clean erasers, to clap them together; you risked your lungs breathing chalk dust. You risked the scorn of those who called you suck-up or sissy — and for what? For a teacher's smile.

It was long since I'd thought of myself as a child, or what I'd thought as a child. Just recently I asked a colleague what he remembered.

"Not much," he said. One or two teachers. One had resembled a horse. He did not speak of the electric clock whose big hand pounced on the next minute, nor of the drinking fountains designed for midgets, nor did he remember the stray dogs gathering around the flagpole on the playground.

"Now let's pretend," Liz said. "We're seven years old. We're alone in your room. It's on a weekend in the middle of the afternoon. Thunderheads over the mountains and we know it's going to rain so they won't make us go out and play. We've got new coloring books."

"Yes, and we've locked the door against them even though we know we'd have to open it if they knocked."

"Oh, they'll knock, afraid we're up to something vile. Well, so we've got these new coloring books and a brand-new box of crayons."

At seven or eight I already knew that the grown-ups had assigned certain colors to certain seasons; with appropriate flowers or gourds or leaves or branches they made telling centerpieces and changed the tapers to mark the dying year.

Now that we had descended into the blue grotto of childhood, where everyone has three wishes, I wished that my crayons had been given me by someone rich and that my box held not only the primary colors and black and white and brown, but vermilion and cerise and rose as well as red; olive as well as green; cobalt and aqua, sienna and ocher. And apart from these, which created special worlds and heavens, was one marked FLESH. At seven I did not see that the hue it lent human skin was not nature's but the undertaker's idea of flesh. But I knew that whatever I touched with that crayon came alive.

WHEN LIZ TOLD ME her father had taught animal husbandry, I didn't know what to make of it. I had never known anybody who taught animal husbandry and wasn't sure what it was, but assumed it was a knowledge of and a concern for beasts whose hair, hide and flesh or brute strength could be exchanged for money, and that one who taught it might write for *The Horse* or the *Hereford Journal*. And Liz had so fixed me with her eyes — as if speaking to someone a little deaf or emotionally unstable — had so fixed me with her eyes, that in telling me what her father had done, she seemed to be making a confession, getting the worst over at once, indicating that I could continue to see her or not, as I would, and that either way she would understand. The phrase "animal husbandry" might have had some devastating meaning either to her or to her father and, of course, it had.

I think my face showed no surprise, but for a moment I felt I should take her hand and explain that my own father had sold Hart, Schaffner & Marx clothing not very successfully, and that wasn't the whole story, either.

"He taught it in Bozeman," she said.

I knew the country around Bozeman. "The country around Bozeman" was a subject for postcards lavish with fabulous colors like those in seed catalogues. Tall pines in the background, cold rushing streams, a lonely fisherman casting his Royal Coachman into a lake reflecting such clouds as made the sky appear even more vast in contrast. Among the postcards were broad panoramas of ranches shot from a high point over the valley, hayfields of clover and redtop, willows winding along the creeks, sagebrushed hills in the middle distance and the Rockies beyond, shadowed by the drifting clouds.

"Here," somebody might say, lifting a glass in Boston or New York, "is where we spent that summer."

Because certain ranchers who had failed at ranching had opened their gates — if not their hearts — to dudes. For several hundred dollars a week, dudes might eat oatmeal, pancakes, eggs and steak for breakfast, learn to call lunch dinner and dinner supper. "Lunch" was a deviled-ham sandwich wrapped in a brown paper sack and carried along with an apple in a saddlebag. For certain monies a week, dudes might wear Stetsons, Levi's and Justin boots and pretend to be who they were not. Sometimes their daughters fell in love with cowboys who might promise a real emotional life, and there was hell and sometimes the cowboys to pay. But such relationships have worked out. Daddy sometimes bought the cowboy a ranch, and out there that made a man of him. Many an eastern girl who had begun by sleeping with the help is called blessed by a little town where she did her shopping and where she established a hospital or a public park.

But it was not "the country around Bozeman" that beckoned those like me who lived in shabby failing towns like Grayling, but Bozeman itself. Bozeman was a residential little city, not a ranch or farm town. Wealthy families who had long since made their money in ranching, mining or timber had built their second and important houses in Bozeman. Locally known as "mansions," these houses, although constructed of perishable wood, had turrets and crenellations and towers to cow the envious poor; broad, treeless lawns allowed friends or enemies to be identified long before they reached the strong front doors. Some houses were occupied by wives and schoolchildren and joined only on weekends by the men of the family, except sometimes in midweek when the beast stirred. Friends from out of town who visited lesser people were invited inside automobiles and driven slowly through Bozeman to see what money and pride had built. The houses were entered by but few of the faculty of the state college.

A stigma had long been attached to the college. True, Shakespeare was taught, and Spanish and French and Latin and philosophy to boggle the mind, but the dignity of the curriculum had been compromised with the inclusion of courses that had nothing in common with culture or even with the business of business as business is generally understood. The college offered — which the state university to the north and west would not — courses in the management of hogs, in sugar-beet culture and in the facts behind a seemingly healthy sheep's toppling over in a faint. In the complex of red-brick Gothic buildings and far-flung barns and sheds, students learned horseshoeing and earned credits. In such circumstances, a degree from the state college appeared questionable; a man skilled in the identification of range grasses had as much right to declare himself a member of the learned community as one who professed the metaphysical poets.

Not surprising, then, that a schism developed. The agricultural people — the Aggies — sat apart in the cafeteria. They sat to the rear in faculty meetings and murmured when it was ruled that students must have a reading knowledge of a foreign language and that all students must pass freshman English. Yes, they rose to their feet, some of them in neither jacket nor tie, and asked who, in the state of Montana, would be reading a foreign language? And if a man could make himself understood, why be concerned with the subjunctive mood?

Some thought the Aggies had no right to a cap and gown, let alone a hood. They were noisy supporters of the football team, which alas routinely trounced the state university; they had organized a horseshoe team and the bright tone of iron shoe striking iron stake was familiar when the snow melted and the bluebells came up around the sagebrush outside of town. No wonder the place was dubbed the Cow College, and that many of the Liberal Arts people felt second-class when they visited their colleagues at the state university. ~Missoula

Liz's father felt second-class, but for a different reason: although he wore jacket and tie, hoping to be accepted by the Liberal Arts people, he was not; and because he wore jacket and tie he was not acceptable to the Aggies. He could not get it through his head why one branch of learning was not as worthwhile as another — to know why and how things grow, what becomes of things that grow, that seeds planted upside down right themselves like sentient beings, and thrive. He was looked on as mad because he believed that plants grow faster if music is played to them.

His name was Frank Chandler.

He called Liz his Bestie Friend, a salutation that underlined a peculiar relationship; they looked on each other as singular. How singular he was became clear when Liz was fourteen. How singular she was, became clear when she was eighteen.

He was tall and gangling, big of joint, his movements slow and angular, his eyes customarily so mild one had the impression he had had an early and successful dialogue with Christ; an expression of gentle puzzlement sometimes fled across his face like that seen in Holman Hunt's *The Light of the World.* He was accident-prone; tools escaped his fingers; he forgot to open doors; he tripped. His feet flew out from under him on the last ice in the spring. He often looked at his hands as if he might find an answer in them; his legs crossed, he would waggle his foot on the end of his leg, and watch it.

People crossed the street to avoid him, or turned into doorways. He was thought to want something; it would not do to let him get too close; he might appear at a door at midnight with a request not exactly obscene but one that disturbed, and brought into question one's own values. Out of gratitude (if you let him get too close) he might come bearing some awful gift. In truth,

[*39*]

all he wanted was friendship, the right to speak to others and receive in return a word and a smile.

From the time he was a child the name Ichabod Crane had been hurled at him. "In fact," Liz said, "he closely resembled the young Lincoln. One could think of him, in his last years, as wearing a shawl."

Some found it puzzling that a man so tall and slow had married a woman like Flo, who was so small and quick. "My mother was described as 'lively,' " Liz told me, "a word that suggests birds or squirrels, creatures whose swift movement taxes the eye, and leaves one feeling one has missed something. But 'driven' would have been a better word for her." Driven as one without rudder or anchor, Flo Chandler wanted little but to be thought a pretty woman, and to have five dollars and some loose change in her purse. As a pretty woman, she felt that flowers were a true expression of herself, and having little money to satisfy her love for coddled blooms, she was the first in the spring to walk out into the nearby fields gathering bluebells and Indian paintbrush; she grieved at how short a time they survived in jelly glasses and bottles; she was as gentle with their withered remains as with a beloved invalid.

She was one who prepared lunch at the last possible moment, somewhat distracted by the enormity of preparing food. Then her hands went quickly to the Campbell's tomato soup, to the can of tuna, to the mayonnaise and the soft, yielding bread in the gay, waxed wrapper.

When Frank Chandler's salary was cut in 1930, she began to play the piano in the small orchestra for Saturday night dances in Pioneer Hall up over the Bozeman Implement Company.

> *Five foot two, eyes of blue,*
> *But oh, what those five foot could do . . .*

Bozeman society was correct in having been chary in asking her into their rooms. In following her new profession, she differed little from the dancehall girls who had entertained the miners in the goldfields and had sold their bodies for an ounce or two. But she would not be snubbed; she spoke to one and all on the streets: and there on the streets she found her own level.

She made friends with the manager of the five-and-ten, and was often observed entering or leaving, by a door at the top of steep, rubber-matted steps, an apartment over the store itself. It is people who live in apartments who lead strikingly disorderly lives. These people refuse responsibility for cigarette burns, cracked mirrors, falling plaster and doors torn off hinges. Party after party went on up there after store hours, long after, and included riffraff like traveling salesmen who answer to nobody, out-of-town mining men who think of nothing but good times, and a Mrs. Hale whose husband, if so he was, had taken over the meat market and had presented her, if you please, with a black Packard sedan — one of the new small ones, to be sure, but a Packard. It wasn't hard to imagine that the fresh blood staining his white pants and apron wasn't always bovine.

Over the five-and-ten a phonograph could be heard as far away as the Ford garage; automobiles suddenly pulled away and laughter fell behind like shattered glass. Flo Chandler's high heels clicked here and there.

"A pretty little piece," men said.

They wondered at the college if Frank Chandler knew; a note to him, maybe. Because of the little girl, as much as anything.

But how would he not know? Does not a man know where his wife is — doesn't he care? When he looks up from the paper in the morning, up from his book, or removes his pipe from his mouth or returns from the bathroom to find her gone — does he not at least inquire?

"Where were you?" he might ask. "I was wondering where you were."

Or had the two of them come to some kind of ugly arrangement after harsh words — even violence? You hear about these things, these awful arrangements that neither would have countenanced but a few years before, arrangements arrived at through a slow or even headlong moral attrition — these I'll-go-my-way-you-go-your-way affairs, and you know they always lead to trouble of some kind, some tragedy because there is no real arrangement. You are forever hearing about this sort of thing and so often a part of it takes place upstairs, or in a basement, and there are those roadhouses that look so withdrawn and shuttered in the sunshine.

Of course a woman as lively and pretty as Flo Chandler who played piano would be welcomed upstairs anywhere; and since she was scarcely thirty she still danced, shook a mean leg, some said. Frank Chandler did not dance; he did not dance because he came from a background where dancing was opposed as suggestive, and they were right, it is. Where he came from was a rundown, dispirited part of Iowa, a land of cruel sun, sin and secret shame and overcooked vegetables, a land where it was to a woman's advantage if she tatted and quilted, and to a man's if he could whittle and tie fancy knots. Funerals were well thought of. How the body was laid out, and in what, and who was on hand for the final viewing. In our end is our beginning. Life had been disappointing; surely death and subsequent translation into heaven offered pleasanter challenges. If not, what was it all for? (And do not forget the photographs in the album before you, nor the shrub planted under the south window. Notice the early shadows and the rising wind.)

It both embarrassed and delighted Frank Chandler, Liz thought, when his wife would for no reason at all suddenly dance up to him as if he were a mirror, making little beckoning, primping gestures and then she would twirl and dance away, leaving him with his hands at his sides and his face in the ghost of a grin.

"Her hands trembled when she fastened on her earrings. She had several pairs."

It was thought-provoking to consider that she, like him, had come from a background where dancing was opposed and hymn singing encouraged, and yet she had learned to dance, and to dance as if it mattered, that only in dancing (and in flowers) could she express herself. Oh, that was a country back in Iowa where the mandolin was acceptable because of old, past associations, fried chicken and hayrides, but the ukelele was not.

"Nor should the ukelele have been countenanced," Liz said, drawing herself up with hauteur. "Those dusky Hawaiian dearies shimmying and drawing attention to their crotches."

What might have been expected to happen, happened.

It was April; at the college they were between quarters; the M picked out in stones on the side of the mountain cried out for fresh whitewash. The rich boy from Nebraska had the top down on his Ford convertible; all morning he drove up and down College Avenue with those students lucky enough to know his favor. The front doors of the fraternity and sorority houses were open to the sun.

There had been unaccustomed activity in the Chandler bungalow, one of six quite like it on a new street west of the campus. Between it and the next was a driveway, unused because the Chandlers had no car. He had never learned to drive, and there was the money angle. The door was reached by a steep set of concrete steps, and the roof of the shallow porch was supported by two A-shaped — well, supports. Photographs of such modest houses appear in newspapers as the unlikely birthplace or former dwelling of some famous name, or as the scene of something so frightful it cannot be reconciled with such innocent architecture.

Frank Chandler was off to the state of Idaho by train — Pullman, mind you — at the expense of the college. He would meet with other animal husbandry people in Idaho and come back to report to somebody who needed the information. He had had no previous experience with a Pullman car and was enchanted by the idea — he mentioned it several times — that there was a special basin over which you washed your teeth and into which you spat. He took a taxi to the station a good hour before the train's arrival.

[*43*]

"I saw nothing strange in his wanting to use that little basin," Liz said. "I should have liked the chance to spit there myself, and to think, Here I am on a Pullman spitting, and when I finish I shall be somewhere different from where I started."

He was to be gone three days and three nights, one of the nights on the Pullman car. He promised to bring Liz what small cakes of soap he could gather in the hotel. Liz was charmed by miniatures, and from the time she could write her name and address correctly she "sent away" for free samples: tiny bottles of perfume and shampoo, flat, round metal boxes of salves and unguents no bigger than a twenty-five-cent piece, cans of Jonteel and Djer Kiss talcum powder no bigger than your thumb.

"It's simple enough to understand the appeal of bantam roosters, Shetland ponies and jockeys," Liz said. "They allow us a fine opportunity to feel protective. But I'm not so sure about tiny, inanimate objects, like teapots and dolls nestling inside a peanut shell. It may be that we sense in the infinitely small a special refinement, as if the object had shed the dross that accounts for largeness. I'll have to look into the matter."

It was into such matters that she looked. Why, for example, did most women choose blue as a favorite color and men, red? What a paradox that tradition assigned blue to males and a shade of red to girls?

The toothpaste consumed in the Chandler household was Colgate Ribbon Dental Creme; the aperature in the end of the tube constrained the paste to ooze out flat, that it might not roll off the brush, if that had been your previous trouble. But — apparently to savor an entirely new experience on the Pullman, her father had bought a gaudy red and yellow tube of Ipana.

"And there it lay," Liz said, "after he had gone, on the bed where he'd been packing his suitcase. His grip, he called it. And then I realized he had deliberately left it behind. He would use the excuse of having no toothpaste to strike up an acquaintance with a stranger. He was so guileless, so unlike me, that it would never have occurred to him to ask a stranger for toothpaste if he had his own with him."

She hoped he had found courage to speak to that stranger, and that the stranger had been kind.

At the time, Liz was eleven and in the last grade of Gallatin Grammar School. "I skipped the second grade and the sixth grade and have never since been at home with six times nine and eight times seven. And I alone of my intellectual peers still wore bloomers that matched my dresses."

She hated bloomers because they marked her as a child. "I saw no reason for them except as a humiliation, part of a far-flung conspiracy among the grown-ups to keep one forever an adolescent. But one morning two days after her father had left for Idaho she understood the reason for them. That morning at ten the pupils were considering geography and she was attacked by her first menstrual period. "The bloomers were an effective blotter." At the end of the class she whispered to the teacher that she was sick; Miss MacGregor the school nurse was prepared for the situation, bound Liz up properly, and sent her home with a doctor's sample of Midol. "I had heard menstruation hit you after age twelve, but I was not much surprised at the early onset. I was mentally precocious. Why not physically and sexually?"

Having five cents in the pocket of the bloomers, she stopped at the candy store across from the railroad station and bought five tiny wax milk bottles filled with green citrus-tasting fluid to get through the day. She wondered if little girls threw themselves under the wheels of railroad trains on learning they had become women, and how awful for the engineer, who probably had a little girl of his own he wouldn't want to see crushed. Well, the thing to do was keep away from railroad tracks.

She took her time walking home; this fairly shattering experience was too vast to be contained within the four confining walls of her familiar room. The associations there now had absolutely nothing to do with her. Her new world included high heels and sorority girls and proms and rumble seats. She was going to have to learn to dance.

"Who is that lovely girl dancing there?"

[45]

"That's Liz Chandler, and she's brilliant as well."

"Do you think she might care to meet me?"

"Idaho, but Alaska."

The Chandler bungalow did not look the same, nor was it; in the ordinarily unused driveway — two strips of concrete each hardly larger than the tread of a tire and with grass growing in between — a dark-green panel truck was parked. No lettering on its sides identified it as belonging to the telephone company or any other service that ameliorates human life. No windows in the body, not even a rear one; whatever it carried, contraband or worse, was beyond prying eyes. She believed such trucks were used by kidnappers and grave robbers and spies. Had she had a pencil, she would have jotted down the license number on a gum wrapper. She stood long enough to memorize it — 809997 CALIFORNIA, land of oranges and sunshine, close to Mexico, land of tangos and flashing eyes. If she were Mexican or Spanish she would be known as Rita Manzanita and she would click her castanets and flash her eyes and dance up there until she was exhausted and fall in something resembling a faint, and a young man she had her eye on would pick her up and carry her off. He didn't realize she was a spy and that her beauty would be his undoing.

Or the truck may have had something to do with the house on the other side, but in neither house was there any audible activity; strange, because whatever the profession of the driver of the truck, it could hardly have been carried on in total silence. Something certainly had to be moved or adjusted. But there was no movement inside the Chandler bungalow; no shadow cast altered the quality of the light that entered the windows.

She was intimate with all the doors in the house, knew the sound of voices or the cough of the toilet flung against the ones that were closed, the ones that were open and how far open; all the doors were silent on their hinges; the oiling of hinges and doorknobs was one of her father's dearest commitments, and one household chore that did not result in bleeding.

[*46*]

Opening, the front door made no sound at all.

Because the house was so small, the contractor had wisely kept the hall to a minimum; there was scarcely enough room to extend the elbows when removing a coat. A tall table with a small round surface and long cane legs was precariously balanced and appeared to fly in the face of physics. Visitors often carelessly nudged it and sent the telephone crashing headlong on the cheap piece of turkey-red carpet. Then came the profuse apologies, as if a visitor never before had been responsible for such a mess in a hall.

To one side was a shallow closet in which was her father's black umbrella, never unfurled in her memory because in Bozeman umbrellas were looked on as English and effeminate; real men pulled their hats low and strode into the falling water. Opposite was the glass-paned French door meant to set a Continental tone, but the skimpy fumed oak paneling and false beams spoiled all that.

Directly from the hall, the carpeted stairs rose steeply to save room, so steeply that when an occupant was seventy he must surely forgo the upper rooms and the bathroom and settle for a daybed below and a chamber pot.

Liz went upstairs.

"I was aware of sounds," she said. "Of rhythms."

At the top of the stairs she paused.

"I believe now that I knew what I would find, what I would see and that I had never seen it before — somewhat as if one had heard of an ape but had never seen an ape nor the picture of an ape. I did not want to pass that partly opened bedroom door, and yet I did, and as I passed I paused and I looked."

The tan window shade had been pulled against the Rocky Mountain morning, and the light inside was powdery and ocher, and the picture that remained always in her mind was that of a faded sepia print.

"I had not realized just how tiny my mother was. It follows that clothes add bulk and stature except to the dead. They were whispering — or he was. He was dark and mildly furred and he was there in my father's bed working over her on hands and knees as a gentle engine might, pumping away. I suppose it is something perverse in me, but what first crossed my mind was that this was an odd activity to be going on in the daylight. You see, I had never before witnessed it nor seen pictures of it, had never speculated what followed kisses and fondling, what was the ultimate message of the valentine and the Whitman's Sampler. I knew people did it and I knew my father and mother had done it because I was standing there with warm blood between my thighs, but I had not known before how they did it and I believed that when they did it, they did it in the dark when everybody was asleep. I didn't believe my father and mother did it after I was born because there would no longer be a reason to.

"I heard my mother sigh, as if she'd just pulled off tight shoes."

The atavistic horror of what she had witnessed seized her a few minutes later, when she reached her own room, now a room of heartbreaking innocence. She lay face down on her bed, eyes tight shut. Her mother would discover that she was in the house and then what? Somehow she must get back past that adulterous door and down the stairs to the outside, and wait in the alley across the street until the panel truck had driven off. But that was impossible because before long they would be through with what they were doing in there and she would be caught and the man might kill her in some way that would look like an accident so she would never talk.

The next best thing was to pretend to be asleep, sleep so akin to death, but now she felt an overwhelming need before she pretended sleep: she went to her closet and reached up on top and brought down her doll.

"I hadn't touched that doll in years."

 "IT IS LIKELY," Liz said, looking into a milk punch, "that human beings hide when they copulate because of a rooted fear that — while oblivious to anything but reaching a climax — they will be found by ravening beasts or cranky neighbors, and that they will be destroyed before they can untangle themselves. I think I could have fallen on my face in the hall before they would have been aware of my presence there. But following orgasm, an awareness of the real world descends like vengeance; evidence must be destroyed, wiped up, hidden or burned; then the roast must be put in, a light bulb replaced.

"Their furtive parting in the hall was brief and in whispers."

Liz had waited until she heard the green panel truck drive off, and then she began to sob.

"Uncontrollably," Liz said. "This is awfully good gin, and I will have more of it. It must have given my mother quite a turn, my sobbing, for of course she would believe it was a result of what I'd seen. My mother must have been on a dilemma's horns — whether to rush right in to me, whether to dress and rush out of the house and never be seen again. But within a minute she opened my door and stood there in the house dress I had last seen her in before seeing her quite without it. She stood wide-eyed, the palm of her right hand pressed against the side of her head. 'Oh, my baby,' she said.

"For a good sixty seconds I let her stand there believing her behavior had caused my weeping, and that she had perhaps damaged me irreparably which, as it turned out, maybe she had. I allowed her to stand there wondering if she any longer had the right to touch me, to comfort me.

"Then I took a long, shuddering breath, and paused. 'It happened at school,' I stage-whispered. 'Right in geography.'

" 'What happened, baby?' Seldom have I heard such relief in a human voice. 'What, what happened?'

" 'I got the curse.'

" 'Oh, my baby.' She came forward now able to believe that in my anguish over a perfectly normal happening I had charged into my room looking neither to right nor left. 'We all — '

" 'I don't want to be a grown-up lady,' I whimpered. And at that moment I drew my doll out from under the pillow. 'I still want to be a little girl.'

" 'Now, now, now,' she crooned on the descending scale, 'you'll always be my little girl.' She then took me in her arms and petted me.

" 'Oh, Mummy,' I said, and began my snuggling.

" 'That's my baby,' she said. 'Now why don't we go down and make us both some cinnamon toast?'

"So many little things end with cinnamon toast or peanut butter."

They were an arresting tableau — the mother cradling the little girl, the little girl cradling a forgotten doll.

"What were you thinking all this time?" I asked.

"I don't know the desperate contortions of my poor mother's brains," Liz said, "but as for me, I was convinced at that moment that I had a career as an actress."

Liz wondered what form her mother's guilt or compassion would take, and assumed it would include a changing of the bedspread. "Unless, of course, she figured a changed spread would alert my father to hanky-panky. And the morning after the night he got back she prepared French toast for his breakfast and made a point of adding a little sugar to the batter. He liked that."

Her father was silent about his part in the animal husbandry proceedings. His wife urged him to divulge it.

"You just sit down right there and tell me all about it," and as she spoke she put her arm around his shoulder and rather guided him to the shabby Morris chair as if he were an old, old man.

"It was just a meeting," he said.

His wife did not bring up the matter of the small metal basin on the Pullman car; it might be dangerous to encourage him to dwell within a private fantasy of spitting into a metal bowl; he had enough difficulty adjusting to the real world as it was. He could not be trusted to leave the house without first making certain that his fly was closed, for once he had urinated, the act seemed to him to have been totally accomplished and his mind went to other things rather than to the gaping slit in his pants. *He did not follow through.* And that is certainly why, once again, he was overlooked for promotion: whatever had been his performance in the state of Idaho, he had not followed through. His mind was elsewhere.

He had, he said, met a man — "a crackerjack of a fellow" — who was sitting in a green leather chair in the hotel lobby.

Liz felt that any man who responded to her father's social advances was at once suspect, for who in the world would want to know her father, but for that very reason she was fiercely protective of him and told herself that when she was rich and famous she would require those who sought her out — who urged her to grace their parties and otherwise be seen with her — she would require them to include her father. She would point out to them that had it not been for him she would not have felt it necessary to become so rich and famous.

But, if her father were to be believed, it was the man in the green leather chair who made the first advance. Leaning forward he had said, "Are you acquainted locally?"

Her father denied being locally acquainted, but that did not stop the man from pressing on. It transpired that the man grew apricot trees and apple trees in the state of Washington in a land he described as a "paradise." He had scores of trees and sold their perfect fruit to a company that made candy bars, one called Applets, after the apples, and the other Cotlets, after the apricots.

"They would be a healthful candy, made from that good fruit," her father said, and as he went on in this vein, his speech became slightly slurred, and his eyes rested on the middle distance. Several times he said "paradise."

The man in the green chair lowered his voice and suggested that the two of them visit a place he knew and drink a bottle or two of beer.

"I couldn't believe," her father said, "that the man didn't know that to buy beer was against the Eighteenth Amendment to the Constitution of the United States and I was surprised that he would make this suggestion in a place where he might be overheard. I spoke to him about the duty of a citizen to respect the law of the land, and he said nobody gave a tootin' about the law and he bet that in three years' time the whole caboodle would be repealed."

"The man was exactly right," Liz told me. "Three years later, beer was legal again and I gather that the national reaction was something like that of a man who has recovered his own soul." Legal beer brought with it an affection for Germans and German Americans that had been abandoned at the beginning of the First World War. Now an entire generation who had never before been inside a saloon could stand at a bar and simply by raising one foot and resting it on a brass rail attain the comfortable insouciance so often observed among cud-chewing beasts. The genteel among them filed into the Sugar Bowl Cafe where booths fitted with green baize curtains were provided for ladies, and they ordered the Dutch Lunch — sliced ham, liverwurst, limburger cheese and potato salad — all washed down with Bavarian Club. "Heretofore their Teutonic experiences had been only with the Christmas tree and the frankfurter."

"And I couldn't see," her father had said, shaking his head, "why the man thought I was locally acquainted."

"Wasn't it only that he asked you *if* you were?" Flo Chandler asked.

"Yes, but asking seemed to mean he thought I was acquainted locally."

"Maybe he thought that if you were in a hotel, that was because you didn't know anybody in town."

Frank Chandler was suddenly alert. "And thought I looked like a fellow that even if he was acquainted locally wouldn't be asked to spend the night in a private home?"

"I'm sure he didn't think that, Frank. He was making conversation. And he asked you to have a beer with him. Don't forget that."

"Well, yes. Acquainted locally could mean did I know a good place to go for a beer. Sometimes I think Repeal wasn't a good thing because lots of people have to be kept from harming themselves or other people. You see that everywhere, and in the prisons."

Now he often napped before dinner, or said he did. When he returned from classes, he closed the door of the bedroom behind him, not in anger or really in anything. He simply went in there and shut the door. As one dinnertime approached, and he had not come downstairs, Flo opened the door quietly. He was not napping; he was sitting on the far side of the bed, back to the door, and the inclination of his head on his neck indicated that he was reading, reading something, tilting a text of some kind against the fading light. He started; she heard something fall; she heard his feet push something under the bed, a little hiss of something as it slid.

"I'll be down directly," he said mildly.

Whatever it was, was not under the bed next morning. Whatever it was, was not a letter, for a letter would not have made that little sound, floating down as letters do when released. A book? Pamphlet on religion? His background was fundamental-

[53]

ist; his mother had not hesitated to ask a stranger, "Are you saved?" and the woman had expected an honest answer. His father, too. They believed in a personal Savior, Who, if accepted, was prepared to forgive blasphemy, incest or rape as matters of no ultimate concern but, if denied, revealed Himself to be as vindictive as a wounded grizzly and would see even the good screaming in Hell.

Pornography?

Whatever it was, it was threatening. To him? If to him, to them. It was as a threat that Flo Chandler began searching for it; as a threat it concerned them as well as him; as a threat it became their property as well as his, and as much *their* right to classify it and dispose of it — tearing it up, burning it — as it was *his* right.

She did not believe he had taken it next morning to the college because *there* it was a greater threat than here in the house. There, if discovered, it might lead to shame and dismissal. *Here*, only a family confrontation — words, tears, promises, perhaps a compromise. She had been alert to his movements that next morning; he had gone to no unusual part of the house, opened no doors, no drawers, had scarcely been out of her sight from the time they woke.

"Your father's been reading something funny, I think," she told Liz. "I want you to help me find it."

"It was my mother's method," Liz said, "to involve me in projects she thought would draw me closer to her. Many's the cake I helped bake, chopping up the nuts and being 'allowed' to beat the eggs. Some kids jumped at the chance to beat eggs: there was the mystery of the gears in the utensil itself, and the opportunity to be legitimately destructive. My mother would devise a game about washing windows, and the one who finished the greatest number of panes won. So many games one wins offer no prize. 'Now, let's just see which one of us finds it first,' she said. It was more important to her to find it than to have my eyes not fall on couples engaging in sodomy — if pornography it was."

Liz had flinched at opening the drawers of his bureau and had

[*54*]

flinched at touching cloth that had touched his private parts. She was struck by how shabby his underclothing was, and how numerous the holes in his socks. She wondered how long ago her mother had stopped caring whether or not her husband's heels and toenails had direct contact with shoe leather.

Nothing under the edges of the carpet, nothing in the recesses of the clothes closet nor in his shabby suitcase stored there. Nothing among the Christmas tree ornaments, a location he might have chosen because we hesitate to touch Christmas ornaments at the wrong time of year and assume nobody else would.

In the kitchen below, beside the breakfast nook stood a skinny steam radiator behind which Liz as a little child had dropped toast and bits of egg her mother insisted on and which her stomach refused; it said something of her mother's housekeeping that the extent of the cache was not discovered until Liz was nine years old. A similar radiator was in the bedroom where they hunted for whatever they hunted for, and there behind it was the publication they sought. Between the covers was material more dangerous to them than texts dwelling on an outrageous God or unspeakable perversions. It was a real estate catalogue.

The desire to own land is as basic as sex and religion, and as likely to get out of hand. Lust for land sends savage hordes raging over the face of the earth, stumbling over frozen tundra and perishing in deserts. It accounts for the Oklahoma land rush, old folks and children abandoned, pistols drawn. It lay behind the hysteria of the Florida land boom that enriched some and left others fleeced and in water up to their hips. It accounts for absentee landlords and rioting peasants. Laws are drawn up concerning the inheritance of land; younger sons are sent off to the provinces. Covered wagons lurch across plains. Brother turns on brother and women forsake their virtue. A lust for land accounts for gentlemen farmers who look with pleasure over their landscape and don't know a McCormick Deering from a John Deere. It accounts for the flight from the city and the rise of ghettos. It is behind the vegetable garden and the annual plethora of zucchini.

"If only I had a little piece of land." Land is security. You can tell people to get off it. If they don't, the police will come, or you can shoot them.

You can leave land to somebody, and be remembered, be immortal because it was you who left it. There may be something under it — oil, precious metals. How would that be!

And you can have your own cow and chickens and will never be at a loss for snap beans.

The danger in the real estate catalogue was not only that it advertised land, but that it advertised cheap land. It appeared that forests were available for a pittance; a thousand dollars bought land as far as the eye dared see, a dollar an acre. Six hundred and forty acres equals a square mile. For six hundred and forty dollars you could buy a mile. Imagine owning a mile. And the land was everywhere—east, west, north, south.

"And over the cuckoo's nest," Liz said.

You had only to step in and see the local representative. He was at hand. Did you require a lake or stream? Did you want the high hills that rolled into the sunrise or a mountain that stood before the sunset?

"So that's what he has in mind," Flo Chandler said.

The catalogue was limp with use and fell open to a certain page. She replaced the catalogue behind the radiator. It was not yet time to make a scene. She didn't yet have sufficient material for one.

Frank Chandler had taught animal husbandry, now, for nine years and had made more money three years before as an instructor than now during the Depression as a passed-over assistant professor. The earliest years of the Depression had brought into question the value of higher education, and the Liberal Arts people were the first to feel the cold heels of economy; their forces were trimmed. To save the French department, the head dispatched

Professor Emeritus Clark over to the legislature in Helena. He was a gentle old soul with a feathery voice, but years earlier he had published a volume, *Villon, Trouvère or Prophet?*, which was known far and wide among the literate and was earthy enough, perhaps, even to have reached the eyes of a legislator or two. On campus, he was a familiar sight trotting along College Avenue wearing a navy-blue beret like one he had worn in Paris some fifty years earlier; he was pointed out to visitors and sought after as an ornament for both faculty and town parties.

The chairman of the legislative Committee on Educational Finance wore cowboy boots with the heels slightly modified so he could walk. He had only one question to ask Professor Emeritus Clark as Clark stood among them in a circular room of cruelly varnished oak, and the question was, "What's French good for?"

The stupidity of the question left the old man quite speechless; he showed them his palms in, alas, a Gallic gesture. How explain to these peasants the towering figure of Racine, and he quoted in his still-moving voice a line that has chilled the hearts of men for two centuries — the words spoken by Phèdre, sick with love.

On dit qu'un prompt départ vous éloigne de nous. The line was not without significance for old Clark himself.

Silence. Had he moved them as Orpheus had moved the Furies in the Underworld? Could not Racine move a stone? Then a legislator from Beaverhead County spoke up.

"Doc," he said, "I think you better talk United States." And there was affable chuckling. After all, the old fellow was harmless.

A few months later the entire French department was sacked, an earnest of what might be in store for the remainder of the humanities division. Only the Aggies had the best chance of continuing paychecks. After all, many legislators in Helena were farmers and ranchers acquainted with swill and manure, and those who were not all had a cow or a horse or a privy somewhere in the background, and were grown men before they knew there was such a thing as a warm bedroom in winter and a fork used for salad only. It was the Aggies who could afford to keep their automobiles and to fill them with gas and shoe them with rubber. The best hamburger and even an occasional steak continued to be served up to them.

Every two weeks for nine years, Frank Chandler had handed over to the Gallatin Savings and Loan Association ten dollars along with his black imitation-leather passbook. The passbook they handed back each time, and each time more valuable, each time more of a loss if lost, a little black book of dreams. He kept it in the inside pocket of his jacket and felt it — as some feel their hearts, and some their balls.

$2,160.24!

Standing before a mirror because her hair was suddenly at fault, Flo Chandler told herself she was a pretty lucky girl, and for a moment she didn't believe a word of it. She loved him — he had been good. But oh, that ambling walk, as if he stalked something — himself? — those knobby knees, the frequent failure of the circulation in his hands that left them cold and their touch that of death. The hair that grew ignored on the long lobes of his ears, his awful compulsion to be liked! And she had betrayed him. Yes, we must see the betrayed in the worst of lights.

She never knew, never knew whether something had got back to him — it was the only time it had happened, she had only wanted to be liked — but the world is rotten with people who whisper things and send unsigned letters. They have nothing to do with their lives but to ruin the lives of others who wish only to be left alone.

He turned to her not a week after he'd come back from Idaho.

"There's a little piece of land, a little place out in the state of Washington. A little place for the three of us."

So somebody must have said something, something that had so damaged all three of them that they must hide in the state of Washington.

She had smiled. "What do you mean, Frank?" She spoke as if he had just remarked, "I'm thinking of doing away with the storm windows."

A good thing she'd found that awful catalogue and had marshaled up arguments against investments in land in the year of our Lord 1933. She had thought what he had in mind was investment, a place in which to put away his money rather than in the Gallatin Savings and Loan.

A wonder she didn't scream.

"... do you mean, Frank?"

"I'm forty years old, Flo."

"I guess I don't understand."

"Don't you really, Flo?"

"But about being forty?"

"I'm no good here. A man can't live somewhere being no good."

"But your job — your — your position!"

"Man does not live by bread alone."

"But first you've got to have the bread."

"Oh, there will be bread. Together we'll be bringing in the sheaves."

"But how, Frank, how?"

"I mean to raise fruit."

"You don't know the first thing about raising fruit!"

"I have two hands, Flo."

You have two hands, have you? You have two hands marked with little scars because you fumble. Your right hand makes your signature no better than a hen scratch. Your two hands look in the wrong places for what you have lost, and they feel for the wrong things, expect the wrong things. Now I can't bear the touch of your hands. I lie in the dark and know you might touch me and take what you called your marital rights that time, and now you speak, you dare to speak of your two hands!

So she thought. "Frank, you must promise me something."

"Yes, Flo?"

"Promise me you won't give up your position until you've thought about it again."

"I can't promise that, Flo."

[59]

"Frank, when was the last time I asked you to promise me something. You can't remember and I can't remember."

"I can't promise because I've already quit my job."

"Please. Ask them to give it back to you. Say you changed your mind. People can change their minds."

"I've already bought the land out there, signed, sealed and delivered."

Now a different montage, a horrid montage, fled across the dark of her mind's eye, snippets of loss and poverty — cold radiators, unpaid bills, threats, an empty icebox. A door opens on nothing. She stood alone in a snowy waste crying out to someone who would not answer.

"Think of your daughter."

"I have."

She did not dare say, "Think of me." Did not dare because that could be exactly what he was thinking, thinking to get her out of that town where he walked under a vile set of horns. But unless she pushed him that would not be mentioned. For there was in him a broad stripe of kindness, and he would forgive her, look on her as foolish, silly, but little worse. Why oh why had she not prepared herself for a life alone. But she had no real means of making a living. You can't live on ten dollars playing the piano once a week in Pioneer Hall. The ads you saw in magazines and inside match covers were for men, not women. They thought it was men who needed money, not the women — selling shoes from door to door, subscriptions to magazines, raising rabbits in your spare time, be an electrician by mail and make Big Money, get into Radio.

She might have had free tuition at the college, learned to type, do shorthand, bookkeeping. Hadn't done it because it would have hurt his feelings, advertised his failure. So you see she had thought of him. Why hadn't she left him years before when she knew it was no good?

Here's why. Because once after a drink or two a friend of hers had put it very, very crudely about her own husband. "He's a meal ticket, Flo. That's what it amounts to. A woman puts up with a lot for a meal ticket." And that was Mabel Horrocks, whose husband managed the five-and-ten, and Mabel was a lot more capable than she. There were cute things in Mabel's apartment like some of the ashtrays, what it said inside them and the shape, and a stuffed doll almost life-sized on the bed for a pillow, and there were serious things, too. Mabel had four lamps, two bridge ones and two table ones; the light from these lamps made everybody look her best. They all sat in chairs Mabel had fixed with pillows she'd made out of a stuff that was green one way you looked at it and purple another, and she couldn't help thinking how comfortable it all was and how a woman likes to be pleased — she did, anyway. Mabel had all the ingredients for pink lady and orange blossom cocktails that the men laughed at, and whiskey, and later on one of the men would rise to his feet. Flo liked to see certain men rise to their feet.

"Now, then!" a man would say, rising to his feet. "How about putting on the old feed bag?"

Their slang was real catchy. It was awfully hard to get ahead of them. They didn't give a hoot, those men. Then the ladies would go to the bathroom to powder up and then they would all get their bags and out they'd go! But sometimes they'd send out to the Golden Pheasant for Chinese food or to Sammy's for clubhouse sandwiches.

In Mabel Horrocks's rooms she hoped some night to meet a man who could halt the dangerous drift of her life.

"I'm so frightened," she told her mirror. "So frightened."

If such a man she met, she would put her cards on the table, have it out with Frank — not have it out, really, because Frank was a kind man, he truly was. But he must sense she was unhappy. If she weren't unhappy, she wouldn't have done what she did. Was it so bad to have people want you? If it came to that, she would tell Frank what she'd done. It wouldn't be the first time a man was told. Let him get the divorce, but she knew he wouldn't because he was a kind man.

[61]

Now it looked as though the chance to meet the right man in Mabel Horrocks's rooms was up the spout.

And Frank Chandler was no longer even a meal ticket.

She had four dollars in her purse. She had three slips to her name, not one good enough to see the doctor. She had lived a hundred and fifty miles from Yellowstone National Park and had never yet seen a bear or a geyser.

And she hadn't the skill to make it alone.

Twenty-eight, Frank was, when she married him. How he had aged in a dozen years. At first she saw in his long silences, in his deliberate ways and slow gait, signs he might one day amount to something. It was those traits, she bet, that her mother believed would help Frank keep her in line. She really wanted to be in line, too.

She had been proud of her engagement ring, glad that it was not a diamond; even as a little girl she had been drawn to rubies, as above diamonds. At one time Frank Chandler's family had had quite a big farm and she believed (something he said?) the ring had been his mother's, had been handed down to him — the way people do — for him to use for her because of family sentiment, a sentiment that did not exist in her own family.

Frank took her to Kansas City for their honeymoon; they stayed in a hotel there, she'd forgotten the name of so it couldn't have been the good one, and she was in fear and trembling that he would notice she was not a virgin, but then of course he didn't notice.

One hot afternoon she left him in the hotel room with his magazines he'd bought downstairs and went window shopping.

"You go along, Flo," he'd said. "I'll catch up on some reading." He didn't care to look at things he couldn't buy.

In the window of a jewelry store was a sign that said RINGS APPRAISED which they do because of insurance, or just to know. It would be a good idea, she thought, to know what the ruby was worth in case sometime later on she got into some kind of jam and needed money.

She told the jeweler, "It's an old family piece." The jeweler was one of those bald men you can't tell the age of. She slipped the ring off and set it down on a square of black velvet. "I'm going to get it insured."

The jeweler picked it up and didn't even look at it with that little glass they use. "I wouldn't consider having this piece insured," he said.

"You wouldn't?" Maybe he was going to say it would cost too much to insure it, that she'd do better to salt it away in a safety deposit box and maybe have a fake made, like she'd read.

"It's not worth fifty dollars, and that includes the setting."

You could have knocked her down with a feather. "I thought a ruby was worth more than diamonds," she said.

"A good one is, indeed," the man said. "But this is not a ruby. This is a garnet."

Let me tell you, she slipped out of there with her tail between her legs! Fifty dollars, and her going around with her chin so darned high. Truly, he had never claimed the ring was a ruby, but he had let her believe that, hadn't he? Wouldn't a girl believe a red stone for an engagement ring was ruby, that a man thought ruby of her and not garnet?

But it was not that Frank Chandler might have thought so little of her that he had fobbed off a garnet on her that frightened her, but her awful need for the security of affection, why she'd gotten into trouble in the first place.

"I know exactly how my mother felt," Liz said. "For one thing, she told me. Told me exactly. My mother thought that whenever two women got together, no matter what the disparity of their ages, they were just 'Us Gals,' and as 'Us Gals' we were bound to exchange confidences — usually in the bathroom where you let down your hair as well as your pants. She was scared to death. And at the age of eleven, I already had an eye for poverty. The poor, like the rich, are always with us.

" 'Once upon a time there was a poor woodcutter . . .' Stonecutter, church mouse, chimney sweep. Old Mother Hubbard. We are weaned on lurid stories of the poor, all calculated to make poverty loathsome, all reminders of what can happen if we don't keep our noses to the grindstone and heed the advice of the *Reader's Digest*. But I should be hard put to suggest what other recourse the Little Match Girl and Old Mother Hubbard had, other than prostitution.

"There were poor kids in school with their crackers and Kraft cheese at lunchtime, and they "took milk" the state sent in little bottles, and there I was, Elizabeth Chandler, with my classy Bumble Bee tuna sandwich and hot Campbell's tomato in my very own thermos and Hostess cupcake to boot. Poor kids have chapped hands and a thin smell like boards that have lain for years in the weather. They can tell each other by the hands and the smell, and they stay off there to one side of the playground at recess, and when some girl did it with a high school boy, she was always poor. Well, of course we all know the poor have no morals. They have to fall back on sensuality because that's all they've got. I remember how shocked and puzzled I was when a boy name of Walter Leach beat me out in a spelling contest. He was a poor kid, damn it, but he spelled 'perish' better than I. It had never occurred to me that the poor could have brains. If they had brains, why were they poor?

"And now I was going to be one of the poor — or worse. And as a woman of eleven, it was time I took a gander at economics. It had not yet been my luck to run into Daddy Warbucks; I was a little too old to sell matches and still too young to be a whore except in kinky circles. I was no good at making paper flowers. Not once was a cardboard turkey of mine pasted on the windows of the Gallatin Grammar School.

"There was always acting, of course."

It was as well they didn't know then that Frank Chandler was going mad.

CALL IT A PERIOD OF ADJUSTMENT, call it a time of transition — the time between becoming and being, between getting and having; but whatever you call it, it amounts to spending a large part of life in waiting — glancing first at watches and then at calendars, and while waiting, we have time to look back with longing and affection, and time to look ahead with a rosary of emotions running through hope, apprehension, dismay and terror. We wait in lines. We wait in hotel rooms, we gnaw our nails and pace. Will the telephone ring? We wait in anterooms. Can the tooth be saved — will it be drill or forceps? A woman waits nine months and wonders if the child will have the required number of toes. A man wonders when the first symptoms will appear. Is the growth something or other or is it cancer? But is the doctor lying?

"Even death," Liz reminded me, "is slow in coming, and hope only underlines despair. And after death, what? Funeral arrangements have got to be made, and if in church, what church, whose church? Funeral home? And what about flowers. They look pretty and show respect but something has got to be done with them later. And by God, somebody has got to go into a musty closet and choose the final garments, or is it best to buy new togs because they must last a long time?"

As Liz and her mother learned, there is a lot of time between being somewhere and getting there. It would have been easier had they piled into a Greyhound, she said, and hightailed it to the state of Washington, but no. Her father had to have a car, and since he didn't drive, he had to learn. It stood to reason he had to have some means to drive out to get supplies in the state of Washington, and they would have to get to the post office, although whom they would write to and who would write to them was a mystery. But one can hope. And he would need a means to haul his fruit to where it would be bought. So he purchased a Model T touring car; it could easily be converted, he said, into a truck.

Now, the last Model T was manufactured in 1927. Since then, the Model A had appeared, greeted by cries, and in five years it, too, vanished, succeeded by the V8. The old Model T, when it rattled into town, was not yet accorded the respect for the antique, nor was it yet a symbol of nostalgia, but greeted by whistles from the rude among the young.

The picture of their preparing to leave Bozeman, Montana, and drive to Washington was framed, as it were, by the walls of Liz's five-flight walk-up apartment in New York City; for there she sketched it all, one snowy, winter afternoon, the flakes all but invisible behind the sooty windows. I was thinking that it was odd that I, unlike most men, had not as a child been able to identify the makes of automobiles, and that she, unlike most women, could. When she had spoken of the old Ford and of days that used to be, she fixed me with her eyes and began to sing softly.

" Among My Souvenirs

> There's nothing left for me,
> Of days that used to be . . .

You couldn't stump her with a song.

She knew the words to "Who's Your Little Whoo-Zis?" and "You're Driving Me Crazy" and God knows what all. Because the sheet music was under the lid of her mother's piano bench

[66]

and the records were stacked like the Leaning Tower beside the Kimball phonograph, she had absorbed the popular songs of the First World War, and since they caught the ephemeral nature of those lost and curiously innocent days, she was at home in that generation as well as our own. She was thus on the best of terms with both "Rose of No-Man's-Land" and "Flat Foot Floogie."

"There's nothing left for me," she was singing, "of days that used to be." She crushed out a cigarette. "Thank God," she finished.

Frank Chandler bought his Model T from a farmer outside of Bozeman. The farmer, no good driver himself, taught him to drive as a part of the deal.

"My father's affair with the automobile was a cosmic collision."

While he was learning to drive, Liz and her mother had time to choose what to leave behind; the choosing was painful. No room in the Ford for the Hoover, no room for the Singer — and anyway, Frank Chandler said, maybe there wasn't electricity out there yet. He called it "juice." No room for the Kimball, of course. They spoke of objects by brand names. Beech-Nut was peanut butter; Hills Brothers was coffee. They slept on the Beautyrest and dropped their slice of Calderwood into the Toastmaster. No room.

Nor for the Ivers & Pond.

Now came talk of putting things into storage and reclaiming them by freight "when things settled down" out there in the state of Washington, but it transpired that storage was costly, and if you didn't reclaim your things, couldn't reclaim your things, and hadn't the money for more storage bills, the storage people sold them. You had to keep on paying and paying for the use of space. Before long, the storage cost more than what was stored. So the Hoover and the Singer and the Toastmaster went for forty dollars to the local pawn shop whose windows offered lavish evidence of other people's disasters. The Beautyrest and the Ivers & Pond were advertised in the Gallatin *Recorder* among other advertisements prompted by intended flight, divorce, scandal, lost jobs, foreclosures, sloppy living and plain bad luck. The Beautyrest had no takers, for it is understood that a used mattress has long since conformed to other people's bones and the coil springs weakened by God knows what lewd gymnastics, and there are stains. Its fate would be the dump at the edge of town where smoldering fires cast off sickening vapors; it would become an object of some interest to hoboes in search there of the amenities.

Flo Chandler had bought the Ivers & Pond secondhand for two hundred dollars; as a faculty wife, she had been granted a loan from the bank; she considered the piano a bargain each time she paid off the loan five-dollar bill by five-dollar bill; she had been somewhat disturbed by the fond way the old people who had sold it had glanced at it. She hated taking advantage. Now it was she who was in trouble.

A piano in a house speaks of culture and of good times, of a house acquainted with a little leisure. Its high, flat surface is a fine point of display for photographs and arrangements of flowers, and since that surface is above the level of all but the highest eyes, it need not be dusted. But now there were no takers at the hundred dollars she felt bound to ask. She had not realized that people who want pianos already have them, and that if a piano is not a Steinway or that other make, it is indeed an immovable object, for the mind boggles at the cost of hiring men to move it — those straps they use, the possibility of back injury and lawsuits, of damage to doorsills and banisters. The Benevolent and Protective Order of Elks called to say they were willing to move the piano to their premises provided no charge was made for the piano itself, and the Church of Jesus Christ of Latter-Day Saints, whose congregation had substituted group singing and hoedowns for smoking, drinking and foxtrotting, made a similar diffident offer.

The universal tragedy of forced sales was beginning to dawn on Flo Chandler, and there in the house remained the piano at whose keys she had expressed her thoughts and through whose pedals she had transmitted her anxieties. No longer an object of value, it was now worse than worthless; because the house was rented from the college, she was afraid she would be required to have the thing moved at her own expense to make room for some other, better piano. In the end, the college — acting as if they were doing her a favor — allowed her to abandon the piano at no cost to herself. They would use it, they said, in one of their practice halls. She was grateful, but the world now wore a new, smirking face.

Liz made a point of packing her doll to keep the lid on her mother's suspicions, to assure her that she was so fond of the flirty-eyed toy that she had run to it past a partly opened door that framed *in flagrante delicto*. Apart from the doll and an empty heart-shaped locket, she had nothing to pack but her clothes. Indeed, the old Model T was stuffed with cloth — sheets, blankets, pillows, clothes, and a canvas tent her father had bought from the Army and Navy Store. They might need it, he said, until he got things into shape.

"My mother cried," Liz said.

They were on the road a week. They spent three nights in roadside cabins advertised as Modern, since each had a toilet; one scattering of cabins was known as the Shady Nook Cabins in reference to a sickly stand of cottonwood trees. "Judging from the number of cars that pulled in and pulled out within the hour," Liz said, "A more apt name would have been Shady Nookie."

Four nights they spent on the road, the rain falling too hard to make pitching the tent feasible, the rain lashing in through the side curtains. One bright night they were stranded with a flat tire and no flashlight; the coyotes howled off in the distance announcing the end of the world.

Yes, they had thirteen flat tires before they reached the Washington border. Liz's father, of another generation, called them "punctures" after those wounds inflicted by nail or vile stone. Off at the side of the road, sometimes beside a mountain stream where in other times they might have picnicked, listening to the water purl over the stones, sometimes in the sagebrush, Frank Chandler jacked up the car, removed nuts, pulled tire and rim from the wheel, removed tack or whatever from tire, removed rim, disemboweled the tire of its collapsed tube, found the puncture, scraped over it with an object resembling a tiny nutmeg grater, applied a liquid cleaner cold to the touch, waited for it to dry, peeled off the protective coating from a patch similar to a Band-Aid, pressed down the patch, worked the tube back into the gaping tire, grunted and sighed and worked the rusty rim back into the inner circumference and yawning lips of the tire. Then he attached the slender, flexible hose of the hand pump to the valve of the tube that protruded smartly through the rim — "a vaguely suggestive operation" — and then he began to pump, his long, angular body rising and falling at the hips until he was glassy-eyed and sat to rest on the running board while the rest of the world rolled by.

And blowouts that shocked them to their senses with the explosion, and Frank Chandler fought the steering wheel to keep the car from plowing into the ditch or down the side of a mountain.

"I loved my father," Liz said. "Sometimes I wanted to hug him close and tell him it would be all right because one day I would be rich and famous. I think I loved him because he was unable. I am attracted to unable, inept people. That could be why I like you."

Her terrible candor struck like lightning, but she was not cruel, simply honest. I am lucky in having early accepted the fact that nothing much would become of me and that I was not likely to be among the invited guests, and so I have freed my mind to exercise what small gifts I have: an ability to faithfully record conversation and sometimes to interpret it.

* * *

Because of the trailing shrouds of fog that persisted that day, the image of the Washington "property" that Liz retained was ghostly — the beginning of something unfinished. A dozen apple trees, their limbs frozen into gestures of agony, bore a few scanty blossoms. The dark woods was about to reclaim a rickety frame house so scaled down in size that midgets came to mind. The sharp-pitched roof was concave from rot and colonies of moss clung to the north side. In the weeds, a human shoe had so shrunk from exposure, had so turned up at the toe, it resembled a troll's. There was a well and a hand pump.

Fifty feet away stood the privy.

Apart from having been spanked once when she wet the bed and having observed her silly mother locked onto a stranger, Liz had had but one other childhood trauma. That trauma was vicarious. It had nothing to do with her, but with a little girl her own age named Marian Parker. Marian Parker had been picked up off the streets by a young man named William Edward Hickman. He had driven her off in a black automobile, and in a barn or a garage had disemboweled her and stuffed her previously innocent cavities with rags. Then he had trussed her up with baling wire.

"To the tune, in my mind, of 'My Blue Heaven,' " Liz said. "The song was popular at the time.

> *Just Molly and me*
> *And baby makes three . . .*

Those families in America whose literacy was so advanced they could make out newspaper prose were alerted to the fact that every city block might reveal another William Edward Hickman who, even as a man shaved or a woman did up her hair, was saving up rags and testing knives. Thousands of Mommys and Daddys, having lost sight of a child in a crowded store or in the woods, were sick with apprehension; thousands of children woke

[71]

screaming and begged to sleep in the same room with Mommy and Daddy; many homely sexual routines were so interrupted.

Pictures of little Marian Parker and William Edward Hickman appeared together in the papers, joined as it were in ghastly wedlock — hers taken as she entered the fourth grade, face frozen into a smile as she faced the merciless camera; his, presumably a high school graduation picture of a few years before, showing a clean-cut, even pretty young man whose eyes looked out on the troubling world of Christ, sex and business, but a face so blurred in translation to cheap newsprint it might have been any young man of eighteen who had signed a copy, his name joined with the word "Lovingly," and presented it to an aunt.

Liz saw him everywhere.

Her father stopped the paper.

She read it in the house of a friend whose family believed there was no way to keep a child from knowing what the world was, that to know was to be prepared.

"It probably wouldn't have happened to her, darling," the woman of the house said, "if she hadn't been a bad girl."

"I'm not sure what the woman meant by bad, whether she was using Marian Parker's experience as just another example of what happened to children who sassed their parents and refused to clean their plates, or whether she meant that Marian Parker had been sexually promiscuous. I know now that she must have meant *that*, but it's hard to know what being sexually promiscuous is, unless you've been sexually promiscuous yourself, and I was nine years old," Liz said. "Surely she didn't mean that a child who was simply naughty might expect to be torn up and stuffed with rags.

"For the first time I knew despair, thinking there is really no hiding place, especially in the mazes of the mind, and that if something is going to happen, it is going to happen. And of course, I was right."

Well, the thing died down — other matters demanded attention: miners trapped in caves, Follies girls bathing in champagne, a minister attempting to walk on water. Anyway, it was absurd to think that such a thing could have happened beneath Montana skies where every morning began with cornflakes and every night ended with hot cocoa. Marian Parker had lived in California, the land of movies and make-believe; what happened in California did not happen, least of all to somebody who brushed her teeth and didn't squeeze the paste out from the middle of the tube. In a few months' time her stomach didn't knot up when a black car passed. At night she no longer listened for the hiss of a gloved hand brushing the glass just before it raised the window.

"And now the tune on the radio was 'I Found a Million-Dollar Baby.' It's rather ugly, isn't it, how grown men will refer to grown women as babies."

Liz had never before used a privy, although they were common enough around Bozeman, Montana, on the farms of the poor, who were often foreigners of some kind and didn't know what was what. Their children, like anybody else, had access to the gleaming white flush toilets at school and the sons of the poor could stand up proud to the urinals Liz had once seen on a dare. She knew that privies were a staple of bucolic humor, of jokes one yokel tells another with many a sly wink, but it was unclear to her why evacuation should be amusing. Later she "looked into it," and concluded it was funny because shitting was the lowest common denominator and that — looking on a man we feared or admired or stood in awe of — we had only to picture him straining at the stool and he was instantly brought into proper focus.

She had come to believe that those who used privies were not quite human, that their English would prove faulty, their religious customs absurd and their hair tangled. But here she was, young Elizabeth Chandler, having to use a privy in the state of Washington.

When she reached to her right for toilet paper she found only a piece of newspaper; it appeared to be not for the required purpose, but a last scrap remaining after a curious job of wallpapering: all four walls and the door of the privy had been covered with newsprint, each page neatly overlapping another, in a vain attempt to render the place gracious and to cover the cracks and so foil the inquiring eye. A compulsive reader even as a child, she drew the door inward to allow entrance of the pearly light, and she read. Oh, what she read.

To her right, where the light was most effective, she read on a page continued from page 1 a detail of the Hickman murder she had either overlooked or had rejected at the time. The sharp ends of the baling wire with which the body of little Marian Parker had been trussed up had been pushed up into the skull and very neatly through the iris of each eye.

They were not long in the state of Washington. "Didn't you already know something was wrong?" I asked. "Your father's buying a place he hadn't even seen? Leaving a place at the college in the Depression to grow fruit?"

"No. Mother and I were a couple of naïves in spite of my knowledge of porcelain urinals and my mother's random experience. We felt dependent on my father. He was a man. We did not ask questions. I believe he may have believed he was about to be fired. Maybe he was fired, and flight was an answer to humiliation. What greater humiliation can there be for a man, such a man as he was, than to be fired. A man with such terrible pride. It's heartbreaking to see a man proud when he has nothing to be proud about."

"But the lack of logic . . ."

"You forget. Nothing was logical then. Women you knew offered to come to your house and wash your hair and set it for fifty cents. The Willys-Knight dealer in Bozeman was mowing lawns and shoveling other people's snow. Young wives vanished for days and came back with a few dollars they'd made on their backs. There were ten miniature golf courses set up on front lawns. The only thing we knew we had was my father."

They were in the state of Washington so briefly she never

knew the extent of the property, whether it was more than the clearing with the fruit trees or included the woods and the land across the road.

They got their cloth inside the house, their pans and bowls, cutlery and the pancake turner seldom used for its true purpose and so soon turned to a horrid one. The two tiny rooms upstairs required the head to be inclined as one approached the eaves, and a sifting of dead flies lay across the floors. As Liz made up her bed on the straw-stuffed mattress of the white-painted iron cot, she saw her father through the dusty, distorting window glass. He was wandering through the weeds among the fruit trees. He paused before each one. "Seen through the wispy fog, he might have been a gaunt Druid."

In the kitchen a rusty stove had been dismantled, the lids stacked in a corner; fire door and oven door had been lifted off the hinges, the lid removed from reservoir. It was obvious that the former owners had meant to take their stove with them. Wherever they went, whatever happened, they would always have Old Friend Stove. Old Friend made raw food edible and was partner with the heart in warming the body and keeping you alive. But something had happened, something else had happened. The stove remained behind, a part of a failed or interrupted enterprise, an object of memories that hovered about it like disappointed shades.

Reassembling the stove seemed to raise Flo Chandler's spirits. "She often recovered from her frequent depressions by looking at the bright side. 'Why,' my mother said, 'it's just like camping out!' It may have been camping out, but your true campers have some place to go back to."

"'Now let's see how quick we can get up the drapes.'"

Among their cloth were draperies to clothe the naked window. And that was the first day.

Frank Chandler drove the Model T into the little town a mile away. In a store there, a woman had stared at him.

"And then she whispered to another woman."

"Why, I imagine that's because you're strange here," Flo Chandler said.

"How could I be strange here when I own this place?"

"She might not have known that, Frank."

"It was a rude thing to do, whisper like that. When she whispered she had her eye on me. She didn't pretend not to whisper."

"You're tired, Frank."

"Yes, I am, Flo. I'll go up and have a nap."

A nap in the middle of the morning, the brittle green shades pulled.

Even those unfamiliar with the body of Verlaine's work will recall Eliot's use of a quotation from *Parsifal: Et O ces voix d'enfants, chantant dans la coupole.*

Those familiar with Liz's work will recall her preoccupation with children; one critic has suggested that this preoccupation is a blemish on her art, but I suggest it is a strength; most writers view children as mindless puppets jerking at the end of strings manipulated by grown-ups; it appears that few writers accurately recall their childhoods and see themselves as children through the wrong end of a telescope — small puzzling strangers. Liz saw children as under the microscope, and like Verlaine and Eliot she was enchanted by the sound of children's voices, found in it something false, something inhuman — and in children's innocence, in their dependence, in their selfishness and cruelty, children are indeed not quite human. As if members of a savage tribe they chant rather than speak the language; they adore the expected rhythms of the ballad; like the Bantu, they relish alliteration for itself, and one is never sure they are aware of meaning, but only of the sound. What child would not cherish the Bantu line "Ba*loo* babba-*loo*va Ban*tu*" (the *lion* he *eat* the *man*)?

The ethereal quality of children's voices grouped in song is, like that of angels, quite sexless, and it is the sexlessness of all but the most precocious children, Liz felt, that let mothers go unpunished who dressed their sons in ribbons and bows until the very day when their voices broke and they took a fresh feel of their balls.

"And we are all of us only old children, the bloom gone from our cheeks, our teeth tusks as the gums recede; fat settles on our bellies and buttocks, meant to be absorbed in the lean years but it only invites heart attack. Like children we spy, inform and vilify, tell tales. We elect clowns, some of them vicious, to lead morons. We long to emulate those who are clever at throwing or hitting balls and pucks. We long to be rich and powerful so we can punish those who hurt us along the way."

On the second day, Liz heard children's voices in the woods; in a little while the children themselves appeared, materialized as if from trunks and branches; they had no way of knowing how dangerous the Chandlers might be, what evil might be wished on them.

"A child likes nothing better than to scare himself out of his wits so long as he knows it will turn out all right. Life — as those children knew it — had been impinged on by a strange, tall man who wandered among the apple trees and a small quick woman, and a child. The child might have some horror to relate, something best left unsaid. Who could say but that she had had that favorite disease of children — leprosy. Your fingers, then your hands, and finally your nose drop off. Leprosy would explain our isolation in that lonely place."

For why would people come to a place that others had left? A place abandoned by others for their own good reason? "We had violated their squatter's rights to the place, would discover their paths through the milkweed, uncover their buried treasure, dig up the bird they had buried with full ceremonies, rampage through the little house they had made quite their own by scrawling on the walls in red crayon the perhaps-yet-untried word FUCK.

In them, Liz saw allies.

She knew better than to approach them directly; just as a man

[77]

will strike up an acquaintance with an attractive woman by inquiring about the book she has been seen reading or feigning
interest in a dog attached to a leash — just as a homosexual will
ask another for a light — so children become acquainted through
objects: a new bicycle, a small box with something in it. Liz had
her doll. There was nothing extraordinary about it; it did not
murmur "Mama" nor open and close its eyes; neither did it wet
its pants. It was noteworthy only in that it was fondled by a child
obviously too old and too tall for such nonsense, who must now
know where babies come from, and had done better to experi-
ment with Tangee lipstick and with Ponds Two Creams.

She wandered slowly toward the children as if unaware of
them, cradling the doll.

"Pugh!" the boy said in greeting. "P and U."

Liz said nothing but smiled down at the doll.

"I'm too old for dolls," the girl said, and twirled around twice
to make it plain she was about ready for the dance halls. Liz said
nothing. "And you're too old for dolls, too."

Liz continued to smile down on her doll, knowing that the best
way to ruffle others is to remain unruffled. "I know something I
won't tell," she crooned. "Two little niggers in a peanut shell."

"Anybody knows that," the girl said, and struck a pose that
emphasized her little ass. "Wire briar limber lock."

So they were bent on proving that they, too, were brought up
on nursery rhymes, were familiar with Georgie Porgie whose
relationship with girls was natural enough — but not so natural
with boys; with the blind hope of Old Mother Hubbard and the
Man who, refusing to say his prayers, was taken by the left leg
and thrown down the stairs. Liz was about to make the proper
reply to "Wire briar limber lock" when the boy finished it for
her: "Girls got a pussy, boys got a cock."

The girl was outraged. No longer the Dance Hall Queen, she
had become Little Mother. She cried out. "Leroy Cooney! I'm
gonna tell Mama!"

"La Verne Cooney!" the boy mimicked as one who had heard
all this before. "Go ahead and tell."

At one stroke Liz knew their first and last names, that they were brother and sister, and that although Mama threatened, Mama never struck — particularly her son.

"What won't you tell?" the girl asked Liz.

"The awful thing I told my dolly."

Leroy was unmoved by the secret. He reached into the pocket of his faded overalls and drew out a pocket knife, opened it, tested the blade with his thumb, closed it, and returned it to his pocket. La Verne's eyes were fond on him.

"He can skin things," she said. "If he wants to. He can be awful mean."

"Who's mean?" Leroy murmured.

"Sometimes you are, Leroy Cooney." Leroy made a faint smile. "Our father drives truck for the paper company. I guess he's the strongest man in Kitsap County and every Christmas he buys us heaps of things and Mama a comb and brush set with a mirror in their own box."

"He gets drunk," Leroy said.

"Do you want to see where we live?" La Verne asked. "He built it himself."

"I don't mind," Liz said. They seemed drawn to her insouciance. She bet they'd never heard a girl say anything like that before.

"But first you got to tell what you know and won't tell," La Verne said.

"Ha-ha," Liz said as if suddenly overcome with fatigue. "How could I tell it if I won't."

"Who cares?" Leroy said.

"Oh, poop," La Verne said, and showed her profile.

"Goop," Liz said. "Let's play we're the Three Goops." And they walked into the woods.

The house was a cabin of cedar logs; as they approached it, the odor of the fragrant oils, released where the logs had been wounded, drifted over and cast a magic spell. Liz was at once

[79]

alert to danger. Just so, the witch's cottage had smelled of inviting gingerbread. Did this aroma that told of antique garments, of ecru lace and whispering satin . . .

> *Some letters tied with blue,*
> *A photograph or two*

. . . this odor masked what danger?

The mother stood just back from the screen door, knowing that screening is fine for seeing out of and poor for seeing into; she had time to form her phrases. She then held the screen door wide and allowed them to enter under her outstretched arm. ". . . let the flies in," she said. "So you're the new girl they saw."

"Thank you," Liz said, and saw a shadow of confusion across the woman's face.

"She still plays with dolls," La Verne said.

"You'd be better off, Miss Snot Nose," the mother said, and to Liz, "Do you want a Nabisco?"

"They're better'n Fig Newtons," Leroy said. "They got named from the National Biscuit Company."

The mother smiled on him. "Well, Mr. Know-it-all."

They had no running water, but the cedar cabin had been cleverly built over a well, and beside the sink was a pump. The mother had an extraordinary imagination: she had cut off the big end of a carrot, hollowed it out, made a cup of it, pierced opposite edges with two holes, inserted string, filled the cup with water, and hung it in the sunny window. From the underside lavish, fernlike, green pubic hair yearned toward the light.

And then something brushed Liz's ankle.

"That's Mr. Kitty Cat," the mother said with a certain warmth. He was one of three kittens that stretched and tiptoed on the bright, new-laid linoleum. His two sisters were both Miss Pussy Cat. Mr. Kitty Cat again brushed against Liz's ankle and began to purr. "Mr. Kitty Cat likes you, young lady." The mother cocked her head, looked at Liz and then down at Mr. Kitty Cat.

And then the mother cried, "*Here* she comes!" as if the arrival was at once expected and desired. She opened the door wide to allow the perfect entry of the mother cat, who carried in her jaws a mouse. She laid it before Mr. Kitty Cat and herself retired across the linoleum where she assumed the posture of the Sphinx. She watched. The two Miss Pussy Cats moved in for a look. Their brother glared at them and hissed a warning. He raised a threatening paw. They retired. Then Mr. Kitty Cat moved in to serious business.

The mouse had been carefully maimed, that its last struggles might offer at least token resistance to Mr. Kitty Cat and arouse the bloodlust he would need later on when his mother no longer cared. The mouse lay still, perhaps playing dead, and when nothing happened it dragged itself a little forward with its front feet; the hind legs had been rendered useless by a clever nip in the spine. It lay still, and then covered its face with its front feet, a curious instinct to protect that part of the body that alone proves identity. Now again it moved. Who could know what hope it had, what was the unbelievable best thing that could happen, maybe that it would be left alone to die. It moved again.

Mr. Kitty Cat gave it a good left hook.

"It was like a room enchanted," Liz said. "You remember in *The Past Recaptured* Marcel pays attractive young thugs to torture rats with hatpins while he watches. Cruelty and pain are sexually exciting. I felt Leroy's eyes on me, and I blushed. Out of the corner of my eye I saw his lips move silently and I knew what words they formed. "You've got a pussy. I've got a cock."

The mouse lay still, and covered its face again. Would not the Mouse God intercede? Mr. Kitty Cat glowered above it, and then gave it a gentle, almost affectionate pat which the mouse apparently took for a tap of dismissal, for it tried to move again, simply twitched, and Mr. Kitty Cat moved in to kill. His little growl was terrible; he sank his small sharklike teeth into the mouse's neck just at the base of the skull. And there, on the new-laid linoleum, picked out with gaudy flowers, a tiny life expired.

The room held a collective sigh.

The human mother spoke with something close to a giggle. "He's going to be a good mouser. How would you like to have him, young lady? You must have mice over there?"

Liz took the fierce young tom; to refuse him would be insulting, and she needed allies.

Her father was consistently hopeful — that a dull ax could be sharpened if only he could locate the whetstone, that whatever was wanting in some human being could be found. He was slow to express negative opinions.

But he did not like cats.

Unable to refuse his daughter — his Bestie Friend — Frank Chandler simply smiled and said softly, "Just keep the little creature away from me."

Earlier in the day, after a trip to town, he had remarked — and Liz and her mother pretended not to hear — that the same woman in the same store had again whispered to her friend.

"You simply refuse to believe that your father is mad," Liz said. "A daughter must refuse to believe a father is mad or a murderer or a pervert. You know there must be some mistake because you do not *feel* like the child of a madman, a killer or a pervert. You do not know *how* to feel that way."

From the top of the steep, narrow stairs, one midnight, she watched her father cast weak cones of light about the kitchen with the failing Eveready. What was he stalking? What was he thinking?

A literate American child walked proud in those days. He knew — *he* knew and not *she* knew, because there was no quibbling then over the greater importance of the masculine gender — he knew that America had the largest population in the world except for Russia, India and China, all three of which could be comfortably dismissed: the Indians were the wrong kind of Indians and did crazy things like disposing of their dead on the tops of towers where they were eaten by buzzards; the Chinese were so ignorant and far-flung they could hardly be expected to hand in an accurate census; and the Russians, feeding on roots and simple cereals and tearing around the country on tractors had little more right than beasts to stand up and be counted.

Americans had millions more telephones than anybody else, and the wires that connected them one to another could reach to the Moon and back, and over them American was talked — a language admitted to be the international language, because if you didn't talk it you didn't stand a Chinaman's chance at parties or in business. No country approached America in the number of railroads, and no other railroads led to such good places — Death Valley, the Grand Canyon and Yellowstone National Park, where in Old Faithful Inn, the largest log cabin in the world, you could buy sterling silver rings with bears on them. Railroad bridges crisscrossed the Mississippi–Missouri river system, the longest in the world, and Mark Twain was an American and very funny, and New York was the largest city in the world, and it didn't at all matter that London was a close second because they talked the same as us. The Woolworth Building was the tallest building in the world and when they got around to building a taller one it would probably be in New York.

"I grieved for the Woolworth Building when the Empire State Building was finished. I knew how the people in the offices in the Woolworth Building felt — suddenly second best. I was not sorry that many offices in the Empire State Building were unoccupied — I thought to myself, 'They bit off more than they could chew' — and I hoped that people in the Woolworth Building would be loyal and not move into them."

It was sadly true that Victoria Falls somewhere off in Africa was higher than Niagara Falls, but a colored picture of Victoria Falls did not, like Niagara Falls, appear on the box of shredded wheat, the best breakfast food, very good with cream and straw-berries.

When the Chandlers moved to the state of Washington, shredded wheat for breakfast was one of the few links with the past. In Bozeman they had had cream, too, but now only milk, which Liz's father bought from a farmer single quart by single quart — they had no refrigerator and no ice.

Mr. Kitty Cat's nose was sensitive to milk and he arched his back and purred and rubbed against Frank Chandler's leg when the top was screwed off the quart fruit jar. Mr. Kitty Cat did not understand Frank Chandler's hatred of cats, or assumed this hypocritical show of affection would soften Frank Chandler's heart.

"So far as my father knew, the cat had no name," Liz told me. "At eleven, I was at least six years too old to call or even think of a cat as Mr. Kitty Cat, and not for at least another six years would I be old enough to legitimately pretend I was a child again who called cats Mr. Kitty Cat and to speak without blushing of Mrs. Cow."

She thought it might be a smart move, so far as her father was concerned, to call the cat Felix after the cartoon for which even her father had a grudging affection. He admired Felix's aplomb. As for herself, recalling the desperate mouse, she thought of the cat as Satan.

They were sitting at their shredded wheat, the box right there on the table — something of a lavish touch — and beside it the jar of milk.

"There must certainly have been token conversation at break-fast," Liz said, "because my mother couldn't endure silence. Si-lence lead to thought and thought sometimes led to unwelcome consequences, and in the whole Washington experience we were frozen into contorted shapes like the fruit trees, and as silent, but there must certainly have been noise of some kind at that last breakfast table other than that of consumed shredded wheat. Do you remember a song called 'Doodle-De-Do'?"

At her household chores or picking up the telephone, Liz's mother often went "Doodle-De-Do," and when not at that, she was a hummer. Humming, like chewing gum or smoking a pipe, sets a tone of insouciance.

She may have hummed at that last breakfast table, or she may have begun the meal, as she often did, with the words, "Guess what I dreamed last night?"

The question is unanswerable; for who can know what another, groping in the narrow alleys and far horizons of sleep, has come upon? What door opened, what the answer was, at what moment an old chemistry professor was revealed as father or as toad? To hope to prevent the narration of another's dream with another question like "That you were in marble halls?" is futile, for tellers of dreams are as determined as those who relate the plots of moving pictures; they will not be silenced and ignore your tight lips and glazed eyes. Tellers of dreams expect their dreams to enthrall the hearer, who must ask nothing less than to understand every nuance of the dreamer's personality. Who has the courage to leap to his feet and cry, "I have heard enough of your God-damned dreams."

It may have been a frantic wish to escape "Doodle-De-Do," it may have been to escape the relating of yet another dream — to prevent the expected — that caused Frank Chandler to rise suddenly, to take a step. His weight was on Mr. Kitty Cat's paw. Mr. Kitty Cat vomited a scream.

Now, the reaction to such insupportable noise is to silence that which makes it; so child abuse is explained.

For a moment, Frank Chandler stood quite still as the cat's scream ricocheted against the walls like a mad bird. Again the cat screamed.

He crushed the cat with his heavy shoe.

"The skull cracked like a nut," Liz said.

But her father was not finished. He stood — cranelike — over the dying cat. Like a human pile driver he regularly brought his shoe up and down on the twitching body, his face a mask of indifference as the corpse turned to red jelly shot through with felt.

"Not even as a child," Liz said, "had I the tidy instincts of a housekeeper — ask my husband Hal, who writes me notes in the dust on the table — but as my father finished off the cat I wondered how the mess could be cleaned up. The area of death was considerably larger than the body of the cat itself; the pores and cracks of the old splintered softwood floor were thirsty for the body juices."

Now her father wielded broom and dustpan. The straws of the broom left a grain in the ruddy liquid, and the dustpan was not big enough. What remained of the cat her father removed with the pancake turner and scraped it against the edge of the dustpan. Just so, many years later in New York a policeman scraped his shoe on the running board of a taxi in which Liz was riding. A suicide had leaped from the top of a midtown hotel; his body had exploded on the policeman's feet.

Then in silence her father left the house, cranked up the Ford, and drove away. They knew he would think, and then come back. To what? Unfinished business? "My mother was certain that if he could crush the life from a cat, he could crush ours."

These things happen, of course, and they are printed in the papers. It seemed to Flo Chandler that the rickety little house, the weeds that pressed against it, the stunted apple trees and encroaching cedars were but props and flats for tragedy.

Females in sudden flight may not know where they are next going to sleep, but they take care to know what they are going to sleep in. Thus they stood outside the screen door of the neighboring log cabin with a small suitcase containing those articles a woman might suddenly need — compact and lipstick to fix a suitable mask, pins for repairs to torn garments, aspirin to dull pain, and a picture snapped on a happier day. Liz carried her doll, her lost childhood.

"We need help," Flo Chandler said through the screen. "My husband has gone crazy."

The woman on the other side of the screen did not appear surprised to see them. Possibly the departure of an earlier family from the rickety house had prepared her for this visit. A kind woman, acquainted with the worst, she was as unruffled as if Flo Chandler had run out of sugar. She was in something "loose," a kind of housecoat, and wore mules. She had not finished with her hair, and in kid curlers she appeared a pleasant Medusa. The movies or an evening of pinochle were in the offing, for it was Sunday.

"Come in." They passed in under her arm.

The husband, only fairly alert at this hour, was a well-coordinated primate whom one could imagine stripped in the shower off the locker room. He was so comfortably masculine that he disregarded his figure; his thinning black hair was another matter; he felt it with the flat of his hand. It was his day off, an occasion that excuses select license. He sat at the table with a brown bottle of home-brew before him at ten in the morning. Now, Americans are taught from birth — although most reject this lesson as not applying to them — that to drink before five in the afternoon is an advertisement of selfishness and irresponsibility; as his wife opened the screen door, he covered the bottle with his hand and set it out of sight on the floor. Whatever his pressures of the previous week, they did not excuse a man's enjoying himself so early when some other husband has gone crazy.

"If I could please use your telephone?"

"We don't have a telephone," the woman said. "But we're going to get one."

"Is there any way to telephone?"

The husband got up. "I'll drive you to town."

"Oh, please."

"You won't have a cup of coffee?"

"We're afraid he'll come back," Flo Chandler said.

"We don't need one," the woman said, "because we don't know anybody here yet."

It would have been more sensible to let the woman drive Liz's mother to the telephone and leave the man behind to protect the house against the return of Frank Chandler, but the woman was one of that class of women who don't drive, having married to one of that class of men who consider driving a male privilege, like slicing up the meat for company. As for her, she believed it would never have crossed a woman's mind to invent the automobile. A man's answer, of course, is that it let you get to places faster. Her answer would be, "Then start sooner."

It might have been a better idea had Liz not remained behind with the woman and the two children, for while the man and her mother were gone her father did return.

"I was in the bedroom with La Verne and Leroy," Liz said, "but I could almost feel my father sniffing around the house. My hair stood on end because my mother's hysteria had been convincing. There was only the latched screen door between him and the woman. She, however, spoke to him as if he were a child." The woman did not appear to believe that he had gone crazy, that he had been termed crazy by Liz's mother, perhaps because he had crossed her once too often and that was enough to make some women label any man crazy.

"I tell you," the woman said, "nobody came here."

"They're mine," Frank Chandler said, "and I want them."

"I don't let strangers in," the woman said.

"I'm not a stranger," Frank Chandler said. "I live back there."

"It's strangers who want to get into a place," the woman said. "I've got a big gun in here."

"I don't want to be a stranger to anybody."

"You don't belong here. What if I had to shoot you?"

Playing a strained game of Parcheesi with La Verne and Leroy, Liz heard her father mumble something, but she didn't see him go away. "I wish I'd seen him once more. I wish I'd seen him walk back into the woods, and I hoped that a voice would speak out of the woods promising him something. There he had been, a stranger at the gates. He had come for us in fear and trembling, hoping for comfort and forgiveness. Good God — we all come on as strangers and remain strangers even to ourselves until we have proved ourselves. My father had no one to turn to because he had not yet had time to prove himself loyal and trustworthy. He had hoped to prove himself among a few fruit trees out there in Washington."

 I TOOK MY DEGREE a month after that evening Liz told me of her father's walking back into the fog. I went into New England to teach. I sent Liz a card I felt to be in good taste well before Christmas, and was hurt that I hadn't one from her in return. Then I realized that friends must have more in common than the state of Montana, and I realized that I am not an interesting man.

I meant to move out of this cramped apartment five years ago, but the thought of moving even my few possessions into other quarters tires me; I am not physical. I don't cope well with new situations and fresh inconveniences. I have come to terms with steam heat, which is most reliable when it's not needed. I no longer suggest that Mrs. Voisin replace the light bulb in the hall with one of heftier wattage — I can find my way in the dark. It is easier to listen to the quarrels and accusations of the transients above me than to complain about them: listening carefully, I sometimes find myself taking sides. Once I would have been bitter about the toilet. Now I accept it — for centuries the Japanese have fancied the sound of running water.

I have serviceable bookshelves of bricks and plain pine boards; I was among the first on campus to hang up prints of Toulouse-Lautrec's posters, and Etta Murphy was among the first to bring me a maidenhair fern.

"And would you like an African violet?" she asked. "They're not much trouble."

"I am suspicious of what is not much trouble. "What do you mean by not much trouble?"

"Well, you can't leave them."

"I don't want anything I can't leave."

"I assume that's why you never married," Etta said. "Anyway, you don't go away much." I had not realized until then just how much is known of the movements of those who teach in a small freshwater college, how it might be said, "You see, he's left his violets."

"I'm afraid I don't want to be tied down, not even the idea of being tied down."

"When I go away," Etta said, "I have the woman downstairs come up."

"That's all very well if she is down when you go away to come up."

"I see you still haven't a television set," Etta said.

"Nor will I have one."

It was some time before they started calling television TV. It was a mark of grace among intellectuals not to have a set. Television was thought to be for those without interior resources; to own one was to confess an empty head. The students were lobbying to have one placed in the lounge of the Union building, but both deans and the president were opposed on the grounds (they said) that television would distract those who preferred to study in the Union, and later on that's exactly what it did. In those days the administration was afraid that the trustees would cry out at so capricious a distribution of funds and begin, through the pages of the journal of the American Association of University Professors, a search for a more responsible administration.

But the battle against television was lost early on. It was whispered in the faculty lounge and in the student store that some really fine things were televised, that the Philistines were not exclusively in charge. Shakespeare, Beethoven on Sunday evenings, *The Stones of Venice*, mind you. One was suddenly in danger, it seemed, in closing one's mind, of becoming provincial in not watching selected programs. When the president himself had a set installed (the lettering on the delivery truck left no doubt of it) the game was up. Those who now spoke against television were speaking against the administration and their days might be numbered—not that that in itself was enough to demand dismissal, but it was an opening wedge that might lead to a close review of one's overall loyalty to the administration.

"I can't afford one," I told Etta.

She patted my wrist. "I hear ducks," she said, and smiled. "What financial responsibilities do you have? You have a fair salary and you have your clothes, and a little radio for your music. Really, you're going to have to start doing something about yourself." She did not mean that. She preferred people who did nothing about themselves so she could start doing something about them. "What do you do with your money?"

My brother is not able to work because of an accident. There is a little boy and a little girl. "I'm saving it for a rainy day," I told Etta.

Etta looked shrewd; her eyes sparkled. "Methinks I already feel the first droplets."

This conversation was held when I didn't know Etta as I know her now; her words left me feeling threatened, as her words so often did, but Liz's first letter to me in my new teaching environment — it arrived that afternoon — restored my amour propre. As an extravagant admirer of Liz's work, I took comfort and strength from her friendship — as if it made me germane to her gifts.

Hello, you son of a bitch, that letter began. *How's the stem end of your bladder?*

She renewed our relationship with a reference to Helen who, along with Montana, was a common denominator. I did not then see her concern with Helen as compulsive, for I did not then know Helen's place in her life.

"Helen has been busy with her nature notes." Helen had taken a set of time exposures of the opening and closing of flowers and likened their movements to that of the ballet. She had spent a weekend with rural friends in Connecticut who had four fireplaces and a horse; sitting quietly on the edge of a slow-running stream, she had observed a tiny frog half in and half out of the water; suddenly the frog's eyes glazed over and it collapsed like a balloon. The life had been sucked out of it by a huge water bug. She hurried to New York for pencil and paper to record this natural horror before the frog's final expression escaped her. She found that her papers had been disturbed.

"Aside from seeing one's name misspelled, being told that one has no sense of humor and having one's place lost in a book, nothing is so enraging as finding one's papers disturbed, particularly those that concern one's money or one's thoughts. It was clear that Claude-Michel had been reading her nature notes."

Helen had confronted him. He shrugged in that impossible French way and said yes, he'd been reading her nature notes. "Why not?" he'd asked.

"But the box was locked!"

"I knew where the key was."

Helen believed passionately in privacy. Without privacy, without the right to privacy, one was simply not a human being. She didn't know about Frenchmen, but Americans are guaranteed the right to privacy. It was in the Bill of Rights or something. "One might just as well be dead," Helen said. Why had he done such a thing?

He explained that in reading her work he might have an opportunity to know her better. Hadn't a man a right to know his woman?

Maybe it was his use of the word "woman" instead of "wife," his assumption that she was chattel and no better than a mistress that moved her to order him out of the house. He had looked at her in amazement, as if recovering from a bizarre insult or a strange hand at his private parts.

Had she, then, lost her mind? Did she not realize that what she had said was clearly grounds for divorce? Did she not understand that no sane woman would order a husband off her premises? He paid half the rent, did he not?

He must realize, Helen told him, and at once, that the laws of the state of New York are quite other than those of the Code Napoléon, thank God, and although he had sometimes in the past paid half the rent, every stick of furniture in the house was hers except his God-damned armoire.

"And I have never before heard you curse!" he cried out.

"You drove me to it. Get out, or I will leave and take every stick of furniture." She looked on him a moment, and then turned to the telephone.

"Of course," Liz wrote, "if he hadn't skedaddled, getting the furniture out of there would have been somewhat more difficult than picking up the telephone. Helen would have had to look up a number and make arrangements, for no movers in New York I ever heard of come in less than a week. The threat could have been effective only if at that very moment a van pawed and snorted at the curb.

"And suitable apartments are not easily found in New York City. I see Helen, trembling and angry, riding about the streets of New York for weeks with her furniture, something like the Wandering Jew, noting with despair the passage of time and the changing seasons.

"She allowed him back, of course, because she couldn't imagine what he would do about his laundry, but she transferred her nature notes to an olive-green steel box with a combination lock, and after she'd learned the combination by heart, she tore up the little slip of paper with the numbers on it."

Liz urged me to come to New York over Memorial Day. "We can go out to potter's field and set flowers on the graves of the poor."

The college where I taught had in the beginning been dedicated to the Baptist faith and plaques on the walls of several of the college buildings gave evidence that more than one Baptist missionary who had been educated there had been killed by natives and, one assumed, eaten. But as times changed and even some Baptists had little stomach for religion, the trustees deemed it wise to dedicate the new chapel to an all-purpose God. It had a tilting floor and a portable altar that could be stored away and the space made available for plays and for a large silver screen that could be pulled down for the projection of motion pictures. But few minstrels wandered to our campus, few string quartets and few professional actors. Our budget denied the fees that might tempt them to travel so far from Boston or New York, and when you have seen *The Blue Angel*, *Potemkin*, and *The Birth of a Nation* two times each, that is enough. Apart from the dismal cocktail parties where every brain had been picked right down to the skull, where the quantity of liquor was always uncertain and the California dip inevitable, there was scarcely any distraction except in eating out at the one good restaurant in town, the Madison — referred to by those in the know as the Mad. Had the Mad depended on academic custom for its survival, it most certainly had failed, but it was a meeting place for visiting parents and successful traveling salesmen eager for bright lights, lobster Newburg and vichyssoise. I have not fathomed (I'm sure Liz could) why one feigned surprise at seeing colleagues dining at the Mad; there was table-hopping and careful, grave conversation among people who had met for coffee at the student store not hours before.

I can't make a move without having some practical reason, and I excused my going to New York by making an appointment there with a dentist who had looked in on my teeth while I was a graduate student. It is my belief that the best professional people do not set up shop far from the urban centers, and the argument I have so often heard among local professional people — that they prefer the sticks because only there are they free from city pressures — is too foolish to be given credence. Only in the city can one be anonymous, be oneself; it is rare even to know a next-door neighbor. Only in the city can you be sure no one is anxious to "help" you; only there you need not fear a knock at the door.

"Hal's on the road with a play," Liz said. She wore white Japanese socks, somewhat soiled, that had a separate nook for the great toe and whose true name I do not know, and a light-blue kimono tied behind with a big bow that rode and quivered over her buttocks like a monstrous butterfly. This costume was part of an extremely limited wardrobe I came to know over the next few years, which included the black skirt and orange scarf for the Halloween holidays, the black tailleur for formal cocktail parties, the wide black hat and the secondhand coat of unimportant fur whose sateen lining was kept in check by safety pins. She did not dress: she played "dress up" and, retreating into make-believe, need not face the fact that she and Hal were now desperately poor. "Are you ready for your sherry yet?" I did not then know that sherry is often a part of the picture of poverty.

She leaned Geisha-like over the bottle of sherry, pouring. "You remember I told you . . ." And we were back in the state of Washington in the fog.

The departure of a young person into the real world from family town house or homestead or cabin is not unlike being torn from the womb. At best he faces an uncharted wilderness where hideous compromises are the rule. At worst, he goes into that wilderness with ugly words ringing in his ears or burning on his lips. Either he is urged never to darken a doorway again — or he vows never to darken one. And never is a long, long time. One of the compromises is that a man or a woman must stand again in that doorway with his tail between his legs and his hat in hand, or whatever a woman does with her hat in vile circumstance.

It is understood that they have got to take you in, after a certain amount of wagging of heads and murmurings about the thickness of blood, the relative thinness of water, and what people might say. For only beasts refuse entry to their young.

At no other time in American history were so many doorways redarkened as during the Great Depression, and darkened not only by oneself but by strange wife, husband or child. One thing can be said for the Old People: they were usually good for a bed and, as the nasty phrase goes, three squares a day.

While Frank Chandler wandered back through the fog into the cedar woods to the rickety little frame house where he must hear the silence and ponder the stains left by a murdered cat, his daughter, his Bestie Friend, played out a game of Parcheesi and his wife cooled her heels in the Western Union office. Except for the beer parlor where the unredeemed hung out, and the Union Oil service station where young men, unhappy away from the internal combustion engine, hung out — and anyway Floyd who owned the place was a lot of laughs — except for those, the Western Union office was the only place open on Sunday. Sunday is a day for contemplation, a day to review, to count one's blessings, and to get at something that had not been gotten at.

Urgent messages of the sharpest emotions — love, loss, need and greed as well as welcome or unwelcome announcements of arrival or departure and words of congratulation — were in those days almost exclusively relayed by telegraph. It was cheaper than the telephone.

Flo Chandler cooled her heels and listened to the muted clickety-clack of the telegraph sounder; the operator, behind the heavy, varnished table, had his dark-green visor — mark of his trade — pulled low. He read a newspaper. Suppose he didn't hear — suppose he failed to attend when the permission to release precious money came through? And suppose the sender con· cluded that the intended recipient no longer needed the money? Should she speak? But telegraph operators, like train conductors, had been granted a vague but powerful and usually untested authority; they were seldom instructed in their work. A conductor might throw you off a train for your impertinence; a telegraph operator might refuse to send or receive a message. By the time *your* rights were established, it would be too late. The operator's indifference to the telegram sender argued that in his experience the beseeched on the other end was in no hurry to part with his money, that there's many a slip 'twixt the cup and the lip; that in any event he hadn't much use for a grown woman who wired home for money and smoked one Chesterfield after another.

Flo Chandler thought first to telegraph her father at his feed-and-seed store; in her panic (would they be destroyed like the cat?) she had forgotten it was a Sunday, that her father would at that Iowa hour be sitting down to carve the pork — done to within an inch of its life, for worms that inhabit a swine's flesh will not otherwise be destroyed, and you die of trichinosis as they do down South where they don't pay attention to things. We all have to go, but not that way. Let worms wait their turn.

So she had telegraphed her mother, thinking to throw herself on her mother's mercy; mercy was a word of importance to her mother, scarcely less important than the word duty. It mattered little whether it was her mother's mercy, or God's; both amounted to the same thing. Mercy was a commodity to be granted or withheld, most often granted when asked for, never granted when unasked for, and its price was some form of humiliation — a promise to do better, to be better, to admit that one was evil or weak. Liz's grandmother was powerful, powerful in the way of one who knows the nature of priorities and convictions, has sorted them out. It was through her that Liz and her mother were eligible for the DAR.

Waiting in the Western Union office was harrowing — it was waiting on the nature of one's future, if any. Unlike the dentist's or the doctor's office, no distracting periodical was at hand, no *Liberty*, no *Collier's*, and the two varnished oak chairs were indifferent to the needs of the human spine. Flo Chandler knew little of checks and money orders, but had heard — read somewhere? — that in extremis you wired for money. The process, as Liz learned later, was like this: you sent a telegram PLEASE WIRE

FIFTY DOLLARS ABOVE ADDRESS STOP LOVE STOP. As if anyone who had to send you fifty dollars cared about your love. The sender of the money, at a distance, handed over a check to Western Union, or cash if he was not to be trusted, and Western Union put the cash or check in a strongbox. Then Western Union wired at a distance that it was all right to hand over the same amount of money out of another strongbox (minus the charge for the telegram, of course) — provided the person who wanted the money could answer a question only he could answer.

"It was like a fairy tale," Liz said. "The testing question to see if one is worthy, the testing question of the Sphinx or Rumpelstiltskin. I wonder now, when I think of my poor, frightened mother waiting in that bleak office — I wonder that as a child on the playground in Bozeman, Montana, I was not alerted to the future when the boys chanted an incomprehensible ditty:

> *Corn-beef hash, corn-beef hash —*
> *Three dots, four dots, two dots, dash.*

"The result of 'corn-beef hash' is of course s h i t. And it was the dots and dashes that relayed the question only mother could answer and would put fifty dollars into her empty purse. I wonder how often somebody, in playful or punishing mood, asked a question that could not be answered, and so branded a recent pauper a fraud in the eyes of Western Union? 'What is the penultimate pillar of the Seven Pillars of Wisdom?' That would put someone on his mark."

At the end of three hours, the Chesterfields gone up in smoke, the testing question came through: WHAT IS YOUR MIDDLE NAME?

"How like my grandmother," Liz said. "She knew my mother disliked her middle name and had long ago disowned it, even the initial. It was Agnes. My mother said 'Agnes' and got her fifty dollars."

The husky, balding man who had brought her there had appeared from time to time. He had had three hours to drink in the beer parlor. As they drove away, he said he knew someplace they could go for a little while. My mother told me that many years later, and that she had said no. But maybe she had felt obligated. God, how we do feel obligated.

 ON RETURNING "home" because you have no other place to go, you may expect them to say "I told you so," and you are lucky if they do not, but you know that is what they are thinking. Look at *their* side of it for a moment. Forget yourself — something you simply would not do. So just for a moment, look at their side of it.

For the first eighteen or twenty years of your life they did everything on earth for you, everything humanly possible, as they put it. You don't remember, but your mother was in labor more than thirty-six hours having you, and she might have died except for old Dr. Johnson, who all his life used to drop in. How he did love a good cup of coffee.

"I thought I was going to lose your mother," he would say to you. They don't make them like that anymore. If a person could just have back those old days.

When you were sick, they sat up night after night with you; they were literally beside themselves. They were young, then, but it would never have entered their heads to have done otherwise. It could never be said of them that they shirked their duties, but they did what they did because they loved you. Never a birthday, never a Christmas — even after you ran off — without their remembering. They showered you with gifts, showered you. Remember the tricycle that time? Oh ho! Did your eyes bug out! And your father right there down on his knees showing you how to oil it and he said to remember to bring it in every night so it won't rust or get stolen because that's what they do. And what happened? Do you remember what happened? It was stolen. No wonder that's the last tricycle you got. Your father was not made of money, and you left it out and it got stolen.

You had no notion of the value of a dollar, never had, no matter how often you were urged to drop coins into that little bank that looked like a house; you hightailed it downtown and squandered every last cent on crazy phonograph records. Why can't they write tunes the way they used to? Now it's no better than dragging garbage into the house.

It wasn't just a phase, either. Phase, my eye, because later on, when you were older and should have known better, you wouldn't pull your own weight or put your shoulder to the wheel. Oh, no, it was fancy duds on time and out all night drinking and carrying on, your lack of respect for what decent people believed in. Why, you wouldn't even spend a little time with your grandmother, who just kept lying there, waiting; you couldn't even forgive an old lady because of what she said when she wasn't herself. Did you think she was too old to have feelings? It was your pleasure to drag the family name in the mud and it would not be too much to say that you caused your grandmother's death. At the last moment she sat up.

But all that wouldn't have been so bad if people hadn't had such hopes for you. Where was the person that Mr. Collins, in the seventh grade that time said such fine things and sent a note home?

And they did not fail to write you over the years and even sometimes tuck in a five-spot, for all the thanks they got, and the time when they sent the shirts and you were so long thanking them they had to go down to the post office (the new one over on the other side of town where it's so hard to park) and put a tracer on them. You can imagine how they felt when the post office said that so far as they knew the package had been delivered because they had a slip or something.

When the children go away, the Old People adjust: why, it's almost like a second honeymoon; better even, because they know each other so much better and what to do and what not. The bills are less, for one thing, and there's no longer the need to go around turning out lights somebody has left on, and listening and listening for the car in the driveway and being afraid of the telephone. It's nice to sit back and think that if they wanted to go to Florida or California to one of those places where they have boats with glass bottoms and you pick your own oranges, they could, and your father's power tools. Skimped and saved all those years for your education, and then what? Well, it's all water under the bridge, or so they thought. It did seem sensible in these times to rent the upstairs; they came or went so you hardly knew they were there, and they had no children. They had that much sense. She had the nicest way about her, none of those halters, and one thing about *him*, a week didn't go by he wasn't there with the rent *in cash;* you'd see him out there washing his car; it was his idea to help your father with the yard. He wasn't any older than you, and according to her, he'd had a terrible time as a child. Your father told him, "I wish I'd had a boy like you," and he just blushed. Something out in Colorado. They were going to be sorry to lose them.

With the children out of the way, they could open the icebox and there you were — no planning, none of that getting dinner on the table for somebody who'd be late, none of that business. And then, bang! When you should be settling down in your sunset years, this letter comes, or this telegram.

The Iowa town they approached by leaping Greyhound bus was huddled on the prairie as if in fear of its life. There was hardly more footage between stores and houses than on the island of Manhattan. In a land so vast, with such distant horizons, why did the town cower? It might have been ringed about with an enchanted circle over which one stepped at one's peril, clutched at one's throat, and fell down dead.

"But there was a threat, of course. One might not fall dead beyond the town — although that, too, was possible, for every so often the Burlington brought in an inhabited coffin. One might not fall dead; but stranded in that void outside of town, away from one's peers, one might be struck with an original thought, be marked like Cain, and never be allowed to return."

For all the green farmland beyond the horizon — the alfalfa, the clover and nodding corn — it was a treeless land. Lacking lumber, the natives — like the Babylonians and the brighter of the three pigs — built some of their houses and all the public buildings of brick. Brick lends itself to fanciful constructions of towers, turrets and crenellations; the courthouse resembled an arsenal; the Civil War cannon and the neat pyramid of balls (welded together to confound thieves) might have been a defense rather than a souvenir of those who died because that's what you did. Miss Innes, the librarian, from her tall tower, might make out the distant approach of an angry rabble armed with pikes.

Liz had several times used the phrase "my wicked old grand-mother," which brought to my mind a mad old harridan loping along the river bottoms — a hag, a witch, a caster of spells, one with Purcell's wayward sisters, and such, indeed, is many a grandmother in a child's mind, and she has only herself to thank if one day she wakes up in a Home without her portable radio, and with a snippy nurse.

Liz said one thing for her grandfather: he met them at the bus stop in front of the City Drug Company, a spot chosen because the City Drug Company was open on Sundays and on that day, too, carsick passengers could step down and buy soothing nostrums and the hale might enjoy a ham sandwich and a cup of coffee, had there been time, and admire the jars of colored water behind the counter.

A small crowd had gathered as the bus pulled in — not to

[*104*]

claim anyone on it, but you never could tell. Once they carried off a dead woman, and once somebody got arrested on it, and they took him to the jail under the courthouse. Lots of crazy things.

"I don't suppose my grandfather, in 1931, wore starched collars, but that's the impression he gave, this stranger of a grandfather who had lived a life parallel to mine in time and was my own flesh and blood and without whom I would not have been."

"Oh, Papa," Flo Chandler cried. Hugging her father, she began to weep. He stood a bit back from her dampness.

"No, Florence, now, now, now. Not here."

She was going to have to learn all over again that there are places for tears — bathrooms, bedrooms — that the corner of Elm and South Pacific streets was not one of them.

"And who is this young lady?" he inquired.

"Oh, Papa, you know perfectly well."

"I do not, Florence. Who on earth can she be?"

"I am the West Wind, Grandfather, fresh with questionable tidings of the man you never were, fulfilling dreams you never dared. Come, let us embrace and as time allows we will reconstruct the past."

"I didn't say that, of course," Liz told me. "I wish I had, for then, once, I think I should have seen him astonished.

" 'I'm Elizabeth,' I said.

" 'Ah-ha!' my grandfather said. 'She's got a tongue after all!' "

It was only four blocks to the house, but her grandfather was not one who would be seen carrying a piece of luggage through the streets, nor would he walk with anyone who did. "Many men feel that to be seen carrying anything, dragging it, pushing or pulling it, is to advertise that they are too poor to afford servants," Liz said. "Women, on the other hand, having no position anyway, have no face to lose in becoming beasts of burden."

So her grandfather had come for them in his car — his machine, as he called it — but had had to abandon it at some distance near the Burlington depot because of the curious oafs who had parked their own cars close by the better to observe the bus pull in. Walking to his machine was something of a progress; he expected people to make way for him and since most people are awed by anyone who expects anything, most of them did. He acknowledged their deference by inclining his head as if he were ticking them off and by speaking their surnames, tilting his voice up into a question so that they might, if necessary, deny them- selves — protest that they were not truly the persons he took them to be.

"Mr. Blake? Mr. Converse? Mrs. Lubin?"

There were no introductions. Liz and her mother might have been no part of his life, and indeed they were not.

The machine they approached was some years old, an elderly car bought in boom times before the Depression, when the feed- and-seed business was thriving and hens and hogs were offered rations beyond their wildest dreams. "It was exactly the color of sagebrush," Liz said. "It was a Buick Special Six Coach. What was Special about it was that it was not the Master Six — that was the good one — and it was a coach because it had two doors instead of four. It was, I'm afraid, called a Tudor because of the two doors, and who would need more, since there were only two of my grandparents and each could use no more than one door. There was no need for the back seat, which you entered by tilting the front seats forward. I think my mother and I were the first passengers ever to sit there; the pile of the gray mohair was erect and alert."

Even a Buick Special set her grandparents above the Chev- rolet–Oakland–Pontiac crowd in the General Motors hierarchy, and it afforded them a precarious hold on the Cadillac slopes. Only two families in New Hoosic had become rich; they were spoken of as "well-to-do." Since it was not much fun to see only each other's rooms, silver, napery, and playing cards they had relaxed their standards to include Buick, Nash and Hudson peo- ple, many of whom had never been east of Chicago and used but a single toilet.

Her grandfather held open the door of the Buick and "helped" them into the back seat. "He called it the tonneau." Inclining his head, he closed the door and tested it, went around and climbed into the driver's seat and cleared his throat. "All right back there?" he asked. "When we get to the house you'll have time to freshen up and maybe nap before supper." The Buick moved off like a huge baby carriage.

"Some people regard grandmothers as valuable institutions. Grandmothers are not only a heartening example of survival, but are perceived as both wise and permissive. Having at different times been both child and parent, they often serve as experienced buffers between father and son, mother and daughter.

"My grandmother was an institution of another stripe. She stood in the hall."

Whatever has become of halls? Halls were where you stood. Halls were an introduction to your house and the stage for introductions. In your hall you had an opportunity to judge and to be gracious or not to those who had gained entry; a small entry won't do — graciousness wants adequate space. In a fine hall the welcome can be made to feel more welcome and the unwelcome held at sufficient bay. Many, many people never get beyond halls, and they never will. They can be stopped in halls and left to wonder for the rest of their lives what lies beyond.

Liz's grandmother was a small, plump woman. In her navy-blue crepe-de-chine garment she appeared packaged. She had none of the bloated appearance of those who had once been spare — one knew she had been born a plump baby, had been a plump little girl who prompted cuddling and had been saved the best piece of cake and the rest of the lemonade with the result that she had come to expect deference as her due and with it the right to judge. She had become a monster of selfishness and rectitude. She stood now in the center of the hall from which good position she could either come forward or retreat. It was for her to say. She was in command. The choker of imitation pearls was just right for the occasion, a grudging welcome to a black sheep. Her feet were so tiny they might have been bound, and one assumed a rosary of complaints concerning the niggardly stock in the shoe store.

"Oh, Mama!" Flo Chandler cried — she who until this moment had been the mama. She ran to her mother, arms out, and with them attempted to encircle her mother's plump shoulders and to bury her face somewhere in the short neck, but a skillful maneuver prevented any such display of hysterical affection and Flo Chandler simply found herself standing there. "Oh, Mama."

And then the woman spoke. "So here you are again, Florence."

There was in the word "again" a suggestion not only of another return to her mother's stingy arms, but many other, shorter escapades, some lasting no more than a day or two, some only a few hours. Liz realized she knew her mother not at all, that it was the girlhood of her mother that was important, that then she had been what she really was.

"I'm surprised," Liz said to me, "that my grandmother did not say of me, 'Look what the cat dragged in.' Her conversation was laced with cynical clichés. I have never known another human being whose expectations were so often fulfilled and whose low opinions were so often justified." Her grandmother expected people to be self-seeking, and they were. She expected marriages to turn out badly, and they did. She believed people wanted something from you; they tried to get it. What might appear to be generosity, she knew to be a means of obligating. One had to be careful about accepting gifts or compliments; you can be sure something will be expected in return.

It is curious, Liz observed, how certain people achieve a moral ascendancy over other people; a part of it seems to be that most people feel unworthy and a very few feel worthy, and the reason for that is that they are worthy. That is not to say that being worthy makes them gentle or kind, for both gentleness and kindness excuse license. It is the habit of the unworthy, when exasperated with the worthy and angry at themselves, to try to imagine the worthy in a compromising circumstance — in bed with a neighbor or nude in the street, the light playing on their defects without the clothes that fit them so perfectly and lend the hated dignity. We hope to imagine them in some impossible situation that makes them throw up their hands. But it is hopeless. There are the worthy and the unworthy just as there are leaders and followers, as there are the good and the wicked and the rich and the poor, the gifted and the ungifted.

The bus to Chicago passed through New Hoosic, Iowa, at an inconvenient evening hour — six-thirty. In a land where supper was on the table at six and the first slab of bread was buttered a few seconds later, supper went on at seven in New Hoosic to allow time to go down and watch the bus pull in.

By nine o'clock in New Hoosic, the dishes were done, domestic animals let out to relieve themselves against the long, confining night; radios murmured the last news and the first yawns were patted. The thoughts of some fled to the cups beside their beds — the water must be changed again before immersing their dentures; of others, to initiating and fulfilling marital duties and, if a Saturday, to the winding of clocks.

That first evening, Liz's grandfather retired to his den for an hour; he was not suffered to smoke elsewhere in the house. Liz and her mother had been shown by the grandmother into Flo's old room; the presence of a trunk and a few cartons neatly tied up with heavy cord was a reminder that they were intruders in a room that had long since been set aside for other purposes.

"My mother stood in the middle of that room holding her poor suitcase — like a waif. My grandmother left us there, trailing the scent of violets behind her, and closed the door. She might as well have locked it."

There Flo Chandler stood. After a few moments she said, "Well, here we are, honey." She set down the suitcase. Then she sat on a little chair before a small dressing table — a vanity with a mirror and two smaller flanking mirrors, a piece of furniture dear to little girls who can't see enough of themselves and from too many angles. If, in the mirrors before her, Liz's mother hoped to find her lost identity in a remembered image of herself, she was bound to be disappointed; for the child we were is a stranger to us, and there is a reason the child is a stranger: identity is the sum of experience, and a child has so little experience his identity is shadowy. When we speak of some one as "childlike" we are saying he has had little experience or hasn't recognized experience, or profited from it. He is vulnerable.

That was hardly the moment for Flo Chandler to search in the glass for herself. Perhaps, Liz thought, her mother was using the mirrors to pick and choose among her various selves the one that could bear what had happened to her — a gauche, mad husband, herself an unwelcome dependent whose mother had often observed that those who made their beds should lie in them. She had no skills anyone required. And she had a child.

At that vanity she had preened before going out on a high school date; on returning from it she had watched her lips from various angles repeat what had been said to her and what she had said; it is likely that before those mirrors she regarded herself regarding herself as one for whom the only answer was to marry a man who would ask no questions.

It was as one who appeared to be preening that she was discovered by her mother a few minutes later.

"Florence. I'll have a word with you now."

Flo Chandler followed the old woman out.

This time, as the grandmother walked into the upstairs hall, she trailed not only violets, but words. ". . . get a few things settled right now."

When the session was over behind a closed door across the hall, Liz heard the old woman speak in measured tones. ". . . running around. And get yourself something decent for church."

It is safe to say that most churchgoers have found earthly life disappointing and by regular attendance wistfully assure themselves of a happier heaven where the worst of the personal problems may be solved and where, at least, money is not so important; but Liz's grandmother had a more practical view of church. It was her opinion that human beings lied and that they stole, that they cheated and bore false witness. Those who did not stop at fornication moved right on to adultery, drunkenness and murder — and of course she was right. To ensure that she herself did not fall into these errors, she was faithful in her attendance at the Methodist Episcopal Church and she expected similar attendance of those who were related to her. We are sometimes judged, she knew — if quite unfairly — by those adjacent to us. She had been faithful to her God and had done many things for Him; she expected Him to treat her with similar consideration. For Him she had gathered old clothes and healthful canned goods — creamed corn and peas especially — and these she had distributed among the poor across the Burlington tracks. In God's name she set aside a dollar a week that, with similar dollars contributed by the similarly dedicated, was dispatched overseas to foolishly sanguine natives who had virtually no notion of sin, if one could believe the Fox Movietone News.

Her God was not easily described, there being three parts to him — a human part, an inhuman part, and a ghostly part. It was only the human third of him you could get your teeth into. That third was a young man of thirty or so whose face showed he had been bitterly disappointed but had gotten over it. In his brief career on earth he had walked on water, cast out demons, changed water into wine, and raised the dead — to what purpose is questionable since they later died a second death. He waded in among people in the temple who were selling doves and he scattered them with a whip. All along he had a hunch he was going to be betrayed, and he kept dropping hints.

The inhuman third of the old woman's God was a harder nut to crack. He was all-powerful, all-knowing and everywhere present; He was there at every coming in and going out. There was no escaping Him. Utterly convinced of the value of Free Will, he did not deter the wife beater or the child molester. The woman who stepped down from her car to aid a stranded traveler should have known in her heart that a second car would run her down and leave her paralyzed for life from the waist down. A man should have thought twice before he offered his hand to another who lay on a live wire. What is the purpose of the hideous pain of terminal cancer if not to teach fortitude and prompt an examining of one's sins? If there were no wars and famine, the earth would seethe with people like maggots on a wound and many of the worthy would starve.

The last third of this God brooded and floated, lurked among the cassocks and cottas in the musty, dim vestry of the Methodist Episcopal Church — most active, surely, when the church was empty and the doors were locked.

After church, New Hoosic ate roast pork. Her grandmother put the raw, bleeding meat into the oven early.

"When we got back from church that first time, the house smelled like a death chamber. I associate that house with death and humiliation."

Liz was a stranger in a strange land; as a stranger she was suspect, for all we know about strangers is that they were not a success where they used to be or they would still be where they were.

Few, except among the rich, are sent to dancing school, but all the young must learn to dance, for the alternative is sitting at home within earshot of grieving parents who see no social future for you, and the bleak possibility that you will never leave the nest. How can you make friends? How can she marry who cannot dance? How explain the middle-aged spinster with dry palms?

Except among the precocious or the rich, dancing begins in a high school gymnasium under swags of crepe paper; a boy pushes and pulls an acceptable girl about the room with but little relation to the music. If she begins to guess some pattern in his movements, she is said to "follow." He leads, as men are said to do. If she follows well, she is much in demand; she convinces the awkward male that he is a graceful dancer. Many quite plain women who are good followers find themselves eventually in circumstances so enviable that cut flowers and crystal are routine. It comes as little surprise that later on they correctly anticipate and gratify more subtle demands. "She's a good dancer" is a more important accolade than cooking smooth peanut butter fudge and finding one's name on the honor roll. Too bad.

Liz guessed early on that she would not be a social success. She was too tall; she was twelve when she entered high school and looked at least fourteen. She had no familiar background, had never played post office, nor had she roasted marshmallows with her present peers. Worse, her brilliance was shocking. In her junior year, her essay "A Thought for a Windy Afternoon" was paid for and printed in a student newspaper with a wide circulation. Her "thought," admirably supported by facts, was novel at the time. It was her belief that young people, though different, are at least the equal of adults in sensitivity, if not more so since their feelings have not yet been blunted by experience. She handily won a contest sponsored by the state for the best sonnet written by a high school student. "Effigy" concerned the death of a doll who longed for an affection that no longer existed except in memory. The sonnet began

> *Who comes to mourn this late beloved?*
> *Who knows what love her presence proved?*

And ended:

> *Unloved at last, but free to go*
> *Under the lilacs, under the snow.*

"Oh, Elizabeth," Miss Nugent in English had cried. "You will go far, far!"

"You're quite the little poetess, aren't you," Liz's grandmother remarked. There in the kitchen her grandmother was entertaining Donald, her grandmother's beloved dead brother's son. His arrival caused a change in her nature. Her love for her dead brother — she was the last one to have seen him alive and his last words were to her — excused in Donald a style of life she would have condemned out of hand in anyone else. "He never really had a mother, you know," the woman often said. In excusing Donald, she had an opportunity to believe herself broad-minded and at the same time to reaffirm her belief that blood is usually thicker than water. Donald was thirty-two, but not yet afflicted with the belief that his youth was gone. He was some years younger than his cousin Flo, and he alone of the family had the run of the house when he dropped in. He often dropped in during the afternoon to "flap his lip over" his aunt's baked goods. He was a handsome, blond young man with something of the rogue in him; his lazy smile suggested secret knowledge that he might quite innocently turn against you. He now sat backward in a kitchen chair, resting his arms along the top, drinking his coffee.

He expected to be waited on, and he was. "Sure, I'll have a touch more, Auntie, please and thank you," he said. In spite of his deliberate movements, his slow crossing of his legs when the usual use of a chair permitted that, and his careful offering of his profile, he was known in New Hoosic as a "live wire" and a "go-getter." He and another, similar young man whom he called his "sidekick" had, five years before — the very year of the Crash — set up a small radio station right there in New Hoosic, the natural outcome of an early obsession with crystal radios and outgoing personalities. Certainly neither Donald nor the sidekick had foreseen the Crash, but it had been lucky for them; in straitened circumstances, people found cheap entertainment in radio.

That cheap entertainment had been around ten years, but until the Crash there'd been enough cash on hand to trot on down to the Tomahawk Theater on First and Main and take in Janet Gaynor and Charles Farrell in *Seventh Heaven*. She was a little French girl; she called the garret she lived in her Seventh

Heaven. The Crash was about the end of *that*. Desperate, the Tomahawk cut the price of tickets and then began offering double features. Later on you got a chance to win sets of china, free passes and turkeys. Next thing they knew, Mrs. Hart herself was selling tickets in that little glass cage out front there. And still people sat home before their Atwater Kents, their Spartans and Stromberg-Carlsons to hear Kay Kyser's Kollege of Musical Knowledge. The more intelligent, deprived of visual stimulation, discovered they had imaginations and sat enthralled with the *Theater of the Air* and *Just Plain Bill*.

"It's not for nothing that poor kids of our generation had better minds than the previous one who grew up with films, and the one after us who were weaned on television."

There was nothing so grand as the *Theater of the Air* nor so maudlin as *Just Plain Bill* on KNEW, the station owned by Donald and his sidekick, nothing so jolly as Kay Kyser nor so hilarious as Ed Wynn the Texaco Fire Chief. Honestly, you could split a gut. KNEW was strictly local. Local news — a brick through the big window of the Ford garage — reports on the worth of grains and swine, a calendar of events — the county fair, club meetings, Elks, Masons, Eastern Stars. Hours of popular records, and KNEW was among the first of the local stations to take "requests."

"Now here's a little bit of 'Stardust' for you out there, requested by Joey Halberson, and it goes out for Jane and Susan and all the rest of you gals."

("Say, I heard you on the radio!")

And, "This goes out to Grandma Porter. She's laid up in the hospital after a fall. She'd like to have a line from you there."

What, aside from seeing your name in lights, is so ennobling as hearing your name on the air? Who would not walk proud in the halls?

Donald might be said to have been kind, for he hired his cousin Flo Chandler as a receptionist, a noun just coming into vogue, an occupation that even today offers hope for women who have no assets but engaging features. He had hired her "for peanuts," as he described the remuneration to his sidekick. Flo had nothing much to do, really, except greet people who visited the station, tell them to wait if Donald or the sidekick was busy, scrub once a week and keep things dusted, and see that coffee was ready, answer the phone and read the news. "Anyway," Donald told his aunt, "it'll get her off your hands, at least for a while."

Because he and the sidekick were live wires and radio broadcasting was sort of racy, it was not expected that they marry, nor was it thought strange that they rented rather than owned their rooms. They could be tied down neither to mortgage nor to wife. Donald had rooms and kitchen privileges at the Plains Hotel and there he bedded down migrant waitresses and telephone operators; some few of those who could be trusted not to get their hopes up remained to prepare his breakfast and were sometimes allowed to return for further congress. The lot of them were young women of whom his aunt would have expected nothing better, simply conveniences, and if they made Donald's lonely life bearable, they served their purpose.

"Well," Donald said, "I don't know much about poetry. I'm just an uneducated hick, but —"

Liz had often noted that the stupid who have made some little financial success often boast of their lack of education as a means of putting down those who have disciplined their minds. *If you're so smart, why aren't you rich?* And so they equate money with success.

"Oh, now, *Donald*," his aunt said. "There you go again!" She had in mind his year at the university at Ames, from which he had been expelled. She believed he had blundered into some kind of scrape involving women — Lord knew he was so handsome the women couldn't keep their hands off him — but what had happened was that he had filched and copied and meant to sell the final examination in English to the unprepared. Luckily for him, he had been apprehended before money had changed hands.

"All right, all *right*," Donald said. "There I go again. But it

[*116*]

'pears to me that my young cousin once removed here ought to do less writing poems and more learning to dance. She ought not be sitting home when girls her age trip the light fantastic. Tell you somethin', Liz me lass — you can't get anywheres in New Hoosic without you learn to dance." He handed back her poetry.

"Did you ever hear a finer line?" Liz asked me. "So clear a statement of homely wisdom? 'You can't get anywheres in New Hoosic without you learn to dance.' And by damn, I believed him. Women believed him. I believed him because he had a place in New Hoosic and I didn't. I'd have given my right arm — as he'd have put it — to be able to dance. To be helped into a car by somebody other than my grandfather, to have a silk wrap held. Writing verse I then thought a poor substitute, and so was the public library. That last year in high school I'd much rather they'd have made way for me in the halls because I was a nifty dancer than because my verses scanned. I hated Donald because he had spoken the truth, and I was determined to learn to dance — but how, unless he taught me? And in that direction he made nary a move."

She remained the tall girl with heavy chestnut hair and huge, questioning eyes from somewhere out west who had won something and thought she was smart. As for her appearance, in a very few years her height and her face — the high, prominent cheekbones, the wide, sensuous mouth — would recommend her as a fashion model; she dropped easily into arresting poses.

Those in the lower classes in America are not much concerned with creativity — they are too busy with the problem of survival. But the middle and upper classes instinctively close ranks against the creative, for the creative bring into question middle- and upper-class values that are ultimately based on money, and money is not as exclusive as they dearly wish it were; money is available to anybody who wants it enough. Those who have put their faith in money perceive in the creative world a world money will not allow them to enter except as patrons or audience. The hand painting of trays, candlesticks tooled on lathes, mosaics of shells and arrangements of beach grasses are vain attempts to seduce the Divine Afflatus.

New Hoosic adored the high school football team, the New Hoosic Warriors; Indians had once whooped it up around the town and the sharp-eyed found arrowheads of flint on the flat prairie. Except for the Warriors, who over the years had played fine games, New Hoosic had remained unknown; but even strangers, frowning in concentration, remarked, "Isn't that where the Warriors hail from?" How fine it was to hop on down and see the team off, to greet it coming back with the old bacon, how moving to see the young people join hands and snake-dance through the town in and out of stores and on out to the stadium, where under the everlasting stars bonfires leaped and cast long shadows, where tomorrow the Warriors would again fight for old New Hoosic! In those lean, broad-shouldered young men they saw themselves when young, whether or not they themselves had ever fled with the pigskin. In the Warriors older women saw the young men they might have married and didn't, but those who did marry them need not have been surprised that things hadn't worked out, because those halcyon years on the team were the very apogee of life; after that, no place to go but down, clutching on the way at unspeakably lovely memories of overnight bus trips, waking to the dawn, screaming crowds, the smell of sweat and steam, bear hugs, the feel of delicious, willing flesh, tears of happiness and smiling gods. They had not much needed to trouble their heads in those days with English and algebra and physics, and over the years many a muleheaded young teacher who believed life was something more than "playing the game" found himself out on his ass.

It may be that the New Hoosic Warriors thought no more of fucking than their less physical brothers, but as local celebrities they could expect admiring girls to more readily accept their promises and semen. One such was a boy named Roland Gann, whose past was hardly more known than Liz's was; shortly before he entered high school he had arrived with his mother, who took over the Pony Cafe and made a going thing of it; this she did by serving a good cup of coffee, joshing with the customers, and attending to their stories. Well, redheads are often a lot of fun. Mary Gann had a raw, husky voice that one day might wake a man — if he played his cards just right, played them close to his chest. She was often seen at the Haystack, a roadhouse fifteen miles west of town, with this one and that one. But, tearful and in her cups, she maintained that her son Roland was her real boyfriend, and since Roland was a big, sullen fellow, it was not wise to get fresh with her unless she made the first move. This she did by feeling your muscle. The ladies of the town had no reason to speak to her; they had no truck with the Pony Cafe, knowing it as a place where New Hoosic's dozen or so whores gathered to eat fried oysters in the wee hours when business was over.

As a football player, Roland was spoken to — and Roland knew why. And he knew he had another two years to be worth talking to and to get a revenge he needed: he intended to jazz, as he put it, the high-toned daughters of the State Bank, the New Hoosic Hardware and the biggest farms, whose owners had a second house in town so their daughters might attend New Hoosic High. Rape was not out of the question. He had not yet reached his goal, but by the time he was seventeen a dozen lesser coeds knew the thrust of his cock and his breath in their ears when he ejaculated. Each girl was but another notch in his gun. Sometimes before he slept he summoned up images of those he stroked until they cried out for it, and more than once he had pulled on his pants and left them panting there. He honestly didn't give a shit. Few young men could avail themselves of so effective fantasies, the creatures of his revenge, revenge for not knowing who his father was, if his father's name was his, for having lived here and there, and for recalling whispers and murmurings whose meanings only subsequently became clear.

In New Hoosic but two years, Roland Gann was puzzled by Liz and her position in the town. Her grandfather drove an old

Buick, but that was better than a new Ford. A lot of rich people drive old cars — they can afford to. Her mother worked, but she worked in the radio station, and her uncle owned it. Her mother was still a good-looking broad.

No, he didn't go for tall girls — he liked them short and sweet, built like a brick shithouse — but this Liz was the smartest girl in school and excellence of any kind must have the damned props knocked right out from under it. He had several times smiled at her in the halls; she had smiled back, but her smile was no more interested in what was between his legs than if she had been a boy.

Then late one morning when she was coming out of typing class and he was on the way to the gym, she smiled in a different way.

"Hi, there," he said.

"Hi, there, yourself," she said like any other girl. He didn't move in then, not him, not old Roland Gann. They got more interested if you didn't show too much interest. But he wondered about it, what she was up to, and he thought he knew. The spring dance was coming up next weekend.

"Kee-rist," Mary Gann sometimes told sympathetic customers hunched over their cups at the Pony Cafe. "I might just as well have no wheels at all." That was her zippy lingo for having no car. "But what are you gonna do when you got a punk, good-looking kid? Hell's bells, I was young once, too."

"You're still a mighty pretty lady," they said.

"Thanks a bunch, you liars," she said.

"There's a lot of guys, believe me, just as soon have your shoes under his bunk."

When she smoothed back her red hair with both hands, her breasts lifted. "Now just a cotton-pickin' minute. You just better watch it, buster."

It was all just kidding. She had a steady, then, some guy from out of town, but she wasn't really sore. "I'll be a sister to you and stand you to another cup of java."

"All I knew of Roland Gann is that he smiled at me as no other boy had, and he played football, and I knew you couldn't get anywheres in New Hoosic without you learn to dance. I didn't put it all together then, but I put it together when he pulled alongside me in an old Ford coupe."

"Hi there again," he said, and Liz was moved and flattered that in the repeated words "Hi There" he was re-creating the scene in the hall quite near the drinking fountain. Did he too recall the faint gurgle of falling water, smell again the dry odor of chalk dust, and feel the new spring sun falling through the window, yellow as ripe corn?

"You gotta date for the dance?" he asked. Had he been more polished he might not have asked a question that required of her an answer that revealed her as one yet undesired.

"No," she said.

But his awkward question indicated a further question, and she thrilled.

"He was a handsome animal," Liz told me, "with that wolf grin of his. I think he was born bad. I think there are criminal personalities, that these personalities have nothing to do with heredity, nothing with environment, with slights and humiliations — that there is a race of criminals who look on others with amazement, and as the enemy who would destroy them."

"Then how's about it?" Roland Gann asked, skimming a phrase from radio.

Liz skimmed a phrase from *Of Human Bondage*, the frequent words of Mildred.

"I don't mind."

Nor did he move in then. He gave her a ride home. As she turned to open the door he pressed her hand hard down against the seat, and his fingers found and stroked her palm; she did not then know the significance.

"I was innocent. And nothing mattered except that a boy had asked me to a dance. What else at sixteen could matter? With the exchange of a few words, my life had changed. With a few words I had been elevated into an exclusive company that included Helen Wagner, whose clothes came from Marshall Field's, and Margaret Lacy, whose mother wore diamonds besides an engagement ring and whose father each year bought a new La Salle. Margaret Lacy's boyfriend might be president of the junior class, but he was not a football player, nor was Margaret Lacy the smartest girl in the class. For Roland Gann I would have played dumb and tied a ribbon in my hair as Helen Wagner did."

Her worldly answer to Roland Gann's inquiry of whether she would go to the dance with him — her "I don't mind" — was quite at odds with the sickening fact that Liz couldn't dance. Suppose at the last moment she pretended to be ill? Then she could cherish the memory of having been chosen among many — and people did get sick. Suppose she — but that would leave him sitting alone that night, he who by a few words had made her feel feminine and desired and the equal of Helen Wagner. For better or worse, she must go through with it. If he never asked her again — so bad was her dancing — that was the price she must pay.

Clear that she and her mother would be longer than temporarily in New Hoosic, her grandmother had assigned her a small room on the third floor under the eaves and there, sliding her feet instead of stamping, she practiced all she knew of dancing, murmuring One, Two, Three, Four and moving forward and moving back. It was not beyond possibility that once a girl was in a boy's arms she was transformed, was suddenly given the gift of dance as naturally as a woman, inexperienced though she is, becomes a mother.

One, Two, Three, Four! Reverse! But *One*, Two, Three? She was at a loss with the waltz. There was no reverse. In the waltz, the female was always going backward.

In those lean years, Hollywood tried to pry people's minds off their pocketbooks and stomachs. Oh, the movies about dancing feet, doing the tap. The cameras attended the feet, the loose swinging arms and the rapt eyes; for an hour you sat in the dark and believed you could tap your troubles away.

Providential that a musical starring Ginger Rogers and Fred Astaire came to the Tomahawk a week before the dance; Liz sat through it twice, observing, observing. As she watched, her brain fled her head and lodged in her feet. Rogers and Astaire danced as lightly as instructed moths, each drawn to the other's lambent flame; up they floated and down a broad stairway that led to or from apartments never revealed but fit for beings as ethereal as they. Astaire swept Rogers into his arms and bore her aloft with an ease that suggested love had strengthened him and lightened her. Oh, then, they waltzed away from the stairway and into a garden lush with formal plantings and over near a reflecting pool. Rapt, they waltzed around the edge — faster and faster — lost in their love and delicate art, and then — just like you and me — she in diaphanous tulle and he in immaculate tux — they fell right in! No matter how rich or grand we are, we're likely to get our comeuppance.

Besides this dancing, what would be required of Liz was as nothing. As for the waltz, she would tell Roland Gann she preferred to sit the waltzes out.

"That way we can get to know each other," she would say.

But it was Roland Gann who suggested they get to know each other.

At eight-thirty each weekday morning, all four classes of New Hoosic High School sat at their desks in the assembly hall, a huge room with windows so tall their tops must be opened by a long stick with a hook on it. It was a sign of grace to be chosen to open a window and to return the stick to the far corner behind the bust of Caesar on the side where the freshmen sat. Before the rows and rows of desks — the back of each one was the writing surface for the one who sat on the seat behind it — was an expanse of blackboard that ran from wall to wall; it beckoned those who would compose graffiti, and Mr. Koch the janitor was responsible for seeing that nothing unauthorized remained there when the students gathered each morning. Some years before, alas, teachers and students had had time to read an astonishing piece of pornography set in couplets that covered the entire board. Miss Kirkpatrick, Mrs. Willis and Mr. Wahl the principal turned as one — as if practiced — and began to erase the hateful, moving stanzas — Miss Kirkpatrick on the right, Mr. Wahl on the left, and Mrs. Willis — whose husband was the court stenographer and wore a green eyeshade — in the middle. Miss Kirkpatrick, who had once been seen weeping in the girls' toilet, used both hands. In five minutes' time they had destroyed the evidence that might, after examining each student's handwriting, have led to the culprit, but it was Mr. Wahl's opinion, expressed in a hastily called faculty meeting, that the vile text had been chalked there by an adult — a word that in itself is faintly reprehensible — and that this depraved beast of a man, probably a stranger, one of those you hear about, had somehow gained entrance by night, possibly by way of the skylight over the physics laboratory, and with flashlight in one hand and chalk in the other he had exposed his longing to corrupt.

But now the warnings, revelations and injunctions chalked there were blameless; each bulletin was signed with the initials of the teacher who had composed it; initials do lend a text an immediacy, an important haste sometimes lost by signing an entire name. B.O.H. — Bernice Hirschmann — reminded her business administration students, in flawless Palmer Method, that their double-entry bookkeeping projects were due that day. V.M.E. — Violet M. Eastman — reminded her little band of dreamers that tryouts for *The Merchant of Venice* would be heard Friday afternoon at three-thirty. Olive M. Scholz declared that the long-awaited copies of *La Tâche de petit Pierre* had been received. She affixed her entire name. Her handwriting was a far cry from the disciplined script of B.O.H.: it was a personal, printed script that flew in the face of authority — a bright, willful child's. The tail of the z trailed after her signature like memory. Small wonder there were rumors. Detestable that so many fell under her spell, aped her stark *o*'s and commanding *m*'s, smiled and frowned and smiled and frowned and affected her quick little movements and cutting remarks.

Liz was considering the word *tâche* in the title *La Tâche de petit Pierre*, the curious fact that the circumflex accent had replaced a vanished *s*, as in *hâte*, *hôte*, *hôtel* and *bête*. How had this come about? What advantage . . .

At that moment, very briefly, Roland Gann stood beside her desk. He let fall into her lap a folded bit of paper.

 SPOKEN WORDS VANISH like mist, but the inflection that perfumed them leaves their meaning in no doubt. Written words are as permanent as ink; but wanting inflection, invite interpretation. We make of them what we will, what we require.

"And maybe that's the charm of poetry," Liz said.

Notes moved swiftly in every study hall, passed hand to hand, tossed and caught in a smooth system of whispers, nudges, hisses and quick glances. Not even responsible students refrained: for almost four years Liz had been a cog in the intelligence machine but not once had she received a note of her own. She was astonished when Roland Gann dropped a note on her desk as he passed to the dictionary, where he had never been seen to go before; he remained leaning over the big book in his football sweater as if he, too, were susceptible to the nuance and sheen of words. But certainly he knew that his maiden visit there had alerted the prowling teachers, who must watch to see if he returned by the same route to pick up an answer.

Liz unfolded the bit of paper.

I got to talk to you. Meet me seven o'clock out behind the library.

Liz hesitated, but remembering the pressure of his hand, she scribbled a note.

All right.

However, he did not return by the same route, but by way of the bust of Caesar.

Well! She tore up the note she'd written. It was an embarrassment. It was a note unwanted, not required. His own note was not a request — it was a command. She would see about *that*.

She had been close to disaster, close to tossing off what she was — a bright girl — for what she wanted to be — a popular girl.

And she was flattered.

Was there not something appealing, something vulnerable in his bad grammar? His *I got to talk to you*. Was it not a cry for help? Read another way, the words were not a command at all, but an appeal.

"I must have known even then," Liz told me, "that if we can convince ourselves we feel sorry for somebody, we feel we have the upper hand."

He had not passed by for an answer. Fearing there would be no answer. In not knowing whether there was an answer, he could believe, he could hope.

The April sun through the tall windows lay flat on her desk and it was the longest day she remembered.

It was believed that the New Hoosic Public Library was a safe and inspirational destination for little children and high school students on week-nights. The children's reading room was furnished with long, varnished oak tables and chairs fit for dwarfs.

"Furniture scaled down for children," Liz remarked, "strikes me as obscene, like a shoe made to accommodate the clubfoot. Of course children, yet lacking adult powers, are themselves cripples." At those tables and in those tiny chairs little people who had but recently learned to read moved their lips and followed the histories of selected animals who spoke the English language and got themselves into amusing scrapes with other animals, with angry farmers, zoo keepers, provident insects and Old Mother West Wind.

Miss Innes shooed out the little ones at eight o'clock and saw to it they didn't leave mittens and overshoes behind. Remaining for another hour was a tall old man in a ruined frock coat who lived at the edge of town in an abandoned bus; he came at noon when the library opened and read newspapers; Miss Innes believed he came there for warmth, and although he was the kind of derelict who might turn his hand to something unspeakable, he had not yet done so. And along with him remained the earnest, the friendless and the unpopular, Liz among them.

In New Hoosic literature was thought a poor substitute for life, but Miss Innes thought otherwise. Had she not, she would have married like anybody else and would not have become the librarian and gone on living with her mother and all those plants. But as librarian she was privy to works that New Hoosic would declare indecent whatever their scientific or artistic worth, and it is likely that she would have been discharged by whoever it is who discharges librarians had it been generally known what she kept in what was known as the receiving room, a room out back, cold in winter, stifling in summer. On a platform outside, the express company left boxes of books to be processed and put on the shelves out front. It is hard to believe that Miss Innes, who every so often in navy-blue crepe de chine and altogether without jewelry publicly consumed a marshmallow sundae alone at a little table with wire feet at McFadden's, was an ardent admirer of Faulkner and had read *Sanctuary* more than once.

But it is not much pleasure to have access to forbidden materials unless somebody knows you have such access. Into her confidence she had taken the Episcopal rector and the Roman Catholic priest, both of whom might profit by the secret texts in their capacities as counsellors and confessors. The president of the First National Bank was in her confidence, the president of the State Bank was not, nor was a Mrs. Morse who lived in a great house. But a Mrs. Drake was, who lived in a small house. As the years passed, Miss Innes created an arcane little aristocracy. She knew exactly whom she could trust; those she admitted to her circle enjoyed the pleasant responsibility of keeping their mouths shut; the power over her she granted them lent her own life a racy precariousness enjoyed by few women in New Hoosic.

"In here," she would say, "I think you might find things of interest to you. You will understand why this room is not for the general public." Her eyes met theirs and a pact was sealed. Just so had her eyes at last met Liz's. She recognized and honored precocity, and accepted it as a quite sufficient passport.

In the far corner of the receiving room was a half-sized plaster cast of the Dying Gaul, whose presence there was not much understood. To reach the shelves you sidestepped cartons and newspapers tied up with twine. On the shelves you found Krafft-Ebing and Havelock Ellis, Boccaccio and Rabelais, Pepys' *Diary*, the little-known works of Mark Twain, poems of Robert Burns, secret journals of the Austrian court. The illustrations for *Modern Embalming* were as appalling as the text they confirmed. Those who have read the chapter headed "Complications" are never again the same.

Liz found a little-known story of Huysmans. It concerned a failing actress who, in the last line, justified her vicious behavior with the words "*Je suis artiste.*"

In the years I knew Liz, I'd heard her use that sentence a hundred times, but in the days of Miss Innes she need be excused only her ignorance of dancing and her lack of friends.

"And so we borrow the disguise of one," she said, "and we hide in the music and the poetry of another, cherish the last words or philosophy of others and we go on and on and on . . ."

". . . the years snarling at our heels," I finished for her.

At five minutes to nine, Miss Innes snapped off the lights in the reading room and at once snapped them back on, a warning that the place was about to close and that each must leave and face again his own four walls. But there were those who left the library and went elsewhere. It could be said of the New Hoosic Public Library that it was a house of assignation.

A narrow alley ran between the library and the Ford garage,

and there Roland Gann had parked his mother's wheels. He sat in the car with an insouciant slouch. He straightened and reached across the seat and opened the door for Liz.

"Hop in."

She hopped.

It is usual beyond the Mississippi River to name a cemetery Mountain View, but the land around New Hoosic was as flat as that around Sodom and Gomorrah. They called theirs Homeview. From Homeview the dead might, with a stretch of the imagination, jackknife up and look to their houses in New Hoosic or up to heavenly quarters. Best of all, Homeview had the only real stand of trees for forty miles around — cottonwoods and alders stood thick on all four sides of the field that swallowed up the New Hoosic dead; less formal trees and bushes grew among the graves. The roads that crisscrossed in there were reinforced with carefully tended gravel, for the infrequent but heavy rains made ordinary roads impassable, and when a hearse must get in, it must get in. Windmills stood like guards at the four corners of Homeview and spilled water into irrigation ditches.

It was a pretty oasis in the Iowa desert and attracted those bent on fornication. Homeview was spacious enough to accommodate a score of cars without crowding and the shrubbery rendered it so intimate one need not be aware of the rustlings and groanings in the neighboring sedan unless one wished to be. Young men of families long established in New Hoosic, who could boast of some tiers of family bones beneath the soil, parked near their family monuments, but as members of old families and with a sense of family pride they tossed their oozing condoms on neighboring plots.

"Many ladies of New Hoosic known everywhere for oatmeal cookies, petit point and apple butter, and men gone through the chairs of the Scottish rite, were time and again reminded as they followed a funeral party into Homeview that here they had first been laid, if not to rest."

Roland Gann had begun to talk some time before they approached the rusty iron arch that supported the rusty iron letters HOMEVIEW.

"Sure glad you didn't back out."

It was not clear then whether he meant she might back out of dancing with him or riding with him. That she was to be ridden never entered her head.

"Why should I?" she asked, *Of Human Bondage* all over again.

"I guess I don't much believe in myself."

He was a clever one, knowing at his age that most females jump at the chance to make a male believe in himself. The old need business.

"I spoke shyly," Liz told me, "as a maiden would."

Liz said to him, "You play football."

"Sure, but what's that?"

"It's something in New Hoosic."

Roland Gann stared through the windshield, frowning, considering. "But then what?"

"After football?"

"Yes, after football. All the others —"

"All the others get a job in town. They buy a radio and listen to the music and remember the past. The past is all we're sure of."

"They what? Oh, you're a hard one to figure, baby."

"You'll do what they do."

"But they got a place here."

"Here, you mean? A family plot?"

He was silent a moment. "Uncomfortable," Liz told me, "uncomfortable with death. His passing would be hard."

"No," he said. "I mean in town."

"I expect you'll take over your mother's business."

He laughed a tired laugh. "Oh, no, baby. I'm just a rolling stone."

"Do you hope to avoid moss?"

"What's that?"

"A turn of phrase." She considered his infantile image of himself, a profile fleshed out with myths passed on in poolrooms, lyrics played on portable phonographs — Man lost and no place to lay his head, Man, the Wandering Jew, a rolling stone. And a female — keeper of the flame, kisser away of tears — is bound if not to stop the rolling stone at least to set up a temporary roadblock until a man comes to his senses or gets too old to roll.

He had parked in a tunnel of brush. "We both came to town about the same time." He shut off the engine and turned and took her hand. "I guess we're both rolling stones."

Liz believed that his rudimentary brain had warned him to establish some common denominator. "We're both strangers."

His animal instincts were another matter. "Oh, baby," he whispered.

"In the dusk, in the green gloom I could not see his eyes. He touched my face and with a finger felt my lips."

And then his mouth was on her mouth. "He held me against him with his left hand and his right hand unhooked my bra, and then his fingers nipped and nipped my nipples.

"There was no point in putting up token resistance. From the moment the car crossed into Homeview, I was damaged goods and not worth taking to a dance. And suddenly I wanted to happen what was happening. I knew there were thousands of bright girls like me who end up as Queen of the Stacks in good libraries, who smell of cloth and talcum powder, maidenhead intact but for their own fingers.

"Now at least I would know what all the shouting was about — and not just secondhand, if you'll excuse me. I would know the act that was the face of love on the one hand and that of murder on the other — the ultimate subject of every novel from Boccaccio to Kate Douglas Wiggin, every love song, every valentine. My temporary shock and dishevelment was a small price to pay.

" 'Oh, baby,' he kept repeating, as so many of them do. 'Oh, baby!' How ugly in that so addressing you they would seem to be molesting an infant! I filed away the pitch of his voice.

"I was on his lap, and facing him, facing Good Old Roland Gann, quarterback for the New Hoosic Warriors, a putative bastard, and his fingers found and used my clitoris. Dearie me! This, mind you, in a day when few men, let alone boys, knew a girl *had* a clitoris, let alone its precise location. In those days what pleasure a woman got was largely in passing, if you'll excuse.

"Now came the loosening of the belt, and the merry music of the tongue of the buckle. He was not so transported that he failed to use a condom — rubbers, they called them out there — Merry Widows. 'Just a sec,' he was saying and he pulled out from his shirt pocket this thing and rolled it down over his flirty cock as a woman rolls on a stocking. Had he been the parfait lover he would have asked me to do the job, the parfait lover or the parfait bastard.

"He was one of the vast unwashed who is uncircumcised, of that rabble who, having so little of their own, cannot bear to part with what might mark them as Jews in common shower. So the rolling on of the Merry Widow was preceded by the easing back of the Gann foreskin.

"Don't let them tell you copulation was difficult in Model A Fords, that the space was inadequate and the gearshift hampering. Facing him I had of course to draw up my knees, but what the hell. And after that it was a breeze. Feeling no pleasure, I was free to observe, as the oculist might, his vacant eyes at the moment of ejaculation, the moment they're so helpless."

Speech comes hard after sex. The drab human voice — a suitable enough instrument for demanding potatoes or remarking the time of day — cannot convey the mysteries of sex, sleep, music and death. "Speech after Beethoven? Roland Gann's postcoital words were classic in their simplicity. 'OK,' he said, as a signal I suppose that I should detach myself from him and avert my eyes while he attended to the cleaning up.

"He looked glum as we drove back to town, perhaps expecting I would attempt to touch him, hoping for some affectionate response that would allow me to excuse myself or to hope. He pulled up behind the library. " 'Seein' you,' he said, and I pictured him at eight or nine standing quite alone in a vacant lot longing to be one of his betters.

" 'Ta,' I said.

"We never spoke again. There was of course no dance, nor did I expect one. I was not left waiting in a party dress of dotted Swiss or racy tulle. I understood the situation. I can be accused of but one piece of sentimentality. On the night of the dance when the attractive and the desirable stepped to the rhythm of 'Moonlight on the Colorado,' I longed for the touch of my poor mad father who had called me Bestie Friend."

 HER GRANDMOTHER OFTEN SAID, "I'm not at all surprised." Thus, she had seldom to alter an opinion or to account for some turn of event that would leave another dazzled. Death, disease and disappearance were all right there in the cards from the first. She was one of very few who only nodded when Mr. Gregson, who taught band at New Hoosic High and appeared to be such a happy man, threw himself, festooned with automobile tire chains to help him sink, off the bridge into the river. She had from the first thought it strange he hadn't married.

"She was not surprised at the rise of Mussolini in the twenties nor of Hitler in the thirties. Somebody, she felt, had got to take hold of things. If things were not taken hold of, chaos set in. Their mistake was that they tried to take hold too long. She may have been a cynic; on the other hand, she may have possessed unnatural foresight: she predicted the Depression and caused my grandfather to sell what stocks he owned and to buy bonds a good year before the Crash and the several thousand in the bank allowed her to walk with unhurried, even tread when she moved down North Street in her dress ties."

As a grandmother, she might have offered to supply Liz's tuition at the university. She knew Liz was bright, and her quarrel was with her daughter, not with Liz, but she was of a generation that didn't think much of college education for women; she had not had one herself. As she saw it, higher education for females led no further than teaching, filing papers or, at best, sitting the livelong day behind a desk, and you didn't need an education to do that. What every one of those women wanted was a home and food and a husband to service her — they jumped at the chance quick enough when they had the choice. College for women was but a costly place to mark time.

"The maddening thing was that there was truth in what she believed, and truth is bitterest when it comes from someone you don't like. As a cynic she brought your dreams into question, and she was right in believing that most of them had no more substance than smoke."

But she and Liz's grandfather were not without plans for Liz. Mrs. Blynn, down at McCabe's Feed and Seed, could not last forever. Nobody can. Mrs. Blynn's arithmetic was — or had been — faultless.

"My grandfather, nodding his head in amused bewilderment, liked to tell how Mrs. Blynn had caught the adding machine in an error." But if you have presumed to put yourself into competition with a machine, you are bound to be treated like one, and frankly, like a machine, Mrs. Blynn was wearing out. "Getting on," as they say. She had been getting on for a year or so and there she sat on a high stool, bent over the accounts, her eyeshade like the blinders on a horse shutting out worldly distractions — color, movement, sound, life itself.

"It was in the nature of a kindness that my grandfather took her on in the first place." He and Blynn had been in the Lodge together, had seen each other dressed in fancy robes — had possibly even adjusted each other's ceremonial swords, weapons meant to remind a fellow that once upon a time there had been more satisfactory means for a real man to settle differences than through courts. Blynn, kindness itself, had been an ineffectual little man who would cross the street to shake your hand and never forget to send postcards. "He'd talk a leg off you if you didn't shut him up." He smelled of failure. "But my grandfather made it possible for Mrs. Blynn to hang on to the house, such as it was."

Now it was about time to put Mrs. Blynn out to pasture. Surely she had put something aside in those ten years; her wants could have been but few, and now she would have time to enjoy the house, and fix it up a bit.

Liz grasped what they were up to when her mother took her aside and in a tense whisper, as if she were explaining sex at the last minute, suggested that Liz take a course in bookkeeping.

"But I was ready for them," Liz said.

To allay suspicion, she enrolled in bookkeeping. "I was about to be put in an intolerable position — the girl who couldn't dance, who would get nowheres in New Hoosic without she learned to dance — was about to be condemned to New Hoosic, to a high stool and a green eyeshade. The enormity of it shocked me into a shrewdness I have never since recaptured. I summed things up."

She had no money; her mother had only a pittance from Donald. But she was the brightest girl in the school, she was Quill and Scroll and about to be elected to the Honor Society. On the strength of her triumphs and letters from teachers she applied for a full scholarship to the University of Iowa. "I thought it reasonable to believe that anyone with a full scholarship would be given an opportunity to work for her room and board."

That she had had the audacity to think of arranging her own life — she who had been beholden to her grandmother for roof and food — was bound to cause a row. Or maybe not a row. The mailman came to the house between ten and eleven each morning; only on a Saturday would she have an opportunity to be the first to put her hands on a letter addressed to her. She could not be sure her grandmother — in the role of monitor — would not open and read anything addressed to her, might simply destroy it or — if the news was bad — smile and remark that there was many a slip and so forth.

The letter did arrive on a Saturday. "My grandmother had a curious relationship with the postman." She treated him as a public servant, which he was; she suspected that because of an entrenched bureaucracy his job was safer than other people's and that he received fringe benefits denied ordinary workers.

She did not retrieve her mail from the box until his shadow had fallen like fate against the gathered lace curtains at the heavy oval glass in the front door, and had disappeared. Having never heard his voice except at a distance and knowing no more of him than his retreating backside she did not feel called upon to remember him at Christmastime.

"It was unthinkable that anyone but my grandmother should retrieve the mail. Hers was the right first to touch and inspect all foreign intelligence." Should anyone stand in the hall with her, she drew back near the wall and turned slightly to forestall another's eye falling on the handwriting until she had time to consider it.

Six weeks had passed, and Liz imagined the letter crumpled and tossed into the trash. She watched her grandmother for some sign of triumph, some sign of anger, but saw nothing.

And then the Saturday.

" 'For me? Oh, Grandmother!' I clapped my hands and then held them to my heart like a child before unexpected delight."

And before the old lady had a chance to retreat and turn, surely regretting she had spoken out, Liz skipped up to her, all innocence, all flustered girlishness, all impulse, and snatched the letter from the old woman's hand. The enthusiasm was so untoward in that house of sighs, the assault so sudden and unexpected, that the old woman tottered on her small inadequate feet and saw to her hair with a free hand and then to her beads.

"What have you there, Elizabeth?"

Liz beamed. "Oh, Grandmother, lookee!"

The old woman read the detestable letter that released Liz forever from her power.

She nodded and allowed a humming to escape her nose. "I'm

not at all surprised, Elizabeth. You do have some good blood in your veins."

"My grandmother wouldn't have been surprised that so many girls at the university were camp followers; but to remain in camp or anywhere near it, duties were required of them not expected of your regular camp folowers. They had to take courses and they had to pass them."

The curriculum had certainly been planned with the boys in mind. The boys might be able to use what they learned later on in their business or their life's work, but there wasn't much a girl could use. You had to take a language and it was best to choose Spanish because at least if you see it you can pronounce it once you know about the double *l*'s and the double *r*'s. They don't pronounce *h*. If they want to pronounce *h*, they use *j*. And taking Spanish makes some sense because it is sort of more a part of our own country, and it is funny to think of the Spaniards down South there discovering things and looking for gold and converting people before the Pilgrims were even heard of. It was almost enough to make you think. Some friends had been in San Antonio that time and reported that the Mexicans were very poor. The hotel there is the St. Anthony.

As for literature, you'd think that would be a good course to take because everybody is used to reading before they get there and have done book reports, but now it was all dull things and the American literature was just as bad. Emily Dickinson makes no sense. She stayed up in that room of hers and she never married, but there was somebody who used to come and talk to her father. *Moby Dick* goes on and on and on, and then people wonder why people don't read things like that later on when they get out. Boys have more organized minds because they understand math better, and they have to because of their businesses later on and their life's work, and are more interested in adventure and sea stories, but they had the same trouble with people like Emily Dickinson.

And that wasn't the worst. Everybody had to take a science. Physics and chemistry weren't like high school and if you took it, it was better to drop it after six weeks because then it didn't count against you, and you could choose botany. It explains why flowers lean into the sun.

If you survived, there was a good side of college, the fraternities and the sororities and getting to know people from other areas and making lasting friendships and memories. You could look back on them. Three were good fraternities and three were good sororities. They were called the Big Three, and three not so good, and they were called the Little Three. People who couldn't get into them got into local fraternities and sororities that weren't even listed in the book about Greek letter societies, but they wanted to get in somewhere. Way down at the bottom were the Barbs, which is short for barbarians and different from the Greeks. They were often poor people who couldn't afford the initiation fee or maybe they were grinds who only studied and didn't understand the need for a lighter side, or were just unattractive. There are a lot of funny people in the world.

Fraternities and sororities gave dances every weekend but the really very important dances were once in the winter and once in the spring. They were called Formals because you wore your formal and the boys sent gardenias and wore white flannels. They didn't have Formals in the summer; summer was filled with old teachers who came back to take courses so they could keep on teaching because if they didn't they couldn't. So they were all old people in the summertime. Almost everybody else went up to the lake where it was cooler.

"For the first time they were out from under the Grown-ups. For the first time they could think of themselves not as children or as girls but as women, and unanswerable, except for money matters, to anybody but themselves." Real life had begun, and as always the popular songs of the day expressed life for them — some condition, some emotion, some fate motivated by love. Rejection. The delights of surrender. Search, disappointment. An-

[*140*]

ticipation, doubt and bewilderment. Love always at the center. Love explained the pretty dress and the white flannels. Love looked for, love found and lost. They existed to find love and to follow it to its conclusion under the man of their dreams.

"Apart from the ten-second delight of orgasm, what is the purpose of love and what is the end? From the first, Nature seems to have some long-range plan in mind for the race, but never yet revealed. And apart from a final mass destruction, when every corner of the earth is crawling with humanity — a brilliant Götterdämmerung, a final whing-ding — I can't imagine what it is."

Meanwhile, the good sororities had houses with pillars, houses once the mansions of rich townspeople (land, banks, lumber yards) who had died or moved to a more sophisticated social scene.

"They were houses of dreams," Liz continued. "I was never in one, of course, but I imagined high ceilings, carved chimney-pieces, the tinkle of ice in silver pitchers and the rustle of taffeta as some proud beauty swept down a staircase. Oh, I'd have settled for that world, but I had no taffeta. I had three skirts and two sweaters and an extra pair of oxfords in a new cardboard suitcase embossed to resemble leather. No room in that society for a penniless smarty who worked in the library and typed up other students' themes for cigarette money. No room for the artist in Plato's Republic. No, the artist was crowned with laurel and then turned away. I had not even been crowned with laurel."

The laurel, such as it was, came in her junior year.

In that year, something horrid happened not a mile from the university; there in a gully huddled a dozen shacks of board and paper, the desperate shelters of the hungry. For years the police in town had been untroubled by much nastiness and were re-membered because they made so fine an appearance marching proudly just ahead of the Boy Scouts in the Armistice Day Pa-rade; the police had virtually washed their hands of the people in the gully and seldom ventured into that neck of the woods. The plight of the people in the gully was so hopeless they might be excused a portion of their unspeakable behavior, but surely not all of it. Is not to be born a human being born to be somewhat responsible? They had no electric lights. Kerosene lamps and candles knocked over in brawls set fires.

A man lived there with his fifteen-year-old daughter.

His wife had run off with a trucker but not before the trucker had beaten up the man for talking back. His wife had stood watching. His daughter was somewhere or other.

He had been a handyman, a carpenter a few years before, when people had the money to build. Now it was repairing steps, cleaning out rotting leaves from gutters, digging up cesspools. Those who had recognized his humanity had time and again offered him a cup of coffee in the kitchen; now they wondered which cup it was that had touched his lips. Better get rid of the entire set and be sure.

For his daughter had given birth to a little boy in their shack and shortly afterward he had taken it by the heels and knocked its head against the wall. Murder is bad enough, but it was his own child, a child whose father was its grandfather, whose mother was its sister, and the heavens cried out for vengeance.

Incest by the man's own admission; maybe he thought that admission would excuse his braining the child. He told the police. If he had thought a moment, he would have smothered the child and it might have looked as if it had been born dead. They had had to touch him, the police had, to take his arm and get him into the car.

"Like touching slime," said a sensitive one, with a face.

They shut the girl up in the hospital for a few days because of the way she was bleeding, and then a car came and took her off to the reform school; it wasn't likely that she was entirely innocent, either. Girls who grow up like that come to know a thing or two.

They locked the man in the local jail until they could get ready for him over at the State Prison. In the local jail they had to put on extra men because there was talk in the town of lynching, and killing a man is up to the Authorities and not up to lynchers.

"They might better have let him go his way. It wasn't likely he would repeat his crime — father another child. Not for another nine months, anyway."

Novelists are sometimes preoccupied with a class of people set somehow apart. With Scott Fitzgerald, it was the rich; he stood in awe of their motorcars — the Locomobiles, the Cunninghams; he cherished their view from windows on the Riviera, their wicker lunch baskets and lettuce sandwiches, their stylish indolence. Drinking, he may have imagined he was one of them. He once remarked that in some years his income was equal to theirs.

With O'Hara it was the cheap and the crass. With Hemingway it was soldiers of fortune and bullfighters, those reckless of life, who laid their lives on the line; he was fascinated by death.

"It's not strange he took his own life. As he grew older it became clear he was not likely to achieve a stylish death in the bullring or by a sniper's bullet; he brooded over the fact of a natural death in a clean, white room; to forestall it he blew his brains out with a shotgun."

As for Liz, she felt herself drawn as into a whirlpool to the man in the jail. In murder piled on incest, he was at least as compelling a subject as Fitzgerald's vapid rich or Hemingway's brainless toreros.

"I wanted to *see* him. My motives were mixed as motives are. I felt compassion, but my compassion has often been misplaced. Maybe I saw in him something of my own poor father.

"My wish to see him was mad, of course, but as necessary for me and my future profession as for an intern to dissect a corpse."

She had a penchant for the damned. "Who isn't damned, death being the end of it, the final damnation whether on the gallows or on the Beautyrest? I thought the authorities might be so astonished at my request to see him they might grant it. I loathe authorities because they stand in the way."

She could think of nothing better to offer the wretch as a gift than two Milky Way candy bars. She had them in her purse.

Downtown at the police station three men with guns sat at a round table behind a breast-high oak desk. One of the men chewed a cigar; they had done with their coffee sent over in paper cups from Chet's Place across the street. Once it had become clear that the threats of lynching were but passing fancies, they had fallen to playing rummy. "There's a whole class of stocky young men with small eyes who wear guns and have things sent over from Chet's. Without their guns and clubs, they turn up in bowling alleys. They are known to weep in secret for the children they were. They are not educated and are at a loss when an educated female comes among them. Had I been a boy from the university they would have been contemptuous because they wore guns and he did not."

They had paused in their game of rummy. The one supposedly in charge laid down his cards in a neat fan.

"Good afternoon, gentlemen," Liz said. Along with her purse she carried a note pad. A note pad looks important. Something might have to be written down.

"What'll it be?" the man asked, coming to the oak desk.

"I hope you can help me. I'm from the university."

Doubt and stealth stood in the man's eyes. Why would anybody at the university need help? "I don't get you."

"I'm writing a paper on human behavior."

"So what can I do for you?" He was still on guard; he had never before been asked to be a party to human behavior.

"I want to interview your prisoner." She had borrowed horn-rimmed glasses for the part she played, and her difficulty in seeing through them gave her the grave, intense mien of one who doesn't fool around.

"I don't know about that," the man said, for her simple request raised impossible questions of decency, privacy and authority.

"You're not the chief of police?"

"He's over to the prison getting things set up."

That would be the scaffold?

"He left you in charge?"

"Well, yes he did."

"I see," she said, and turned. In charge, her voice told him, but not free to make decisions.

"How long'd you be?" he asked. "He wooden talk a reporters."

"Twenty minutes. Half an hour. You could be right there with me."

"And I got to check your pocketbook," he said. To prove he was indeed in charge, he let her go alone into the basement to the incestuous father.

She descended the spiral iron steps into the netherworld, into the tomb, and tomb it was, for by all laws both holy and secular the man down there was now as good as dead. The cellar was fitted with steel cages to keep people from doing what they did. There were but four cages, since the local law did not expect things to get out of hand all at once. Only one cage was now occupied. Overhead in the corridor, unavailable to a prisoner who might wish to electrocute himself, a fluorescent tube like the sun perceived from far under water cast a remote, sickly, flickering light. In the damp, archaic silence the light played over a small man in a wrinkled gray suit; highlights revealed it to be of shoddy gabardine. Instilled with the dogged sense of propriety of the genteel poor, he had dressed for the occasion of his arrest. His necktie had wisely been taken from him, for it was the state's right and not his to take his life. The shoulders of his jacket were padded. A small man — no match at all for the trucker who had beaten him. "But then it is true," Liz wrote me, "that something about small men brings out the worst in us. He sat hunched on the coat, his head in his hands. Then he lifted his head.

"Some men as they grow older come to resemble their dogs. Other men, as their hair turns white, as their features soften and their hips spread, come to resemble their mothers and we are uneasy with the truth that men, too, have nipples which though they offer no nourishment do respond to the lover's touch.

"Other men — and he in the cage was one of them — are but

gently touched by the years. The clothes they choose are young men's clothes. Lambent youth sits in their eyes and then one day they shrivel. They are husks."

As the little man raised his head, Liz caught the faint smell of Lysol meant to mask some detestable human odor. But at that moment — like incense — it called up a mystery beyond human understanding. It called up Love.

"I wondered if such a thing might have happened to me and my father sometime after we had walked hand and hand in the woods. Of course it could have. My father would then have been in a cage. And I? Where would I be?"

Yes, the man was watching her, the light from the tube playing over him like the ghostly miasma that hovered over the creation of Adam, when man had yet no concept of morals and was quite unjudgeable by our own. The man in the cage was as remote as Adam; his experience could be expressed in no known tongue. When he spoke, it was not of his experience but of her future. "What do you want?" he whispered.

"He had so removed himself from ordinary human experience he was ethereal.

"Standing before that cage I felt as if I stood at the grille of the confessional. What I wanted was his forgiveness, his blessing. I think no one except him who has suffered horribly has a right to forgive."

"What do you want?" the man had asked. That was the eternal question, and that was the question put to the Cumaean Sibyl; she, too was in a cage, and she foamed at the mouth and knew the future. "What do you want?" they had asked her, and she replied, "I want to die."

In her free time Liz hung out at a tavern at the end of the town smoking Camel cigarettes and drinking a single beer. "I was more comfortable there than at the lunch counter in the student store, and I began to make notes for a short story. The place was called the Stable and it was dark and shadowy as stables are said to be, and windowless. Three stale bales of hay all but blocked the door; other bales had been pushed against the walls. Worn horse collars hung from pegs, and kerosene lanterns, bridles, singletrees, coils of rope, and hames — objects meant to lend the place tranquillity because they represented an era almost forgotten."

"What on earth are hames?" I asked her.

"They are made of wood and they fit into a horse collar and the traces are attached to them."

The barn effect had been pushed a little far with a wagon wheel that had been fitted with little electric lights molded to resemble candles; this hung from the rafters. In a dark corner of the room a jukebox radiated bright, shifting rainbows that repeated a pattern every few seconds; fed with cash, the machine countered with songs of love, loss and longing. It sang of prayers and mothers and babies, and of flowers, especially of roses; it sang of early death, roadsides, and of all the heavenly bodies. Both local and foreign riverways were celebrated — all timeless motifs certain to find quick refuge in easy hearts.

"I sat there in my booth, a spider with her web of dreams."

One day on the cork-faced bulletin board in the student store there appeared the announcement of the McCutcheon Prize for Creative Writing.

Worthwhile prizes — the Pulitzer, the Nobel, Guggenheim Fellowships, the Indy 500 and elevation as Pope — all come with money attached. Otherwise, what is the good of prizes? Money makes cut flowers available and fruit out of season. Money silences witnesses and keeps the police at bay. Money makes it all blow over, and in the right hands is said to promise Salvation.

The McCutcheon Prize existed because of interest-drawing funds given to the university by a woman named McCutcheon, whose husband had been working on one of his poems the very day he died. That one she had set aside. He had married late in life, had met his bride on shipboard and very shortly turned to poetry. But because of the delicate nature of his art, his work had found no commercial publisher and had been privately printed on attractive stock, each poem illustrated by an old friend. He had presented several copies of his work to the University of Iowa, where he had spent a year before something happened and he went east to Harvard.

The Prize, as conceived by the woman who appeared one day in black, was to be for poetry alone, but she had been persuaded, by the president of the university, who had been talking to some of the English people, that since so little fine poetry was written these days there might well be years when the prize went unclaimed; he urged the woman to extend the scope if not the amount of the prize and to include prose, which because it is easier to write is more often written.

The English department, an outfit that must have its hand in all things and didn't give a hoot where money came from, made it clear that although of course the woman must be on the board of judges and receive copies of all entries, the department itself must be the final judge of the worth of a work, and if no worthy work was found, no prize would be offered.

The woman's position was that the Prize was to encourage art rather than to crown excellence, but in the end, over lunch at the hotel, the English department had its way and she herself, so long as she lived or cared to, was to be present at Commencement, and in person would hand over the check for two hundred dollars concealed in an envelope.

"A Descent into Hell" was the disturbing title of the story Liz submitted in triplicate. One copy went to the McCutcheon woman, who was away somewhere. Liz wrote under a pseudonym.

"Called myself Nelly Bly," she said. Her true name and her pseudonym were on a card sealed in an envelope to be opened only after the winning piece was selected; the judges didn't want it thought someone had won because of personal reasons.

"A Descent into Hell" opens as a young reporter — new to the community and unfamiliar with local morals which are based on the literal interpretation of Scripture — goes down into a prison. Each step down was seen by the sensitive among the judges as a yet darker aspect of love — but love, nonetheless. He interviews the prisoner, who cries out, "Jesus, how I love her."

The state hangs the incestuous father in a corrugated tin building with the dimensions of an airplane hangar and the temperature of a morgue. Under the fluorescent lights the sheriff, the coroner and the prison doctor look no less mortal than the man who stands on the gibbet, hands tied behind him, and no less condemned to death, as indeed they all are. All look like corpses — the man about to be one, the rest with a few more years to cherish earthly limbo — the sheriff to insist on death, the coroner to verify it, the doctor to pronounce it.

Some minutes later, after an official cuts down the corpse and nails it in a long pine box, the reporter and a friend of a few hours meet for a drink in an all-night place. The reporter's nails are bitten to the quick. Shaken by the execution, he makes observations about love. He questions God's judgment.

"Not much is known about love," he remarks. "Abraham and Isaac. Could a sane man excuse a God who would suggest to a father that he kill his son? Would a sane man listen to such a God and reach for the knife?"

What is Genesis teaching? That God an abstraction is dearer to a man than his own flesh and blood? "But suppose there is no God — and we have no reason to believe there is. We are only told so. By whom? By men who have their reasons — men who live off the gullible and frightened. If there is no God, then it's man himself who makes up stories to excuse those times when for one reason or another he sacrifices a son like that cooling corpse in the box. However you look at it, neither God nor Abraham nor any father is to be trusted. We find out later just how good a father the invented God is when Christ cries out in vain from the Cross. As for Christ himself, he was less praiseworthy or pig-headed than a host of martyrs who followed him. Those poor duped sheep went happily to their deaths without even the comforting conviction that they were sons of God.

"And they tell me God is love. Is love?"

In love and loneliness the man mounts his daughter, a child is born, a life begins and is snuffed out against a bedpost. Why? Because a man can't father his own grandson. So we are told, so we believe.

"If the child had lived he'd be in a home, no worse, no better off than any other orphan, no better off, no worse off than you or I because what have we got but a life to lead?"

"It's life that matters. What doesn't matter is who puts whose cock into whose cunt. You've got to look no farther than that fly on the pie, good for nothing except to be sucked dry by a spider. Fly says it all. Fly's got a plan. To stay alive. He can fly straight up and sideways and he can fly forward and backward. He's worth nothing, but he's got a thousand eyes to escape the spider and the swatter."

"You're drunk," the new companion says. "You're excusing him. Let's just get the show on the road."

"Excusing? Oh, no. But brother, he wasn't the murderer. He was the instrument. He killed the baby because of our opinion. You and I, we're the killers, Al."

Some English departments are liable to believe in art for art's sake. This one had allowed and even recommended the reading of *Ulysses*. It was not disturbed by that scene in *Sanctuary*. In such lofty mood the judges unanimously chose "A Descent into Hell" for the McCutcheon Prize. In their unanimous opinion, Miss Chandler must have the prize even should the McCutcheon woman vote against them. She appeared to be in Europe. But there was a problem and the head of the department knew it, and solving the problem required letting Liz know she had won the prize before the appropriate time. The head of the department himself wrote Liz the letter; he saw no point in getting his secretary mixed up in the thing.

"A Descent into Hell," he wrote, was one of the best pieces of student writing he had ever had the privilege to read and there was no question but that she must have the prize. However . . .

"I could imagine his pausing there, and looking into the middle distance, and then getting back to his unpleasant task."

She could not say she was surprised she had won the prize; she knew that dozens of popular writers get their material from newspaper files and police blotters, that with such sources closed to them they couldn't write a line; they were dependent on fact for both character and plot. The material was foolproof: it had the mass appeal of violence that had proved attractive even before they had appropriated it to their typewriters.

. . . however, there were a few words that were a bit "gamy," as the head put it; were they necessary to the story or the tone? Would she mind stopping in at his office for a few moments at her convenience?

She had not used the words *pour épater le bourgeoisie;* the middle class does not like to be twitted and, alas, it is the middle class who makes the decisions. She had hoped the judges would see that the words were exactly the words that a reporter would have used at that time and in that place. In using them, he had been whistling in the dark, a frightened young man, appalled by the destructive power of public opinion (she must look into the matter of slogans, sometime), a young man who had attended an execution out of loyalty to the condemned.

Well, they could do with the words as they wished — alter or remove. It was just then — and later — the money that mattered. Bereft of its overtones, she thought her story no better than journalism, but the fulsome praise in the note left her wondering if she had a gift she didn't know she had.

Two hundred dollars! Twenty fives. Ten twenties, four fifties. How many in America are offered the opportunity to know at first hand who looks out from a hundred-dollar bill? The money was not in her hand and wouldn't be until June and the ceremonies, but the merchants of the town were generous with credit; they had a comfortable arrangement with the university: no student who owed money in town could be graduated and in the past there had been sad scenes and understandings of the dangers of credit.

She bought a handbag of genuine leather and fitted it with a lipstick from Elizabeth Arden — none of your Tangee, thank you — a small vial of Paris de Coty, a compact and a cigarette case of tortoiseshell. Her mother was careful never to be seen without a purse and she had never had a good one.

A farm was attached to the madhouse that had claimed custody of her father, and his gifts as a onetime farmer were there utilized. He had his own plot of ground, he wrote, could plant and reap anything he chose. Although the animals had in the past belonged to the state of Washington they were turning the animals over to him one by one as a reward. He was a friend to the birds and had learned their language just as anybody learns a new language, by listening to it.

One of these days he had a mind to get on some old bus and hike right back to Iowa and wouldn't they all be surprised.

It would not do to send him what might be withheld from him as destructive or self-destructive — no razor or pocketknife, nothing that might be stolen from him — no watch, no camera. Time as told by a watch could have but little meaning to him, nor could the smiling likeness of his keepers.

So clothes it was; it had been painful to consider his dependence on stiff uniforms or others' rummage. She bought a heavy wool sweater in green, his favorite color, mittens lined with fleece — the institution was on the cold side of the Cascade Mountains. In a wallet she tucked five dollars. Surely they allowed him a little money. She bought him Fatima cigarettes, and for herself a skirt and blouse and pumps with the new Cuban heel.

"There is no more selfish pleasure than anticipating the delight of someone who receives an unexpected gift."

She had a hundred dollars left, or would have when she got it.

The McCutcheon woman was apprised of the judge's decision. "Since our vote was unanimous we can but think your own vote would be similar. We look forward to your presence and know you must look forward to meeting Elizabeth Chandler."

That opportunity the woman rejected out of hand. "When I was informed," she wrote, firmly astride her high horse with the word "informed" and the passive voice, "when I was informed of your decision to honor so filthy a piece of trash, I was absolutely beside myself."

Her absolute proximity to herself had indeed been unpleasant. "In these times when the world is flying to pieces and the hungry cry out for help we need a literature that prompts hope and faith. We cannot countenance writing of the Chandler type. I will not mention the vile language. What I object to most strenuously is this gratuitous attack on the Deity."

True, she was writing at a time when men walked hungry in the streets and died unnoticed in alleys, when the roster of the churches grew long because there was no warm place but in the church. She was writing when the Hays office felt it time good people saved bad people or saw to it that others didn't become bad because of what they saw on the screen, and certainly a first step was to prevent people from seeing couples in bed or about to retire there. It was time for more wholesome entertainment — stories of old people smiling and seeing it through, of young people getting into amusing scrapes that worked out all right because of humor and good-fellowship. Because animals make so direct an approach to life, their stories are illuminating, and it is not surprising that one of the actors most popular at the box office was a manly dog. *Rin Tin Tin*

The McCutcheon woman was writing at a time when man was

groping for a reason why the world was rotten, and one reason was that God was punishing him for his excesses of the twenties, when he turned his face away from Him and preferred to go to hell in a handcar. Now was the time to turn back to the old faith, to bell, steeple and creed. Would God not then in his infinite mercy again offer His face to the humble and speak the word that would revive the factories, green the fields, pay the mortgage and bring back the children? And so it seemed He spoke. Hitler appeared, and a war and everybody benefited but the killed, and sometimes death itself is a benefice.

But when the McCutcheon woman wrote, Hitler had just come to power, and what men knew were lost jobs and hunger, and what they feared was the impersonal power of authority, and among these authorities were the trustees of the University of Iowa.

"He who is not with me is against me," a man wrote who thought in black and white. Those who were with him presumably had carte blanche to root out those who were against him — Communists, pimps, perverts and all the rest who won't straighten up — but especially atheists who are not only heedlessly but avowedly against him.

"I urge you to reconsider," the woman wrote. "Several other entries merit your particular attention. I was touched by the tale of the family who at Christmastime gave each other exactly what each wanted, but only a picture of it cut from a magazine, and lo and behold! each found in his heart that the picture sufficed, that it was giving and not the gift that mattered.

"You may think me an 'Old Ninny' but it is my opinion the Chandler girl should not be rewarded but expelled. If you do not reconsider I feel bound to place a copy of the piece in the hands of the Trustees."

"The judges backed down, of course," Liz said. "It is to his credit that the head of the department came to me himself. What could they do? It was their jobs, perhaps. In the end it was Authority and it was Money."

MONEY.

She thought of going to the president of the university, "of throwing myself at his feet, but as an upright man with a duty to protect the morals of the state of Iowa and especially of Iowa's flower — her educated ones — he would no doubt have kicked at me but not so accurately as to sully his shoe."

The day was close when the authorities would hand out diplomas to the music of Sir Edward Elgar; gorgeous in caps and gowns, they would walk serene in the ghostly company of Alcuin and Abelard, serene and proud as many never again would be, and perilously close to the day when the merchants must have their money. Money — must it always be money? Money to make the collect call, the dime dropped in, graciously returned by Operator, gratefully received. Money for the frantic telegram, to replace the window, to buy a stale loaf. It was the moment for Liz to pull herself together, take stock of her assets — her brains, her story, a letter of praise.

Teaching a history of the drama in the theater department was a man who looked younger than he was; many do who are so occupied with make-believe they are untouched by the aging burdens of reality; such men have no reason to lie about their age. Early that semester he had astonished his class by entering the room as if preoccupied, sitting with purpose at his desk, and then sweeping the class with his eyes to demand absolute attention and utter silence. Then in a hushed voice he began to recite "The Shooting of Dan McGrew": "A bunch of the boys were whooping it up in the Malamute saloon."

His voice called up the faltering lamplight, the drunken babble at the bar, the mindless whorehouse music, the need to forget. Outside the wind howled like a beast wanting entrance.

The music stopped with a crash. The door flew open.

The class sat transfixed until he had finished, and then his usual prosaic voice rose out of the silence. "So you see that even trash can be effective."

Trash? Liz disagreed. Could trash endure like this verse? Endure the searching test of time? Be so far-flung, so moving, so universal? For Service's verses spoke to the violence in Everyman, clarified his loneliness, rejection, poverty, his guts. Trash because it appealed to his primitive instincts. Everyman's music, folk music — trash? — was at the heart of Bach, Beethoven and Brahms. She would like to discuss the matter with him.

At thirty or so — broad gestures, quick speech, sudden frowns — he had begun to direct one-act plays mounted by the Masquers — a fey outfit — and so had freed his superior to put his mind to more serious drama. He had sometimes smiled at her in a way that had excluded the others. Indeed, he had winked. Well, she was his best student. He had come from Massachusetts and had done his undergraduate work and graduate work at Harvard. Her academic excellence and his New England background had linked them.

A peculiar attitude toward life and society was evident among those who had been even partly tarred by the brush of Thespis; it showed in their pointed lack of support for the football team, in their scornful rejection of both words and music of the university song. The young women wore earrings to class and carried umbrellas and not a cloud in the Iowa sky. The young men sometimes wore overalls. Both sexes adopted irregular footwear, espadrilles, huaraches, tennis shoes and moccasins. All scoffed at the Reserve Officers' Training Corps. Understandably untouchable by any recognized fraternity, the young men had organized a club of their own and had rented a rundown mansion of spools and dormers and weeds at the end of town where supervision was next to impossible, and there they lived in a loose fashion and entertained whom they pleased. Even girls. The sound of strange music and broken glass was reported and rumors abounded. They had so firmly established themselves as eccentrics they were suffered to smoke cigarettes not only in the theater workshop but in class, and more than one who might better have fitted in modern European history or business ed had opted for the drama to enjoy the privilege.

Smoking, the laden gas oozing from his mouth and up into his nostrils — French fashion they said — the instructor from Massachusetts had once announced to the class that it was his ambition to discover a student-written play he could direct, but none so far had come to light.

"They're all shit," he remarked.

At the word a frisson of delight eddied among the students. What might he say next? So this is what life was, saying what you liked. God, to move east of the Mississippi.

Liz was no playwright, but her story was not shit and its structure lent itself to theater — the depths of the cell in the first scene, the height of the gibbet in the second, both brought into focus at midlevel in the drab, everyday world of the tavern, where appetite takes precedence. Stage left, behind a scrim so thin as to suggest recent memory, a man twists in space.

"Depth, height. Good, bad. Black, white. Pleasure, pain, birth, death. The mind responds to the paradox of opposites. Is, is not."

Liz believed it was not the business of an artist to reconcile opposites — that was the business of a philosopher. It was an artist's business to manipulate, to orchestrate opposites into a fresh pattern the human brain will respect as an arresting truth.

Wouldn't her instructor be flattered if she turned to him for

[157]

suggestions for turning the story into a play? Communication would be established. Following that, she would show him the letter of praise. Then she would tell her tale of woe. Behind his banter, his show of boredom, a weary aloofness, she sensed a gentle, vulnerable man-child who still believed in promises.

"Sure," he said with no particular interest. "I'll read it over the weekend."

She knew that as a play her story had no more chance of being produced at the university than it had of winning the prize. She counted on his first enthusiasm.

It was not then thought appropriate for instructors to associate socially with students; under condoning lights in hall, bedroom or bar, hair is likely to be let down and feet of clay exposed. It is wise to let the young believe for as long as possible that the years bring wisdom; later they may understand that what years bring is resignation, failing powers and disappointing children, an increasing anxiety about one's own last words. Instructors have set atrocious examples in appearing to condone the life style of young people.

He called her at the library on Sunday evening. Any particular place she'd like to meet him?

"How about the Stable?" Her turf.

He had taken a booth. He rose at once. "Frankly," he said, "I'm as excited as hell."

"Speak more."

"I know how some instructor felt when Edna Millay handed him or her the manuscript of 'Renascence.'"

She handed him the letter of praise. He held it close to the palsied flame of the candle. "Fine, but I don't need his opinion. What the judges saw without knowing what they saw was the structure." He spoke of arches and flying buttresses. "You can't let them get away with reneging on the prize."

"It's a lost cause. You know the atmosphere."

He grinned. "You could blackmail the old man. He admitted you won the prize."

"Hurt him?"

"No, you wouldn't hurt him. Neither would I. But we'll never get anywhere thinking too much of other people. Anyway, it's not really the money that counts. It's that you won. What your work is worth."

"I thought it was worth the two hundred and fifty dollars. I started spending it. I went into stores and I charged things."

"Jesus," he said. "Your family? Would they help?"

The sound of music haunted her recollection.

Before she could answer, a figure in a booth on the opposite wall, unable to endure the chastening silence, had moved to the jukebox. His choice was a song about suicide called "Nobody's Darling but Mine." It was a perfect statement of despair set to a tune as haunting as one by Mahler or Franz. In a room now charged with the possibility of self-destruction, she spoke.

"My grandmother hates me. My mother has five dollars a week. My father is mad." So she spoke who had been called and chosen because she had written with authority of an indifferent God.

"There must be a way." So spoke the young man in the grip of that dangerous generosity often felt as love, so often regretted when the bank statement arrives. "There is a way. I've got a hundred dollars."

Actress that she was and a close student of the Method, she summoned up an image of herself — brilliant tall girl, her liquid eyes and heavy hair her only ornaments; no little watch at her wrist named her lonely hours; no tiny ring with birthstone declared once a year she was worth chocolates and pretty blossoms. She let tears spring to her eyes and her mouth trembled.

"I wish I could say no," she said.

Her hand lay within his reach.

"You know," he said, "the time will come when people will come here because you once came here."

Her eyes fixed him with her fear of poverty, of the flophouses, of the morgue and a numbered tag and potter's field. He had put into words a thought, a hope, she had often nourished. *When I am rich and famous.* When the cards are down, it is not enough to be an artist. She was prepared to let him take advantage of her — if that was how he wished to put it to himself. She thought he might now make some erotic move, to suggest a night in a roadhouse. He might think she'd be glad of an opportunity to be of service, to perform for a hundred pieces of silver little special things that the unobligated would refuse with a great show of outrage — flashing eyes, lifted chin, the brain pursuing and the mouth speaking the words that would forever after devastate him and mark him as a beast.

He was speaking again, but he had dropped his voice and again he was quoting a verse of Robert Service's:

There was a woman, and she was wise; woefully wise was she;

He paused, then continued:

She was old, so old, yet her years all told were but a
score and three;
And she knew by heart, from finish to start, the Book of Iniquity.

"For a moment I thought he was speaking of me, calling me a prostitute even before I might become one. But then I followed his glance to a female at the bar."

A young woman and quite alone, but committed to accepting strangers. The woman at the bar was known at the Stable and so far had been tolerated. The two stools on either side of her were vacant. The men talking on either side of her were standing. The young woman was known for what she was: to sit beside her was to accept her invitation.

"Her business is poor tonight," he said.

Liz resented his notice of the young woman, his condescension, his judgment of someone the facts of whose life he could not possibly have known — his dismissal of a human being as trash, his making small talk of human tragedy. But she smiled. "Her business may look up tonight. As mine has. Maybe there but for the grace of you go I."

"You wouldn't do that."

"I don't know."

"Meet me here tomorrow night, same time?"

Before he helped her out of his old gray Chevrolet, he gave her a chaste peck on the cheek. She wondered if he were queer, if that was why he had gravitated to the theater, where nothing and everything was surprising.

It is not unusual, over a third glass of alcohol, for a man to ask a woman to marry him nor for a woman, looking into the disappointing depths of her handbag, to accept him. The one has something to give; the other, to receive. Is that not the human relationship? The marriage of Liz Chandler and Hal Phillips was remarkable in that the groom chose and bought the bride's suit; it is not unusual for a man to feel he has better taste than a woman because in choosing for her it is his taste he is pleasing.

"A man believes a woman chooses her perfume to please him, which is true. He believes a woman chooses her clothes to please him, which is not true. She chooses her clothes to please other women because they are interested in the clothes themselves and not what is underneath them.

"A man intimate with Props and Wardrobe assumes his taste is good, but what he chooses he chooses for a woman playing a part — in this instance a young woman getting married before a justice of the peace in Des Moines, Iowa, where we had removed for the occasion."

Her Halloween costume and Japanese kimono came to mind.

The suit he chose for her was trimmed about the collar and hemline with bits of fur. "I think his choice was based on primitive man's pleasure in dressing his woman in the skins of the best wild beasts, but whoever had supplied this fur had gone off into the woods at no great risk to his own life, for it was indefensibly rodent."

In a small room, on a small pole, an American flag insisted on allegiance, an Underwood Standard set a cold, bureaucratic tone, and they were married.

"Marriage!" Liz said. "A Mr. Louis Kaufman Anspacher who was born in 1878, addressed a crowd in Boston, Massachusetts, on December thirtieth, 1934. He said, 'Marriage is that relationship between man and woman in which the independence is equal, the dependence mutual, and the obligation reciprocal.' I don't know who Mr. Anspacher was or is, but he certainly had his head in the clouds." She tore open a pack of cigarettes; women are said to be the gentlest of the several sexes, but show a cigarette pack small mercy.

"Marriage!" she continued. "Insisted on by the Church, who recognizes it as a state so difficult that every available ghostly power must be summoned up and propitiated, an institution so impossible the very priests who recommend it remain single, an example set by Christ himself that he might be the freer to harangue and to pontificate. Christ had the mother wit to know that no man can stand to have his wife hear him speak in public though he speak with the tongue of an angel, especially if he speak with the tongue of an angel, for *she* knows his true tongue.

"A civil ceremony to protect a child's inheritance is hollow now that birth control is so effective there need be no child to need protection. And so many have moved off the land there isn't much left to inherit. The equity in the house? And what became of the silver and the brooch with the tiny seed pearls?

"Marriage is a leap into the dark." Marriage is thought to be an escape from the tyranny of the family, or from poverty. From one's image of himself, or what one knows about himself, or to prove that one is wanted or worth wanting. Marriage is often revenge; sometimes another face of pity. Seldom is there equal commitment — there is the lover and there is the loved one. Sometimes neither. "Two human beings," Liz said, "feeding on each other."

She married Hal Phillips for several reasons. "I married a boy-man. Briefly I fell in love with his paleness, his blondness, his ghostliness and thin, lost sweetness, a man who already knew that struggle is useless, a disembodied fairy prince who could get his hands on a hundred dollars. And married, supported, I could become an artist."

Like Mr. Louis Kaufman Anspacher, she had her head in the clouds.

They checked in at the best hotel in Des Moines, Iowa. "You have a reservation for me," Hal told the clerk. "A corner room for Harold Phillips." That was her first acquaintance with the importance of a corner room. There you have a view of a hundred and eighty degrees, and not your ninety degrees, settled for by the stingy or out-of-pocket.

The aging bellboy stood quite speechless on receipt of a crisp dollar bill and showed his appreciation by backing across the room and reaching behind for the doorknob. What a lesson in the power of money! Nor was this the end of Hal's puzzling extravagance: after a steak dinner downstairs — moved into with a thin soup — he called from upstairs for a bottle of champagne. Liz was struck at the size of the silver tub of ice that cooled it. She supposed the champagne was meant to weaken her inhibitions "when the time came," but she had no inhibitions at all, only interest. "I was twenty when I was legally bedded, too young yet to have any idea where my lack of inhibitions might yet lead me."

Hal had equipped himself with a paper pack of Four X Skins, each meant to be soaked in warm water and pulled like a sock over the alert penis. "They are said to be cut from sections of the intestines of sheep, but I saw no evidence that the end of the thing had been artificially closed, and I could think of no part of the intestine that ended in a natural blind alley except the appendix. Did sheep, then, have appendixes? Then who can say the appendix is useless?" The superiority of the skin over the latex condom is that it allows more sensation to pass to the glans of the penis. With reasonable care, it could be used again and again, rinsed out after each session and kept in a glass of water where it floated, disembodied, a little womb.

"Which it exactly was." One or another of them floated in several glasses in the Des Moines hotel, and later on much farther afield.

The light from a single lamp caught on the green bottle of spent champagne. Lying propped up on one elbow, Hal confessed that through his mother he was descended from Anne Bradstreet, the Tenth Muse of colonial days. It was then that she understood the corner room, the thin soup and the champagne. Winthrops, Bradfords, Carvers and Bradstreets — however diluted their blood — look on first fruits as their natural right even if they can't afford them. If necessary, they expect others to supply them. Their natural world turned about corner rooms, strange soups, leather bindings and grape shears. They were most at home at summer places on the water and most themselves on board yachts with sails like wings.

"I felt a *frisson*, a singular apprehension, as if touched by déjà vu: I not only understood the privileges expected by first families, but why in grammar school I had been so inexplicably impressed by the Pilgrims wading 'ashore' onto the stage. Our marriage, it seemed, was the last link in a chain, the first of which had been forged some centuries before we were born."

Their marriage was a link in that chain, all right. And it certainly wasn't the last one.

Over breakfast — room service, another tub of ice (this time under the orange juice), shirred eggs and a fresh carnation — he told her of his plans to leave the university and go back to New York, where he'd practically been promised a job as stage manager for a group of players on the Subway Circuit.

Subway! New York: teeming millions, Empire State Building, brilliant minds, studios, art. She knew nothing of the practical side of the theater, that the rewards are seldom financial; for in

[*164*]

the theater as in the Church and other such realms of fantasy rewards are unearthly. The future of his job can be deduced from the economical means by which they approached it — the Greyhound bus. The bus is the transportation of the damned — the unwanted old and the unwanted young — and it carries them across the Mississippi as across the Styx; they wait for it in chilly stations of cinderblock, in failing all-night drugstores where cruel light falls on their haunted faces, their paper bags and suitcases kept whole by bits of clothesline. It was not lost on Liz that she and her mother had approached New Hoosic by the same system.

They first stopped at the house of Hal's mother in one of the many Newtons in Massachusetts. She was, after all, his mother, and then while he searched for an apartment of some kind in New York City, Liz could become acquainted with her; as women, they would no doubt find much in common — a love of cloth or a mutual concern for his welfare. Was he not an only child as he was an only husband?

"Don't mind," Hal told Liz, "if at first she seems a little stand-offish," and it was clear to Liz that so far as his mother was concerned, theirs was not a marriage made in the stars.

Few who live in Boston speak of living there but rather in Back Bay or in Chestnut Hill or on the water side of Beacon Hill. Failing these, there are the incorporated communities of Brookline and Newton. Newton is certain to be a disappointment to anyone who has something else in mind; the character has been bred out of it by the deadly similarity of the big brick houses, some of them timbered above the second floor, some with porticos supported by the pillars that do creep into a man's mind when he has money enough and prepares himself for the stylish indolence once practiced in the Deep South.

But there are Newtons within Newtons, and as the roll is called, the houses get smaller, the garages have only one door, the materials become less durable, and taste deteriorates. On a street that leads directly into Boston one has only to look to the right and see a cast-iron donkey of almost life size between the shafts of a sky-blue cart, which is filled in the summer months with petunias, in the fall with a heap of gourds, and when the snow flies in from Springfield, with a stuffed Santa.

In the least of the Newtons, the family sedan, when it is at leisure, goes unhoused. In the least of the least of the Newtons, Hal's mother lived so perilously close to the Waltham line that foreigners who worked in the watch factory drove through her street as the quickest way to get to their Catholic church; they frequently returned, whole families of them, in party mood by the same route. True, the houses on the Waltham side of the line could hardly be distinguished from those on the Newton side, and those on the Waltham side spoke of themselves to new acquaintances as "living on the Newton line." The heartless described it as a "modest" neighborhood, the small houses of a design so similar they might have been the storm of a single brain — the result of some long-ago project in which profit and not human comfort or pride was of chief concern. They had not grounds but yards, each one neat, well trimmed, and made personal in the peculiar arrangement of flower and shrub, choice of material and style for outdoor fireplace or birdbath. Many houses were faced with shingles of white cedar that had long since turned silvery — a pleasant consideration for Hal's mother. So covered were the houses on Cape Cod; as Bradstreets, she and Hal considered Cape Cod their true home, and for a month each summer she lived there in a cottage and walked the beach at low tide. The house in Newton she had declared singular and made clear the Bradstreet relationship to the sea by having had attached to the roof a weather vane in the shape of a clipper ship under full sail.

Hal's father, a general practitioner, had died while Hal was still in Newton High School, a school, some insisted, as good as Kent or Groton. Dr. Phillips could have made a great deal more money had he specialized, but he was a kind, gregarious man; he enjoyed visiting patients. He had left Hal's mother enough insurance and securities to allow her to do nothing, but not enough to do nothing as she would have wished to do it. As a doctor's wife with a certain position — and she was almost forty at his passing — she could not be expected to do whatever it was working widows did; to work would have made a farce of the fact he had so wanted to leave her independent.

It followed that when it was time for Hal to enter Harvard like his father, he had had to scout around to find a friend of his father's who was willing to cosign a note, and one did — one with whom his father was said to have fished. So maybe kindness counts after all. The alternative was that his mother go into capital and that was clearly impossible; she often described herself as a nervous woman, and the nervous cannot weather apprehension about the future.

"She thought it strange that Hal had gone into drama, for as a child he had given every evidence of being a manly boy. She thought it very strange. She thought many things strange," Liz said.

She thought it strange when people in town for the day didn't telephone. Strange when her name did not appear in the parish bulletin after she had contributed icebox cookies; strange when she had received no word, strange that she alone had been kept in the dark, and strange how some people prospered.

"I'm going to be perfectly frank," she told Liz. "I think nothing is gained by not being frank. I think it very strange Harold didn't write me about his getting married."

"It was the both of us who got married, Mammy," Hal said. "It was sudden."

"I distrust impulse. Your father didn't. Sudden is right."

"You always said I'd know when the time came."

"I hope you both knew," Mammy said. "I'd think there was something you could do about drama here in New England and not kite off to New York. Couldn't you teach it again?"

"It's teaching it I don't want to do. I want to *do* it."

"Teaching it out there, yes, was of course strange, but teaching it here would be different. Exactly what is it like out there?"

[*167*]

"I couldn't say exactly," Liz said. "But there are hogs and it is flat."

"I've understood that, too," Mammy said. As she spoke, her eyes were on Liz's feet done up in wedding shoes — green suede with a brass buckle that concealed a band of elastic that kept them from dropping off. "Shall I call you Elizabeth or Liz? Harold mentioned both names in a letter he wrote before you decided on what you did."

"Liz will do nicely. I keep Elizabeth for special."

"A dear friend of mine is called Elizabeth, and I hope you will think of me as Alice."

Liz and Hal did not rise next morning until after eight; by that time Mammy P, as Hal called her in the third person, had made her far-earlier rising known by several trips up and down the stairs, pausing each time outside their bedroom door.

"She gets up to watch the birds," Hal whispered. "She and the birds have a thing going. There's a Mrs. Robin and a Mr. Robin. She thinks she can tell."

"You two must have been awfully tired to sleep so," Mammy said at breakfast. "I never know what people eat. I have only juice and toast and coffee."

"That's ideal," Liz said. "It's next to impossible to think on a full stomach."

Mammy looked at her.

It was thought better all around if Hal went alone for a few days to New York to see about his job and to look for shelter. "You'd just be hanging around," he told Liz.

"New York is not much of a place to hang around," Mammy said. "You read awful things about the minorities there. You'll see they're more in line around here."

For a couple their age and with their education and indefinite future, nothing but the Village would do, or maybe Brooklyn Heights.

"Are all you people moving in there now — the Heights?"

"Frank Buzzell did," Hal said.

"I never cared for his handshake," Mammy said. "Wasn't he going to do something about his music?"

"Not after he met Ruth," Hal said.

"Oh yes, I remember now," Mammy said, and looked levelly at Liz. "Ruth is enormously wealthy. They've already been around the world twice."

So Hal threw a few things in the suitcase, as he put it.

"Aren't you forgetting something?" Liz asked him.

He looked into his suitcase. "Forgetting?"

"To give me a little money."

"Oh." He stood with his feet quite apart, hands on his hips, a characteristic stance, his face blank. "Of course." He took out his wallet, held it close, and carefully removed a five-dollar bill. "Sort of take care of this," he said. "You won't be needing much."

"I won't run hog-wild."

"Nobody really needs cigarettes," Hal said, and he grinned like a sheep who can't explain himself, "including me."

Liz thought Mammy P had had her hair professionally disturbed especially for their arrival. "First impressions, you know. No woman wants to feel forever remembered for her atrocious hair." Mammy's hair was a pale-blue nest of curls so tight and perfect that they might have been applied with a pastry tube, but it turned out this was the perpetual and not the occasional state of her head. She attended it in secret and protected it through the night with a stiff flannel coif. So rinsed and curled, she appeared to Liz to be armed for expected struggle she had no intention of either avoiding or losing. So curled and rinsed, she sat straight on a Victorian settee and spoke across the room.

"Hal says you do writing."

"None to speak of."

"Hal seemed impressed."

"He shouldn't have been. It's simply what I do best, I think."

"Has Hal told you anything at all about his stomach?"

"Virtually nothing."

His stomach, then, was a nervous one — a not unusual stomach in a man who thinks deeply. He was too easily touched. Following the death of his dog when he was seven, he had remained a week in bed and no other dog was got for him. A poor mark on a report card had caused his temperature to rise and him to vomit. This had been pointed out to his teachers, who in turn pointed out the relationship between cause and effect, and from that time on he received honor marks and except for the existence of a Jewish girl would have been salutatorian of Newton High School.

"They have nothing better to do than study," Mammy P said. "They're getting into the Cape, some of them who have changed their names." Then suddenly Mammy P smiled and offered the palm of her hand as if in friendship. "And yet you know, I have always loved their rye bread. I have Mr. Simpson save it. I wonder sometimes what he thinks. I think it very strange that Harold hasn't called."

He had been gone three days.

"I cut my time short at the Cape to drive up and greet you two," Mammy said. "There's really not room there for three, and I'm anxious to get back to the sea air. Since Harold hasn't called I think you and I will go on back there. A little shopping, first, though."

"Suppose he calls?"

"When he can't get us he'll know we're not here. He can call the store. They're pretty good about that and send somebody across the marsh and then we can go call him wherever he is."

From Simpson's Market, Mammy brought back lettuce, mayonnaise, canned milk, potatoes, canned corn and salt pork. "For corn chowder. I don't imagine you're familiar with our chowders, either corn or clam. When you get to New York you'll find they put tomatoes in and use the wrong clams. I simply send it back untouched. On the Cape we dig our own but of course the natives would much prefer to dig them and sell them to us. They make a living of sorts."

She packed the groceries in an insulated wooden chest along with a block of ice. She filled four gallon jars with tap water. "I like our Newton water better than the Cape water but I wouldn't tell anybody there that."

The Model A Ford coupé, some eleven years old, was immaculate. They had tried, it seemed, to get her to buy a sedan, but she would have none of it. "People who need to be taken somewhere are usually couples and in a coupé there's no room for them and the question doesn't come up. It's not at all that I mind helping people, but then they feel obligated and the first thing you know they've got a foot in the door."

She was dressed for the thirty-mile trip south in a faded denim skirt, a white matelot, a straw boater and sneakers. "Don't tell me a tanned skin is a healthy skin," she said.

She drove just under the speed limit, both hands on the wheel, and those who overtook and passed her she labeled fools for expressing themselves in excessive speed.

I remember Liz's describing the Cape. "Flat, sandy landscape. No map of it was accurate for more than a moment. Severed from industrial Massachusetts by the Canal, it died slowly, twitching like a snake in death throes. The beaches shifted and changed, waxed and waned out in the hollow sibilance of the Atlantic."

Both Hal and Mammy P had spoken of their seaside abode as a cottage. It was approached off the highway by a short road that was periodically inundated by tides; unless one was there to look out the window, an almanac had to be consulted to find when the road was navigable.

"But navigable isn't the right word, is it?" Liz asked me. "Navigable is for rivers and other waters. Passable?"

Automobiles were abandoned at some distance from the cottage; to go farther was to risk sinking into the sand. The word cottage suggested a more elaborate structure than what Liz saw. It was a genteel hovel constructed of vertical boards turned silver by the elements. It had a shed roof.

"It's only a shanty in old shanty town," Liz said. "One might expect to see in front of the place a scrawny child in rags whining for alms. The dunes had so encroached that one could have walked through the window." It had but two small rooms.

"In a little cottage like this," Mammy P said, "things have got to be shipshape," and indeed things were. The plates and saucers were neatly stacked in an open cupboard of raw boards, the sometimes-matching cups hung in sequence according to size from little hooks. On a second shelf a shallow wooden box was partitioned to accommodate cutlery, forks and spoons. "Harold made that box in manual training in grammar school," Mammy P said. Everything in the shack had a history, however recent — cattails extracted from a nearby marsh were arranged in a low pewter bowl, one of the few remaining Bradstreet treasures.

"Suppose somebody broke in?"

"Who would believe the piece was genuine? And there's little theft here. Strangers are spotted instantly and watched."

Small starfish had been dried and glued to a board and hung on one wall. Cooking was possible on a two-burner kerosene stove; two kerosene lamps nested in fancy brackets on opposite walls and a third, with a fluted shade of milk glass and said to be valuable, rested on a high round table with splayed legs of bamboo. The ancient leather-covered Morris chair had surely been a fixture in Hal's father's office, a silent witness to tonsillectomies and such bloodlettings. On a card table lay a worn deck of cards.

"We eat there," Mammy P said. The chairs were of a style found in dumps and were painted a sunny yellow. The floor of wide boards was scoured smooth by the sand swept out each day and the knots, more resistant to abrasion, were raised, like cameos; in the bumps and whorls the sensitive might make out human heads and faces with shrieking mouths. A remnant of Turkey-red carpet added a warm touch.

A door let into a shallow corridor leading to a single-hole privy, the cracks in the shrunken boards covered with newsprint to prevent flying sand from troubling the private parts. The masthead could still be read: *The Evening Transcript*.

The whole place was ephemeral and the whole was charming. But for the pewter bowl and perhaps the lamp, nothing was of any value — was of less than value; almost everything had been retrieved. The mind was free of all concern over breakage, theft, ripping, spotting, tearing, and could fix itself on the spiral descent of a gull, the dive of tern or osprey, the hiss of the incoming tide. Nothing in the little bookcase was likely to stir up ideas — the detective novels of Mary Roberts Rhinehart, the novels of Gene Stratton Porter, said to have been killed by a streetcar in Seattle, those of Albert Payson Terhune, James Oliver Curwood and Harold Bell Wright — all comfortable with three names that scanned like verse and loyally identified their natural mothers. It was a literature that summoned up a past of cigars and brandy, of lace handkerchiefs, parasols, violets and smelling salts, pious animals and the Fourth of July. The *Old Farmer's Almanac* warned of storms long since weathered; a field guide to the birds identified fowl long since spied upon and jotted down. The limp *Boy Scout Manual* proved that Hal had at least hoped to embrace purity, to refrain from cursing and spilling his manhood. A threadbare cotton Indian blanket covered a spare army cot. It had probably once been a savage red and had been woven with designs by someone who knew of aboriginal art only that it was based on angles and fir trees.

From a covered box under the bed in the second small, dim room, Mammy P removed and displayed snapshots, among which was one of Hal at seven with the very long-tailed mongrel whose death had caused Hal's fever and confinement. In the snapshots the sea was ever in evidence — seen flat and gray from the beach, supporting dinghys, rowboats and schooners, the sea at high tide and low, angry and calm. But equally omnipresent was Mammy P, always she and Hal together: she touching or touched, she in profile as she turns to look at him, she smiling, she serious, she with lifted chin and once, without the sea, she and he in Harvard Yard. Her persistent presence made clear that the photographs were not so much a record of Hal's growing up but of her own ability to outwit the years: she looked scarcely older when she stood in Harvard Yard than when she was with Hal and the tragic dog.

"Surely," she must often have been addressed, "surely you're not the mother but the sister!"

Why the doctor father did not appear in the photographs following his early death was clear enough — he was dead. Anglo-Saxons stop short of taking the likeness of their defunct; though they may whistle in the dark in reciting the Service for the Dead, they are not so sure as other races that life exists beyond the grave and do not wish to be reminded, on opening an album, of the black fact of extinction. But why was the father not included while he yet lived? Had he been required over and over to spring the shutter? Was it because, though an M.D., he was no Bradstreet and not worth developing? Was his photograph among those loose ones with curled edges that had not been glued into the book?

A final photograph had a page to itself. It showed Hal while still in college at the helm of a racy yawl. His face was a mask of ownership, of pride of possession, and the wind in his face was his, the spray his spray and Portugal his destination.

Mammy P dropped her voice as some do who are bound to tell a truth but do not wish to alarm. "It belonged to some very, very wealthy people," she murmured. "He always wanted a boat, poor boy."

So it seemed it took more than being a Bradstreet, and the doctor father had not supplied the lack. With but five dollars in her purse and a few cigarettes, Liz felt a kinship with the father, both of them alien to certain plans. What was her place — what shutter was she meant to spring?

She slept, under the thin, false, Indian blanket.

The morning was cold and damp; she woke to the primeval bawling of a distant fog horn. Where was the husband she scarcely knew?

Mammy P had brought out from her bedroom a round kerosene heater with a bail for carrying. "Now we can all be cozy." She squatted before the heater with a lighted match. "Will you want something more than coffee? Then you can find something to read." For some time the heater cast out only an odor of chilly smoke.

Liz picked up a novel of Eleanor S. Porter's, published in 1910. Now, just as the damp little room released the mind of the responsibility of attention to itself, so almost every object in it allowed the mind to dwell comfortably in the past — hardly an object there but had existed in 1910; the arrangement of cattails recalled a time when America was rural; the lamps a time when electricity was a novelty; the Turkey-red carpet a time when such was the proper covering for the front stairs. Pressed by the monotony of the rain, the years retreated; a faint odor of mothballs and heavy woolens hung about — and it was 1910.

She started at Mammy P's voice. "Why Sumner, you scared the living daylights out of me. I didn't hear your truck."

She was speaking to Sumner Thomas, the local handyman. Many of the natives of the district bore given names that had been surnames. There were Warren Duncans and Duncan Warrens, Linsay Wendells and Wendell Linsays. They kept alive names whose founders had long since gone under the dunes; some of them, like Sumner Thomas, were so inbred they evidenced the traits of their remotest ancestors — silence, acuteness, vengeance and stealth. He sensed he was part of the independent, unspoiled and authentic American ambience the summer people paid for, that he was more needed than needing; he was ever prepared to tell someone who crossed him to go fuck himself.

He was a rugged, black-haired man of forty — or sixty — who could say? Age sat on him with the indifference it sits on an animal—all the years between youth and age are similar in appearance. He had a reputation for strength, for straightening horseshoes with his bare hands, ripping the Sears, Roebuck catalogue right down the middle. He was lazy and slow and he leaned against the doorjamb in his rubber boots; his olive-drab trousers bloused out over them; he appeared to be wearing grotesque knickerbockers. His heavy, muscular jaws allowed him not so much to eat as to devour, but the striking note of his appearance was his large horn-rimmed glasses, exactly like those of the men who employed him when they could — the writers, artists and professors who fled each summer to the Cape and formed a long, orderly line outside the grocery store every Sunday to pick up their marked copies of the *New York Times*. These spectacles as worn by Sumner Thomas were at once comic and sinister, like those, in a moment of fun, that are pushed back on the face of a dog. Thomas could sometimes be counted upon, if he liked you, to change your spark plugs, repair leaks, clean out the privy, deliver kerosene, and run errands. His wants were few, and since he was the only handyman available, he saw no reason to be particularly responsible.

Now he laughed. "Snuck up on you, did I? S'pose I was some crazy old murderer?"

Mammy P pretended to be exasperated and put her hands on her hips. "Now why would a crazy old murderer want to come down here to Dennis? We all come down here to Dennis to get away from crazy old murderers."

"Can't never tell, though," Thomas said. It would not be forgotten — it could not be forgotten — that Thomas had accurately and publicly predicted the hurricane of '38, had stood right there in the store and predicted it when out the window the day was bright and the water as undisturbed as the face of a silver dollar.

"It'll be a regular corker," he'd declared. "I feel it in my bones."

Such was the typical, irresponsible prediction of one whom many considered a half-wit; he suffered not only from the customary inbreeding; his mother was by no means certain which of the Warren Thomases his father was. She had been a woman of short memory and soft heart. But twenty-four hours after Thomas's prediction, the whole Atlantic seaboard was in the jaws of the ocean. From then on, Sumner Thomas's sentient bones did not go unheeded. Some thought that Thomas had been compensated for his lack of more formal background by an awesome gift of prescience. He had set himself up as a dowser. With a forked stick held lightly in his huge hands he now foretold water.

"You take that walk of yours this morning?" he asked. "Whole damn beach's alive with dead squid. Never seen anything like it. Comes hot, gonna be some real old stink."

"Ugh," Mammy said. "Horrible things. Italians eat them."

"Well, there's some big old feed for the wops this morning."

"What do you think happened, Sumner?"

He showed Mammy his empty palms. "Don't like the looks of it. Bad luck."

"Pooh," Mammy said. "Oh, pooh. What was your errand, Sumner?"

His eyes went blank, his mind apparently still on the beach. "Oh, say — Hal called Fred to the store. Hal wants his new missus to hop the bus for New York City first thing in the morning. Says he'll meet her at the bus stop there six-fifteen tomorrow evenin'."

Mammy opened her purse, holding the mouth of it toward her, and handed over fifty cents, the usual fee for carrying intelligence across the marsh. Sumner Thomas ducked his head, turned, and stalked out.

For a few moments the air was heavy with things unsaid. Then, "I suppose you haven't any money."

"Virtually none."

"I suppose I can lend you some."

"I'm sure Hal will pay it back."

"How can you be sure when you know him so little? I'm sure he would intend to." Her smile was cynical. "Let's leave it there." The air was damp with past good intentions, promises, sheepish smiles, shruggings of shoulders.

A dialogue finished. Done. Liz picked up her coat. "I'm going to walk on the beach."

"In those shoes?"

"They're all I have."

"You'll get it on them."

"I walked down to the shore," Liz wrote me, "where some find solace in returning to the site of our beginnings, hoping to discover a new one.

"But the sea had vomited up death, not life. Hundreds upon hundreds of squid lay over the beach like a blanket, a pinkish, putrid quilt of flesh oozing into the sand. Out of their element they were shocking, dehumanizing. Like human entrails splashed against the concrete.

"Why do we shudder at what attacks its prey with suckers? Because parasites suck? Attach themselves unwanted to the host? The squid is no parasite. It fastens its sucking, tumescent tentacles on its prey and hands it to its many arms, and they direct it to the gaping, beaklike mouth. But in 'sucking' we see the lamprey and the leech, both drawn to blood as if by smell, so sly the host wonders at his failing strength.

"Thousands of slimy deaths stranded where life first crawled to land on little weak feet, choking on unaccustomed air. Escaping What? What had been so fearful in the sea?

"But whatever it was, it quickly followed life on little weak feet of its own."

 AFTER HAVING HUFFED and puffed up five flights, Liz looked around the apartment with the excitement of a birthday child. She stood that day in a room larger than she had expected; in time to come she learned that the room was fey: when she was encouraged, it was larger; when she felt she had lost her direction, it shrank. "The room is fey as the past is fey," Liz once wrote me. "When we look back on childhood and feel all its airy spaciousness, the rooms we played in but especially party rooms — balloons and streamers, masks and favors to take home — those rooms are larger than they were, and the piano was not a Steinway. It wasn't a grand, but an upright, and out the open window there was no garden, only a tree. We alter the past to suit our egos."

Into one small closet a kitchen had been forced, the sink no larger than a bedpan; in a closet slightly larger, a bathroom. "You had to duck and sidestep." Hal watched as she moved about from kitchen to bathroom to a little bedroom he meant to furnish with the very bed he'd been born on; and he did. "I believe he needed proof that he'd been born. It was a bed made of many brass pipes, like Proust's. You know the photograph — Proust lying bearded and dead, a little pile of manuscript on the bedside table."

The place was every romantic's idea of a garret, the ivory

tower where Art lived. "I was a hick from Montana and Iowa by way of the state of Washington, and I knew Verdi and Puccini and Gautier and art for art's sake and I believed myself touched with genius."

"Do you like it?" Hal asked her. "Is it all right? Can you write here?"

"Oh, yes, Hal, oh, yes." As she spoke she stood beneath that feature of the place that moved her most. Above her was a skylight, the first she had ever seen, constructed of thick glass reinforced with chicken wire and almost opaque from years of tobacco smoke roiling up and urban grime drifting down. But it wanted only a stepladder and a brush to become their private glass on heaven; open, it was her pathway to the stars.

"Pathway" was the wrong word, she told me years after she was first concerned with pathways and stars. The word, she said, should have been "passage" to the stars since "passage" is a direct route and "pathway" is a dilatory way. "Passage" was a shot — and an echo; "pathway" only two echoes.

I believe it is such attention to sounds and rhythms that makes her prose arresting, but as she spoke that day, I think she was giving me no lesson in the power of words but begging me to see that she had changed for the better, had a tighter grip on her art. "I have changed, haven't I?" she asked.

The true change was in her appearance; she had thickened, was getting a double chin. The tremor in her hands was now pronounced. My silence, as I considered this, was a little too long and she was quick to guess what I was thinking.

"It's booze," she said.

The long, frequent letters to her I typed on Railroad Bond, a cheap yellow paper once used by railroad telegraph operators for typing up into ordinary English the clickety-clicks they heard. Serious writers use it for first drafts. In using it myself I had at least one thing in common with them. Railroad Bond, perishable as it is, is the despair of biographers, archivists and collectors. It rots. Liz's biographer will be in luck: her letters, no matter to whom, were written on sturdy white stock with a high rag content. Not so her notes, which are voluminous and written down in her childish hand on laundry lists, matchbook covers, paper napkins, and in the margins of whatever book she happened to be reading when an idea struck her. I once suggested that she regularly gather her notes together and speak them into a dictaphone. As a graduate student at Columbia, I had tried to use one. Each was in its own little booth, which gave no more privacy than public toilets under whose short doors one's feet can be seen and oneself identified by anyone sensitive to footwear. I had found myself tongue-tied before a dictaphone, afraid someone would hear me.

"You were afraid someone would think you thought your voice and thoughts were important enough to be made permanent," Liz said.

"Have you ever tried to use one?" I asked.

"I seldom even use the telephone," Liz said, "and your words on a telephone are not much in danger of being played back to you, as they are on a dictaphone. Hearing your words played back, you suddenly exist at once in two different places and at two different times — then and now — and one of yourselves, your airy self, you can no longer control. Some Indians won't allow their pictures to be taken."

I was writing to her one afternoon when Etta Murphy stopped by. "It does seem to me," she said, "that when I come here for a little chat, you're at that typewriter. You never used to type so much."

"Autre temps, autre moeurs," I said and I smiled, thinking of one of Liz's stories: for years a man had had first one and then another German shepherd and suddenly one year he bought a collie. Questioned about his choice, the man explained, "Autre temps, autre cur."

"Why do you smile?" Etta asked. "And what are these times and ways you speak of? These typing activities? I swear, half the faculty is secretly at the typewriter." I assume she thought the Railroad Bond meant some creative or scholarly activity, that whatever I was writing I thought important enough to prepare a first draft.

"As secretly as possible," I said.

"Now aren't you the funny one! But you're not the first, my dear, nor the only one who takes to heart our president's hint of a week ago that the faculty must publish more. Contracts are coming up, coming up, coming up. People will be advanced! Salaries raised! God's in his heaven!"

"Who is to know? Who has said so?"

"Browning, dear. Robert Browning said all things that make us to clap hands and live. I have always loathed both Brownings and their little dog. What a vile little dog was Flush — what a sycophant! But aren't we all — licking hands, standing on our hind legs. Sloan himself is again wooing the muse. Said to be rewriting poetry he wrote as an undergraduate at Princeton. He feels his *Study of Exit Lines in Beaumont and Fletcher* is not likely to be immortal and it transpires that he had one more than his usual highball and remarked that no man wants to be remembered only as an academic type.

"I have the distinct impression," she went on, "that when I come you're afraid I won't go away."

"I know you will at last go away."

"What takes you to New York so much? You are seen on the train."

"I have friends there."

She glanced at the folded letter beside my typewriter. "Some little affair?"

"You might call it that."

"Others will. Don't get yourself into trouble. I know you don't yet have tenure, but even on tenure you can be dismissed for moral turpitude. I'm just joking. But what an awful thing." She helped herself to an apple from a bowl. "I remember once when I was a child I took an apple and somebody said, 'They're Delicious

[*182*]

apples,' and I said, 'Did you already try one?' and they said, 'No,' and I wondered how they knew they were delicious if they hadn't tried one. Do you know that lovely little waitress with the soft voice I try to get when I take people to the Mad for dinner? Well, she and her husband had an argument the other night and he dropped dead. She spelled her name Alys on that little tag they make them wear so you can call them that. I understand the Mormons make up names like Darlene and La Merne, but I knew an interior decorator in Chicago who shaved his head absolutely and spelled his name Jac."

The letter from Liz that had suggested to Etta an affair concerned the early days in the New York apartment. At that time Hal was certain that her story, "A Descent into Hell," was a natural, as he put it, for the *New Yorker*, for which nothing is a natural. "And they pay up to a thousand dollars," he said.

"I was appalled," Liz wrote. "And a thousand dollars. His grasp of money is hardly more than mine. I was afraid of his confidence in me. I had supposed — we all so supposed in Iowa and Montana — that I was the one to be taken care of. In return for being taken care of, your ordinary woman is expected to perform the duties of a wife — to copulate, cook and comfort. I was willing to go along with that so long as I had some time to write, but I knew instant money was beyond me. So sophisticated — if fairly popular — a magazine as the *New Yorker* would instantly see through undergraduate material praised by a few midwestern professors. I was appalled by Hal's ignorance of what salable material was, but I am not sure it was his ignorance. He so wished to believe that I was a source of fortune that his belief became fact. Oh, the gulf between fact and belief." She knew, she wrote, that she'd never be a popular entertainer. The vast public would reject her complicated images; their own lives were complicated enough. They did not wish to read the unpleasant truths about human relationships. Like Hal, they preferred belief to truth.

Hal was not discouraged when they did not hear from the *New Yorker*. He was encouraged. "I am a little frightened of people," Liz wrote, "who perpetually put a good light on a situation. They are likely to be taken by sad surprise; they are unprepared for failure." Hal had, she said, known people who had been published, if not in the *New Yorker* then in other good places. "This delay probably means it's going to the next-up editor," he said, and on the strength of that he brought back steak on one occasion and canned vichyssoise on another. He was forever doing something on the strength of something — of a letter, of a telephone call, of a premonition, of a particularly vivid dream, of the fact that it was New Year's Eve and the next year was bound to be better or anyway different in such a way that he could handle it.

Many evenings while they waited on the *New Yorker*, Hal — like the Pied Piper — brought his little troupe single file up the steep narrow stairs. Assembled on the top landing, they then burst in, darting and descending like jays, scolding, warning, shifting, defending territory. They kicked off their shoes and sat cross-legged on the floor in their dirndls, their chinos, their denims, and the light from the single lamp caught their glass beads, their silver. They pushed their hair from their faces so they might speak.

"The word *darling* had just begun to be used as a common salutation.

" 'Darling,' one of them said, 'I hear you're to be in the *New Yorker*.'

"And by God, I found myself doing as they did — pretending. I fell afoul of belief and fact because I wanted to be treated as a published author. I didn't explain. With them it was not the actuality but the pretending that mattered. And so for a moment it was with me. They were dedicated to pretense, but not the legitimate pretense of the legitimate theater." They were not good actors; they didn't have to be. They lacked the spur of poverty, but dressed and acted as they imagined the gifted poor would dress and act. They had fled Buffalo and California and Wyoming, from which sites they received checks from parents for tuition and board and room at Barnard or Bard. They behaved like boarding-school girls making secret fudge over a spirit lamp. They might defer to some older one of the group — a woman who provided sets and props and had a leotard under her dress; or an older man in a cape who hired the halls, paid Hal's precarious salary, among others, and took out his own salary in trade.

They shifted and changed from month to month and year to year like patterns at the end of a kaleidoscope, but the pieces of the pattern were the same whether they spoke their lines around New York or in a recent barn in farthest Long Island. Like falling leaves they drifted, and young as they were they smelled of dessication.

Pearl Harbor did not disband them, for women were not even briefly considered as cannon fodder; and the men — doe-eyed and easy with faintly Egyptian postures, hands at right angles to the wrist, the breast presented, the face averted — the men could not but corrupt our soldiers who, bereft of loved ones, might be open to seduction. In any event, they were bound to prove unsatisfactory killers.

"As it turned out," Liz wrote, "I was grateful to them all. Except for them I had no book; my book you liked, my book that made you sit at my feet. Remember? You did like it, you did, you did.

"I saw them as Poe might, saw them as selfish, as vicious as children, guests at a masquerade. I knew them. They were I. Running from Something, finding a bed for a night with a stranger, finding in a phrase of music an excuse for egregious behavior, in drink the courage to face the mirror, believing a costume is effective disguise, a mask, dark glasses, colognes. What I knew, what I know, what I wrote is that they and I are everybody everywhere, and that to them as to me must one day come the ultimate knowledge that almost nothing we believed in is true. We took the façade for the reality and didn't even bother to find the reason for the façade."

As for Pearl Harbor, the shock of it spared Liz the full force of Hal's disappointment when "A Descent into Hell" was returned from the *New Yorker* along with a courteous but printed slip.

Thank you for letting us see your work. Sorry we can't use it. An editor or a reader had written underneath in pencil, "Don't let this discourage you." And it didn't discourage her. She was alive! She had a skylight, and the slip had been signed by a human hand.

Pearl Harbor was another thing for Hal. Quite simply, he didn't want to be killed. He was thirty years old. He was too young to die. Or worse, to be maimed. What a word, *maimed*. He had done nothing he really wanted to do, had accomplished nothing, made no money, never owned a boat. He did not understand the larger concerns: Shell Oil, the debt we owed France once again for Lafayette and the French appreciation of Benjamin Franklin, the debt we owed the British for lending us their language and siring so many of our fathers. He was thirty years old and obliteration was distasteful. No doubt when one was older something would happen to the mind, some enlargement, some understanding that would make death, if not acceptable, at least bearable.

"Jesus Christ," he said.

"Maybe they won't take you," Liz said.

"What's to stop them? Jesus, if only we had a kid."

"There's hardly time."

"Do you think maybe a pregnant wife's an excuse?"

"I have no idea."

"Maybe they won't take me for a while. They'd be after the young guys first."

"And if you got me pregnant right now, it might pay off."

"Come on, Liz. Don't joke."

"God knows I'm not joking."

"It's all very well for women." He saw himself as alone, fatherless, apart even from a wife who was clearly unsympathetic; he had suggested what any man in such circumstance would suggest.

He was no more than a reflection in a store window. Women, who had never fought a war.

"You could pretend you're queer."

"And me married? They'd check."

"Queers marry."

"It would kill Mammy P."

"I seriously doubt that. And you could explain."

"She'd always wonder. She's never believed in what she calls 'homosexualists.' Even if I could explain, she's a patriotic woman."

"Then come along into the bedroom and we'll see what we can do."

"I couldn't even get it up now. Anyway, they say when a fellow's worried he's impotent."

"Sterile."

"It amounts to the same."

The United States did take the young ones first. The young ones are so busy with their music and crazy dancing and their first cars — so close to their pasts, still half fond of model airplanes and marshmallows and peanut butter — they have no clear concept of the future and don't so much mind losing it. It may be that it's easier for parents to lose someone who is really no more than a child. Parents are bound to miss someone more who has begun to achieve and has been around longer.

The plan had been, following her failure at the *New Yorker*, for Liz to go to work. Surely with so many young men gone more jobs were open. She had all this time on her hands.

"Like dirt."

"No, but you do," Hal said. "It can't take an hour to clean up this place."

"I had planned to write a book."

He was suddenly alert, and seemed to listen; hard to tell whether his sudden interest or awareness was brought on by concern or hope, and Liz was struck that she knew him so slightly: she didn't know him; she guessed him.

"You had? A novel about what? I'd think short stories would

be a safer bet. Wouldn't a novel take a long time?" He'd once told her that he'd read that Scott Fitzgerald had made thirty thousand dollars on short stories in a single year.

"A novel about your friends," she said.

"What's there to say about them?"

"Everything."

He gazed at her, then blinked, then frowned. "You hardly know them except as a bunch of people sitting around, and that time you were with us a month at Montauk."

"Writers make things up. Writers know without knowing."

He was torn. A wife who worked looked worse (or better) to the army than an idle wife. He could fairly hear them down there at the draft board. "Oh-ho!" they would be saying. "It appears this wife of his works!"

The United States, recognizing the ultimate importance of children in its scheme of things, might look with kindness on a man with a pregnant wife. Homosexuals are condemned and rightly so because their lust is sterile. Without children there can be but race suicide, crumbling houses, untended fires, no laughter, no promises, no tears — no more than the whisper of the surf, the howling wind on the prairie, the last sun against the face of the last mountain. No United States, no hope. Hope for what? Something.

The truth about sex, according to Liz, was at once dull and astonishing. Dull because it was often an answer to boredom and because it lasted so short a time. "Oh, you can light candles and space your drinks and cigarettes and vow to wait until the music stops playing and you can control your foreplay. But then suddenly — it's all over." The woman moves to the bathroom and returns to find the man pulling on shorts or socks and everything is as it was, the same road ahead, the past no less puzzling.

But sex is astonishing because of the force and breadth of its drive.

"Do you suppose there are female Peeping Toms?" I once asked Liz.

"Of course not," Liz said. "Women are afraid to go out at night.

"But he in the black raincoat hardly differs from those who buy or rent the permissible trash in the bookstores or watch it on the screen. Without sex, there would be small call for cut flowers and no point in jewelry and pretty shoes. With sex, there is an opportunity for self-gratification. Who thinks of children at the moment of orgasm? Who considers the future? The future is more of the same, your children doing the same, but the drive is there whether it leads to happiness, divorce, murder or suicide — the mindless drive that in its intensity sends us searching the streets for an answer. Surely some future generation will stand in awe, thrilled at what has been revealed and will thank their long-forgotten forefathers for their persistent rutting."

Hal wondered what was the better bet — a wife who worked or a pregnant wife? Not certain what he was up to, he put his mind to it and got it up and by the end of February, Liz was pregnant.

"We were an unlikely pair of prospective parents," Liz told me. She had thought her children would be her books. He knew nothing of insurance or of bonds, cared nothing for baseball or stamp collecting. There was no spot in the apartment where a crib would look other than egregious. Anyone come for a drink would stand amazed.

And yet Hal was jubilant. He was going to be a father. What a piece of news to carry to the draft board, and not the least of it was the comfortable fact that the Bradstreet bowl would pass into the hands of another generation.

"Wait till Mammy P hears this!" he crowed. "I can see the look on her face."

Liz could, too, but perhaps another one of Mammy's faces, for she suspected that Mammy in her heart of hearts hoped that Liz, unpregnant, would move in with her in Newton and sort of help out. After all, Mammy P was getting on. "I don't want

[*189*]

anything said to your mother until we're absolutely sure, and when anything's said, I want to say it."

"Well, it's up to me to tell the draft board."

And he did. "There's this big old bull dyke sitting behind the desk there," he told Liz. "Christ, they'd just as soon slit a man's throat as look at him. Now look: there's this American flag in a corner in case you forgot your nationality, I guess. You'd think they'd of had some old geezer there, the ones that are behind the war, but I guess no old geezer wants to show his face, the ones who got us into this."

The big old bull dyke made it clear with a book of rules that a pregnant wife didn't count. The proof was in the birth.

"I wouldn't think you'd just want to sit around until the last minute," he told Liz. "You could get some kind of job in the meantime, a few months or so anyway, until it began to show, if you had the kind of job where they cared when it began to show." Something where she didn't have to bend down or like that.

"Has it ever occurred to you to get something a little more profitable than being a stage manager for — shall I say ephemeral — players?"

"What would you suggest?"

"You know everything about electricity, about lighting."

"You'd want me to be an electrician?"

"Why not? Or arrange lights in stores. Altman's? And with your theater training . . ."

He grew shrewd. "They have to set up lights in defense plants, too."

"Yes," she said, "and with a child *and* a job in a shipyard or whatever."

Just so, couples thought in those days of some way to outwit the United States, of some way to stay together, of a way to keep from being maimed or slaughtered. Circumstances differed, the end was the same, and one always heard of those who pulled strings.

Or had strings pulled for them.

Lighthearted, he took the New Haven to Boston, where he had a nice visit with Mammy P. She described herself as worried sick, of course, about the whole thing, the whole world, but she knew that even if he didn't get a place in one of the shipyards in Quincy or Hingham he might get something somewhere else. If he didn't, he would certainly do his duty as an American, but for the life of her it seemed a man was doing as much building ships as in the trenches. This was a war she could believe in.

" 'A date which will live in infamy,' " Mammy remarked. All the women she knew had been certain war was coming, and were somewhat relieved that there was more — well, more point in war work now than just Bundles for Britain. Believe me, they now had their work cut out for them. Twice a week they met under a garage where sewing machines had been set up. They sewed bed jackets for the wounded.

One thing, though. It didn't seem economically sound to her from a national point of view to put the best-educated young men in the country into the trenches.

"I don't think it's trenches now," Hal said.

"Well, whatever." She could understand why it was common practice in the Civil War for an educated young man to hire a substitute to fight for him. A substitute very probably had never had so much money in his pocket before. Of course it was wrong because we are all in a way equal, but it did make a kind of sense or the government wouldn't have put up with it.

The employment office of fresh, rude cinderblocks was identified by a fresh-painted sign and stood just outside the main gate where a man in official uniform inspected notes and badges and allowed entrance to the favored. In the employment office a great many hopeless men shuffled about the cement floor or sat dejected on new folding chairs. Newspapers open to want ads lay on the floor fouled with footprints and cigarette butts and spit.

It appeared that the well-paying jobs in both shipyards had

already been gobbled up by those who had been granted an earlier reading of the handwriting on the wall. Nothing remained but poor, menial jobs, jobs as janitors, security guards, jobs at the bottom of the heap and available because of the turnover among drunks and floaters who had found the pay inadequate even for muscatel. Hardly the place for a Harvard man, a Bradstreet. The uniform of the security guard who had directed him to the place was among the most shapeless garments he had seen; of olive-drab felt, it looked not so much official as institutional. Hal had seen in the man's eyes a profound acceptance of boiled cabbage, naked electric light bulbs, dark halls and sniveling children. And that was the end of that.

"To be perfectly frank," Mammy said, "I don't think you'd like a job there anyway. And I shouldn't like you to have one there. Those places are full of cement fumes and sooner or later they get silicosis." What good would he be as a father, dead? Had he thought of that?

The view through the windows of the day coaches of the New Haven Railroad depressed him; as the train crept through the slums of Bridgeport he saw through the grime and distorting glass a thin young woman with a big belly hanging up diapers under a rotting porch. He considered for some time the squalid inevitability of life. And death.

It looked as if he were going to be dead one way or another. The draft board sent its clammy message.

Greetings . . .

He was ordered to report for a physical examination in a building seized by the United States for that very purpose; he was commanded to strip naked except for socks and shoes and so was instantly recognized as male and declared desirable by a gamut of doctors who joked. Why in God's name hadn't he thought to apply for Officers' Training?

"Well, that's that," he told Liz, and he was face to face with an image he had hoped to avoid, having to defecate in the presence of other men, like an animal.

"They're bound to put you somewhere where you won't see action, with your education," Liz said.

"Where I won't get shot, you mean," he said.

He had been granted a month's time to "settle his affairs," a hint that he should prepare for the worst and not leave things for other people to do, things about money and cemetery lots. To do less was selfish. It was selfish to neglect making a will, even if signing it is concrete evidence of your mortality. Did you think you would live forever?

Yes, you did. You thought in a sunny corner of your mind that when it came your turn to die science would have abolished death or so extended life that you would have another chance to hope that science would do something.

His gold-plated Gruen wristwatch was hardly worthy of the stiff, white paper a proper will is written on. It was not worthy of the lofty legal phrases. Useless as a timepiece for a woman, it would end up in a drawer. He had no property; the cottage on the beach and the house in Newton were both Mammy's and so was the Ford coupé. His model airplanes? Birds' eggs? What had he to leave? The snapshots? They all showed a boy scarcely recognizable as the man he was.

That was it — Liz must have a recent photograph, and if he were killed she would remember and the child would know himself to have a father. Have had. Tears sprang to his eyes.

The taking and processing of final photographs was a business not overlooked by professional photographers; they understood that time was running out. Like all business people, they were quick to profit through fear, despair and sentiment. Little shops had sprung up just below the street, little shops up over something, side by side with the dens of mediums who called up the dead, dark halls where strange gospels were preached, cubbyholes where skin was tattooed that some name, some sentiment never be forgot.

NO WAITING! ALL PRINTS READY IN TWENTY MINUTES!

The cup of weak, cooling coffee was his five cent excuse to sit a few private moments at a counter in a dismal drugstore; the wan waitress had clearly hoped he might order a sandwich listed on the board over the coffee urn in movable plastic letters. The *n* in TUNA was upside down. So was everything. He bought a pocket comb to arrange his fine, thinning blond hair. Without seeming to (he disapproved of men's grooming themselves in public—it shrieked of no self-confidence) he touched and straightened his tie.

INSTANT PHOTOGRAPHS! ONLY $1.oo!!!!!

He was told to go right on in there, into a dark little booth entered around a black curtain that had clung a moment to his face like a cobweb; he sat straight and arranged his jacket. In a few moments a voice as sterile as a dentist's said, "Ready?" He said he was. It was over in a sudden, blinding flash. The photograph caught the likeness of a young man horrified, as if he had just seen God.

A block away was a hand-lettered sign. RECORD YOUR VOICE FOR A LOVED ONE!

To enter under that sign was as good as condemning yourself to death: you had made a first step, set in motion an arcane series of events that could end only one way. A recording of his voice was not likely to give either pleasure or comfort to Liz; he could not remember once in the past year when the word love had passed between them. The reason for their marriage had been vague, a fumbling based on unspoken mutual need. His need may have been domestic security with a little financial security thrown in — but financial security for what? He had never looked hard at the future but supposed the theater would somehow lead somewhere. He would stumble into something — isn't that the way it was everywhere? — stumbling into something. Who really knows what he wants and if he does, does he get it? How many work at something they have chosen? Who at twenty dreamed he would end his life as a postman, or selling trusses or insurance?

Who can love whom he envies? He envied not only Liz's sex,

which set her beyond the draft, but her belief in herself and her own powers, which set her apart and beholden to nobody. But that he was capable of love he was certain and that love was an anchor: he might fail as a husband, he would not fail as a father. He loved a child as yet unborn. It was cowardly to deny that child the sound of a father's voice.

He passed under the sign. Again he was told to go right on in there into another booth — this one soundproofed, he hoped. He was told to talk into the microphone when a red light glowed. Typical of him that he had not planned for this moment as others must have planned, writing down some sentiment or exhortation or prayer on the back of an envelope. It would seem that one who had prepared himself for the theater would have a hundred curtain lines at his tongue's tip that might serve as epitaphs — where are you, Aeschylus, where Homer and Spenser, where even George Gordon, Lord Byron? But nothing came.

It would seem that a man who had stood before a thousand classes would not now be stiff with stage fright. He sweated, and nothing came — or almost nothing. The red light glowed and his mind fled from one and then another meaning of scarlet — danger, warning, stop, distress. Blood. And nothing came, or almost nothing. Hardly aware of the words, he began:

There was an old woman, and she was wise; woefully wise was she;
She was old, so old, yet her years all told were but a
*   score and three;*
And she knew by heart, from finish to start, the Book of Iniquity.

Such was Liz's reconstruction of those few hours; what she had in her hands, given her with a studied diffidence, were the record and the photograph, but such tangibles are springboards for the creative mind and what it imagines is very likely to be the Truth. Just so the mathematician solves the Unknown.

"Oh, Hal," she murmured, and very nearly said, "You shouldn't have!" as a woman might on accepting a small ribboned box. Her face froze in a smile like that of a woman with a gift neither expected nor desired from someone who seldom crossed one's mind, to whom one really ought to have written or telephoned except that one didn't want to be encouraging and get all that started again.

Wise as she was, she was sometimes no better at understanding or explaining the instability and unsatisfactory nature of human relationships than anybody else. "Whatever I felt for him," she wrote, "I no longer felt. I couldn't forgive his using my body to escape being drafted."

Because that's what he'd done. She was bitter not because he was going but because he was leaving his growing seed inside her. Morning sickness next, then the swelling and the angry veins, backaches, and at last the involuntary rending of her flesh, and blood. Her will had nothing to do with it; acted upon rather than acting, she was face to face with a faceless authority.

"And that was our marriage.

"No, never a marriage. A need we both had, a need hard to honor and hard to refuse. Perverted generosity on both our parts, maybe out of a fear of being alone, of no one's caring. As for me, I felt that Hal would forgive me anything so long as I could be of some peculiar use to him, but what that was I wasn't sure. Maybe I represented something more permanent than that little shack built on sand."

The center where Hal would be instructed in war was by way of Boston, and that might have made it easier for Mammy P, who hated New York City as filthy and vast but did want to see Hal again before the army had swallowed him up. He wrote, rather than called her, when he would arrive at South Station, for Mammy P disliked calling or receiving calls and held the telephone company responsible for the decline of letter writing as an art.

Ten days passed before she replied, time enough for her to have had taken and developed the snapshot of herself she included with her letter. Liz believed Mammy must have been the last woman on earth to fix the flap of an envelope with sealing wax to prevent all but the most determined from examining her words. "I had thought of getting a little steak in," Mammy wrote, "the way we used to, and rosé from Pierce's." She had looked forward to his little visit, but that was not to be. "For the past year or so Koussevitzky has been conducting the music — if you can call it music — of Stravinsky, Honegger and Ives." Truly, it was enough to drive one right up the aisle.

Since Hal loved music as much as she did, if only of a different kind, he would understand her joy when Koussy posted notice he had scheduled an all-Brahms program. It appeared he had come to his senses. She hadn't heard Brahms in a coon's age as the boys used to say, and to hear Brahms was akin to going home. But drat it! Wouldn't the performance fall on the very evening Hal was to arrive in Boston and she, alas, had already asked the Carvers to join her and they had planned a simple supper later on. "Biff" Carver hadn't been at all well — the doctor seemed to think it had something to do with his blood and she understood it could be painful but he had continued to garden and to golf. Incidentally, Maude Carver sent her best wishes to both of them for a rosy future.

Mammy P understood that the government allowed at least one leave before a soldier was sent across the water, so there would be that time to look forward to. He was to convey her dearest love to dear Elizabeth.

The photograph was accompanied with no explanation and it required none. It was a final statement of one who wished to be remembered exactly as she was — trim, pretty, lean, controlled and vapid. Mammy's pale-blue hair was at the ready, the cashmere sweater picked out with sequins lay light on her shoulders. Her pretty slippers urged attention to her slim ankles. Here was a mother worth fighting for; here was a picture to give a son courage; here was a picture to carry into battle.

"Gorgeous shoes," Liz said.

[197]

"Mammy always said shoes were her one extravagance."

"How could she admit it? But thank God for it. A true extravagance makes her almost human, and I can think of nothing more effective than fancy boots to conceal feet of clay."

"You're being too hard on her."

"That would be impossible."

"She really has very little, Liz."

"Very little brain, very little feeling. You must tell me about your father sometime."

"He was — something like me, Liz." Tears had sprung into his eyes — whether for the past or for himself it was hard to tell. "And you love me, Liz?"

"Yes, Hal. I do."

"I've got to believe that now. I'm scared."

One among hundreds of thousands of scared young men. Reduced by terror, transformed by fear into a child clutching at memories of mothers and fathers and puppy dogs, about to risk his life because he is ordered to do so by men who will never hear the screams nor gag at the stench. "There are principles," Liz wrote me. "Of course there are principles — courage and duty and dignity and even patriotism — but always underneath is money, money. Somebody profits. Somebody gets rich. One of the truths is Money."

That night in the brass bed she held him close until he slept.

"NATURE HAS A FISTFUL OF TRICKS," Liz wrote. One man is singled out to die a violent, untimely death. Another man is debatably fortunate because he will expire in a hospital bed from which he has observed the ruthless survival of potted plants, and is prepared for the fact of death by a benevolent Nature. The passing years act as a cumulative anesthesia; the disappointment, tragedy and loss that would have been intolerable but ten years ago are accepted as inevitable, and inevitable that what one once thought was possible and true was neither true nor possible and that it is wise to prepare for tragedy. Until you are prepared to face tragedy with grace, you are subject to blackmail. A father should be prepared to dress (socks, shoes, pants, shirt, and tie and jacket) and go down to identify his daughter who lies on a slab. This was not expected many years ago when across the river on a summer's night the band played "Stardust." The moon came up, remember?

Just so, Nature prepares the pregnant mother for her role. Her mind is opened to the half-forgotten world of childhood, a tinkling music box, a lacy Valentine, a morning in spring with the sun full in her face. She feels her womb an ampule holding a precious burden whose submarine dreams will come true. Oh, how she will dress the child and how she will fly at those who dare to hurt his feelings! She is moved to smile at little children in the park, and to ask their ages. When did he walk, when did he talk? She will read aloud to him and by merest chance she's come on a Mother Goose with the very illustrations she recalls. Little Boy Blue.

Christopher Robin. She will buy cloth and thread and needle and cut out and stuff a Kanga, a Tigger. And then at last, Dickens. They will read him each Christmas.

She will be waiting for him (darning something of his, baking something, waiting for his step) when he comes proud with his report card, staring at his growing feet because he can't bear her pride in him and yet demands it. When he comes in tears with a skinned knee or a tale of unfairness or of the death of his dog she will take him in her arms.

Dreaming, she pauses before shop windows, speaks to pregnant strangers, examines dollhouses (it could be a girl), and toys that explain the color spectrum, and shapes and angles that explain the world.

And see! He has brought her a flower pot of clearest red marked with a stencil — who would guess it had begun as a coffee can? He has brought his father a tie rack from manual training class. So alike they are, father and son, and with them gone on one of those little trips of theirs she is lonely, but she'd have it no other way. See how he grows. And what is this — what is this in so huge an envelope? An acceptance to Harvard, that's what it is. Who can blame her for tears? She is a candidate for heartbreak.

"Is it incredible that I thought like this after two months of pregnancy?"

Yes, I thought, incredible that the most cynical human being I'd ever known could be seduced by sentimentality.

"I wore my pregnancy like a blanket — it was no less than a type of insurance; if I failed as a novelist I could fall back on motherhood, as on a cushion." Careful not to tire herself, she sought out leafy spots in the city to acquaint the child in her womb with nature, and for the child's sake she drank but little.

But the check the government granted wives and widows of enlisted men was hardly more than the rent. She had known nothing of New York rents and she and Hal had failed to realize that already the Village was becoming fashionable, invaded by a laity with fat wallets — brokers, car salesmen and insurance executives whose wives thought that down there below Fourteenth Street they might escape their pinched life-style and touch hands with the creative and those otherwise anointed or damned.

Liz was lucky to find a job so undemanding that there were hours when she appeared to be doing the work she was paid to do when in truth she was writing about Hal's actor friends. She had no sooner filled out the application than she got the job with Reuters, a British news agency based uptown. There she had her own desk; she had access to teletype machines, fluorescent lights, a coffee maker and a clean toilet. She worked with diffident men and with other wives who had been abandoned for the war.

"What we were doing was translating English into United States and releasing parts of it to the American papers. Sometimes we colored it a little.

"British news was never so appealing after the Battle of Britain, when it did seem for a time that the island might really be invaded by the Hun. That was their finest hour, when England owed so much to so few." Who was not proud of his Anglo-Saxon blood and who but the heartless would fail to buy a cigarette case of white enamel bearing the arms of the House of Windsor? But with the entry of America into the war and the result then a foregone conclusion, a deadly sameness infected the news, and the global scope of the conflict strained the mind and left it listless. "So stupid of the Japanese!" Liz said. "And they are called a clever little people! Had the envoys they sent to confer with Roosevelt crossed America by Greyhound bus or by the Northern Pacific Railroad, changing in Chicago to the Pennsylvania, instead of zooming overhead in the clouds, they would have understood that the state of Montana is not much smaller than Germany, that Chicago alone would take years to conquer, that they must fight their way from 245th Street South to 7600 North and then they would have to deal with Evanston if ever they got that far. It was likely that they'd bog down somewhere near State and Madison. These treacherous envoys would have seen that Ohio alone is capable of supporting fifty million people, that the Rocky Mountains are impregnable and all in between north and south and east and west was the vast rich land where people couldn't be starved out, who knew the sacred nature of private property and would gladly die for it."

To the readers of the newspapers it seemed almost like old times when an ancient, titled Englishman was murdered in Bermuda or the Bahamas, where all those people are who have drifted away from the mainstream. There had apparently been a wild party. The old man had been knighted because he was so rich it was hard for the Crown to avoid doing so, and he had either been an American or a Canadian so it was possible for almost anybody to get his hopes up about knighthood. His pretty wife was immediately suspect, and then the young wife's lover, who was — to no one's surprise — French; it is believed that your ordinary young woman blanches and falls back on cutting throats no matter what the provocation — for cut the old man's throat had been. But it transpired that the wife and the Frenchman had an alibi and could prove it by a maid who had seen them dallying on a bed the very night of the murder. It would seem there was little reason to perform an autopsy on a man whose throat had been slashed from ear to ear, but one was ordered and one was carried out. Cut into, the old man's stomach disclosed a peculiar treasure of objects undreamed — buttons, cloth, shoe leather and scraps of what the microscope saw as human skin. Several people including servants were examined for wounds made by human teeth.

"These nifty facts we suppressed." And suppressed also that the old man had taken not only his wife to bed but a doll meant as a voyeur to heighten his flagging passion. To print such "news" must bring into question the caliber of men the English raise to the peerage.

[*202*]

Being privy to such morsels was a singular bond among those who worked at Reuters; they had many a little chat around the coffee machine. Among those who sipped coffee from paper cups was a large, cautious young woman with quite small feet named Doris.

"In her wake was the odor of Ivory soap and Johnson's baby powder." She knew herself from childhood to be haunted and hounded by small, sudden crises and in her unusually large patent-leather handbag she kept tools, drugs and devices to meet them — needle and thread, pins of both kinds, aspirin, iodine, cigarettes against sudden need, five dollars secret even from herself, dental floss, matches and a candle stub, a coiled length of copper wire, a fresh razor blade and a tiny vial of smelling salts. It was from Doris that Liz borrowed a Kotex when she began to bleed in the Reuters' clean toilet just before lunch. So, she had been wrong — not pregnant, had merely missed two periods. Well, that was that. She looked ahead. She never allowed (or did not then allow) the past however recent to acquire the importance of nostalgia, a sickness that distorts truth.

But Doris had but the one extra pad and one was clearly not enough, even after having been several times wrung out. She looked into the mirror as one does who for a moment has lost track of himself. Concerned, she walked out among the tables and desks and knocked at the door of Mr. Cummins's office. He was the supervisor and had direct contact with London but did not fancy becoming involved in personal problems. He rose, alarmed.

"You're as pale as a ghost," he said, and glanced at his watch as he did when no more than "Good morning" had been said to him, should he later be required to place the words in a frame-work of time. "Let me call a taxi for you."

She was barely able to get up the five flights of stairs into the apartment. The fifth and last flight was circular but wide enough for only one person; it led to what had once been servants' quarters; servants were expected to go aloft single file.

Liz was grateful that she could support herself not only by the banister but by the opposite wall. She felt she had lost a good deal of blood, much of it on the impervious cushions of the taxi where by now either the driver or a new fare would be appalled. "It's hard to say whether we are more troubled by the sight of our own blood or that of another — in either case it is a stirring symbol of the passing away of life, of the scene where violence was done. Does that account for the universal fear of blood — that it be shed or is caused to be shed?" Red, red, red, the hue of violence, adultery, anger and death. Had she been thinking clearly — or at all — she'd have directed the driver to a hospital. Instead, like a frightened animal, she had directed him to her peculiar hole, where at least she might suffer in familiar surroundings. Now she must get to the telephone and call the doctor, a slender young man who had first declared her pregnant. He had been kind. He would come.

The Manhattan directory was heavy and her vision began to fail. Then, as her numb middle finger dialed the digits that would call up the doctor's voice, the first spasm of true pain lifted her; the muscles of her stomach and her groin contracted like a sudden fist and her face twisted.

"I'm afraid I'm hemorrhaging," she gasped, and dropped the phone.

She obeyed an instinct that warns a woman to be scrupulously clean and in a clean white slip before she offers herself to a doctor. She thought the flow of blood was lessening.

A second spasm seized her as she moved under the skylight towards the bedroom. She dropped to the floor. In a moment her arms and legs worked and she crawled and pulled herself onto the brass bed and there, an hour later, gasping and choking she was delivered of a half pound of amorphous, nameless tissue. What she had for her pains was a massive clot of her own blood.

"And so does Nature interrupt the full-term birth of what would most certainly have been an imperfection."

"Certain fictions are abroad," she wrote. "There is a fiction that school days are the happiest of our lives, that age and wisdom go hand in hand, and that water drunk after a night of champagne makes you drunk again. There is a fiction that the killer returns to the scene of the crime—just why, it is not for me to say. No — wait a minute. It *is* for me to say. Otherwise, where is a place for this determinedly childless woman, this careless wife? It must be my business to attempt to explain the inexplicable, to suggest order behind instinct and to detect even in madness a pattern—a design that repeats itself at least once. The killer, the criminal, if he returns to the scene, goes there because only there could he have remained innocent; only there could he have prevented from happening what happened."

Another fiction is that women quickly forget the pain of childbirth, and once again allow themselves to be penetrated. "A fiction fostered by men who won't shoulder responsibility for causing pain, who compare using a condom to washing their feet with their socks on. I first heard that comparison voiced by a halfback on the New Hoosic football team. No, it is not women who forget the pain, but men — even those who stand aside and hear the cries in the upper room.

"As for me, never again. Never again risk aborting a monster." Such wasn't the business of the artist.

She saw no reason to disturb Hal somewhere in the Pacific with a gaudy account of her travail; it was not likely that he who had not experienced it could conceive through the written word the violence of her pain and her subsequent depression — perhaps Nature's way of pointing out that some possibly correctable flaw in her anatomy had been responsible for the loss of a potential human life. But knowing that he may have had recent if fleeting thoughts of electric trains and Erector sets, she told him, and then closed the letter on what she thought an appropriate note.

"I'm truly sorry, Hal. Truly." At such a distance she felt she could so speak and not have her sorrow challenged.

A V-mail letter came and she opened it with dread, slitting it across the top with a nail file instead of ripping it open to give it the importance it deserved. She was going to dislike reading that he would return not to the family he had expected but only to a status quo, that his time in the Pacific theater was not a time of growth and change but of standing still. And he would certainly hint that they were both growing older.

"My dearest wife," he began, and it appeared he had not yet received her news, but then she read, "Things like this just happen."

Just happen, she thought. Good God!

"I know this may be a foolish request," he wrote, "but I wish you'd send me a dozen cakes of Ivory soap." The big bars, he thought, would be the better. They could be cut into smaller pieces after he received them.

After a moment of disbelief, she was furious. "Exactly why," she wrote me, "I'm not sure I could have said. I understood that a man in his circumstances might get things out of proportion and begin to think of Ivory soap and Spearmint gum and potato chips as links with home. I even tried to convince myself that his casual dismissal of my miscarriage was a crude attempt to make me feel better."

I believe her anger was not allowing her to think. I believe her anger was at his setting himself up as a practical philosopher who would suggest when he got back that they give it another try.

I've read much about how novelists work, read many interviews, and by the time I knew Liz well I had talked with several who showed up at some profit to themselves at the college where I teach. Some were amused, some complained that on every lecture circuit, on every campus, at every writers' conference the same questions were put to them.

Novelists are sometimes approached and propositioned by someone who offers to reveal the story of his life for fifty percent of the profits on the book. We all think our lives must be of interest — what the open door revealed, what the light fell on, what the whispers meant. I think Liz would have agreed with me that it is the order imposed on life that might make it worth living and worth reading about, the art of including and excluding. If novelists would only tell us their secret — but we go to our graves untold.

Novelists are often asked if they use an outline or if they make up things as they go along. One novelist told me he knew the last line of the book before he began it. But all of them maintained they went through a first draft as quickly as possible, skirting those places where they might get stuck, and then went back and revised and revised.

Liz's first novel, *Masquerade*, she finished while still working at Reuters, three years after Hal went overseas. The theme of the manuscript was that we are different people with different people, different in different rooms and at different times of day. We cherish old friends because they had a first impression of us that is possibly the correct one. We live our lives playing parts when what we long for is a role.

The manuscript was a single draft; she labored over it sentence by sentence, word by word, instead of rushing ahead like the rest of them, and then revising. She wrote it as a poet writes poetry, as a painter — particularly a watercolorist — paints, having seen the whole in his mind's eye before he begins, working within a mental framework. I think what she wrote was more poem than novel — everything felt, not much happening.

She might have carried her manuscript directly to a publishing house and handed it to a receptionist, and thus have seen what a publishing house looked like on the inside, but she was suddenly shy; she did not wish anyone to associate her face and her voice with her work. Should the manuscript be rejected, it would be the manuscript that was rejected and not her. She herself would go unimpaired and able to write again. The manuscript went through the mails, as if she lived in New Hoosic, Iowa.

Once the package was out of her hands she felt like a child who has lost a doll to a rushing stream, understanding now what it is to finish a book and not yet have another to write. Except for writing, the years meant nothing; had she been asked on a witness stand what she had been doing a year or a month before, she would have been struck dumb.

The years without Hal had been meaningless moments and hours with various others; she ate out with this one and that one, let them bring her home, and slept with them, but only on weeknights. Weekends were hers for writing. None of the men she knew had any more importance than a stranger sidling by in a darkened movie house. They were older than she, men who had escaped marriage or those who had come to regret it. The dearest wish of one was to nurse her. Another, a doctor with a fringe of red hairs about his bald pate, chastely kissed her on the street below and later called with obscene suggestions. She filed them all away among her notes, the suggestions and the men themselves, in cheap ledgers with marbled covers. In pencil in her childlike scrawl she wrote

> *Christ and sex. Apostles queer?*
> *Men, womens' breasts. Infantile? Jealousy?*
> *Why moon appears larger horizon, shrinks as rises. Importance*
>   *first appearance anything. Familiarity, contempt.*
> *Why Chinese, Japanese all look same white people.*
> *Some men jealous wife's Tampax.*
> *Model T Ford like huge baby buggy. Rocking motion.*
> *Howl of coyote, reverberation like starlight on water. Chalk cliff.*

She was most comfortable with the gay boys. They sensed she did not judge them; she did not put them off by playing the professional female — the right to hysterics, visits to the hairdresser, headaches, birthdays, charge accounts. Her humor attracted them.

"There was not one of them," she once told me, "who wished to be what he was."

"Jesus Christ," a David said who worked beside her at Reuters. He was a cadaverous young man with a large head. "Who wouldn't want to be anybody else." He had several times been beaten bloody on Eighth Street by sailors in attractive pants. "No woman," he complained, "would beat you up if you propositioned her."

One she knew had married to force himself to be straight. "I thought I could learn how. I could understand," he said, "why my wife would blow up if I'd gone after another woman. But why did she blow up over a man?"

"Because she was helpless against a man," Liz told him. "She might compete with another woman."

Some of them, sick with shame, had gone to psychiatrists who dressed in heavy tweeds and made broad gestures, and ever before them on their desks were sobering snapshots of wives and children.

Some had wrapped themselves in the gorgeous ritual of the Anglican and Roman churches, praying that liturgical magic might transform them. They despaired that it did not. They were astonished that priests were sometimes damned like themselves and like themselves had fled to the Church where, at least, they were not expected to marry.

Others were attracted to the simple bigotry of the fundamentalist sects, the sects of bumper stickers that warn that Christ is Coming. They had only to be born again, to believe in or on the Lord Jesus Christ, and He would straighten them out — make them want a woman and follow the baseball scores. Well, He didn't.

"Sackcloth and ashes was a washout," Liz wrote me, "and so was total immersion."

They brought her small, exotic gifts — wooden casks of Ceylon tea, lemon marmalade laced with gin, a duster of pink feathers on a long pole for high dirty places. "What the girls might have carried in the Ziegfeld Follies." They brought booze and plump roast chickens from the delicatessen.

The weeks went by.

She knew that in this country forty-seven thousand titles are published each year and that apart from textbooks and learned tomes they are aimed at the popular audience where the money is, at a public wary of prose more difficult than that found on cereal boxes, at readers who find their heroes in cartoons. But two or three houses are responsible in including on their lists a few works of art at little or no profit to themselves; Hawthorne House was one of them.

There arrived a crisp, white envelope.

The occasional trembling of Liz's hands is known medically as an intention tremor; she shook when she put key to lock, hand to telephone; threading a needle was impossible and accounted for buttons never replaced, for the scrap of gray sateen lining that hung just below the hem of an old gray squirrel coat I remember. She had got it from a bin.

"When I finished the note I couldn't stop shaking." Along with acceptance, the letter suggested lunch in a grand hotel whose name called up sables, crystal and attar of roses.

 SIX TO ELEVEN MONTHS pass between the time a novel is accepted and the time it appears in print. "Roughly," Liz wrote, "the gestation period of a she-goat on the one hand and a horse on the other." The delay is laid at the door of the typesetters, who are said to be a proud, perverse outfit.

Masquerade, a novel by Elizabeth Chandler Phillips, was published in May 1945 to what the trade calls "mixed reviews." Puzzled reviews might have been more accurate. They were marked by grudging, cautious praise.

"One reads Mrs. Phillips's novel with awe and delight, as one reads Mrs. Woolf, but it is hard to put a finger on the novel's attraction."

I think I can put a finger on the attraction: those reviewers who had the ability to carry a tune in their heads understood that *Masquerade* was music, that the beauty was in repetitions, imitations and dynamics, and was most effective when read at a sitting, as a symphony must be heard. The review in the *New Yorker*, that publication that has ruffled the feathers of so many authors, was not sympathetic. It printed the entire last paragraph of *Masquerade* under the caption "Rich, Beautiful Prose Department" and drew a furious letter from Liz's editor, Helen, who had become Liz's friend and literary defender from the moment the two met over lunch in the Oak Room.

Liz had stood before first one and then another bookshop window all over the city to be assured her book was there.

And Hal came home. If anything, he looked younger than he had when he went overseas.

"Certain men don't age because nothing touches them."

He stood naked next morning under the skylight, placed his feet wide apart, put his hands on his hips, and said, "Whee!"

Liz felt compunction; she didn't like copulation with him.

"Whee!" he said like a boy out of school. "You must have been damned excited when they took your book. More excited than you wrote me."

"It's hard to write about excitement when it has already passed."

"And isn't it great," he said. "Five hundred dollars. Two great things happening in the same month?" His eyes were sly, playful, demanding an answer.

"Yes, it is," she said, embarrassed lest he compare the publication of her book to the Allied victory in Europe.

He laughed. "Two things — my coming back and your book published." He shook his head. "It must have felt great to get your hands on that cash."

"It relieved the panic."

"You put it in the bank? Most of it's left?"

"I bought a black dress and two pairs of shoes."

"That's not bad."

"I sent fifty dollars to my father and fifty to my mother."

He let himself down on the ruined chaise longue and searched for what he needed to smoke a cigarette. "Isn't a fifth of what you got too much to give away?"

"It was a way of letting them know I'd succeeded a little; they might be happy knowing that."

"Well, sure, but for Christ's sake. It's only —"

"Only what?"

"Well, let's face it. Here I am home, and no job yet, and not even sure what I want to do. And you about to be laid off at Reuters."

"I'm glad," Liz said, "to hear you say you're not even sure what you want to do."

"I don't follow."

"Because your not being sure tells me that at least you've considered getting a real job and not getting mixed up with actors again."

"And what would I do if not get mixed up with actors? I'm not going to teach again, can't stand the backbiting."

She knew he had long thought that stage-managing would lead to directing, but to tell him he did not have the commanding personality of a director would be cruel, to tell him that his contacts in the theater were too peripheral — and those contacts he had, had suffered from his absence of four years. She believed his sense of theater was shallow. "You know almost everything about lighting," she said.

His eyes narrowed; he was pained. "There you go, there you go again wanting me to be an electrician. Women get hold of something and they harp, harp, harp."

"You read that in the funny papers. What women want is a little security."

"Sure," he said. "I'd say sure if a woman was thinking of a child's future."

"That remark doesn't hurt as much as you'd hoped. Somebody has got to do store windows."

"Oh, sure. Altman's, Bloomingdale's. You said that the first time."

"Somebody really good with lights. Creative."

Her suggestion was all the more hateful because it was reasonable, but he perked up at the word creative. "Those jobs are in the hands of the fairies," he said.

"I'll overlook your bigotry." She believed bigots to be a cult and like all cults, an evidence of insecurity.

And so began one of their bizarre arguments, the common

[*213*]

rows of those who have plighted troth. Each partner drags up old things, dredges up old hurts, picks old scabs, and stands in judgment of the other, wishes he hadn't married in the first place, must have been temporarily mad — well, wasn't love a kind of madness — if it was love — and if he had married it should have been to a different kind of person, somebody reasonable, somebody caring who would at least listen, not somebody bent on making you over, somebody using you. And before Liz was the image of some man she might have married: the truly whole man, happy man, athletic man, family man, the Oh, Jesus, shoot-the-breeze man of guts, able to handle other men, the man of pipes and dogs and all the rest of it but at the same time an artist.

But now — so long ago — Hal just back from Europe, he was saying, "When do you get paid next?"

"Friday as usual."

"They pay every week? I thought it was every six months."

"Six months? What are you talking about?"

"Your book. When you get royalties."

"I doubt there'll be royalties. I got five hundred. They'll be lucky if they make that up in sales."

"You mean five hundred dollars is all you get out of three years' work?"

"A lifetime's work."

"And I mean to say it's a piss-poor proposition."

"All right, piss-poor. But there it is."

He began pacing about the room as if it were entirely his. "It would seem to me that as long as you're writing something you might write something that people would read."

"People who count will read what I write."

"Now who's being bigoted? Looking on everybody as if they all had twelve-year-old minds. That attitude drives me nuts. It's an excuse for failing."

"So you think I have failed. And by the way, not twelve-year-old minds. Six-year-old minds."

I was perhaps one who didn't have a six-year-old mind. I was one of the few who bought *Masquerade*. Some who were later puzzled by the book or who did not understand it at all may have bought the novel on the strength of the dust jacket — a background of dead white, the word "Masquerade" in block letters of jet black. Just underneath lay a scarlet domino.

That fall, Halloween hovering over the Village, the mirrors reflecting the sharp flames of tapers, I met Liz at Helen's elegant little house, and I sat at her feet, as I do now.

Hal could not understand, if she was a writer, why it had taken her three years to write a book of less than two hundred pages and why, if she was a writer, she didn't sit right down and begin another one. I think it took her three years because she was breaking new ground. She had no model before her. I think she did not sit right down and begin another because she was empty.

So Hal did take a job with a commercial lighting company, perhaps thinking that this selfless move would shame her into production. But very soon he had what he called to himself Inside Information.

As one in the acting profession — if only by wish, now — he was convinced of the reality of make-believe. He more than half believed in signs and portents; he had a book of dreams and another on the Tarot cards. He was quick to credit whatever might be twisted or interpreted into looking like good luck for himself. His new secret stood in his eyes, in a smile and a faintly furtive look — the expression of one who has discovered how to have his cake and eat it.

Hopeful, possibly gullible, he believed an incredible story that was going the rounds of such places where such stories go the rounds: it seemed that a device invented some years ago was about to be perfected that could catch images on a small screen just as radio catches up sound. When the device came within reach of the general public, no one would any longer leave his chair to see a movie. It would be the end of the great picture palaces of gilt and plaster and velveteen. Even the theater might be doomed.

The company he worked for had been approached by some

people. Lights were needed for this new device, and lights must be arranged. So Hal would be in on the ground floor. That was the floor to be on. He would make contacts. He believed in contacts, in the worth of contacts. Before you knew it he'd be back in the theater again, in such a theater as had never been before. He'd be part of a new medium.

Liz, in the meantime, made false starts and discarded them because each one failed the test that must be applied to any successful novel: in a simple, declarative sentence, answer the question What is this novel about?

Like a woman battered by postpartum shock, she was struck with the stunning idea that maybe she could no longer write, that God or Fate had singled her out to write but a single book, and in her mind's eye she imagined herself as one of a defeated procession of one-book writers who must spend the rest of their lives trudging toward nothing. Troubled, she returned to her habit of making hundreds of notes that might later be of some possible use. They might give Hal the impression she was working seriously. I have seen pages of them:

> *Why did I become a writer? Stories in picture books. Written word only permanent thing.*
>
> *Thoughts about life. Like the melody of songs known only imperfectly, only in part, only in the alto part, etc.*
>
> *The most intimate and at the same time the broadest female sexual image, the coming to life of the dormant — the isolated, hidden and independent object which stirs, functions and explodes quite apart from its surroundings. The erectile penis.*
>
> *The silence of the organs in sexual climax.*
>
> *When we see a mug shot of a thief or a murderer or a rapist, we say, "He looks like a criminal." But what we see is Everyman.*
>
> *Christmas — the look of the word crystal, chrysalis, St. Chrysostom, Christopher, crucible, crucify. Rain in California, night, Woolworth's, primary colors, cheap toys, talcum powder. Old Spice. A scrawny Christmas tree not chosen.*

Personality of a town — imprint left by the people — like me — who grew up there. New Hoosic. College town at once permanent and impermanent, new faces, faculty, students, but same subjects, same houses, buildings. Growth of trees.

Family pronunciations. Skizzers for scissors, skedooly for schedule. Absotively posilutely. "I'se regusted." Amos 'n' Andy. End of blackface comedy. Changing attitude of blacks and whites. Black-face tragedy. Trouble ahead?

The Tiger's Revenge by Claude Balls. The Spot on the Sheet by Mr. Completely. The Open Kimono by Seymore Hair.

First time heard word fuck. The big boys.

What's that lying in the road? A head?

What things too late for. Actress. Baby. What things too soon for. Success. Fame. Money?

A book about growing up.

She looked up from that last note one morning after Hal had gone and she sat with a little hangover and a cup of coffee. She thought she had a novel.

What is this book about? It's a book about growing up.

At the Fourteenth Street library she took out a copy of *The Five Little Peppers and How They Grew*, a book dear to the hearts of children because it proposes a life without the brooding presence of parents — the two big Peppers have died. To be an orphan is not at all a bad idea. You can stay up as long as you like.

She went to her typewriter and wrote the first paragraph:

The hideous accident that orphaned the Bates children happened a week before Christmas. Had it happened in surprising spring, when quite nice people wandered along the road in search of bluebells, had it happened in easy summer, when a glass of lemonade is the thing, or in the fall, the time of flames of reds and yellows and self-congratulatory Thanksgiving, the Bates children might each one have been farmed out and separated forever.

A good beginning? But weeks passed as she worried the material, nagged it, flogged it, pulled, twisted. Something wrong. To write about growing up, you have to have grown up. She thought she had not grown up. Grown up, she'd have lost what gifts she had; grown up, she'd have lost her child's eye, the vision of the world in those primary colors, a child's rhythms — skipping, chanting, taunting in four-four time, a child's cruelty, candor. It was a child who noticed that the Emperor had no clothes. Innocence? Ignorance? A child has no knowledge of consequences. Notes again:

> *The wheel and the zero that changed civilization have the same*
> *   shape.*
> *Bitter green odor of leaves.*
> *Another name for the giraffe (from Arabic) is camelopard.*
> *A tortoise on St. Helena is pointed out as the only living thing*
> *   that ever saw Napoleon.*
> *Only the female mosquito sucks blood.*
> *Cultural inferiority of Midwest, contempt for American authors.*
> *   The lout Mark Twain, bubblehead Thoreau, screwy Haw-*
> *   thorne, dry Emerson, scary Poe, patriotic Whitman, Moby*
> *   Dick (no author), and whoever heard of Henry James? Emily*
> *   Dickinson was worse than Edna Millay because she wrote*
> *   jingles about frogs in bogs and Amy Lowell smoked cigars.*
> *   Bess Streeter Aldrich was better than Willa Cather because*
> *   she never left home.*
> *Title: Let Nothing You Dismay.*
> *We love our dreams because we are not responsible for them.*
> *   Apart from us, wonderful like sex? We can't help dreams*
> *   but of all things they belong only to ourselves.*
> *Names. Miss Woolbreight. Mrs. Bonesteel. Mrs. Aubrey*
> *   Dame. Hosannah Bloodworth. Mr. Birdlebough. Miss May I.*
> *   Sprinkle.*

The telephone rang. "Liz! Liz dearest!" Helen breathing over the telephone. Peter Pan collar, circular gold pin. "Good news, good news!" She had in her hand this very moment a letter from the director of the Vail Colony. The director had read with excitement *Masquerade* and hoped Mrs. Phillips would be interested in a three months' scholarship at the colony's retreat in the Berkshire Hills in Massachusetts?

At the artists' colony a dozen or so lucky people were relieved of turning their hands to anything but their art. Left behind were the dirty dishes, the inquisitive neighbors, squalling children, lazy students, office managers. At the artists' colony the presence of others quite like themselves might have a healing effect and free their minds to create; there among their peers they need not talk down to people — it might be assumed that everybody had heard of Zeno, Phidias, Delius and Sir Thomas Browne, and everybody knew that Hagia Sophia does not mean Saint Sophia but Holy Wisdom.

Creative people were offered an opportunity to mingle a bit with the simple people of the countryside who dropped into the post office or the general store with their droll tales of weather and human shenanigans. It was thought that the crowing of cocks and the lowing of cattle would spark important memories of childhood that might be translated into words, music, color or stone.

The Vail Colony occupied a Victorian mansion of many rooms left to the directors by an old woman who had wanted to write or to paint; social pressures, apparently, had intervened.

"One hoped," Liz wrote me, "that her generosity singled her out for special consideration in the netherworld." Her gift was perhaps not generosity at all, for it was doubtful that the old woman's heirs wanted the house; the towers and crenellations made sense only to a generation fed on Sir Walter Scott, the stained-glass windows only to those who had made the Grand Tour, the porte cochere only to those who knew a Hackney from a Hambletonian.

The artists worked and bunked in the dozen or so bedrooms that had been fitted with tables for typewriters, with bookcases for those who could not live apart from books; rooms were cleared to accept the paraphernalia of painters. Some rooms had been soundproofed and pianos hauled in. Sculptors worked in the cellar, for the upper floors could not be expected to bear the weight of plaster and stone.

A brass gong in the lower hall had once been attached to a Buddhist temple and had called the faithful to prayer; presently it called the artists to meals. A cocktail hour preceded dinner at the long formal table. The artists brought their own liquor which they relinquished to the director. She locked it up in a cupboard with the owner's name on it. A similar situation exists in nursing homes, where old people much possessed by death might drink more than is good for them. The dead old Victorian woman, blind to the new world about her, had stipulated in her will that no liquor was to be served on the premises; she had doubtless observed the effects of liquor — especially among the poor — but the director, somewhat in touch with reality, honored the spirit of the old woman's testament by requiring the artists to serve themselves and so in a manner of speaking they were not served. Private drinking went on in the upper chambers.

Lunch, ordered the night before, was a choice of such sandwiches as turn up in school lunch boxes — egg salad, tuna, peanut butter and bacon, ham and cheese, a choice of soup in a thermos jug. A piece of fruit nodded to the bowels. All was delivered shortly before one o'clock in a small wicker basket outside the door of each workroom by a skinny, dark young man whose eyebrows ran together just above the bridge of his nose. He had been told not to whistle. Worse than the whistle was the waiting for the sound of his footfall in the carpeted halls. Waiting for it, some artists found it next to impossible to create until the tension had been resolved. Orange peels set back outside in the wicker baskets prompted long thoughts of day coaches, coal smoke and whimpering children.

After New Year's Liz arrived by bus at the village near the colony, sick with a hangover and despondent over a quarrel with

Hal about her drinking; no good in explaining to him that when she drank she felt more confident about the future. She brought with her the old fake-leather suitcase from college days, her portable typewriter and the gray squirrel coat she'd bought from a bin, believing it could later be worn in New York, but however suitable it might have been on Twelfth Street and Fifth Avenue, it was a poor choice for the Massachusetts hills; the small hides were helpless against the cold. She clutched a big brown folder of notes that might — in this new environment — tumble into some pattern. Just so do we persist in believing that by removing ourselves in space we can escape grief, disappointment, sickness and confusion — that at the outer edges we will encounter composure, happiness, health, and ideas. Without an idea for a novel she felt herself a fraud.

"And I arrived there expecting a Currier and Ives winter with text by Whittier and found one by Hieronymus Bosch narrated by Poe."

Frank's Taxi was pulled up alongside the drugstore where the bus pulled in.

"Frank's Taxi was a stern reminder of vanished years. It was a maroon Oakland — one step up from the Chevrolet in the General Motors stable. Anyone entering this ancient coach was bound to wonder where Frank got parts for it and if he would need them before you got where you were going." Seven men of employable age had gathered to see the faces of strangers. They wore mackinaws.

"Looks like we're in for it," Frank said, and spit. "She's due to hit tomorrow night."

"Then I'd better stop at a package store first," Liz said.

"One excuse's good as another," Frank said.

With twenty of the forty dollars Hal had handed her to buy overshoes, mittens and slacks, she bought four quarts of vodka, and cigarettes.

"Vail Colony," she said.

"Tell by your typewriter," Frank said. "And stocking up on booze. They all do."

Her spirits lifted at Frank's saying they all did it. "*Così fan tutte*. It made me feel a part of a group."

The storm struck the next afternoon.

During the following three days, the colonists disported themselves like children who feel that a dramatic change in the weather excuses a bit of license. When the first flakes fell they dressed in woolens and walked and trotted to the village for mail, cough syrup, Band-Aids, toothpaste, cigarettes and liquor. They returned rosy-cheeked, eyes sparkling, and imagined themselves younger, and the snow piled up. They pressed against the tall windows to regard the snow that shut them away from their enemies in the city and from whatever else at a distance was hateful.

The winding driveway disappeared, and theirs was the tentative euphoria of people suddenly cut off from the mainland. They were excited when the thermometer dropped below zero — who does not wish successfully to experience the worst earthquake, the most ferocious typhoon, the most savage blizzard, the coldest winter?

"It is incontestable evidence of one's ability to survive."

But it quickly became clear that the Vail mansion had been built as a summer place, a way of saying it had no insulation and that local carpenters had ignored cracks. The ornate radiators of pressed iron were rarely more than warm, and they rapped like spirits as they cooled. Word trickled down that the boiler in the cellar was in so delicate a condition it would burst if the fire under it was properly stoked. Icy drafts stalked the halls; when outside doors were opened the rugs and carpets levitated. The house was haunted by a nagging cold like that one feels on winter nights in bed, but a cold one endures rather than brave an air even icier to fetch another blanket.

Darkness fell early. It seemed that every street in the village, every highway and byway, every farmer's feed pen was plowed out before the isolation of the colonists was considered. They watched the high flashing lights of the plow and heard its purposeful grumble as it moved snow this way and that, but not for them.

Upstairs the typewriters and pianos were still; chipping and pounding were no longer heard in the basement. In the sitting room a fire crackled in the fireplace and shortly after lunch they gathered around it and showed it the palms of their hands, expecting warmth, but the heat was swept up the chimney into the howling afternoon. They demanded their bottles and for a time their spirits lifted, but then the telephone failed. Loved ones in the city would have no idea whether they were alive or dead, nor could they now learn whether their loved ones were alive or dead. Many had left problems in the city that their voices could no longer solve. Suppose a doctor was needed, or a priest? It was weather for heart attacks.

A stately woman with upswept hair had arrived at the colony with a gunny sack of driftwood; she removed the rot from each piece as a dentist picks out decay and then with stylus and paint she emphasized knots and grain and "brought out the spirit of the wood." Now she stared out to the early dark. "I fear for my sanity," she said and her fear was contagious. Word was that the young man whose eyebrows met over his nose had plunged the jeep deep into a ditch in an attempt to reach the village with lists the colonists had pressed on him; he was lucky to have made it back on foot and now he sat in the kitchen blinking with pain as his hands and feet warmed.

A man with the profile of an apologetic parrot was finishing a novel about a mythical South American republic; that locale afforded him a better opportunity to describe such simple cruelties and complicated sex as are hardly practiced in the Northern Hemisphere.

"We're under siege," he remarked.

A man who had come to the colony to complete a concerto for harmonica hoped, with the nasal timbre of that instrument and his angular four-four rhythms, to catch the essentially raw nature of the American people.

"Do you know of the Donner Party?" he asked the company. He spoke with the authority of one who knows a good deal about a great deal, one who knows that Haydn wrote eighty-two string quartets and that in Portland, Oregon, there exists a fine example of the architecture of Stanford White, whose murderer made his initial getaway in a Packard runabout; he spoke as a man who knew that the real name of the Pig Woman in the Hall–Mills case was Jane Gibson, and that she drove a mile at the time she discovered the bodies. "You do know of the Donner Party?"

Some remembered something. He filled them in. It was an unpleasant story to hear at a time and place when thoughts were beginning to be somewhat introspective and to touch again and again on eschatology. On their way to the California goldfields the Donner Party had been caught by a blizzard in the Sierra Nevada; after some days they began to starve and fell to eating one another. The screaming and moaning were lost on the wind. An ugly piece of American history, an ugly piece of human history — but uglier still was that after they had been rescued the survivors turned on one another, accused one another of the horror they had been bound to commit; all were guilty simply because they had survived.

Was the teller of that vile tale making a black joke in comparing the artists at the Vail Colony to the Donner Party? Was he saying that every man and woman in that cold, vast room was equal to cannibalism to save his life? Oh, there are many ways of feeding on each other. Everybody in that room fed on another's presence and another's creativity; they must be with others who understood the agony and the joy of creation, must be with others like themselves, for creative people — unless they have so common a touch they can make money — are not much respected in America. They had all come there to feed. At whatever cost, all wished to be survivors.

From a white plaster medallion of cupids and trumpets set in the center of the fifteen-foot ceiling a chandelier was suspended; eight long, brass tubular hooks supported eight frosted-glass globes. Shortly after the turn of the century the piece had been converted from gas to electricity, but not before alternating current was available; the earlier direct current had been avoided by the sensitive because the newspapers described it as that used in connection with the electric chair, a piece of furniture that has changed but little in design. It was unpleasant to think that the phenomenon casting a cozy glow over the dinner table and lighting the children to bed might suddenly be diverted to snuffing out a human life.

Now the big globes blazed, and the talk was loud. From time to time there was even a bit of joking once they had accepted the failure of the telephone. They had the comfort of each other, and above them over the mantel a full-length portrait of their benefactress in yellow taffeta and pearls looked down upon them.

And then the lights flickered; the globes were suddenly pale as a constellation of eight moons, and then the globes were slightly red. At first it was hard to believe that so elaborate a fixture and one so much a part of the settled past was, after all, dependent on a distant generator, a fallen tree, a snapped cable. They lifted their eyes to the failing fixture. People need time to prepare for the dark; we wish to turn off the lights ourselves and in our own good time. For sudden dark deprives us of sight, that most trusted of the senses, and opens the mind to speculation and panic. We are dependent on our hearing, our touch, our sense of smell — each one of them rudimentary at best without the steadying sense of sight, each one of them capable of a thousand awful interpretations.

Light! Let there be light! To lighten our path, light at the end of the tunnel, let us see the light, light to lighten our darkness. Let us be children of light.

Their hearts and minds willed the lights to recover and — strangely enough — they did. Came murmurs of relief, a clearing of throats.

A man spoke to Liz.

". . . come to my room for a drink? I swear I won't eat you."

She had heard of nobody at the Vail Colony nor, it seemed, had anyone heard of her. Had they been younger than she or even of her age, she might have thought them people who had not yet made a name. She had heard of nobody, that is, except this man who would not eat her.

Because the two poems of his that appeared again and again in the anthologies had never been superseded, she had thought him long dead. He was a contemporary of all those poets liberated by Victoria's far from untimely death, and who for more than forty years were still known as the Younger Poets. When later they appeared on platforms, audiences were shocked to find them old men who sometimes had to be led off. Hearing them recite their work, one was gripped with the embarrassment one feels at spying on the grotesque, the embarrassment at watching old white men play hot jazz — skeletal arms, thinning hair, sharp noses — or at chimpanzees in formal dress and top hats riding bicycles. It would have been better to have locked them up so that one might recall them as they appeared on the dust jackets of their early books, shirts open to the third button revealing unwattled throats.

Struthers Carpenter was surely sixty-five. As a poet he was or had been a metaphysician, one who saw behind the shadow and around the world. He had written of a painter who had happened on a painting by a child, a painting remarkable in that the child had painted not a tree but the light blue space around the tree, a tree that emerged as solid as if it had been the true subject and not the object of the painting. A child experiments, not yet knowing there is a Right Way and a Wrong Way. The poet wonders

> . . . *if only a child can see*
> *Beyond the void who made the concrete be.*

Physically, Carpenter almost exactly resembled an ordinary human being except that, as the toy poodle differs from the standard, he was but three-quarter size, his height, his feet, his fine small hands. He stood a good two inches shorter than Liz. Surely in department stores he was redirected to the Boys' Department where, although the styles and colors like youth itself were ephemeral, he could be more accurately fitted. He wore a faded kelly-green pullover; his gray corduroys were threadbare. An admirer might have considered having his little sneakers cast in bronze for use as paperweights. His smile was apologetic, like that of a good child not yet certain he is welcome. His voice, unlike that of many small men who strive to make up in clamor what they lack in stature, was light and soft. As he spoke, he jingled small change in his pocket.

That two writers, one of whom knew and admired the work of the other, should converge on the same artists' colony might be no more than a coincidence, but it seemed to Liz more than mere coincidence that Carpenter's poem about a child's peculiar vision should have long ago crystallized her own vision of childhood, that children have special eyes that see in a landscape what older eyes reject or miss. Now Carpenter himself was walking beside her. And so, like a ghost, Inevitability stalked along beside them up the broad, carpeted stairs to the second floor and on up the narrower, uncarpeted stairs to the third floor and down the hall to Carpenter's room. He stood aside as she entered.

Something had been set in motion.

Like Liz's apartment, the third floor of the Vail mansion had been the servants' quarters when servants "lived in," having been brought from New York City along with the other Vail portables. The rooms were small, so much of the space up there being required for the Vail trunks and discards. Tucked under the eaves, the ceilings of the rooms sloped so sharply that to open a window one had to stoop and crouch — no great matter since servants had so recently been emancipated from hut and hovel that they did not expect to have the entire run of a room without squatting from time to time. In so small a room, Carpenter's stature worked to his advantage. In the day of the servants, the walls of the room had absorbed countless Hail Marys and Hail

Holy Queens as well as more aggressive prayers calling attention to the needs of simple folk — most of them concerning survival and heartbreak — while below in the master bedroom the master and his lady spoke of their own style of survival and heartbreak. After 1925, when the mansion was handed over to the directors of the colony, the walls absorbed the words Imitation, God, Nature, Aspire and Perfection that figured in the thousand definitions of Art.

"Carpenter's definition was as good as any of them. He believed that the beginning of Art is the desire to make order out of disorder, and the end of Art is that moment when disorder is not only ordered but pleasing to at least one of the senses. A smoothed stone is art to the fingers."

The vagueness of definitions of Art suggested to Carpenter that artists are chasing will-o'-the-wisps. After a moment of silence, when even the wind was briefly still, he said, "An artist is haunted by the prospect that he isn't an artist at all, that he is using art as an excuse for not becoming a lawyer or a broker or a druggist — some useful person. The artist who does not doubt himself is appalled that he has lost his powers overnight or over the years through age or alcohol. He is vulnerable, for he has likely made a mess of everything except his art — divorced his wife, abandoned his children, spent his money, insulted his friends, and behaved in such a way that only his art will excuse him. With that gone — when people draw back at the sight of him . . ."

Carpenter spoke like an old professor who was warning one last trusted class before he handed in his resignation.

But the ambience in that room in the Vail mansion was not that of the classroom; rather, it was that of a small projection room, a movie theater. Carpenter's gooseneck lamp was bent low over his desk and cast a small circle of light so bright it beckoned the eye and so contracted the pupil that the rest of the room was cast in darkness; Liz imagined a seated audience gathered there to escape life in the moving shadows on a screen, safe, momentarily, because they were not alone. "It is unthinkable to be alone when the drama is done and the lights go up."

"And unthinkable," Liz wrote me, "to be alone when the lights go out."

As Carpenter rose to fix a second drink, the lamp flickered. Liz rose. In darkness it is better to be on your feet. Her eye was drawn to the circle of light on the desk. Just within the perimeter lay a piece of mail intended to declare continuing if hasty concern — a picture postcard that was a thoughtful alternative to those lifted from revolving wire racks in the bus station. It was a print of a Gauguin oil Liz had first seen at the Museum of Fine Arts in Boston, where she had been taken by Mammy P.

Gauguin had made the painting in Tahiti; it showed twelve human figures — eleven females and one male — in various attitudes against a broad background that resembled a fantasy of Eden — sinuous trees, broad leaves, lush fruit, blue shadows not of the blue shadows are said to be, but *blue*. In the foreground a woman in a loin cloth stretches to pick an apple. Eve? Close to her feet a child eats a piece of fruit. Cain? Three figures sit on the ground to the right; lying beside them is a baby. Vague figures — memories? — walk in the background. To the left sits a woman. To the far left a woman of far darker complexion holds her temples and appears to grieve. They have erected a blue god with human shape on a round stone altar, presumably a long time ago, for they ignore the arms bent at the elbows, fingers raised in benediction. A dog lies on the right. There is a cat and a goat. A gull stands at the right and a fanciful bird something like a peacock struts across the stage. The human beings no more than the animals appear to have plan or purpose. They simply live — a verb too often a synonym for existing. They have asked no questions. They have not asked the overwhelming questions.

But Gauguin asked questions.

When the lamp on Carpenter's desk flickered once more and then failed, it was not the natives and their animals and birds that were fixed on the dark screen of Liz's mind but Gauguin's questions he had written up in the far left corner of the painting right at the time of his attempted suicide.

D'où venons-nous? Que sommes-nous? Où allons-nous? Where did we come from? What are we? Where are we going?

Carpenter, somewhere in the dark, was speaking in mock sepulchral tones. "And the earth was without form, and void; and darkness was upon the face of the deep. And the spirit of God moved upon the face of the waters.

"And God said, 'Let there be light . . .' "

Nothing happened. But Liz had the theme for her book.

 WHERE DID WE COME FROM? is a question for theologians and archeologists. Where are we going? is one for sibyls and oracles. But What are we? is a question not only for novelists but for each one of us who lives. In asking what we are and now who we are, Gauguin would not even allow us our humanity, for in including animals and birds in his paintings he suggests that animals and birds are our peers and that their beginning, existence and their end have as much significance in the eyes of a created God as ours. That he doubted his humanity may have moved Gauguin to kill himself.

What Are We? — the second novel by Elizabeth Phillips — attacks the problem of how we differ and what we have in common. We differ, her novel suggests, in our perception of Truth. The book begins:

"The house was in the woods; those with a New England turn of mind recalled it as a woods of maple; those who were excited at being somewhat north remembered it as a haunt of spruce and pine, but those who were drawn more than casually to Robert Frost argued that it was a woods of birch."

Ten artists, then, come to a colony with different perceptions of Truth but alike in having been shaped as children by terrors and humiliations. When the house is plunged into darkness — an adumbration of a common Death — each tries to explain himself to the others by describing in exquisite detail that event or scene that had left scar tissue:

A boy of ten watches his father thrashed by another man. Later, the father begs the boy for forgiveness.

A girl of fourteen is seduced by her father and sworn to secrecy. "It would kill your mother," he tells her.

A boy overhears his father beg his stepfather for money.

A little girl's mother is apprehended by a floorwalker for shoplifting in Woolworth's. They are taken up a flight of stairs where the Manager waits.

A girl of twelve watches her father go mad and watches as he crushes out the life of a kitten, and with it what was dark and painful in his own life. She recalls the brief, pointless squalling of the kitten.

No one in love with images and the magic of English could be surprised at the reviews of *What are we?* The *New York Times* carried a piece under the heading "A Haunting Landscape of Childhood." Milton Hindus, probably America's foremost authority on Proust, wrote a review for *Commentary*.

"Ten days after publication," Liz wrote me, "I stuffed Hal's dirty underwear and mine in a bag and carried it down to the Laundromat. On the way I bought a copy of *Vogue* I couldn't afford. My agent told me I'd be surprised. I put a nickel in the slot to get soap and a dime in the slot to start the washer. I dumped the clothes in and then I sat on a bench along the wall and opened *Vogue* to a page called 'People Are Talking About . . .'

"And gee whillikers! They were talking about me!"

Vogue called the novel "a modern *Decameron*."

She raised her eyes from *Vogue* to those who dropped coins in slots, whose hair was in curlers. Some smoked, some popped their gum, some read *Redbook*, some read paperbacks on sex in lofty rooms and sex in the underbrush. She smiled to herself, thinking, They do not know who sits among them.

"It was the finest moment of my life."

[*232*]

Except that I knew she was often blind concerning herself, I should have wondered at her naiveté. Those she sat among were the ones who waited for tomorrow.

One rainy afternoon we were drinking in a piano bar in University Place. "Do you mind if I pry?" I asked her.

"Pry ahead."

I was about to speak of money. She had once remarked that the instinct to keep your finances secret is as deep-rooted as the instinct to survive. To reveal your bank account is to make you either vulnerable or invulnerable; it is clear exactly how you are to be treated. What most people want of other people is their money. Unlike beauty or talent or brains, money can be had — if you play the right card. "Artists alone," she had said, "pretend there is a standard other than money, and that is because they haven't any, and so long as they remain artists, few will ever get any. Unfortunately for them, even artists must survive, and since they don't have any money they must find somebody who will give it to them. They may have to perform little services."

"You wrote me that you bought a copy of *Vogue* you 'couldn't afford.' What became of the advance from Hawthorne House?"

"It wasn't much. Only a thousand dollars."

As Hal had expected, television boomed, and the company he worked for supplied many of the lights, but Hal never even got his foot in the door; those who got their feet in the door and then shouldered on it were hard young people — "Young punks just out of college," as Hal put it, standing spraddle-legged, his eyes appealing. He was forty, I think. He and Liz were no longer young people. Every last man in the company, he said, had a car of some kind, a car of some kind to take his wife and kids to the beach, a car to wash and polish on Sunday, a car to tinker with and take pictures of, a car you could call "My car."

Hal had gone so far, while Liz was working on *What Are We?* to ask Mammy P (after all, she was his mother) if she would

[*233*]

cosign a note with him because the people at the Chase Manhattan did want that.

Mammy P was ready for him and brought up all the arguments against a car they all do. The snow in winter, the parking problem. "And all those repairs," Mammy wrote. "They don't make cars the way they used to. They told me so in the garage, and if I keep my little Ford a few more years it will become what they call a classic and worth more than I paid for it. And anyway, I'd think it would be humiliating for you down at the bank with them, having to have a cosigner at your age."

Was it so much to ask, since he supported her so she didn't have to get a job in a library or something and had all her time to write — was it so much to ask that Liz help with a car? And look: it would be good for her to get out with him into the country and browse around and think, get some ideas for a book that would really sell. "Jesus," he said, "other people write best-sellers. They're on the list every week. There must be some knack you could learn. Jesus, I'd think you could just pick up a best-seller and see how they do it, the sex and everything. I'm not a writer, but I'd think you could do that. They've got hold of some formula."

"The formula they had," Liz wrote me, "was built into them. What moved them moved their readers."

So it wasn't much to ask for, and he and she took the subway uptown to a place with foreign cars; they walked up a concrete ramp into a building that felt like a basement even on the third floor — concrete, narrow windows, echoes. Something in Hal's background recommended English cars, and he had read that in England if you couldn't have a Rolls you bought a Morris Minor or a Hillman Minx, which was at the other end of the scale, to show you didn't care about cars, really, but about transportation. You were rather above cars. You made this statement, and another statement you made is that in the background you probably had a Rolls but didn't want to make a show of it, like a woman with her jewels in the bank.

A good secondhand Hillman Minx they bought; they made a joke about naming it Rodney after HMS *Rodney* and, in fact, the little car was battleship gray.

Sundays, Hal polished Rodney with a Kozak cloth, a rag that removes New York grime without scratching the paint. He lifted a friendly, acknowledging hand to others doing the same thing, and sometimes they gathered in small groups and talked about carburetors and fuel pumps; wonderful how you made friends if you had a car. Finished, he came upstairs and looked down on the roof of Rodney at the curved reflections it caught of the buildings on either side of the street.

"If I had a child," Liz told me, "I think I should feel about it as I do sometimes about Hal. Protective. Indulgent."

There was no question of her learning to drive Rodney; New York was not the place for learning — you have to have open stretches with no hazards until you get the hang of it, and in moments of crisis, she shook. Driving school was out of the question: at thirty-two she couldn't bring herself to expose herself to the condescension reserved for older students. Nor was she mechanically minded; all she understood of the internal combustion engine was that its principle was somewhat sexual and that may account for a man's love of cars.

Insecure, we strive to make ourselves exclusive, to belong to a special group hostile to outsiders. Fraternities, lodges, religions, neighborhoods, occupations and provable ancestors are all means to that end, and almost anybody can achieve at least one of them. Among some, singularity is achieved by owning and sailing a boat.

Hal was a close reader of the travel section in the *Times* when it touched on sailing, and he followed the advertisements headed "Boats for Sale" in the sports section. The pages scattered around the shabby apartment had caused one of Liz's friends to inquire cautiously — as of a secret illness — if Hal was interested in baseball. She could understand why sailboats appealed to him. They were born of the wind, but like the wind itself they were for him quite unattainable. Believing he would be moved, she had once read aloud to him *The Dry Salvages*, the third of Eliot's *Four Quartets*.

"The salt is on the briar rose," she read. "The fog is in the fir trees."

He sighed. "What a beautiful name for a boat," he said. "The *Briar Rose*."

One Sunday morning they drove Rodney out on Long Island. From a restaurant whose windows looked over a marina, Liz watched Hal walk tall and boyish down a pier. At her right hand was the remains of her third martini. They had begun lunch with clam chowder, and as it was served Hal had spoken, as Mammy P had spoken, of the contempt in which your true New Englander holds Manhattan clam chowder. The tomatoes.

"No tomatoes in this," Liz said. "And this is still New York."

"Not really. Long Island's more like the Cape. The cook back there knows he's going to get more Yankees than the New York crowd."

They had gone on to boiled lobsters whose ruined, scarlet bodies and empty claws now prompted unavoidable thoughts of many Kraft macaroni-and-cheese dinners yet to come.

Hal had not pressed her to walk down to the sea with him to the little boats with furled sails, feminine and passive on the bright water. Without his speaking of it, she knew he was critical of her landlocked attire — the old plaid skirt, her brown oxfords, the only shoes she owned appropriate for difficult terrain. Nor would her opinion of the little boats be of any interest to him or of value. Not in the least accustomed to talking a nautical language, she was likely to embarrass him before strangers by referring to a lanyard as a rope, and even if she remembered the term, she might mispronounce it. Boat people, like the British, pronounced certain words as they wished, not as the words were spelled.

But she knew the real reason he had not pressed her to accompany him (and a reason he would keep even from himself) was that he wanted to go down alone and live a fantasy among the boats.

"We cannot bear to have anyone close to us see us and hear us play the fraud. We had rather stand naked in the street."

She watched him move with confidence down the narrow pier — or was it a float or a dock? — and he paused now and then in serious judgment beside some ketch or yawl or schooner. His own garb announced that such judgment was his right; he wore faded jeans, a worn white shirt scrupulously clean — he had washed it himself — dirty white sailor's cap with the little brim pulled impudently down, and dirty white sneakers he called Sperry Topsiders that had once cost the better part of a ten-dollar bill. Something about the efficiency of the tread. An accessory to his costume was a set of binoculars which his father had trained on birds and which he had meant this day to train on the sea, but he had left them on the table.

Now he was standing quite still alongside a boat that apparently charmed him.

In a moment, she knew, he would strike up an acquaintance with a couple doing something on board with ropes; the woman, in a blue, probably denim skirt and a blue and white jersey, was already deeply tanned so early in the year. Liz hoped they would not snub him. He would begin with a flattering remark. "I couldn't help noticing," he would say, "the rake of her beam. How she sits in the water." And the strangers would bridle as a man does whose car has been praised by the service station attendant. If they were kind, they would ask him aboard.

And he would name-drop. "I see you're from Duxbury." Or Marblehead or Mystic or Camden. "You must know so-and-so." He would speak the names of his Harvard friends who sometimes sent him a card at Christmas — she recalled a Santa at the helm of a boat. Then the strangers would offer names and if Hal's luck held out, it would soon be established that he had Bradstreet connections, and as a Bradstreet certainly had a boat of his own somewhere.

And why had he stopped near that particular craft?

"Just then," Liz said, "a power boat — a stinkpot to those in the know — this power boat fled out of the marina and its wake lurched across the water." The stern of the boat Hal was examining bumped against a piling and then swung out.

"The window where I sat was at such an angle I could see gilt letters on the stern. I picked up the binoculars. I felt a chill. The letters spelled out *Briar Rose*."

A letter came addressed to Hal and not to Mr. and Mrs. Harold Phillips. Alerted, maybe, by the slight to Liz or whatever it was, he stuffed it in his pocket. He must have realized that Liz, too, was alerted to something and would make inquiries. On the other hand, is there a law against a mother's writing personally to her own son? Must all be shared? Does not husband or wife still knock on the bathroom door?

She thought he intended her to find and read the letter. If he did not deliberately show it to her, he was not responsible for her reaction to it, was he? And a wife has a right to know what her mother-in-law is up to.

My dear Son:
For some time I have meant to write this letter.

What had prevented Mammy P from writing the letter was that for some time she had hoped it would be unnecessary to write it, that events would take care of themselves as events sometimes do, but events had not. Hal realized, of course, how she was one to practice restraint; she distrusted emotions that led to excess — always had. But a time might come when restraint must be abandoned. One must ever have in mind the larger picture.

What had moved her to "take pen in hand" was her having gone up into the attic; she had ascended there with nothing particular in mind, yet had been drawn to those regions like one in a trance, and once there her eye had fallen on the appealing sight of his high chair.

"It was no ordinary high chair," Liz told me. "Not one of your machine-turned, fake-maple ones or painted white."

"Painted with white lead," I reminded her. "Children cut their teeth on it and died of it."

Hal had once spoken to Liz of the chair. The chair was somehow his due. The piece was entirely of teak, made by an old man on the Cape who as a young fellow had sailed on clipper ships. When Hal spoke of his childhood, he dropped his voice as if speaking of the dead. The chair, Liz gathered, was so elaborately and beautifully carved it might have been a throne for a tiny potentate; the edges of the seat and back resembled plaiting — gadrooning, Hal called it. The arms and legs resembled thick ropes — hawsers — and they terminated in complicated knots — crown knots on the legs, Turk's head on the arms — there is an entire world of knots and splices. In high relief on the back of the chair was a diamond knot Hal said had no use except as decoration. Then the old man died.

"Very likely of eyestrain," Liz said.

Hal, Mammy P wrote, must keep in mind that he was the last of their particular line and as heir to a tradition he and Elizabeth should see to it that the tradition continued.

And incidentally, Liz thought, Mammy P could be assured through a grandson's genes of immortality.

And, Mammy wrote, *Elizabeth is no longer a young woman*.

In a few years childbirth would be dangerous or even impossible. It may be that this was none of Mammy's business, but she was Harold's mother and so was prepared to set up a trust fund for a child's going off to Harvard, although she doubted she'd be alive long enough to see him graduate in Memorial Hall, maybe not even from high school.

"She wrote," Liz said, "that we need not even be concerned about her funeral expenses. She had faced facts and had taken out a Before Need Plan so when the time came we had only to give the undertaker a buzz, and he'd take it from there."

[*239*]

The contents of the letter burst forth the next Christmas Eve, a notoriously explosive evening at best, according to the metropolitan police.

If not actually insane, they have but a precarious hold on reality who turn to religion, a refuge that reveals itself in astonishing gymnastics — walking on water, descending into hell, ascending into heaven, wrestling with angels — in voices out of bushes and from behind clouds, in visions high in the sky and clear as rainbows, in weeping statues and open wounds. And yet, what but magic can make bearable the length and the end of life?

In the name of God millions of board feet of spruce and fir trees are hauled up in freight elevators and set out among the filing cabinets and business machines for office parties, are dragged into heated rooms for private parties and swagged with tinsel — focal points for dismal, alcoholic cheer as Christmas itself is a focal point of the year and some special Christmas the focal point of a life. The new snow was deep, the heart was warm and all was right, and here is another example of our desperate wish for things to have been as they were not.

Guests at Christmas parties have in common a peculiar loneliness, an isolation through the loss of innocence, an understanding that we are no longer what we thought or hoped we were. Hosts cannot bear the thought of friends passing through Christmas alone, nor can they bear to pass through it alone. The hope suggested by the birth of Christ cruelly underscores how those we love have failed, failed themselves and failed us, and how we ourselves have failed. But we persist in gathering, hoping to catch in another's eye and in the distorted image of another's room in a colored ornament on a tree the possibility of another chance — in seeing in the birth of a child a fresh beginning.

That Hal had got such a tree up the narrow-twisting stairway was a miracle in itself, but such a tree was the central prop to Christmas Past.

"Such a lovely tree," Helen murmured. Oh, Helen was there.

Claude-Michel had a tradition of spending Christmas alone with his parents in France. She was pensive, thinking of divorce.

Helen was there and a young man named Carl, whose love had gone off to Pennsylvania, and a pretty dark girl named Janet, a buyer at Bonwit's, a graduate of Barnard and depressed because she had recently had a second abortion within the year. She didn't know what had got into her, allowing herself to be picked up so often in bars — some awful kind of compulsion, she believed. She had arrived a little drunk, having come from another party as so many do. She sat cross-legged on the floor on the small, dirty oriental rug in the first lotus position and so expressed her contempt for chairs, daybeds, chaise longues, and indeed the entire Establishment. "Something nice," she whispered as to herself. "Something nice."

". . . when suddenly," Carl was saying, "when suddenly one by one without so much as an ado the entire bar emptied out through the back door into the alley. Darlings, it was a raid!"

"Something nice," Janet whispered through her hair. "Did ever you once sleep with a soft little woman?"

"Once, oh yes, once yes," Carl said. "It was like sleeping with a corpse."

"Come Death," Janet whispered. "Come Death the Comforter."

". . . not to be spat upon," Carl was saying.

"The harm, the lust, when all we want is love. To be wanted. Something nice."

"And nothing but the memory of strange bathrooms and one's aging face in the mirror. What must it mean?"

"From the Hebrew," Helen remarked. "You know the Midrash on Psalms?" Although the hour was late and the tacky chaise longue invited lounging, she sat straight in her white wool suit and Belgian shoes like one ready to flee.

Hal was in a drunken, thoughtful mood. "So it's all crazy when you think Christ himself spoke Aramaic."

"Or we assume so," Helen said. The conversation at midnight

had gotten somehow out of hand. It had begun with the premise that we are better off knowing as many languages as possible since each one of them is capable of subtle nuances not shared by any other. It appeared that no one could be entirely whole without the gift of all tongues.

"Sumpin' nice," Janet whispered.

There was general agreement, before casual guests began to vanish, that language was sacred. Not much later Helen and Carl and Janet kissed and hugged each other and then kissed and hugged Liz and Hal.

"You must not kiss me, Carl," Hal said. "You must not even try."

The departure of the company left a yawning vacuum in the apartment. In a few moments Hal's voice rushed in to fill it. Liz had begun picking up glasses.

"A real shitty Christmas Eve," he said coldly. "But if you gather together a bunch of shitheels —"

Liz said nothing.

"Helen's a barren nun," Hal went on. "Among your friends a barren nun, a bloody faggot and a streetwalker."

"We're all streetwalkers one way or another," Liz said.

"Oh, you're fucking glib one way or another," Hal said. "And you're a damned selfish wife." He turned and went into the bathroom where he relieved himself directly and noisily into the water and then he splashed around washing his hands; he was meticulous about that.

Coming out he stopped and stood straight, his legs apart, arms akimbo, his hands clenched into fists, a stance often assumed by an understandably belligerent child of whom one might say, "Isn't he a manly little fellow!"

Hal looked long at the wall across the room. "Another bloody year, and no toys under the Christmas tree."

ONE MORNING BETWEEN CLASSES Etta Murphy had burst in on Sloan, the head of the department, with some problem or other and he had not quite time to conceal some papers.

"One tiny little bit stuck out," Etta breathed. "The important part. Important little parts do. He was as flustered as I've ever seen him. His hands shook when he loaded his pipe."

By noon the entire faculty knew or thought they knew that Sloan had applied for a Guggenheim Fellowship. Whispering began around the coffee machine in the lounge.

John Simon Guggenheim died in 1922 just as he was about to enter college; his parents rose above their grief and established the John Simon Guggenheim Memorial Foundation in tribute to that young man of promise, and once a year since that time thousands of creative people have applied for grants — they fill out forms, submit examples of their work and the names of friendly critics and powerful professors. They outline projects they suppose to be worthy — scholarly research, composition of music, painting, sculpture, the writing of poetry and fiction. They dream.

But ah! the following spring when you have only to reach out your hand to touch April! Then a handful of artists in North and South America, some of whom have been driving taxis and living on tomato soup, are stunned to receive a letter advising them that they are about to have credited to their bank accounts a large sum of money. For the first time they can face the teller without stuttering.

"Couldn't you find it in your heart," Etta asked, "to be just a little bit happy for him if he turned out to be one of the favored? Couldn't you rise above things? There now! Of course you could. If you can't rejoice with him, rejoice with the college. We haven't a single Guggenheim Fellow and only one Ford Foundation. They don't lie under every bush, you know. What an honor for us all! What it would mean to trustee and student! I wonder how the honor would sit on him, how he'd carry it off? Were it I, I think I should attempt graciousness. I should think I could afford to. Of course I don't know whether he went after the grant for some scholarly project he's had up his sleeve or for his poetry. His poetry is not really bad, you know." Etta's face screwed up and she giggled. "But oh, when I think how he jumped when I caught him. Nobody likes to be caught practicing hubris. Why don't you stake out a little project for yourself? That wouldn't be hubris, only practical. You'd be much safer." Etta was close now and she touched my arm. "It's not at all surprising he applied. They had their entire kitchen done over at God knows what expense. It began with a breakfast nook. She wanted a nook and it went on from there, including one of those new ovens you can forget and a table made of butcher block in the center of the kitchen. If she's told me once she's told me a thousand times that both she and he hold breakfast to be the most important meal of the day. Your stomach is rested. She was a physical education major at Cornell and they met at a dance on one of those lakes up there where Dreiser laid his American tragedy and she was in charge of something — canoes, I believe. She had learned to use buckwheat."

Now, I think a case might be made for dividing the American people into those who read *The New York Times* and those who do not. And those who read the Sunday *Times* might be divided into those who reach for the news, sports and financial sections and those who reach only for the "Arts and Leisure" section; among the latter group are men who drape their coats and jackets about their shoulders like capes.

One Sunday morning I picked up my copy off that table in Mrs. Voisin's entryway and was struck how a newspaper is a symbol of the transitory nature of human life and I realized that every room except mine in Mrs. Voisin's rooming house had for the last ten years been occupied by first one stranger and then another who had vanished to some peculiar success or failure and I wondered if they ever passed the place, thought of themselves as they had been, remembered the tension of the light switch, the cough beyond the resonant walls, and the sound of the Voisin grandchildren at the keys of the Hammond organ. I had become such a familiar to the place that Mrs. Voisin, who had a true peasant's distrust of the footloose, had thought it worthwhile to exchange Christmas cards with me.

I reached for the theater-arts section. In other years I had read the list of new Guggenheim Fellows with the sick interest with which we read obituaries — we do not expect to see our own names there but we sometimes shudder with recognition. Sometimes I saw the name of someone I knew if only by name; once, someone I knew slightly who composed music. An anthropologist who had actually lived in Grayling, Montana. This year in my typical self-delusion I read the names in careful sequence, as if I didn't care one way or another if I came across Sloan's name. However, I did care. It is remarkable how many of us condemn traits and idiosyncrasies in people we dislike that we quite overlook in friends. Who is well disposed toward those in a position to damage us? Sloan had come directly from Indiana to Harvard Graduate School and had learned overnight to patch the elbows of his Harris tweed jackets with leather and to smoke a pipe. As a graduate student he might have been taken for a professor and yet even then he cultivated the common touch; thoroughly adopting New England, he inquired of students if they knew how the Red Sox were making out. How I hoped he had actually

[*245*]

applied for a Guggenheim and been set back on his heels. Of course, if his name did not appear on the list, we would never know that he had failed; he might not have gone through with his application, fearing failure. He was careful of his ego; it was as fragile as an egg. But if he had applied and failed, surely something would show in his eyes. A tightness about the lips. But suppose he had not failed and I came upon his name? Then I must find words to congratulate a man who didn't give one damn whether I did or not. We care nothing for the applause of those who exist at our sufferance and see in it only sycophancy.

There would be a round of parties for him; Etta herself would give one and serve one of her dips and he would stand there preparing his pipe with a special tool from Dunhill — half tamper and half reamer and of sterling silver. He had more than a dozen pipes — briers, meerchaums, clay. One was carved into a human head. Pipes for every mood and whimsy.

"They say you can trust a man who smokes a pipe," Etta once remarked.

"I feel the same about a man who chews gum," I told her.

He displayed his pipes in his living room in a glass case except for one too large and complicated that rested on a side table, a Turkish pipe that resembled a red glass vase — a hookah, a nargileh, by God. Attached to it was a slender silk-covered hose through which he might draw smoke. I imagine he first got himself into something loose. Oh, he'd be Queen of the May, all right. He might now have another title to follow his name in *Who's Who in American Colleges*, and expect now to be eligible for *Who's Who in the East*.

In the Sloan house, guests were offered wine only — "the juice of the grape," as Sloan dubbed it. I don't think wine was served only because his wife was a physical education major but because wine only had Biblical authority. Looking not on the wine when it is red and so forth. Christ turning water into wine at that wedding — but a small step from turning wine into blood, as I understand some do. For Sloan was a senior warden in the Episcopal Church and once a month he weighed ecclesiastical matters. His was the final say on who administered the sacraments. He had dismissed a priest because the man's wife drank. I saw them the day they left, at the bus station. The clothes hung on both of them.

I disliked Sloan for his brilliance and his security, and there you have it.

I read those names in the *Times* in careful sequence, as one is careful not to step on the cracks of a sidewalk for fear of breaking one's mother's back, but I read from the bottom up as if this perverse approach might alter what I saw — I was now convinced I would see the man's name; the strength of my dislike of him was bound to bring it to the surface. Zimmerman, Lawrence: studies in the southern psychosis. Yost, Thomas: Reconstruction in the border states. Vincent, J. S.: the poetry of *el siglo de oro*. Tennyson, Virginia: painting.

And there it was, the letter *S*. There was but one *S*. My stomach growled. There was but one *S* and it did not belong to Sloan. My hands steadied. Now we might watch Sloan for signs of rejection. Etta with her false innocence was bound to bring up the whole Guggenheim business. It was naturally of interest to academic people.

"How many of the lucky people did *you* recognize on the list?" she would cry in the lounge. Knowing Etta, Sloan was likely to avoid the lounge for some time. His extended absence would in itself be indicative. But knowing Etta, I knew she would bide her time.

So now I read on, pleased with each name there. How generous one can be in spirit when one is in no way involved. I imagined each one of them at the moment he or she opened the letter expecting rejection and finding Treasure, Recognition. Freedom! Oh, many happy households in North and South America.

And there leaped out at me the name of Elizabeth Chandler Phillips: fiction.

My first hope at seeing Liz's name was that she would replace the muskrat coat so I should no longer wince with embarrassment when I took her to lunch at Longchamps near her apartment house. I used to hope that the lofty nature of our conversation would excuse her clothes — at least in the eyes of those close enough to eavesdrop.

And my feelings were hurt. I might have understood her modest silence about having been named a Fellow had I myself been an artist — we are not much pleased when our peers are handed the laurel. But why hadn't she called me?

Assuming she now had money enough for gin instead of the fattening cheap sherry that attacks the pancreas, I arrived at her place next time with flowers instead of booze. I had considered both carnations and roses, but carnations, I knew, she associated with sickness and death. "And they are a cheap posy," she once said. "But showy. And that is why they were chosen for Mother's Day. Even the most destitute sons and daughters can sport a carnation in tribute to Mother. Dead or alive."

It was very early in the afternoon when I arrived, and already she was drinking sherry. "Oh, let me take them," she said of the flowers and for a moment I thought she was going to play Katharine Hepburn and the calla lilies, and that act has been done to death by female impersonators. But it was clear that her apartment was not equipped to receive cut flowers. "What shall I put them in?"

"A vase, perhaps?"

"I've never been given flowers before." I imagine there are thousands of women who have never received cut flowers, thousands of them in the Ozarks and on Indian reservations. "I have no vase."

"How about a milk bottle?"

"They don't put milk in bottles now. Not for a couple of years. I'll run water in the tub until I can think."

While the water ran I telephoned the liquor store and in ten minutes the boy came carrying gin up the difficult stairs and tapped on the door.

I couldn't understand her not bringing up the matter of the Guggenheim grant. I wanted to know how she had felt on applying for it. Had she realized how damaging to her (I see now) faltering ego a rejection might be? How had she been notified of her success? Telegram? Was it a complete surprise? I wondered what she might carry to prove to scoffers and doubters that she was indeed a Fellow — a card to carry in her purse? A bit of silk ribbon to wear? And the worst question of all: How much money? Good Lord — I knew it was a great deal and could see no reason why she should be shy of announcing a figure. After all, I was her *friend*. I had heard a figure of six thousand dollars. She was certain to have settled more than she should have on her flibbertigibbet mother and mad father. She had so little grasp of money she could not grasp the meaning of necessary selfishness. Maybe there was some material thing she longed for — a piece of gold, a jewel, a vase. What that desired object was might be a clue to that facet of her I did not know. "We are what we want." Something like that. Who doesn't covet some perfect object — as a reminder that the perfect exists?

"Why didn't you write me or call me?"

"I was afraid you'd think I was an ass."

"Why? I couldn't be anything but happy for you — proud for you."

"I gave most of the money to Hal."

I stared at her. "Why?"

"The down payment on a boat."

"So that's it. The toy under the Christmas tree."

"Not exactly. A substitute."

The ropes on either side of a boat that support the mast are known as shrouds.

IT IS BUT HUMAN to wish to possess something one can't afford. Poverty is marked with the trappings of the rich — a television set casts colored shadows in a house whose rotting roof sags under the antenna. A Cadillac is parked before a hovel. The poor child who has guessed the number of beans in a jar wins a pony and saddle and bridle to make the animal viable, but can afford neither stable nor fodder and the pony must go.

Liz and Hal were under obligation to that beautiful little craft of a certain age, one of teak and brass and flowing lines, of proud prow and rakish stern, a symbol of restrained opulence. An aging Hispano-Suiza in mint condition could have made no clearer statement. But boats have got to be painted and calked. Barnacles have got to be scraped off their pretty bottoms.

"Hal had no clear idea," Liz wrote, "that those who can afford a boat can afford repairs." The original sails were threadbare and could no longer contain the wind. "Would you believe nine hundred dollars for sails? A suit of sails?"

One year it was a question of getting the boat into the water or paying the rent, and the next the replacement of the auxiliary motor. "Would you believe a thousand dollars?"

Brief friendships were made at marinas on Long Island Sound and up the Massachusetts coast. They were asked aboard for drinks, and they must ask others aboard for drinks, and sherry would not do.

Rope unravels, and storms crush.

Hal's solution, since Liz was not writing, was to get her to work at some job. Her only skill was typing, and as a typist she was accurate but slow. She addressed letters for Planned Parenthood and for an advertising agency. She was late to work and nobody puts up with that. The closest she came to using her creative powers was to compose press releases for an agency that handled monologists, portrait painters and obscure string quartets. She left the place in the middle of the day, depressed by the struggle of artists to survive and the number of people who fancied themselves artists.

It was the beginning of self-doubt — the ravenous worm in the apple.

In the fourth year of the boat, Liz's friend Helen divorced Claude-Michel, and one spring morning not long after, she dressed carefully, gathered up her laundry in a bag and her library books not quite overdue, and left her charming little house. An hour or so later, back in the little house, all was ready for her and in proper sequence — first the calming pills, then the tub of warm water, then the razor blade. The totally reliable cleaning woman found her next morning and called the police, who notified Daddy.

"The son of a bitch," Liz had written. "Daddy notified me, as her oldest friend.

"Mummy and Daddy were late arriving. I went ahead as instructed and chose a funeral home from the Yellow Pages. The Abbot Funeral Home had an unfair advantage in the telephone book. I'm no businesswoman, but if I were an undertaker I'd call my beauty shop for the dead AAA."

In marrying Mummy, Daddy had married above himself insofar as that was possible in that little Michigan city. "What he lacked in breeding he made up in brutality."

They had arrived by train; both were afraid of flying, being of a generation who looked on telegrams and airmail letters as threatening and flying as unthinkable.

"They confided that the situation was somehow easier for them because Helen had been gone so long from Michigan except on brief visits when she was running around so much of the time they hardly saw her. 'Perhaps it's a blessing,' Mummy remarked, 'that parents and children grow apart.' "

They were grateful that Liz had gone ahead and chosen the mortuary. They were the kind of people who say "realtor" when they mean "real estate man." And Liz had talked with the people there about a little-known cemetery, a new and quite expensive necropolis at a distance from New York, where there were trees and even a little brook. An expatriate in New York, Helen had never ceased longing for brooks and birds and trees. A shame she had not lived to publish her "Nature Notes."

"Just past the new wrought-iron gates," Liz wrote, "was a squat, granite building. A temple for a tiny god? The iron door, not yet rusted, was padlocked. I used to think they kept tools in there, lawnmowers and rakes to make things pretty, and shovels for digging. Actually, they store corpses there in the wintertime, when the earth is frozen. They wouldn't want to blast."

The gravestones lay flat on the ground for easier mowing; the other way, you have to kneel and use clippers. The fresh-cut grass would have stained the white linen pumps Mummy had cannily not worn. "The woman tiptoed," Liz wrote, "that her heels might not sink into the delicate new turf and cause her to fall backward. She stood first on one foot and then on another like a crane, and wiped her heels with a bit of Kleenex, and she folded it, and dropped it into her purse."

Daddy wore his Masonic ring. Liz was surprised he was not wearing a short-sleeved shirt with Hawaiian designs. "Too cold, I suppose." The backs of his hands were freckled and the hair on them, like the hair on his head, was red in the sunlight. He had choked up as the earth was tossed into the gaping hole, and he touched his throat where his Adam's apple lurked, but he bore up since he was in the life insurance business, and accustomed to death — without it, his profession would have had but little point. Without it he would possess no Cadillac, no summer cottage at the Lake, no power boat to skim its surface, no monogrammed Spaulding golf clubs and no electric cart to haul them from tee to tee.

Liz wondered what last image Daddy kept in his mind of his daughter, what one he treasured. Did he see her in the swing under the apple trees? Skipping rope or trailing her hand in the water? In cap and gown after being graduated from Wellesley? Or that other long-ago thing?

The last spade of earth was tossed in. "My little girl," Daddy said.

"The son of a bitch," Liz wrote. "He seduced her when she was twelve. Later on he knocked her sprawling to show what happens to little girls who might blab.

"I began to cry, but even as I wept, it occurred to me that the death of someone close is often in some way to one's own advantage. How grateful one is to be delivered from the thrall of Visiting Hours! How in the hall outside the sickroom there is no longer a need to lower the voice and tiptoe. The bedroom is available again for a guest. And so often the advantage following death concerns money. Now at last I was free of the resentment I felt at having had to borrow money from her. I could remember her with an entirely loving and clear conscience, promising myself that somehow I would eventually have repaid her had that been possible, and now it wasn't possible through no fault of my own.

"But Christ! How was I to pay the rent?"

The rent went on, the bills, the food. For a while Hal continued to lunch uptown and then began to carry a sandwich in a paper bag. Liz lunched on sherry and sometimes a peanut butter sandwich, having heard that peanut butter is the perfect food and supplied a vitamin alcoholics needed. The drying sandwich showed a single bite. Her stomach would no longer contain the entire contents of a can of soup and the remaining half she shut up in the thumping refrigerator where the temperature was ideal for the growth on top of delicate, nile-green hair.

Her face was flushed from broken capillaries. She complained of double vision, so there was the oculist, who sent her on to a doctor. Teeth seldom fail to let go at the worst possible time. Have them repaired or removed? Which is cheaper.

She might have cleaned the apartment. Neat surroundings might have helped, but such a complicated project was now beyond her powers of organization — making the list for the hardware store, and getting all those soaps, bleaches, buckets, brushes, steel wool and scrapers up the stairs. Hopeless. But it wasn't the breakage or the grime or the stains that haunted her — it was the years. It was the future. She tucked a bottle into a tote bag and escaped at ten in the morning into a dark movie house and watched old newsreels and Constance Bennett in silken gowns, and gangsters in snap-brim hats.

The city terrifies the poor. It is monstrous that the law allows dark rooms, cold radiators and cold stoves. From time to time Liz heated her soup over a can of Sterno. It is incredible that the law allows human beings to be thrown into the street in the dead of winter. But Liz and Hal had packed their few belongings and gotten two chairs down the twisting stairway and on the sidewalk. I assume it was about this time that she wrote this letter to herself, one I have just now read:

My world is lost. Where is any joy? I have none. Everything that destroys is in me. I have no ground, no home, no clothes, no child, no true husband, no parent. On the thirty-first of January they will turn off the light again and the gas and the telephone. Hal is miserable and working himself into the grave for a boat and so I drink and drink and spend what I can get my hands on. My house is cold and the toilet won't flush and money is at the root of every single terror. It is cheaper to drink sherry than go to the movies, I guess. No, if one can do nothing else one can flee

*from the rain of terrors into the ark of liquor and safely ride out
the storm while not stirring from the spot. Poor Liz. Poor Hal. I
must be well plucked. I must put a good face on it. I must
straighten my green skirt and get my hair cut and call somebody
to pull us out of this hell.*

Poor Liz, poor Hal. Divorce seems never to have occurred to
them. Their marriage had worn so thin, like the draperies at their
windows, that it was no longer even worth destroying. I remember thinking that those draperies, those curtains, would filter the
light that struck their deathbeds.

Liz's telegram did not reach me at once. Etta had kindly invited me to drive with her to Boston to see *Les Sylphides.*

I wired Liz money. The trick question she must answer as once
her mother had answered a trick question long ago and far away
in the state of Washington was this: WHAT ARE THE NAMES OF
YOUR TWO PUBLISHED NOVELS? I asked this question not so much to
allow her the opportunity of speaking the names of her books in
the presence of some nameless clerk who might be impressed, but
to remind her that she was an artist and that I had faith in her and
wouldn't let her forget it. The question was a subtle prod.

When I got my first job at a junior college for women located
on the Hudson River, I asked Liz out to celebrate — it's no good
celebrating alone. I had a French place in mind. I didn't insist on
a taxi up into the Fifties because I knew the food would be
expensive, but before we reached the subway at Fourteenth
Street Liz paused outside a restaurant and read the menu pasted
inside the window that promised paella and arroz con pollo.

"Ah-ha!" she cried, and struck a pose. "We dine here, no?"
And there she told me that she was not Elizabeth Chandler Phillips at all but Rita Manzanita the fiery Spanish dancer. As Rita,
she slept all day but was instantly alert when dusk descended and
shadows fell and once again she took up her place on the stage or
on the surface of that broad table that had been cleared for her.

[*255*]

Dancing the bolero, she was ringed about with local hidalgos and rich vaqueros who had come on for the occasion from all the surrounding sierras and pampas. As she danced, they panted like lovesick dogs and threw gold coins to her and now and then she tossed them a rose or two she swept up from a handy basket.

"But what zey deed not know," Liz said, shaking a finger at me, "was zat I was pure." Not withstanding her flashing eyes and suggestive kicking and stamping around, she was a virgin quite unlike Liz Phillips the tall, literate girl from New Hoosic. As Rita Manzanita she was a tease but would allow no one to possess her, unlike Liz Phillips who if not "possessed" had done time and again and with a great many all those things said to lead to being possessed. But Rita Manzanita was an interpreter, not a creator who must know the stuff of creation.

So the Cafe Sevilla it was. It was appealingly tacky, a rabbit warren of small rooms that brought together almost anybody's idea of Spain and Mexico. On the walls were bright posters hawking bullfights; one wall was covered with a similar fresco in smashing colors on black velvet: the costume of the torero who crouched with his scarlet cape was picked out with real gilt sequins. The bull, who threatened the viewer, had real glass eyes. Faded red plush hung from curtain rods shaped like spears. Low, fake beams suggested that you sat in the hold of a galleon. What the Spanish themselves used as throws for tables is not much known, but here the rough tables were laid over with red and white checked clothes that are most appropriate on the tables in cookhouses on ranches in the American West, but the reasonable will recall that Spain had had a proud if brief history as far north as Colorado. At the end of a short hall, where one turned left to the toilets marked *Hombres* and *Mujeres*, stood a suit of armor — a comfort to those who are uneasy in Spanish surroundings that fail to take into account Don Quixote.

Now, two months after I had wired her money, I called her and asked her to get us a table at the Sevilla. I had no objection to having Hal along, but was glad she said he would be out of town.

At best, Hal was distracting, and I know nothing about lights or boats. The Sevilla was Liz's and my private knowledge and private joke.

"But not the Sevilla," Liz said. "It closed years ago."

I hung up feeling something close to grief, realizing that we don't go back to places because there we had once been happy, but because there we hope to find ourselves when younger.

But oh, with the same dreams.

My dream was the common one — to have a million dollars. Even in dreams, I did not dare to ask for more than that, certain that I would be refused and then even the million denied me. I could just grasp the meaning of a million dollars because that sum, it was rumored, was what the old lady had for whom my mother had worked in Grayling, Montana. The old lady had a nurse, and therefore my mother was able to sleep at home and in a way take care of my father and my brother and me.

The old lady's name was Logan. In her youth she had traveled extensively, as they say, chiefly in the Far East, which accounted for the screens of filigreed alabaster, the gold brocades, the chests of camphorwood, and the snow globe or whatever it was. Her house was called the Logan Mansion and about it hung so important a miasma no child would dare, at Halloween, to approach it to soap the windows; someone — the nurse or the old lady herself — was sure to be watching from the round tower at one corner of the house.

In the carriage house, long since stripped of carriages, was a Pierce-Arrow touring car, the headlights sprouting out from the fenders. It hadn't turned a wheel in twenty years, but I was allowed to dust and polish it, and many hours I sat behind the wheel dreaming my dream. What I would do with a million dollars! Everybody I loved would be safe. No one would ever cry.

When the old lady died, she left my mother a thousand dollars, and that is why I am educated. A thousand dollars and the snow globe.

Whether it was worth a hundred or a thousand or more I had no idea, but Liz's peace of mind was far more important than my pride of possession. I carried the thing with me to New York, where such things are said to fetch the highest prices.

At Grand Central I bought a quart of Booth's House of Lords. I thought Liz and I might visit awhile before we chose a place to eat. When I saw her, I was astounded. She wore a black cocktail outfit of taffeta and I knew it hadn't come from a bin. What good thing had happened?

"You look great," I lied, for I had the impression of a clothing-store dummy behind glass in The Store Beautiful in Grayling, Montana. In those days dummies were contrived to resemble human beings exactly and were crowned with human hair; but the waxy face and limbs and high color gave the game away. "You look smashing. Let's find a place with lights."

"I tried to get hold of you, but you'd already left," she said. "I'm afraid dinner's out."

Her new dress was not the only novelty in that room, nor the bottle of gin in the tiny kitchen.

On the wall was a new painting.

Liz was harsh in judgment of what was said to be art. "It's a sobering fact that there's not — except maybe for one name — a single important American composer. When Bach, Beethoven and Mozart were writing, Americans were clearing forests and killing animals. It wasn't likely those Big Boys or those with a little less talent would leave a comfortable local court and sail west to make music for Protestant peasants." But as time passed and America emerged from a handful of bickering colonies, we found we had not among us a single Schubert or Schumann, not even a Debussy or a Ravel. Why?

"Possibly because for so long we believed that music was the province of females, who had time for such trivia, and by the time that attitude had changed, great music stopped with the death of Mahler. Stopped. Died. Clever practitioners continued and continue to work over the stiffening corpse, but melody, the spirit, apparently has fled.

"Modern music refuses the logic that the human ear recognizes truth, that the human ear recognizes melody as beauty."

She was equally caustic regarding abstract painting. (I understand it is now fashionable to be critical of those who are critical of abstract painting.) Liz was critical of those who dribbled paint or splashed it.

"Art is never an accident." The success of Mark Rothko she thought a result of a hoax like the prose and plays of Samuel Beckett. "Rothko's appeal may be that his champions do understand the limits of a rectangle."

Now, seeing this new painting on her wall, it was I who was critical. Did I speak out of pique because she had other than dinner with me in mind? I thought the painting hideous, an affront. The splashes of pink and orange and black suggested violence. Was the thing a joke? A conversation piece meant to test the unwary?

"I'm sorry I have to go out," she said.

"I'm sorry, too. I came here only to see you."

"Make my bed and light the light. I'll be home late tonight."

"Bye-bye, blackbird. But before you fly, what in hell is that thing on the wall?"

"A painting, obviously."

"Not obviously. Who did it?"

"Someone named Freddy."

"Who is Freddy?"

"Someone I know." Simple acquaintance is not sufficient cause for hanging things on walls.

"Is it so bad? I rather like the feel of it."

"You know it's atrocious. I assume you're seeing Freddy tonight."

"We do as we must. We're meeting at the Bagatelle." The Bagatelle meant nothing to me then. "If you want," Liz said, "you can come along and have a quick drink with us. You might as well meet Freddy."

It was as grudging an invitation as ever I received but I accepted.

I helped her on with her old squirrel. If she had known Freddy long, surely something would have been done about that squirrel.

I let myself back into the apartment with her key and went to the kitchen to fix a drink. Her altered circumstances did not yet include the proper drinking glasses for the several fluids. The makers of cheese spread well understand that many in the world will never own prettier glasses than those into which cheese has been pressed, and many a lonely heart will be cheered by the gay colors. I chose one bearing a wild iris, and poured gin over an ice cube and I sat down and thought — oh, the usual: who I was, what I was doing there, of death and the distant recollection of distant dance music, of sitting on the runningboard of a car and being sick. And I considered Freddy's curious remark to me. In the false candlelight of the Bagatelle Freddy had said, "And just how do you fit into the picture?"

The apartment was almost dark now and I got up to find a light. In that former servants' quarters no arrangement had been made for a chandelier or other overhead lighting such as was taken for granted by those below. No more than lamps or candles were thought required for the meaner life of the help. It had been too difficult to install in the walls the wires needed to bear electricity when the building had been cut up into apartments and they ran exposed around the outer edges of the room near the floor and had been painted over so many times they were all but invisible. I searched for a lamp.

No effort is spared to make lamps appear to be what they are not; it is almost that light is seen as an embarrassment, which it sometimes is. Lamps are disguised as old telephones and coffee grinders, as the hub of a wagon wheel, as statues; polished roots and driftwood hark to a pleasant summer's day, but most often lamps appear to be a container of some kind — bowl or jug or vase that might conceivably contain the oil that once fueled lamps. However, the shades necessary to soften the harsh glare of electric bulbs give the game away: a bare, glowing bulb is the prop in theater and story that means abject poverty. Liz's lamp on the bookcase had begun as a bottle of Lancer's Rosé wine; Hal had filled it with sand from the beach outside Mammy P's cottage to steady it, and he or Liz had pasted wine labels on the false parchment shade to carry out the winy scheme.

Alone in Liz's apartment, I did what people sometimes do when alone in other people's places — I investigated. You find out a good deal about people by lifting lids and opening drawers, by examining phonograph records and books, and the kind of person who does this is a certain kind of person, too. If you find no Tchaikovsky among someone's classical records you can be pretty sure he's a snob, and if you find a lot of Schubert lieder you can be pretty sure he's formidable and probably into Webern, who was shot by a trigger-happy GI. Hal's old jazz records spoke of the spark of youth he felt within him. Liz's Brandenburg concerti helped, she said, when she was sobering up.

The literate poor when they were in college learned to construct bookshelves of loose bricks and raw pine planks. Hal's books were on the top shelves and hers on the bottom; his reflected his attachment to salt water — all of Conrad was there and a tattered volume of Dana's *Two Years Before the Mast* inscribed "To my dear son from his Mother on his 12th birthday Anniversary." *Birds of Sea and Shore*, and *Small Boat Handling* and the complete poems of Anne Bradstreet, should he ever for a moment question his roots.

Most of Liz's book were texts and kept because they had been expensive — *Seventeenth-Century Poetry; The Romantic Revival* — Wilde and all those people; Pascal's *Pensées;* the two-volume edition of Proust's *Remembrance of Things Past;* a French grammar and a Greek; Frazer's *Golden Bough.* Their collection together was hardly more than a reminder of a hopeful past that had unaccountably become a sordid present.

Among Liz's books was a volume of Shakespeare's *Sonnets* that would have given me no pause except for my recent moments in the Bagatelle, the lights so dim there you might make what you wished of the face opposite you. You had only to choose whether a face was anonymous or dear.

It had been a long time since I'd held a copy of the *Sonnets*. Many who have been required to read Shakespeare are glad they do not have to read him again, and some feel guilty that they do not feel the urge to read him again. In high school in Grayling, Montana, Miss Kirkpatrick had insisted on *Julius Caesar* and *The Merchant of Venice;* with the first I became acquainted with the dangerous phenomenon of mob psychology; with the second, the insanity of anti-Semitism. What on earth had that to do with Ethel Jacobson with whom I had mistakenly thought myself in love in the eighth grade? The girl who sat behind me had been required to recite Portia's speech about mercy, something about "mercy's scepter's sway," and the girl had pronounced scepter "skepter" and after a year or so she became a whore along the Salmon River in Idaho. Well, the poetry of Shakespeare is spread pretty thin over the plays, for Shakespeare knew a thing or two: his audience no more than that of our own day would put up with much poetry because poetry makes you think — and it does not seem to say what it means or mean what it says — not much time for that sort of thing in the theater; the thing to do is get on with the story and the pratfalls.

Unlike the plays, the *Sonnets* are concentrated poetry but they have been troubling to many who would wish that things are not or do not seem to be what they are. For the *Sonnets* appear to be written to a young man and it is unpleasant to some to consider that Shakespeare may have been a degenerate. If so, he must be forgiven if only because of his art.

So considering, I replaced the volume. Hardly two hours before, I had been at the Bagatelle — the only man there. I don't know whether Freddy's name was Alfreda, Winifred or Fredricka. I did not inquire. I had only the impression of a graying, middle-aged woman with an aura of enough income to buy anyone who needed to be bought. I am hardly in a position to cast stones, but I disliked her. I disliked her because she was a threat to Liz. A relationship with this Freddy must prove even more destructive to her art than either poverty or alcohol. Liz knew as well as I the limits of acceptable human behavior. Not so attenuated as Helen, she might not turn to suicide but strangled by guilt she would not write again, and to Liz that amounted to the same thing.

Had Liz's background been different, she might have survived this Freddy, but her attitudes and her values, however much she might protest, had been shaped long ago by Bozeman, Montana, and New Hoosic, Iowa, where her behavior was named despicable. To be homosexual was to be damned — God had better seen to it that you had been born with two heads; at least with two heads you were not likely to corrupt the innocent. Liz knew as well as I the incidents they remembered in those little towns beyond the western horizon: Mr. Coyle, who taught band, had thrown himself under the wheels of the Union Pacific locomotive; the scoutmaster had taken poison — and they had deserved such deaths. And that wife of a rancher — she left her big Norwegian husband and went to live with the postmistress up over a store. Who would not wish to punish them for flying in God's face?

Liz knew the cringing boy on every playground — he is nicknamed Hortense or Minerva or Clarissa. The sissy. The very word is charged with the hiss of reptiles. He was set upon by the other boys, the real boys, both they and he only half understanding at that age what the trouble was, they knowing he must be driven out of the tribe and he understanding their power and their right to drive him out. He ran — he always ran — his lungs raw from gasping and later on he reached to feel his bloody knees where he had fallen on the cinders.

For the sake of security, Liz had become worse than a common whore.

As her friend and admirer, I had to see we had a confrontation.

I had to take her back to Square One, and Square One for Liz was this: God in rare instances of goodness endows certain cripples and those marked for early extinction with singular gifts, in compensation. Whether Liz was one or the other or both I do not know. But a gift implies an obligation, and her obligation was to use her gift — to leave the Freddys and quit the alcohol.

The poverty, of course, remained; but she herself had once spoken of the spur of poverty. And I could help a little.

I am not much good at confrontations. I doubt that I had ever initiated one before. I poured myself another drink and then another and waited for her.

Had I been better at confrontations, I would now be more than an assistant professor, and if one is going to confront, one should at least be on his feet. I woke covered over with something and I felt lonelier than I had ever felt in my life. On my next birthday I would be forty and many are already famous and dead at that age. What a waste for the brilliant to die young and what I should have given to be brilliant and dead.

I looked at my watch, the numerals painted over with what glowed. If ever it is quiet in New York City, it is at three in the morning, and in that quiet was the distant subterranean thunder of a subway.

"Did I hear you stir?" It was Liz. I could make her out, sitting on the ruined chaise longue. There was some alcohol in her voice. "I could have sworn I heard someone stir." A match flared as she lighted a cigarette and the black dress sparkled with highlights.

"I see no reason why I should not stir. I was bound to."

"Poor baby, left alone," she said. "Did you think I should not return to you?"

"Please fuck yourself," I said. "And throw me a cigarette."

A long silence. "I will not remain in this room another moment unless you clean up your speech. I will not suffer foul mouths. I had rather walk the streets."

"You might put on water for coffee," I said. "Thanks for the blanket."

"Somebody has got to cover up for you. Want a little whiskey in your coffee?"

"What a hateful idea. Yes." I propped myself up on an elbow and prepared for the confrontation.

"I won't take your abuse, you know," she said. "As a child I promised myself down on my knees I would take no more abuse. Do you know, I once talked to a man who swore by the prose of Albert Payson Terhune. We were eating doughnuts, and the sun lay between us. Later on there was a new moon as thin as a penny and across the town a dog was barking, so you go fuck your own self."

"There was no such person as Albert Payson Terhune, and the dog you heard was old Dr. Rayburn's dog. He was an abortionist."

"The dog?"

"Please be serious. Dr. Rayburn was the abortionist and when the authorities found out they stripped him of his powers. His wife and the children left him and they got into some kind of trouble in California."

"It was in the papers?"

"They couldn't hush it up. A policewoman's mother was involved, and all Dr. Rayburn had left was the dog. If the dog hadn't persisted in barking, the authorities wouldn't have hauled it off to the pound and gassed it."

"God damn all authorities. I assume Dr. Rayburn followed the dog to its grave."

"He stood at the graveside hat in hand."

"Had it yet begun to rain?"

"Jesus. You know everything. The first few drops of what was to be a downpour."

"I know a thing or two. I know Dr. Rayburn didn't feel like eating anything when he got back to that cold, empty house."

"He looked for a moment at the coatrack of elk antlers and at an umbrella stand that stood in the front hall. Later on he did fix himself some canned soup."

[*265*]

"Tomato. What did he do with the dog's dish?"

"He avoided it with his eyes. The dog's name was on it."

"Zeke. So much loss, so much sadness."

"Man is born to sorrow."

"What a nifty idea! I hadn't looked at that side of it."

"That is precisely where you make your mistake."

"Beg pardon?"

"You don't look at all sides. Liz —"

Now I was ready for the confrontation. Our foolish dialogue might have gone on till sunrise and it was typical, a good example of the fantasy life we shared. But I could not shape it as she had shaped it in *Masquerade* and *What Are We?* And at my age, I was afraid to try again.

But sometimes our dialogues were a means of sparring — we reverted to them when either of us believed the other was about to demand something about ourselves we didn't want to reveal or when one of us was afraid the other was about to reveal what the other didn't want to hear. Just so, I think, all people spar, for conversation is as important for what it hides as for what it exposes. We talked of Dr. Rayburn and of a dentist named Sneed who drank to steady his hands, and of a bachelor named Frank who lived with his mother and couldn't get an icebox into the house farther than the porch steps. We talked of a Mrs. Rebish who was so tired she couldn't get a comb through her hair and longed to get into something loose and to get her feet up.

"Liz —"

She rose and stood in profile. The black dress better suited a younger woman or one who had not yet lost her figure; her waistline was gone with booze and fats and starch. Shoes had always been a problem; her feet arched so high they appeared deformed and I thought of those grotesque casings for clubfeet seen in shop windows in side streets where the curious wander. But it wasn't the pretty, incongruous dress nor the shoes that made her appear so vulnerable, but her stance. She stood slightly stooped as some stand who wish to pass as shorter and more fit companions for those of normal stature. To pass — oh, to pass.

She was waiting for me to speak.

Life is a fragile concept and has not the resilience of the spider's web; with a single word the clever among us can shatter it — the rich are told that many wait upon their death; the beautiful, that lines even now appear; the ugly are handed a mirror. The strong are reminded of their brief moment; the simple that they can expect oblivion; the complaisant, that there will soon be horror, and that the God they cherish is their own creation. A father is reminded that a son is ashamed of him; a mother, that a daughter remembers.

And I made no confrontation. I hadn't the guts, just then, even to save her art. For I was that coward on the cinder playground. I was Clarissa, and thirty years later I wake with my lungs raw from gasping, and I reach to feel my knees, and in those thirty years there have been similar scenes.

I made no confrontation. She had a new dress, and there was a steak in the refrigerator. She didn't need my money; she needed my understanding. So I took her back to Square One — but another Square One, the first morning of our friendship. I hope she remembered, for then her confidence was unshaken. Who was I to speak of duty and obligation? Who was I to interfere in a life? Perhaps to do so is also to step beyond the boundaries of acceptable human behavior.

"Liz — I think it's about time for a milk punch."

 A GLANCE AT THE ALUMNI NOTES in the pages of the college magazine reveals that most male students go into business when they are graduated, and the females marry them; by the end of the junior year the sexes are pretty much paired off. The girls have accepted some boy's fraternity pin and some have given thought to having their sorority pins attached to a charm bracelet. Except for the obvious forms of business — the dragging of sample cases from door to door, the car salesman waiting inside the showroom, and the druggist with his obscene rubber goods, I do not much understand business. I do not understand all those who disappear with briefcases at nine each morning into buildings. It is said that the successful among them have their own keys to the toilet. But in what is their success? Money, surely.

Whatever their success, I doubt that any more preparation for it is needed than the ability to write and translate business English, a grasp of figures, and a sharp eye for the advantage, and many colleges no longer require a reading knowledge of French or German or Spanish or Greek, and nothing beyond first-year English. Students are freed to attend to more practical matters. Your regular businessman, after a hard day at the office, won't relax with Keats and won't amused at his wife's prattling away in a foreign tongue. The thing to do is have a drink and unwind. Unwound, he can eat.

But at our little college the liberal arts tradition persisted and a senior was not thought to be amazed by a radical changing verb. He must know, at least in passing (and in order to pass), the theologies of Anselm and Alcuin and to understand the peculiar construction of the Lion Gate. Nor could he escape culture. Pianists came from as far away as New York to play Mozart and Brahms on the big Steinway in the student union building, and a man with a lute came to sing ancient lays of love and violence in the Highlands. All this had to do with the music department, chiefly female, and I don't know what the performers charged.

But Sloan, the head of our department, could get poets for as little as three hundred dollars, and novelists for a larger figure, depending on their popular appeal; novelists with good reviews but with mean royalties could be got for the least. Both poets and novelists read their words in February, when the winds howled down from Canada and created a captive audience. The poets had a certain interest to some students as examples of how some people lived without doing much of anything, and it was thought that the novelists, possibly inadvertently, might reveal how it was possible to set down the story of one's own life for a profit. The questions from the floor were predictable.

"Sir, do you write with a typewriter, or by hand?"

"Do you write early in the morning or late at night?"

"How do you know what to put in?"

"Do you write about people you know or do you make them up?"

"Where do you get your ideas?"

I had not yet heard that last question answered satisfactorily except maybe by one novelist who said, "God gives me ideas." His words caused nervous titters — whether at his presumption or at his profanity, I don't know.

Sloan's aggressiveness in public relations was so appalling he had persuaded that old gray poet who, as a human being, was a vicious old fraud to come and read about hired men and mud and birches and stone walls. Later on, following the reception at the president's house (where a fire blazed in the fireplace), a group of girls sat at his feet. He was easy with them and called them his kids and he winked. Oh, that old poet was a feather in Sloan's cap, and word was out that he had even solicited Mr. T. S. Eliot and Eliot had only been prevented because he had been tied up in a retreat in Cambridge with the Cowley Fathers.

Now the time had come again to call in a novelist. Sloan was fiercely jealous of his right to choose this one or that — he did not welcome suggestions and liked to surprise the campus with his choice. I don't know what got into me except for my desperate desire to help Liz — not only the money business but to give her a chance to be seen, to be known, to repair her self-esteem. I couldn't think of anyone better able to express to students the pain of childhood, the terrors of growing up — what their past had been and what was ahead. She was still a Presence. When she entered a room the air moved before her. If of nothing else, she could speak of the authority of Failure, to use Scott Fitzgerald's words about himself. She herself once remarked that it was failures who most experienced life; successful people know little of what goes on around them.

So I went to Sloan's office. Except that he most certainly would have smelled it on me, I'd first have had a drink.

I hate tapping on doors.

"Come in," he said, his voice resonant against the closed door as in a shower. "Oh, it's you," he said.

"May I have a word with you?"

He looked at his watch. "Go ahead," he said.

Sloan had had his pick of the new offices and his was at once neat and cluttered. He was a liner-up of pencils and pens and papers and paper clips, everything at right angles. As he mulled something over he might alter the position of the angles as some people doodle, but the angles were always right. On his desk was a second collection of pipes in a rack — his working pipes, I imagine — and now at this time of year a huge, gaudy valentine from one of his students was propped up against the photograph of his wife and children. On the floor, attesting to his fondness for the wilderness, was the prepared hide of a black bear with head attached. It had been sent to him by a colleague from the West whose brother, curiously enough, had at some time been a game warden; the bear, in life, had been a nuisance around camp.

Sloan's books accounted for the clutter — two solid walls of them — and he had in truth read all of them, remembered all of them, and they were in English and Old English and Greek and God knows what. Sloan was the only man I knew who could speak Rumanian. When we dislike people as I disliked Sloan, we do hate them to have brains.

I wish I didn't clear my throat in times of stress; clearing the throat reveals to an adversary that you are leading not from strength but from weakness. "It has to do with your bringing in a novelist."

"Indeed?"

"If you haven't already made your choice, I hoped you might consider Elizabeth Phillips. She wrote *Masquerade* and *What Are We?*"

He reached for one of his pipes and peered into the empty bowl. "Oh, yes. I think I read a review of the books, or one of them."

"Then you haven't read them."

"My dear William — how can I possibly read every little book touted by the *New York Times?*"

"They are both little masterpieces," I said.

"Curious that no one else has expressed that opinion."

"But Sloan, the reviews did."

"Then perhaps I wasn't reading closely enough. Perhaps I had already formed an opinion —" and he gestured toward his walls of books — "that the masterpieces of this world have probably already been written."

I was afraid he was about to begin a lecture on the Death of the Novel.

"What," Sloan asked, "did she write after those two books?"

"Those are her only two."

"And the second of them came out more than five years ago, I believe." Sloan often pretended to be vague and then in the next sentence you knew he had forgotten nothing, that his pretense was a ploy to put you off guard. He knew damned well how good the reviews had been. "It's a curious thing, as you know, that the great writers always leave behind them a large body of work. An extensive *oeuvre*. The greatest artists in any field."

He had me there — the greatest artists, yes. But what of Emily Brontë, who wrote only *Wuthering Heights?*

I made the error of appealing to something possibly humane in him. "She's had a bad time, a rough time, and that accounts for only two books. She very much needs the money and the exposure might help give her the confidence to write again."

Sloan looked long at me. "I think this place is hardly a charitable institution. Artists asked to speak here are meant to help us, not we them."

"I think it worthy of a liberal arts college to encourage literature. The making of literature."

"I never heard of a real writer yet who didn't write in spite of himself, in spite of circumstances. Even because of circumstances."

He had me there. Over and over it transpires that somebody was doing his best work knowing he suffered from a terminal illness, from an impossible relationship or from grieving for some loss. Sloan continued: "I'm afraid, William, that I'm not much inclined to honor your artistic tastes." He chuckled. "I recall you once remarked that Bruckner was the greatest of symphonists." And then he became serious. "And in any event, this year I've decided to call in a fellow whose work has more social than literary importance. I have been in touch with a Negro. I think they are now calling themselves blacks, I can't imagine why."

I answered him as I thought Liz would have answered him, and the difference between him and Liz is that she never would have said "I can't imagine why" because her whole being was attuned to imagining why. "I think they believe it is their right to call themselves anything they please. I think in calling themselves blacks they wish to call a new attention to themselves — as you just did."

Sloan looked blank for but a second. "Maybe so," he said.

No one but someone with Sloan's popularity in some quarters and his power would have even considered calling in a black — not because there was local prejudice against blacks but because they were not at all perceived as having much to do with the liberal arts. He might just as well have considered calling in the head of the Teamsters Union. I doubt if many of our students had ever held speech with a black, except in the main dining room of the Parker House in Boston.

Even the parents of our students would have none but the fondest memories of blacks, whom they might have called "darkies." For in those days blacks staffed the dining cars on the great railroad trains, although of course the steward who greeted you after you had passed through the possibly dangerous, draughty small corridor between cars was a white man so that everything was kept perfectly clear. Oh, the white tablecloths and starched napkins and the silver and the flowers, and oh, how the scurrying waiters kept their balance holding their trays on upstretched fingers even as the train lurched into the sharpest curve! It was no less than a ballet. Of course, the waiters were used to it; they had been trained. Sailors are said to be equally agile and steady even when the ship rolls in a storm. It is pleasant to think of both waiters and sailors keeping their feet in difficult circumstances.

The novelist Sloan was about to call in was no Uncle Tom by a long shot, but a young black who believed the native white population to be greedy, bigoted and selfish. I knew the man only for his short stories and had not yet read his novel that had moved the timid in the cities to install extra bolts and chains on their doors, for he promised nothing in the future but violence and flames and revolution — Fords and Plymouths turned over on their backs like helpless turtles. He promised God's wrath. He

[*273*]

called his novel *Dies Irae,* a Latin phrase that is understood even by white Protestants, possibly especially by white Protestants, who have for three hundred years been accustomed to having the best of it. How unpleasant, should the old order change!

Sloan pulled open the drawer where he stored tobacco and began to prepare one of his pipes. Then his eyes narrowed like a clever one sniffing danger. "There's a situation out there," he said, and put down his pipe for emphasis. "There's a challenging situation out there, and it's high time we came to grips with it." He rapped his clenched fist smartly on his desk: that at least was a beginning. I left him brooding.

I wondered if Etta Murphy had seen me going into Sloan's office, for she was just outside the door as I came out. Her eyes were bright. "Did he have you on the carpet?" she whispered, and drew back to give me a chance to open my mouth.

"Not just me," I said. "The whole of white society. He's coming to grips with a situation far larger than I."

"Then maybe everything's blown over," Etta said. "I do hope so."

I certainly hadn't come to grips with Liz's situation. I wondered if her importance as a writer had blown over — if indeed she had ever had any importance. Thinking so, I at once felt disloyal and guilty, but Sloan's opinions had somewhat shaken me, and I wondered if my defense of Liz was due to those personal loyalties that so much influence what we think about anything. I knew, for instance, that Owen Wister's *The Virginian* was trash —"When you call me that, smile!"— but I had an affection for the book because it had been a comfort to me when I was fifteen and had broken my ankle skating. I associate the pages and illustrations with the wintergreen odor of a pale-green astringent liniment called Absorbine Jr. that my mother brought up the stairs.

I knew that the Hudson Super Six was not the best car. The best car in America was the Duesenberg, but my uncle drove a

Hudson and when he came to our house my father behaved better, and I would have bought a Hudson. My enthusiasms, then, had been impure. And now? What was I doing — defending whom I thought to be the underdog? Defending the opinions of those I had loved? Whose image is inviolate? And who am I to have any opinions whatever — what am I? It's a laugh that I could defend anybody.

After my talk with Sloan I picked up Liz's books with apprehension. I would be the cold critic. I would forget the times we'd spent together, dismiss her past, set aside her poverty and whatever mess it was she was now in. And by God, her sentences were more beguiling than on the first and second readings. What is great art but that which gives again and again, which grows as you grow, which alters thought and makes you think in other categories? How she had spoken! What a loss that she was now mute.

As though through time into the Past I looked through the falling snow at the ruins of the woolen mill across the river, each flake as it fell tracing and retracing the letter *j*. Every window had been broken just for fun. Not a wheel had turned there in a hundred years. The mill remained a monument to failure for somebody, and poverty for somebody else; it was a dismal scene. Often I had wandered there and walked alone in the vast rooms where there still remained heavy, rusting machinery too outmoded to be moved or sold. I once brought a sandwich with me and a bottle of beer and thought long thoughts of Cartwright and his spinning jenny and of children stunted from overwork and lack of sunshine.

Up the front of the crumbling brick wall ran a narrow iron ladder, a means of reaching the roof or of escaping fire. The ladder cried out to the daring to be scaled. The danger was in the height of it and the possibility it wasn't secure. Insurance companies call such things "attractive nuisances."

Suddenly there was movement on the ladder. A human figure, probably a boy and probably on a dare, began to climb, and the entire scene changed, came alive, became significant. The ruined mill had a purpose after all. It was a challenge, an arena where bravery was proved. And watching, I now knew why there is a human figure in a clear glass globe or some hint of human habitation. The makers of those globes, tiny worlds of blizzards and calms, understand that the phenomena of Nature mean little except as challenged or suffered by a human being. Man lost in the storm; man willfully building his house too close to the edge of the sea and again and again under the volcano and along the lines of a known fault and called courageous or foolish or stupid, but man always the focal point, the point of reference. It is that lack of focal point, man the point of reference, that makes so many uneasy before the paintings of Buffet. Except as it relates to man, cosmic upheaval is not so moving as a little child's pondering the death of a sparrow found in the corner of a barn.

As a child, I had wrestled with a supposedly unanswerable question: If a tree crashes in the middle of an uninhabited forest, is there any sound? The question, of course is quite answerable. There is no sound. There are only vibrations. For sound is what human beings call vibrations perceived and considered by the human ear. What animals and birds and insects perceive and what they consider is another matter.

It's a small thing, and perhaps insignificant, but I should never have understood the figure in the clear glass globe except for reading the novels of Elizabeth Phillips, which shimmer with the charming intricacies of Haydn's string quartets and the secrets of Cézanne's palette. They prompt a reader to search for answers where answers were not thought possible, and to find them. The search makes of life a sharper pleasure.

I was alone a week later in the faculty lounge. At the tall windows are bright yellow draperies, of velvet if you don't look too closely, they echo the yellows in Van Gogh's *Sunflowers* and his *Bedroom at Arles*, two paintings that are known to everyone, two paintings that do what can be done to obviate the bleak, New England winter. I had poured coffee into a paper cup and reached to take a few Oreo cookies. I like to take a few home, but I think we are not supposed to. Just as I began to slide the Oreos into my pocket, Etta spoke behind me.

"Caught you!" she whispered. "But don't be sorry. Mum's the word. Sloan wants to see you."

"About what?"

"Does he ever tip his hand? It's my opinion he's distraught."

"How could you tell?"

"He was rattling his change."

"Come in, come in," Sloan said. The palms of his hands were flat on the top of his desk as if holding it down. "Close the door, have a seat. This is one hell of a mess."

"What is?"

"This revolutionary. This Negro writer. Oh, if they aren't getting uppity."

"How does he manifest it?"

"He's canceled his engagement with us. No explanation whatever. And when I think that I offered him an opportunity to state his thesis with no holds barred, and the students . . ."

The students, I knew, would have had an opportunity to see someone who avowedly hated them — might even *hear* him hate them. Until they had read his book *Dies Irae* from a stack of them Sloan had ordered for the bookstore they had had no inkling of the mood in the black communities.

"When I think —" Sloan repeated and then for a moment was speechless. What he was thinking was of all the important novelists and poets he had bagged when far more important colleges than ours had gone begging. "When I think . . ."

"Steady now," I said. "You know the consequences of thinking." Had he not been distraught, I should never have presumed to joke. "Thinking can very well lead to action."

"And action is what I propose," Sloan said angrily.

"Would you kidnap him?"

"Please be serious. The chairman of the board and Mrs. Becker wanted to hear him. They've been keen on race relations for some time and think something should be done. It's too late to get another black man. Doesn't that rather surprise you? And now it's almost too late to get anybody."

I suspected he'd been on the phone and that he'd been turned down by both blacks and whites because they realized that on such short notice they were second or third or fourth choice and after all people have their pride and the pay wasn't much and northern New England is a long way off in the woods.

"On short notice," Sloan said, "on such short — insulting notice, if you will — do you think your Elizabeth Phillips would consider filling in?"

I hesitated. I hesitated just long enough to distress him and to make clear that my Elizabeth Phillips was not exactly at his beck and call. "I think she might."

"Please use your influence, William." And then he coughed. "Only one thing. It's crossed my mind — now please understand this — it's crossed my mind that a reason she hasn't been well, more productive, is that she drinks? I've known cases like this with your so-called creative people. She doesn't drink or do anything like that, does she? Can you be responsible? Will you guarantee her?"

"Yes, of course. And if you like, I'll see to the publicity."

"Not much time for that, but you can try." Then he rose and shot out his hand. "Done and done," he said. "Thanks, Bill. Woweee!" And he was a man happy to have washed his hands of the unpleasant. "This is your chance to show what you can do in a pinch."

In high school as an alternative to business English, I elected a course in commercial art and learned to letter in various scripts. I hadn't held a brush in my hand in years, but felt no small excitement as I prepared Liz's publicity posters, an excitement that often attends small, intense projects. This was a labor of love. Liz might like to have one of the four big posters. I knew the place for it on her wall. I knew what on that wall it must replace.

The posters were well designed, if I do say so. In jet black, in block letters, I fixed the titles of her novels:

MASQUERADE
WHAT ARE WE?
And under them a quotation from one of her fine reviews.
"The novels of Elizabeth Phillips are perhaps America's best-kept literary secret."
With the dust jacket of her *Masquerade* in mind, I drew in — as if it had just been tossed down — a scarlet domino. I was astonished at the effect. As an image it linked both her books— underlined *Masquerade* and hinted that the question *What Are We?* is unanswerable until the mask is stripped off and cast down in challenge. It touched the secret of her books, their touching on the little mysteries of living. But more than that. A red domino must strike an almost-forgotten chord in the students' past — a dark chord in minor mode composed of notes that summon memory, a first reading of Poe's "The Masque of the Red Death." Halloweens in little towns, ghost stories around a fire, delightful horrors. Naked boughs moving in the wind before the light at the end of the street — the haunting, retreating horizons of childhood.

Only yesterday railroad stations were at the center of American life; there things ended, and there things began. The spires, minarets, round towers, campaniles, flying buttresses and rose windows of railroad stations were proof that overnight America had achieved what other nations had labored toward for centuries, that America was broad enough and tolerant enough to absorb all cultures. And indeed the trains hauled Swedes and Czechs, Rumanians and Germans and Basques across the country to settle the empty spaces, and hauled back their sons and grandsons as Americans to fight the necessary wars.

Only yesterday the rich and the famous and the beautiful were safe their drawing rooms on wheels; should they feel some little need they had but to touch a button that rang a bell. The envious and the lowly, when the train paused at a station, might watch them picking at chicken salad in the dining car, touching their lips with linen napkins.

But what is more dismal in these latter days than a railroad station? I waited there in the late afternoon; it seems impossible to get from New York City to anyplace else until late in the afternoon. Set deep in the wall of the waiting room like the entrance to a tomb was a huge fireplace of native stone; no living man had ever known a fire there. The long slick, slatted benches were bolted to the floor to prevent the needy or the playful from carrying them off for private use or as souvenirs. Fancy, cast-iron arms distributed at intervals down their length prevented all but the shortest from lying down. All were now empty. The drinking fountain offered a trickle of water; in the drain, several had spat out chewing gum. In the men's room, both toilets were choked and the partition between the two had been bored through with pocketknives; the surface was alive with invitations.

I had gotten Liz a room at the hotel, a Great Inflammable that was about to be torn down for a parking lot. I dared to assume that some of the faculty would think it immoral if she shared my apartment.

Only two stepped down from the train into the new inch of snow — a little girl, first, in wire-rimmed glasses; a couple too old to be her parents waited for and accepted her. I was glad they didn't know me — because of Liz's old suitcase. I should prefer my friends to have peerless luggage, and Liz had closed this wretched old piece on quite a long and identifiable length of stocking. And the old squirrel, of course. I hugged her close and knew again the small-animal odor of the fur. Is it not astonishing how fur does hang on, and a pity that seams and buttons do not.

"Bill," she said, "I'm terrified."

I had been afraid of this. I hoped to comfort or distract her by drawing her into one of our foolish dialogues. "Many go to their graves unaware of terror. You're lucky."

"And the miles were merciless."

It was working. "The cruel concatenations. How about the trees?"

"Bare. Skeletons."

"There is no hope, then."

"Possibly in prayer."

"Then you have found God."

"Because of you, dear."

"Don't bother to be kind. I do what I must."

"Bill, I'm terrified."

The graying couple had departed with the child by private car. A taxi waited at the curb, the windshield wiper brushing off the snow; its lights came on suddenly as a reminder of its presence and purpose. We got in. When Liz spoke again, I wasn't certain whether she was or wasn't continuing the dialogue or whether our getting into the taxi had broken the chain and she was now speaking as herself and not as an actress. "All through New Hampshire a woman watched me."

"That was but a few miles."

"And so intently."

I went to bed apprehensive. Had she become a little paranoid — or had I?

The telephone woke me early. Throughout the years of our friendship the telephone had rung at midnight or three in the morning, calls on Halloween when three or four were gathered together in New York and when I had lifted the telephone I heard only ghostly groanings. Or trouble of some kind. The telephone takes precedence over everything: a doctor not yet too deeply into a lobotomy will drop his scalpel to answer it.

I was relieved. It was Etta with the bright voice of one who's had her coffee. "Friends of mine saw you and your lady friend at the Mad. They watched you for some time and said you were both intent."

"Nice of them."

"Have you heard from her this morning?"

"She wanted to sleep in. It's a long trip up here."

"Then you haven't heard from her. It's a long trip if you're used to New York. Well, I thought it rather rude of Sloan not to have planned something, especially since you're pinch-hitting for him — isn't that the baseball term?"

"I wouldn't know."

"So I'm having the group over here for cocktails before you go to dinner and she does her act. I was on the phone half the night rounding up people. Do you think she's partial to any particular dip?"

"Anything but California dip. Anyway, you're known from here to there as the dip queen."

"At five, then," Etta said, and as the English say, or said, or are said to have said, she rang off.

I had seen no way of getting out of cocktails, and maybe Liz would like to go for cocktails, would not mind the attention. She might like to see a faculty kick up its heels.

But she had said, oh, she had said many times, "I will not suffer fools." And I had been flattered she had suffered me when I was at best no more than a sounding board. And who were fools? Were they those who could not describe a given moment nor see faces in the pattern of a rug? Were my colleagues fools? I expect they were, from her point of view. "I will not suffer people who say 'By and large' nor those who say 'As of now' for 'Now.'"

I could not remember a single conversation at any faculty party that was of much lasting interest. Then why did they meet each other weekend after weekend at first one and then another house or apartment? Perhaps to assuage anxieties by speaking to or of others whose decisions are not always wise.

Someone had bought land to build a house — earnest money had already changed hands: a man had dared put down roots, and it is dangerous to put down roots in a college town unless one has tenure. Someone had bought a car. Another had thrown caution to the winds and thought of California, of which little is known except for oranges and Louis B. Mayer. And so they appeared, each in his uniform, the worn tweed jacket with patches at the elbow, the wives in their little dresses.

I finished my coffee and wondered how long I should wait before I called Liz at the hotel. I waited another half hour.

I called and gave the room clerk the number of her room and got no answer, and I called back and gave her name, thinking the clerk had made a mistake or I had made a mistake in the room number, and still I got no answer.

I called again and got her. I decided it was better to let her believe this was the first time I'd called.

She set my mind at rest. "The coffee in this town is awful," she said. "The coffee is awful all across the United States, except at the Ritz in Boston where I went once when Hal was in Boston on business. There is hardly one in a million who has ever had good coffee and yet they maintain as if they knew that the one thing they do like is a good cup of coffee."

"Aren't they the same people who had lain awake all night?"

"Tossing and turning. They heard two, three and four strike."

"And the night before they didn't get to bed at all?"

"They were up all night carrying on."

"I doubt they can get their wits together. We're to go to cocktails at five."

"Are they a bunch of poops?"

"I'm afraid so, but they're the best we have."

Society has found that more people can be gotten into a small room if everybody stands up. "So happy to meet you," Etta said. "You're the writer. Now, just let me take you around." And to me, slightly lowering her voice, "Sloan called and said he was all tied up and may be in later. If not, he wants you to meet him backstage in the chapel a few minutes before she goes on."

I had assumed that Liz would be the center of immediate attention, if only because she was a stranger. In our little community, a stranger's appearing in the wintertime was unusual and could only be explained by death or divorce, and he or she was watched for signs of loss or woe. Of Liz, one might have guessed either death or divorce. The recent black cocktail gown said death, but the fussy little bows argued for divorce. She carried a big black bag. I supposed her books were in it.

"I hope you've marked the section," I had said, "where the father begs his daughter for forgiveness."

I looked around the room with the detached gaze that sizes up an ant heap until a pattern of movement is discerned, and at last I saw that the women were moving slowly but perceptibly to one end of the room and the men to the other, and the center of attention on the one end was a young faculty wife and on the other a young instructor. The wife had taken this occasion to announce herself pregnant. Pregnancies were most often announced in the middle of winter when much outdoor activity is curtailed by bad weather and long nights offer longer opportunities in bed. Surrounded by curious well-wishers, the pregnant one rolled her eyes aloft to express her own surprise at her predicament; so must Leda have looked to heaven in dismay since, to her knowledge, she had been visited by the worst only by a bird.

At the opposite end of the room, the husband held modest court. He accepted the joshing and restrained backslapping as well deserved; for in spite of future wars, certain heartbreak, a pinched pocketbook and a world already overpopulated, he had elected to continue the race. Despite the drawbacks of fatherhood — they are doubtless many, and fortunately a veil hangs against the future — he could now consider graduation presents and look to some comfort in his declining years. Preoccupied with the glad news of two among them, the guests at Etta's party might almost be excused for paying so little heed to Liz. I saw at once what I had suspected, that they recognized only established genius and her art had brought her neither wealth nor fame. Further, they had been brought up to distrust flights of fancy.

The gathering could not have been a worse experience for Liz, who for so long had lived and thought apart from the world. This zoo of a single species of smiling academic people made it clear that the real satisfactions in life are simple — simple procreation, simple friendship, simple understanding that everybody is upwardly mobile — and these satisfactions do not include exploring the dark corners of the earth and psyche and do not include inquiring into the why of everything to get at truth. They had their philosophy and they could afford to snub her.

In that room she could not have escaped self-doubt, a recognition of her failure both as woman and as wife — even her failure as an artist. Surely she had expected to have written far more. The fallow female artist cannot compete in any room with the woman who smells with motherhood. It is far more likely that the artist will never again come to term than that the mother will cease to bear.

Some few were kind to her, but with them, too, she was quiet and remote, holding her drink in both her hands. In her black dress and big hat and pointy shoes she was New York in the backwoods, or what she hoped they thought to be New York. I thought of a lost little girl playing dress-up. From time to time I lost sight of her.

She had had no more to drink than the rest of them, but they did not have to speak that evening, and they had not spilled one of Etta's famous dips across their fronts. Stains are noticeable on black silk.

Marie Antoinette is said to have called her shoemaker before her to complain that a costly set of shoes had fallen to pieces. After having examined each of the offending shoes he had looked at her reproachfully.

"But Madame," he said to her, "you must have walked in them!"

And so it is today. We have the example of thousands upon thousands of women in sneakers or loafers carrying their party shoes to the car and changing into the pretty things en route. Liz had no sensible shoes in that bag, but I refused several offers of a ride back to my place.

[*285*]

"It's only three blocks," I reminded Liz, and I did not add that I hoped the cold air would do her good.

"Hadn't I first better go back to the hotel?" she asked.

"Why? You can take a little nap at my place and get rested."

"What a peachy idea!"

Because of her shoes and the ice on the sidewalks I steadied her and carried her black bag. I was glad of the gathering dark.

Mrs. Voisin stood watching from the doorway of her place at the bottom of the stairs as Liz and I climbed slowly up, I to the rear in case Liz fell backward. I expect Mrs. Voisin in her lifetime had seen a great many similar ascensions.

The dry steam heat smacked us in the face. I removed her old squirrel and hung it in the closet. "Let me help you off with your dress."

"Why on earth? Are you suggesting rape?"

"You wouldn't want to appear on the stage in a gown that's been slept in. And you've got dip on it."

"What will I do?"

"You sleep and I'll repair the damage."

"But give me my bag." No more will a woman part with her bag than a child with his security blanket. Women climbing into rowboats out of the raging sea do manage to hang on to their bags, and their bags they have with them when they leap from burning buildings. But there was more than a psychological attachment to this black bag. I lifted the thing off the chair.

"Give it me."

We are so conditioned to respect the privacy of the contents of anything closed against us that I hesitated. She stood in her slip, only slightly unsteady.

"Give it me."

"I want to see what you've marked in your books to read."

"All taken care of, my dear."

I pretended ignorance of her commanding eyes. "No, let me see." I turned from her, opened the bag and was not surprised at the full pint of gin. "I'll take charge of this for the nonce."

"You will like hell."

I expected fury; an alcoholic will do or say anything to destroy whoever stands between him and a drink. "If you think you're stronger than I, take it away from me."

She glared at me. I had always admired her eyes. Juno's must have been similar. "Give it me, you God-damned queer."

"Sticks and stones. But names will never hurt me."

"Like hell they won't."

"They did and they do. They still do. But I'm surprised you said them."

"Memory," she said. "God damn memory."

"Yes, God damn it."

I closed the door on her.

In a little while I got out my ironing board and unfolded it; it is cranky and can pinch. I brought out the iron that Etta had found so amusing and the cleaning fluid from under the kitchen sink where such liquids should not be kept if there are children in the house. The basis of cleaning fluid is carbon tetrachloride and many are allergic to it. It is absorbed by the skin, enters the bloodstream, and the entire body becomes one enormous blister. I use rubber gloves. It must not be inhaled for any length of time and must be used in a well-ventilated place. I opened the window to the winter night and got to work on avocado dip. Then I closed the window and went to ironing. A steam iron must not come in direct contact with silk. Use a clean, damp cloth.

Then I sat down and picked up *Time*, but the wars and rumors of wars, the merging of corporations and the collapse of religion did not hold me. I kept listening for Liz. Even asleep she must be aware she was to make a public appearance in an hour. That alone should have been enough to drive her into total sobriety. Then at last I walked into the bedroom and turned on the light, about to suggest a cold shower.

I touched her shoulder. "Liz."

"I'm awake. I've been awake. I can't do it."

"Sorry. You've got to do it. The chapel will be filling up."

[*287*]

"Let it fill. I can't do it. You must have known."

"If I'd known I shouldn't have asked you. I only asked you for you."

"Like hell you did. You did it for you. I was to be the prize sow and you'd get Brownie points. You're afraid for your job."

"Pull yourself together."

"I'm pulled. I couldn't speak a word out there. They want to see me fail."

It is true there is not much joy in the world at another's success or good fortune, and another's failure mitigates one's own. "Then I am to go out there and say you're sick?"

"Say what you please. Or tell them the truth. Tell them I got drunk because I am afraid of them."

So no good. She had been too long a recluse; emerging from her shell she was quivering and naked. I knew the feeling. "In that event, we'd both better have a drink."

"Dear heart," she said, "fetch me my gown, dear heart."

Dear heart? At the words I started as at the passing of an unexpected shadow. Those were among the first words she'd said to me and never until now said again. And pouring drinks I felt something grow inside my head. Tell them the truth. And in my head I began to put together the finest lecture I'd ever deliver. I need not tell them she was drunk and frightened. They would assume she was drunk. That is the usual belief when people fail to appear. Students of college age are often excited about people who drink too much, who dare to shoulder a charming irresponsibility, for in drunk older people they have a sobering glimpse of a world out there but a few years off where many walk in shadows.

Many will, many do and many did. Twisted Pope, syphilitic Delius and MacDowell, Hemingway a suicide, drunken Fitzgerald and Moussorgsky, Poe the drug addict and Coleridge the same. Queer Tchaikovsky, Wilde, Saint-Saëns, Poulenc, Michelangelo and Rimbaud and Verlaine. Virginia Woolf walked into the river; Mozart was a pauper, Beethoven deaf, Van Gogh disfigured, Milton and Homer blind — all a matter of record and the record growing longer. But they were not to be the core of my lecture, rather another truth: that the ungifted as well as the gifted are similarly afflicted; and apart from their afflictions they have only in common with the gifted their mortality.

The awful truth is the price each one of us pays simply for the gift of life. That price is death and pain. That being so, it behooves all of us who have no claim on posterity to act in such a way that we will at least be remembered with affection. The novels of Elizabeth Phillips deal with this ultimate truth and may well be the reason for their unpopularity. Who wishes to accept such truth? Knowing the truth, who can any longer hope? Along the way her prose heightened the ordinary, illuminated the murky, clarified the half-perceived and so subtly that a reader cynical or stoical enough to accept truth is delighted and dazzled by what he takes to be his own new vision. So it is when one is at last comfortable with the C-sharp Minor String Quartet. So it was when I understood the reason for humanity in a glass globe.

As if I had known for a long time that I would be thinking what I thought now — that this moment must eventually arrive — I had marked in her books those passages appropriate to the words I would speak this evening. Whatever else I am, I am convincing when I read aloud what I believe in.

"I will arise and go now," I said.

"Ah, yes. You go to Innisfree?"

"Nope. To fix another drink — I'm not easy on the stage. Then I'll mosey on over to the chapel with my bag of pearls."

"Bully. And cast well, sweet prince."

The chapel, a brick, mock-Georgian affair, was the gift of a rich old dead man. What had been needed was a theater–lecture hall, but the old man's study of eschatology had moved him to promise God a chapel and he had left money for its maintainance, stipulating in his will that the steeple be visible by night as well as by day. In the reflected glow of the floodlights groups of students moved down the hill under the barren trees.

I saw an unusually large number of faculty cars in the parking lot — those of the entire English and history departments. Greek's old Ford coupé and philosophy's old, orphaned Packard coach. I think word was out that Liz was drinking in her black gown, pointy shoes and floppy hat. Would she stumble? Would she outrage? Lectures in the past had had high moments. An old lady and former student had inconceivably made a fortune talking and talking and talking on the radio about home management and the cookbooks she wrote, but on the stage she had been struck dumb. Older members of the faculty remembered Edna Millay up there and drunk. A professor emeritus from Harvard said to have been loved by three generations for his learning, his humility and his droll humor had stepped too near the edge and had fallen into the pit. Agile students got him to his feet and brushed him off and papers were prepared for him to sign, releasing the college from costly liability. Ex-President Hoover had arrived in a black Cadillac followed by two black Buicks loaded with Secret Service men with guns. The burden of his speech had long since been forgotten. The Australian outback? War relief to brave little Belgium? His opinion of the Great Depression? All forgotten. What was not forgotten was his being introduced by the president of the college as "our extinguished President."

I entered the stage door and walked up the concrete steps. "Stage doors," Liz wrote in the first paragraph of *Masquerade*, "exist to further the illusion that actors do not arrive and depart like you and me, but simply happen."

God, it is said, moves in a mysterious way; he does indeed. I believed Sloan, whatever his faults, was man of the world enough to accept Liz's failure to appear as a quirk of genius; he had been studying such caprice for a long time. In any event, no great money was involved, and he had made it clear throughout the faculty that he'd washed his hands of this event, that mine was the responsibility. As for me, I welcomed the chance to step into a cranky breach and to show him I could handle a cranky situation. My trouble with him and his with me was that he believed I lacked aggressiveness. Maybe he was right. God knows I'm not aggressive, but my belief in Liz, my belief in the two books I had under my arm and my ability to interpret them made me for the moment quite sure of myself. The Truth, I said to myself, shall make you free.

I moved into the shadows backstage among ropes and pulleys and flats, among them one much used for comedies and tragedies that unfolded in vast country houses. It represented lofty windows giving on a formal garden walled with fancy topiary. It was meant to call to mind vanished gracious living; dignified help appeared like genies at the tug of a brocaded bellpull.

And like a genie, Sloan now appeared.

"I wondered how long it would take you to show up."

I spoke as lightly as I could, knowing that Sloan was bound at first to be upset and that the audience, expecting Liz to appear and fail, would at first be disappointed. I could hear them out front. The peculiar acoustics of the chapel caught and reinforced the sound of the letter *s*. It resembled the sibilance of an incoming tide. "It appears," I said, "that another one of our performers has been indisposed."

"So I was warned. But I'm afraid I must refuse your use of the plural possessive. Mrs. Phillips was no choice of mine. You vouched for her."

"Who can vouch for another human being?"

"However, you did. I think this no time for philosophy."

"Maybe not. But I came prepared. I've got the thing in hand."

"Prepared? Prepared for what?"

"I have a talk ready for them."

"You have indeed? Indeed you may have, but you are not going to deliver it."

"Sloan," I said, "please understand. I want this chance. I need this chance. I have something to say about people like Elizabeth

Phillips. I think they should hear what I have to say." I put my hand on his shoulder. He flinched like a flighty mare.

"I believe they already know enough about people like Mrs. Phillips. I suspected something like this would happen, and I, too, am prepared. Now you run along and hold her head. You're more needed as a handmaid than as a personality."

That night, according to Etta, Sloan gave the most successful performance of his life.

His little preamble was prosaic enough. "Because of an expected emergency, I stand before you in place of the woman as advertised. I mean to do my best to make worthwhile your venturing out. Your doing so attests to your support of the — shall we say — arts?" He chuckled.

"And then," Etta told me, "before anyone knew what on earth to expect, he launched into the Chicken Story. Of course everyone there had heard *of* it, and now each of them would be privy *to* it. Honestly, I think he could have been a great actor making so much of such sparse material. We were in *stitches*."

When he had finished, the students accorded him that accolade reserved for very few professors when, at the last class of the year, they rise to their feet and clap. "Honestly," Etta said, touching up her hair, "that man can handle anything."

The conclusion to my own evening was quite otherwise. I threaded my way out through the parked cars and walked along the dark street to my place. Everything was closed, but naked bulbs still glowed over the cash registers.

More than a month past Christmas and Mrs. Voisin had not yet removed the wreath of evergreens tied with a plastic bow, continuing evidence that Christians inside had once again exchanged neckties and colognes.

I climbed the stairs. The light from my bedroom lay pale in the hall. Liz had killed the bottle. It lay on the floor beside the bed with her two books. She herself lay on her side on the bed in her slip. Her knees were drawn up. My friend lay like a fetus. So far as the public was concerned, she had never been born.

In March, teaching contracts were dropped into the mails. For some weeks the atmosphere in the faculty lounge around the coffee machine was hot with rumor and gossip. Who was to have another chance? Who would be sacked and who promoted and who elevated to tenure? I did not much hope, as I had not much hoped when at last I did not receive a bid from a college fraternity. But for a day at least I had hoped my mail had gone astray — I think everybody has believed such a thing at one time or another, why the invitation didn't come. We say to ourselves, Mail does go astray. You hear of that every day. My situation is by no means unusual.

All the signs were up. Sloan had pointedly avoided me for some weeks, maybe to prevent my asking him why for so long he had played me at the end of a line like a trout on a hook until I was too old to easily find another situation: as our years pass, doors close.

Etta for some weeks had been unusually kind to me, kind with the kindness we show the dying. She is much closer to Sloan than she lets on. She drove me in her new Buick to watch the breakup of the ice on the river. We parked near the woolen mill. Only a few days ago she ran in to leave a jar of her tomato chutney and assured me that should I need it, she would part with the recipe.

But the blow when it came was not so sharp as it might have been, for I was already stunned by the news of Liz's death. She had had little time to escape the Truth.

Cremation.

She had died of a heart attack. "She'd been out shoppng earlier," Hal wrote. He had been on the road, and found the ice cream long since melted in the unopened carton, the bottle of sherry in its brown paper bag, and I thought of her laboring up the five flights of stairs, her heart weakened by alcohol, exhausted by her weight. Rigor mortis had set in. Tall and heavy and rigid, she was not going to be easy to get down those stairs. But that had not been Hal's problem. In the Yellow Pages there are professionals for everything.

"I hadn't realized the two of you were so close," Hal wrote. "Some weeks ago she said she wanted you to have her papers."

In each one of the characters she wrote about were the several personalities that exist in each one of us — not just those different personalities that appear when we are in love or drunk or under pressure — but that one within us who must believe wholly in something or somebody.

Oh, it turns out that one's total belief is usually quite unjustified. It is not unlike taking lovers who last a night or a month or a year, at the end of which time one says, "What was I thinking of? What got into me?" But while it lasted one felt whole, was even happy — if happiness means fulfillment. Or, descending into religion, we later find that what we believed was worth belief and valid if only because we wished it so; its only reality was our faith, and faith is selfish, but for a time life was bearable and possible.

I believed in Liz.

Her papers arrived in a carton that had once held six half-gallons of gin; I opened it and sat cross-legged before it on the floor and a tap came at the door.

She treated her tenants with respect. She was no snoop; she stood hesitantly. But Mrs. Voisin did keep her ear to the ground, although of course in a small college town the shifting nature of the faculty is soon common knowledge and of particular interest to one who is a renter of rooms.

"Come in, Mrs. Voisin." She took a hesitant step forward and she was not one who usually took a hesitant step. She had a scarf tied neatly around her head and I suspected flying dust somewhere, pierced with sunlight. "Come right on in."

She cleared her throat. "They say you're leaving us."

I doubt that Mrs. Voisin, somewhat French though she is, had read Racine and yet she had used Phèdre's very words and I was transfixed with the memory of a story Liz had told me of an old professor in the days of our youth who had stood shaken and ridiculed before a committee of the legislature of the state of Montana. The past is LOUD WITH ECHOES.

I expected that Mrs. Voisin wanted to know if she could now advertise my apartment. "That's true, Mrs. Voisin."

"I am so sorry, Mr. Reese, so sorry. You're always the one who never gave me trouble."

"That's kind of you to say."

"We're friends for a long time. So I wondered if you would like me to take your plants."

I had, after all, accepted plants from Etta. Something of my own, something to make the place my own, something dependent on me. "I wish you would."

"So I wondered," Mrs. Voisin said. I was touched. This tough, shrewd lady had walked the floor below considering me and the fate of my plants, fearful that in my disappointment I might stop watering them, they might perish along with me in a domestic suttee. "I'd be much relieved if you took them." The nature and extent of responsibility to living things is awesome.

"But you'll want to keep them until the last," she said, and turned.

When she had gone, it was with another sense of responsibility, of paying last respects, that I began to look over the gift of Liz's papers. On top were the first drafts of both her novels with changes in blue pencil that would be of value, I hoped, to some future candidate for a doctorate.

Next down were a dozen folders thick with notes, scraps of paper, paper napkins, matchbook covers, and on them scrawled unusual facts — the date of the first postage stamp (1840, British, one-penny, Victoria in profile, black), how chameleons change color (successive layers of different pigments in the skin that can be projected or altered or suppressed), the probable identity of Jack the Ripper (Duke of Clarence), the birthstones and flowers for each month. She noted that the frozen flesh of the mastodon in Siberia is still edible and that the leaf of the rhubarb is poisonous.

The King of Diamonds alone has but one eye.

One slip bore but a single word: *poontang.*

Cross my heart and hope to die.

Marguerite go wash your feet the board
of health is across the street.

Ollie ollie outs in free.

How handwriting forms, matures, and ages.

Each folder was a scrapbook a bright child might have assembled, one containing key words meant as springboards for calling up time past, past entertainment, past small talk, what the men smoked, how the women got their clothes clean, how they heard the news.

Newspaper clippings fragile and brittle. OWNER LOCAL RADIO STATIONS DIES IN CRASH. So that's what became of Donald. You can't get anywheres in New Hoosic without you learn to dance.

Her mother had sent the clipping, certainly. A line in one of her mother's many letters written on lined stationery. " 'Twas jus' wonnerful hearing from you. I was lucky to get a place with the O.K. Steam Laundry. Remember Fred Burroughs who owned it and walked with a limp? His son-in-law has got it now. He's pretty good to me so everything's hotsy-totsy."

SERVICES FOR PAST PRESIDENT D.A.R. HELD TUESDAY. So that's what became of Grandmother. "Your grandmother wasn't the same after your grandfather's death."

I smiled, thinking of what Liz must have said: "Her recent singularity was that she no longer had a husband."

No clippings about grandfather's end, but I see a bedroom set apart by drawn shades and I smell mothballs and spirits of camphor, while in the garage dust settles like memory over the Buick Special Six that has been jacked up on blocks to spare the tires.

Mementos of her father, a lacy valentine backed with paternal sentiment. "Dear Bestie Friend: Sure did like your last 'effort' and would like another. So how's about it? You're a real lover girl & your old dad loves you bushels and bushels like on the front of this card. They've got me in charge of the hogs out here now." A label carefully torn from an orange crate. SWEETIE BRAND, an orange on a flowering bough.

Close to the bottom of the cartons were my own letters to Liz, unfolded and flat, four hundred or so pages secured with rotting rubber bands. If she had expected to die before me — the sensitive are said to receive delicate premonitions of death — she may have felt amusement at including my own letters in her gift to me. Who recognizes his own voice — whoever wrote a letter that sounded like himself to himself. (Liz might have observed that the fact was a sound example of how little we know or understand ourselves.) Liz and I had once talked of the crawling sensation — the muscles in one's face, particularly around the lips, taut with embarrassment — at reading over one's own words. It is not unlike reading of someone just dead whom we've not much liked, whom now we pity for his bragging, his posing, his whining. Alas, the purple language. the vain attempts at philosophy — the reaching for the moon and having only a fistful of air to show.

But in saving my letters, she had honored me. She had not thought me a fool.

After my letters, but two papers remained. The first was a note about money, the lack of which had surely contributed to her destruction.

Money omnipresent, omnipotent, all-corroding, all-pervading. It rules, holds sway, makes possible, makes impossible. Its language needs no translation. Its rule even among the most ascetic and unwordly is unquestioned. The blind and the deaf, the sound

and the unsound understand its subtlest whisper, nuance, ca-
dence, its ear-splitting roar. It is the conductor of symphonies.
It is the triumphant general of all our wars ...

The last and final paper lay face down, hidden like the hole
card in poker that makes possible, makes impossible. Mr. T. S.
Eliot in *The Waste Land* has written of a card

> *Which is blank, is something he carries on his back,*
> *Which I am forbidden to see ...*

I turned it over. It was not blank, and there was no mistaking
its significance for me. It was her birth certificate. In exposing it I
had transformed the gift of her papers into an obligation. I was
committed to making her name known; she had chosen me her
Boswell, and like Boswell I have not the gift to create, only a
pedantic ability to select and to organize. My burden was to
winnow the moments and years, a thousand notes and facts and
observations and to reveal what a child had become, to answer
the question What was she? Exquisite failure or an important
stranger at the gates?

It is good that I have not collected much, because of the moving. The little radio, my clothes, the ironing board and iron — all
to be taken to some small quarters somewhere. A few books. Liz's
letters and my typewriter.

And of course the snow globe or snow scene, whatever it is.
It's hard to believe it hasn't a name that is recognized the world
over. Some years ago, recalling my first conversation with Etta, I
telephoned the research department of the New York Public
Library. A woman with a pleasant voice was amused and interested.

"I've been here ten years," she said, "and yours must be among
the second hundred calls about the object," and she laughed.

"Strange to say, the answer is that there isn't any answer. If you find an answer, we would appreciate a call or a card."

I couldn't think of another article that had no single accepted name; even the metal frame that fits around the face of an alarm clock is known far and wide as a bezel.

But I think it fitting that the globe we look into should have no common name. For although the several questions we call and call into the storm are always the same, each of us hears in the teeth of the same wind different answers.